Forbidden Zone

Book 11 of the System Apocalypse

by

Tao Wong

License Notes

This is a work of fiction. Names, characters, businesses, places, events, and incidents are either the products of the author's imagination or used in a fictitious manner. Any resemblance to actual persons, living or dead, or actual events is purely coincidental.

This book is licensed for your personal enjoyment only. This book may not be re-sold or given away to other people. If you would like to share this book with another person, please purchase an additional copy for each recipient. If you're reading this book and did not purchase it, or it was not purchased for your use only, then please return to your favorite book retailer and purchase your own copy. Thank you for respecting the hard work of this author.

Forbidden Zone

A Starlit Publishing Book
Published by Starlit Publishing
PO Box 30035
High Park PO
Toronto, ON
M6P 3K0
Canada

www.starlitpublishing.com

Ebook ISBN: 9781990491061
Paperback ISBN: 9781990491078
Hardcover ISBN: 9781990491238

Books in the
System Apocalypse Universe

Main Storyline

Life in the North

Redeemer of the Dead

The Cost of Survival

Cities in Chains

Coast on Fire

World Unbound

Stars Awoken

Rebel Star

Stars Asunder

Broken Council

Forbidden Zone

System Finale (upcoming)

System Apocalypse - Relentless

A Fist Full of Credits

Anthologies and Short stories

System Apocalypse Short Story Anthology Volume 1

Valentines in an Apocalypse

A New Script

Daily Jobs, Coffee and an Awfully Big Adventure

Adventures in Clothing

Questing for Titles

Blue Screens of Death

A Game of Koopash (Newsletter exclusive)

Lana's story (Newsletter exclusive)

Debts and Dances (Newsletter exclusive)

Comic Series

The System Apocalypse Comics (7 Issues)

Contents

What Happened Before

John Lee has come a long way since the System arrived on Earth over a decade ago. From his campsite in the Yukon, he has fought monsters, aided in stabilizing civilization, and finally, taken to the stars to see the galactic society that destroyed his world and killed over five billion humans.

What he found was a society as twisted as humanity's from before the System, one where Levels and Classes are not enough to advance, where speciesism, Classism, and wealth still have an inordinate impact on lives. A society that is constantly on the edge of decay and destruction as Mana boils forth and destroys entire planets, turning entire solar systems into Forbidden Zones.

As he journeyed through Galactic Society, paying off old debts to the Erethran Empire and setting right what wrongs he could, John also stumbled upon a series of secrets. Firstly, about the Corrupt Questors who hid at the edges of civilization, and later, an even larger secret about the System itself.

John gained the Hidden Class Junior System Administrator, and in so doing, he crossed a line he never knew was there. The Galactic Council took action, targeting him and Earth in an attempt to hide their secret.

Rather than let them win, John fought back. He returned to the capital of Galactic society, Irvina, and made deals with politicians and Questors alike in an attempt to save Earth. In the end, John realized he could not save the planet, not from what he had done nor from the forces arrayed against it.

He could only disperse some of the forces and ire directed at the Dungeon World by choosing to betray Earth, to place the target firmly on his back. In so doing, John threw Galactic Society into turmoil as he revealed his Hidden Class. This act pitted Galactic Council members against one another and set off the flames of war.

Now, he and his team have to survive the chaos he has created…

Chapter 1

Gravity greater than Earth normal pulls us down. Still, it's slight, barely an inconvenience for our System-assisted and boosted bodies. Silver and pale blue corridors flash past, the metallic flooring offering amazing grip as we sprint down the vast hallways. The lighting here is just a little brighter, the intensity of the invisible electromagnetic spectrum higher than would be comfortable for basic human eyes. Guaranteed cataracts if the System was not healing us every second of the day. Even the temperature is off—too cold for comfort, though nowhere near as bad as a Yukon winter. It's more like a Yukon summer—a touch too chilly to wander around in a T-shirt, but warm enough that a jacket would be too much.

That's Irvina for you. Everything is just a little off, just a little alien. And while we flee from the chaos I caused in the Galactic Council's chambers, the sound of burgeoning warfare unable to be contained by the building's privacy wards, I can't help but be grimly satisfied. Satisfied and a little anxious.

The building itself shakes as Diplomats and Ambassadors, Bodyguards, Manservants, and Spies all communicate in the best way they know how. Creatures of the Galactic order, violence is in-built into them all. The building shakes and I know that the Weaver and its puppet are retaliating against those who would attack my doppelganger and the council chambers.

I grin as I focus on Mikito as she hurtles down the corridor, holding me aloft in a princess carry. The corridor we traverse takes us away from the Ambassador suites, toward the nearest teleportation platforms. We—and in this case, the "we" includes Mikito, Harry, Feh'ral the Heroic Librarian Corrupt Questor, Ali, and me—are attempting to flee before the Council puts a proper lock into place around the council chamber. We intend to get to the teleportation platforms as soon as possible, since plan A is to use my System Edit Skill to crack the shield and port us out.

A flash, a twist in the threads that connect me. The Extra Hand in the Council chambers is now dead, its presence and speech-giving abilities offering us the distraction we needed. The truth about the System Administrators, about the System Quest now reverberates not just through the Council chambers but the Galaxy at large.

It's why I dragged Harry along. Why the War Reporter, with his Skills that connect directly to the System to allow him to bypass censors, was so important. We needed him here in the Council chambers, where they have lines encoded and systems in place to broadcast pronouncements to the entire galaxy. It's why, even now, Harry hurries along, fingers twitching as he works his Skills and his channel.

"Did it work?" I ask.

He nods, generally smooth skin strained, the tight curls of his hair in slight disarray. "It's everywhere. They tried to stop us, but there were too many Reporters. The news was too juicy. Never mind all the Diplomats and Ambassadors who were sending out the information too. My way was just a little smarter." My inquiring look makes him flash a savage grin. "Encrypted and time delayed and through a backdoor in their own systems."

My health crosses the top third and I wave at Mikito to let me down. Once I'm back on my feet, we resume running. Truth be told, as much as our little distraction has worked, I have every expectation that the Council itself will make their presence known. The only way they don't already know is if the Lady's ability to hide information works on them too. The power play between Legendarys and its results is not something I care to guess at—not even with the damn library in my head.

Considering System Administrators are in play, I'm not entirely sure that we can count on the Lady even if she can beat the rest of the Council. She was evasive when I asked her to block off the information flow to make our little plan work. I can understand her position. After all, we're asking her to put herself in a very exposed position. Even if she has helped us before, nothing she's done is something that she can't explain or hide. This though is crossing the Rubicon.

What the hell is the Rubicon anyway? Always makes me think of those square cubes you twist around to make a pattern, which makes no sense.

Idle thoughts as we run away. Being able to weigh potential problems, play with my Skills, and keep track of the map while having idle, idiotic thoughts is just a side effect of my attributes. Stupid high Intelligence.

As fast as we hurry, we only make it most of the way to the teleportation platform before we are stopped. It's not the guards who find us, but the lady herself. The other lady. The Duchess. A quick search of my memory tells me she wasn't present on the Council floor itself, a fact that mildly surprises me now that I think of it.

"What a fascinating manner of completing your promise," the Duchess says. Her tone is quiet, light, but there's an edge to it.

Flanking her, a half dozen guards watch us, all of them dressed in overlapping jackets, tiny little, small swords by their sides and beam pistols on the other hip. The dark-skinned Truinnar men glare at us, their displeasure mirroring their employer's. In the corner, Hondo stands with arms crossed, eyes fixed on me. Not that he's the danger he was before.

"I always try to fulfill my promises." I glance upward at my health, noting it's nearly at my maximum. With a surge of Mana, I activate Soul Shield to give me an additional layer of defense. Not that the Advanced Skill isn't showing its age, what with my opponents in the Heroic and higher levels these days.

"So the System is truly a program," the Duchess says, eyeing me thoughtfully. "And Administrators run it."

Something in her eyes, the way she looks at me, makes me think she's pricing out my full utility. Pricing and weighing it against the cost of acquisition. She smirks, tall and predatory in a beautiful, elegant navy-blue gown that sparkles with little glints of light.

Her eyes grow cold, and I start talking. "I'm just a Junior Administrator. The little I can do is significantly constrained."

"Still, a Junior Administrator is more than most have," the Duchess says, tapping her lips.

"You might want to reconsider that, toots," Ali says. "You might be powerful, but the Council will be searching for us. And whatever old boy-o here could provide, it ain't going to be worth the shitstorm we've cooked up."

"Like what you brought down on Earth?" the Duchess Kangana says. "It seems it might be better to capture you for them then."

"It would seem like that." I give my best wolfish grin, the one that lets the rage and insanity bleed into my eyes. "They can go after Earth if they want. That's not my problem. You can get in my way, and I'll just end you and your people.

"Because their secret is out now, and I don't give a shit. Not anymore. I finally have a proper lead on the System Quest. A way to get an answer. I'm going to pull on it, pull on it until the entire string unravels. Lady like you, I'm sure you'll figure out a way to make full use of that chaos when I'm done."

"Do you really think that just betraying your planet is enough to convince them you no longer care about it?" the Duchess says. "After all that you've done?"

"No," I say. "I could've voted against it, like I wanted to. I could try to stop them, but Earth would never have stopped being targeted. It's too much of a disruption to the way you Galactics did things for it to be allowed to stay. Earth would always be on the defensive." I grin, smile widening. "Now, I made sure what you all wanted happened. And I managed to pick up a few political favors along the way—not that they know it's mine." I tilt my head over to Feh'ral, who nods at the Duchess.

She startles a little, surprised to realize he was always there, floating along silently.

#CreepyLibrarian and his Skills.

"The Questors have garnered much from this action. More from Questor Lee's revelation. We will be aiding his planet."

"These favors…" Duchess Kangana's eyes narrow on the Librarian in thought.

The Librarian inclines his head a little to the side. It's entirely wrong, as if he's missing a couple of vertebrae, more snake than humanoid.

She laughs. "Oh, well done. I expect I'll have a visitor soon? Or, I assume, my man on Earth."

Again, Feh'ral nods.

Her laugh rises, light and tinkling, filling the hallway.

"Great. So if that's the case, we're going to leave now. The chaos gave us a head start, but it's not much of one, and unless you want to really stop me, we got to move. Or else all of this was for nothing." I pause and then throw her a bone. "Again."

The Duchess Kangana's lips curl up in a sneer.

There are ways of removing memories—Skills and Classes and Spells that specialize in memory alteration. They're all limited by the System, forced to work within strict constraints. If not, Mind Mages and Psychics would have been a major problem already, and not the generally reviled group they are in the Galactic ensemble.

The Questor's library, the one that Feh'ral shoved into my head, is more than happy to remind me of numerous incidents when the constraints created by the System were insufficient. The Somaz incident, the Cull of Putaera, the Viridian Wastelands.

Now, with my own knowledge as a System Administrator, I can see how Administrators dealt with the loopholes afterward. I bet if I went poking, I could even find the patch details.

Not the time though. I push it all away, focusing on the now. Mikito makes a little humming noise next to me, reminding me there are things to do, problems to solve before our time runs out. In the distance, I hear the rumble of explosions, the high-pitched whine of beam pistols, the hiss of loosed spells and the crackle of flame. The smells of roasted flesh and spilled viscera filter toward us, blood coated in the sulfuric stench of torn alien bodies.

Death marches through the Galactic Council building as the Administrators and their allies attempt to cover up their secrets in the most violent way possible.

Seeing that the Duchess still hasn't moved, I speak. "Now, are you going to move or are we going to have to move you?"

The guards tense, but she smirks and shakes her head, making them stand down.

"Go. Bring with you, chaos. I will watch how you run, and I will take pleasure in watching you struggle and bleed as you bring rack and ruin to my enemies and your allies. The halls of power will be emptier after today, and all that bloodshed—of victims and bullies alike—will lie on your head." She pronounces the words with a smile, leaning forward. "Go, and know that I'll be waiting to pick up the pieces. I'll feast on the corpses of those who survive and grow stronger.

"Go, Chaos bringer, with my gratitude and curse."

Her hands, clasped before her, twist a ring. The world twitches and she and her guards disappear, leaving an empty corridor. I take a step before a little blue notification appears.

Title Gained: Chaos Bringer

Some people create chaos wherever they go. Often, this chaos is localized—a messy room, dramatic relationships, a failed kingdom. You, however, have surpassed them all and caused chaos on a Galactic scale. There will be death and destruction in your wake, and all that you have done will reverberate for millennia.

Rewards: Reputation increase with certain factions. Major reputation decreases with most other factions. +50% increase in effects of luck (both negative and positive).

I look over the notification with a wry smirk before dismissing it. Time to go. We've wasted enough time talking.

***

"Out!" I snap at the attendants working the teleportation pad as we burst in, blast doors a shattered ruin that we step over.

The group turns worried and fearful gazes at us, some dropping to the floor, others freezing in place. The teleportation room is all mauve and steel gunmetal, with the teleportation pad itself just a raised dais with arcane sigaldry on its base.

Mikito snaps Hitoshi around, lopping off the edge of a metal shield—enchanted but only Advanced Class—to reveal the guard standing near the doors. He blinks, staring at the destroyed shield and the polearm leveled at his face, the large blade of the naginata still dripping a little blood from the exterior guards who did their duty. He drops his shield and laser baton, soon followed by the rest of his squad.

"You have no right—!" One of the attendants on the teleportation console, a console filled with runic work, shouts through both of his voice boxes. The attendant's humanoid, with a longer than normal neck and two eye stalks but the normal number of legs and arms.

His companion slips a slimy green tentacle over and touches the noisy attendant on the arm, its entire slime body vibrating a little as stalked eyes look at me then Mikito. "That's the Redeemer! He's a Heroic villain. Polonium-level bounty!"

"That's him?" The attendant shrinks back, though his voice is full of doubt. "I thought he'd be taller."

I grunt and cast Fate's Thread. It attaches to the annoying attendant via his chest so that I can use it to draw him toward me. My impromptu action makes the few guards on the opposite end of the room either run out of the secondary doors or open fire. The rest of the attendants—those who haven't already fled get moving—scramble out of the way.

Even as the blasts strike me, Feh'ral and Mikito react. Data pads fly out, striking at guns and crippling legs, while Mikito flickers across the fifty feet separating us, not even bothering to use Haste. She's just that fast. By the time they realize she's moving, she's among them. Hitoshi dips and twirls, cutting apart weapons and breaking hands. The disarmed guards are picked up by swooping data pads and Mikito's hands, tossed out of the room through the open door.

All the while, I clutch the attendant in one hand and keep him safe with Two for One and a Soul Shield extended from my body. I lean in so that I stick my face in his, though I end up staring at his nostrils due to his stalky eyebrows being a little too high. "Take a good look until you're convinced."

The attendant gives off a series of clicks from his secondary mouth, located lower along his throat. I frown for a second, before realization strikes that it is his way of acknowledging my point. To my further surprise, rather than running away, the slime creature has flowed over, making distressed squeaky noises and leaving a trail behind it.

"Redeemer, begs. Don't hurt. He didn't insult, just stupid. It's his time of month. Yes?" the attendant bubbles at me.

"Time of month?"

"Yes. When he lays egg." The slime attendant inflates, then lowers its voice. "We're try spawn once more. Genetic splice. The hoping, the taking, this time."

I look between the tall, orange alien creature and the slime. While I'm pretty open-minded, having spent quite some time in the Galaxy by this point, the mind boggles at times. The mind truly boggles.

"We just need you to work the teleportation portal." Mikito detaches my grip on the tall attendant and leads him back to his post. She's got one hand on his elbow, guiding him, while Hitoshi sits in her other one. A not-so-subtle threat.

"But I… I… can't." At Mikito's glare, he wilts a little but continues. "There's a lockdown. I can't open a connection."

"You just get it ready," Mikito says, pushing him forward. "You there, slimy. If you're staying, help him."

The slime-attendant burbles in a huff, but it does get moving, which is all we can ask. It rolls over to a position nearby while I eye the teleportation pad.

It's a simple hexagram with runic inscriptions carved into the pad. Beneath the metal inscribed plates, I know there's also Tier I matter dispersal technology, a backup for the magic when it doesn't work. There are multiple redundancies built into the entire system to ensure it functions when it needs to.

And also, doesn't, when they so deem it. Like now.

Then again, I'm a Junior System Administrator. As the workers power up the entire thing, I watch the flow of Mana and tap into the data stream back and forth between the System and the pads. I stare as they trigger the pad, track the flow as it gets dispersed and how it all interacts with the System. I ignore the surroundings, knowing that Harry and Feh'ral will keep an eye on potential problems incoming and Mikito within.

Temporary Forced Link connects me to the attendant's Skill that controls the teleporters. Disengage Safeties triggers, giving their Skills and the technology on the platform a boost. Riding on the Skills, I tweak its effects a little so that when the teleportation request hits the global teleportation shutdown, it overrides the safeties there too.

Simple.

Easy.

Evil.

The teleportation pad hums to life—to the attendants' surprise—and we all scramble onto it. A moment later, we blip out, leaving the Galactic Council's building.

It's only as we appear that I wonder if I should have told the attendants to run. Then I debate if even that mild interaction is enough to put them on the kill list I know is forming. I worry and feel a little guilty, but I have no choice but to dismiss the thought.

What is, is. What will be, will be.

For now, I've got other problems. Among them, the fist flying toward my face as I appear in the one location we thought safe.

Chapter 2

Delicate fingers on a slightly wrinkled fist target my nose. It's not that fast, not like the blur I would expect from a real threat. The angle and the way the fist is cocked shows that the attacker isn't used to punching. She probably would hurt herself if she actually struck me. I take that all in in the second before the fist impacts my Soul Shield and bounces off.

A moment later, she's cursing up a storm, cradling her hand and wrist.

"Katherine," I say, moving away from my friends as I scan the area. The field we're in is empty besides Katherine, her boyfriend, and his security team. None of our real enemies, though the look she gives me makes me reconsider my assessment of dangers. Trees rise up in the distance, demarking the start of a new farming location. The one we're in is lying fallow, making it the perfect place for us to port in.

"You bastard. You raging, obsessive maniac. You… you… you traitor!" Katherine snarls at me, face flushed red with anger and blotchy with tears. She kicks me, only to regret her actions a moment later as she hops around on her foot. "I'm revoking your proxy, for now and forevermore. I'm revoking your citizenship of Earth, and I lay a Curse of the Anathema on you. Let no one from Earth, no one who wishes to be our friend offer you aid!"

I feel the Skill take effect, watch as it wraps around my Status. A part of me notes how it feeds directly into the System library, the portion of my Status Screen that the System runs, and in so doing, it gives me a new Title.

Title: Curse of the Anathema—Earth

You have been marked as the sworn enemy of an organization. Any who wish good relations with that organization will avoid you. Any who wish to harm them might seek you out. But it's unlikely. Those who have become anathema to any group are considered dangerous and untrustworthy to the extreme.

Effect: Maximum negative reputation with Earth. Impossible to gain positive reputation with Earth. Increase negative reputation with most other organizations. Reputation gains are penalized.

I discard the notification, barely even glancing at it. I deserve it, even if it is painful.

"A pox on you and all your allies. I should never have trusted you, never have listened. Rob was right. I was right, when you walked away the first time from Vancouver. Once a coward, always a coward!" Katherine says.

"I'm sorry. Sorry I had to trick you, that it had to come to this." I consider explaining what else we got from this, why I chose this option. In the end, I decide against it. Nothing I say would offer a proper explanation. And in truth, I did what I did for personal reasons as much as for Earth's benefit. If there is any good that might come from this. I might think so, but it's all guesses and suppositions, and the future is murky at best.

My words do little to calm the rage in her eyes. In fact, Katherine pulls a beam pistol from her inventory and opens fire. Her weapon, powerful as it is, only sparks harmlessly against my Soul Shield. Eventually she'd be able to penetrate it, but Mikito doesn't let it go that far.

The Samurai plucks the weapon from Katherine's hand, pushing her backward to give us space. The guards beside us react, drawing their own guns. Feh'ral tilts his head, that slight motion enough to freeze the guards as the Legendary Librarian just looks at them. A moment later, they're waved down by Katherine's boyfriend as he pulls her away. He peers at us carefully, noting that we don't intend to escalate the situation further.

I'm glad that Req'm's smart enough to hold back.

I'd hate to kill more people just doing their jobs.

Harry has backed off, hands held up. He's recording every single interaction, his Skills broadcasting the entire thing even as he uses other Skills to hide our location. We still can't stay here long, but for a few minutes at least, we'll be safe from prying eyes.

"And you! How could you let him do this!" Katherine shouts at Mikito, her anger still raging unchecked. "Don't you care about Earth? You were a Champion once, before you threw it away to follow this traitorous fool."

"He is my liege."

"That doesn't answer anything!" Katherine snaps.

Mikito doesn't offer any further answer as she takes the scolding. Katherine barely even pays attention to Harry, who's busy shooting this entire thing. Whether it's because his Just a Bystander Skill is keeping him out of the line of fire or because he's a reporter, I'm not entirely sure.

I move away from the pair, using my recovered Mana to summon Ali. The little Spirit pops into existence, cracking his neck and stretching when he appears, taking the time to look around. He spots Katherine raging and decides not to interrupt. Mikito continues to stand in Katherine's way, taking the abuse for my actions. At least Katherine is no longer violent, having calmed down enough to shout.

Eventually, it's Req'm who takes hold of the situation and calms her down. Katherine is still swearing, tears leaking from her eyes as she's dragged away, out of the field and our sight. In short order, I spot their ship lift off, skimming close to the ground as they leave us in the field.

"Well, that could have gone…" Ali trails off.

I can't help but agree. It's hard to call such a resounding refutation of our shared heritage a success but…

Well. It could have gone a lot worse. Like Galactic Council Champion worse. Or, you know, an actual Legendary Class waiting for us. Feh'ral is silent, knowing better than to interrupt this very Earth matter.

"Time?" I change the subject, looking into the sky. Searching for our ride. Just one of the many deals I made and enforced via the Shackles. It's payment for what I did to Earth, for the secrets I revealed.

"They should be here any moment," Ali says. There's doubt in his voice as he stares at his interface.

Harry, standing by our side, hears Ali's words and bites his lip. Then, resolved, he asks, "Problem?"

"Nah, we should be fine…" Ali says, only to trail off as he senses it.

I do too, at the same time. A surge in the Mana flows, a shift in the System. Light collects and a small thunderclap resounds through the surroundings as air is forced aside.

One second, peace. The next, Plan A gets the blue screen of death.

***

"Fancy meeting you here," I snark as I renew my Soul Shield. A mental command has the Hod appear, the power armor forming around me as I get ready for the fight. I can't help but wonder if Katherine let him know where we are. If she betrayed us as I did her. Another part of me curses the cynicism that makes me think that.

Kasva Dedprom, Champion of the Council, stands before me, flanked by Buidoi, his Psychic partner, and another figure. Not a Heroic, just a late Master Class. A three-person team, or what vestiges of a team they have. A sudden breeze rises, throwing back Kasva's cloak. Gold edging on his armor glints, set off the deep emerald of the metal alloy. I'm surprised to see his armor back in one piece, then I realize he might not be using the same gear.

I cock my head, eyeing the three as Mikito finishes pulling on her own gear. I'm surprised they're taking their time to attack, and I rake my gaze over them. The Psychic's armor is a little burnt, a little damaged. The yellow scales on his snakey body are damaged, even as he twists his earless head from side to side as he stares at me. As for the Master Class, his armor is almost spotless but for some dirt and a tiny rent along one leg, the dog-human hybrid's fingers twitching. A moment late, I spot the Master Class's Status as Ali finishes populating it.

Nuan Keai, Savant of Life, The Tree's Sap, Burden of the Angels, Nesma Chosen, Contested Love, … (Warden of Life Level 41) (M)
_HP: 2378/2430_
_MP: 2365/5330_
Conditions: Healer's Buff, Shared Pain, Lifesap, The Fount of Youth, Mana Tap

"_Son of a bitch, they're buying time to heal themselves!_" I send over the group chat.

Mikito's eyes narrow as she considers whether to attack now or later. Personally, I curse the fact that I'm missing my Extra Hands right now, but I doubt they'd hold off long enough for me to create my doppelganger and refill my Mana.

"No need to rush, Redeemer," Kasva says, his gaze fixed on the tense Mikito. "There's no place for you to run to anyway."

"Oh, really?"

"Your ship was destroyed, the traitor killed when he refused to break his promise to you. Not that he wouldn't have died if he did," Kasva says.

"Fascinating that you managed to make your Skill work like that over such a distance."

"*Ali?*"

"*Looking into it now.*"

"*I have confirmation.*" Harry sends back. "*Cfton Marrow's personal intergalactic yacht was destroyed by the planetary defense system when it attempted to undock. It's not the only one. Any Diplomat, Courier, or Space Runner attempting to leave Irvina is being taken down.*

"*There's more. The global restrictions on Portaling and other forms of teleportation have been amended to remove any loopholes. There's a complete block on movement throughout the planet, even via the System, no matter how many Credits are being offered.*"

"Locking down the planet, are we?" I move sideways, putting distance between my team and me. If they're going to launch an attack, I want Harry out of the line of fire.

Feh'ral does the same on his side, shifting direction so that he can take in the three. His eyes are locked on the healer, which is good. I'm going to be a little busy dealing with Kasva.

Ali hesitates then drifts closer to Harry, his body growing in size till his feet hit the ground. His orange jumpsuit fades as he switches designs. I'm not sure his new outfit is much better, since he looks like a Power Rangers reject now, the helmet missing a jaw piece to allow his full beard to show. But the Spirit looks grim and determined.

"It's easier to start a purge when the locus of the disease is quarantined," Kasva says.

"Won't work. Harry's done his job and gotten the information out already," I say.

"Do you think we do not have precautions taken against those information peddlers? They are a disease, a necessary evil we allow to survive but have always kept an eye upon. Trimming them down again will be good for the System."

Harry lets out a hiss, fists clenching.

The Champion smirks at Harry as he continues. "It was a simple matter to get ahead of his message and enforce a harder encryption on the Reporter's missive. Now, it won't release for months for many distant locations. So long as we manage the issue on Irvina, the purge will be well within acceptable levels. After all, that's why we have the Security Corps."

"And by manage, you mean deleted my recordings and killed my friends," Harry says.

"There is a price to be paid when you choose to attack the organization that sells you your Skills," Kasva says, easily rotating his neck around his body.

Once again, I try to see Kasva's Status and get the same block. But this time, I can feel the block, the way the Skills work to safeguard his Status. I could break through it. A little effort, a little use of System Edit. Just hack my way around his Status and the multiple alterations to his baseline Screen that I can sense. Figure out how he tics.

"You talk big, but you don't have your friends harassing us this time," Mikito says, spinning her naginata in a casual show of intimidation.

Feh'ral is silent, though I wonder how much of their efforts have blocked the Librarian's own play. Then again, we always knew they'd go after the Questors.

While I'm weighing the danger of an active hack in the middle of what will likely be a knockdown, drag-out fight, Kasva replies. "We don't need more."

Social Web unspools with a thought. I watch the threads that connect Kasva to the world around us. I use it to check if he's lying, knowing he could easily beat my other Skills with his own. Social Web is a little harder to fool.

To make use of it, I keep walking around him, watching as the web shifts. I get a feel for the way the strings move even as Kasva turns. My movements let me work on triangulating any changes if someone is closing in on us, though I'm a little worried that he's letting me do it.

"His troops are busy. You really kicked the hornet's nest out there, John. The local guard and peacekeeper channels are flooded. The Council is attempting to suppress the information by killing anyone who has found out the details—including all the Ambassadors and Diplomats. They are fighting back, mostly by spreading the secret farther throughout the capital. Most of the Adventurers and other dungeon runners have been informed, and they've gotten involved in the fight in a preemptive attempt to keep their lives." Harry sends the report in a flash of downloaded text, and if the written word could sound breathless, this would. *"It's a civil war, and not all the troops are staying loyal. They realize they might be silenced when it's all over. The rest of Kasva's compatriots are all caught up, and I've got reports that at least a couple of Master Classers have fallen."*

"And the Council itself?" I send. As powerful as the people on Irvina might be—and more than a few Heroics have made the capital their place to live—the Council is a force unto itself. Especially if they act in concert. And that's not counting the Shadow Council.

"No news."

"I wonder, are you sure you should be here?" I say, pivoting my thoughts.

Could I beat Kasva? Maybe. Feh'ral is here, and he could easily take out their healer. It might take a little longer, since Feh'ral isn't a Combat Classer and healers at the Master Class level are notoriously hard to kill. I bet this one has more than enough enchanted gear to make it extra hard.

That leaves me to take on Kasva directly. I have some ideas of how to do so. But fighting him is a gamble at best. And more importantly, it'd take too much time.

"Can you afford to leave your employers unprotected at this time?"

My words freeze Kasva as he keeps pivoting to keep me in sight. It's only for a fraction of a second, but for that moment, he's truly surprised. It probably never occurred to him that his employers could be threatened. After all, it is not as if most things can harm a Legendary.

"Didn't think about that, did you? Why aren't they here? By now, I've crossed every line they might have. They should be here pounding me into the dirt themselves," I say. "Instead, you're here. And you probably weren't even told to do so. Just running on your old programming like a good wind-up doll."

Kasva gestures and the thrown blade of light cracks against my Soul Shield, piercing through it partially and penetrating the Hod's armor. My health slips a little, but none of his Affinity is embedded in the attack.

Mikito moves forward, only to be blocked by Buidoi. Polearm and incorporeal figurines outlined in purple and white energy clash as Buidoi deploys his own Skill, forming his psychic puppets. They keep clashing, spinning from side to side, but Mikito's checked. At least for the moment.

Feh'ral doesn't do anything, just watching. Neither does Ali. They both must have guessed my train of thought.

Even after taking the blade of light that slowly disperses, leaving a hole in my shield, I don't attack. Nor does Kasva follow up his attack.

"So. You going to fight me or you going to watch as your employers fall?"

"What did you do?" Kasva says.

"Just told a little truth, that's all." I grin, knowing I have him now. He could fight me, but Penetration's Evolved Skill means he won't be able to finish me fast. He knows it, I know it. And he doesn't have the benefit of hiding what he can do anymore. I saw his Skills in our last fight. "Truth. Weightless, insubstantial, impossible to grasp. But with the ability to change reality itself when revealed to the right people at the right time. A snowflake on the mountainside, causing an avalanche of… chaos."

Kasva growls and steps forward.

But the Warden of Life grasps his arm, shaking his head. He whispers, but I read his lips anyway. *"He speaks truth. One of the Council Members is dead. Another is close."*

Kasva stops delaying. A fist clenches and he's gone. His abrupt disappearance catches Buidoi by surprise, though not Nuan. She blips away, and as Buidoi triggers his Skill to leave, I slam the door shut with Quantum Lock. A fraction of the second later, I feel his teleport bounce off my Skill, setting my teeth on edge. Of course, he's got his own way to penetrate teleport locks, but I don't let him. I make use of the planetary locks with System Edit and keep his attempts at escape shut down.

"Wha—?" He spins toward me, looking worse for wear as he bounces off again, the very fabric of his body tearing apart and coming back together again and again in short order.

His Skills have begun to disperse because he let the phantom figures go. After all, he'd need to resummon them when he followed Kasva. Too late, he realizes his mistake. Mikito does not wait for Buidoi to recover from the pain, the surprise.

Blitz turns on, combining with Charge and the already cast Haste spell. She slams into Buidoi with a vengeance and pins him with Hitoshi, the polearm bursting through his chest and holding him aloft, blood dripping down his sinuous body. The naginata is glowing, sucking at Buidoi's lifeforce as he struggles weakly while impaled.

I'm not done either, for I throw one of my daggers at him. I imbue a Grand Cross in it, shoving it down such that its area of effect is tiny, no more than a few centimeters wide. The dagger enters just above the left of where his hip would be, piercing his defenses with ease. And then the Skill triggers and parts him from his lower half. The tail thrashes and flops around while blood pours from his chest and lower torso.

Pushing forward, Mikito takes them forward, still connected by the naginata. Mikito spins through the air with cat-like grace, landing first and hoisting Buidoi upward. Hitoshi keeps sucking down his life, never letting him detach himself while Mikito triggers attack Skills through the connection.

Buidoi recovers from the surprise and pain of our attacks and blasts area effect attacks at the both of us. It's a real headache, but it's not enough. Especially when Ali throws himself into the battle and messes with the electromagnetic charge in his brain. Feh'ral's eyes go blank as he taps into my connection and reinforces my Dimensional Lock, putting a stop to any escape attempts.

In the end, finishing off the Master Class is a matter of stabbing. Emergency Skills and enchantments patch him together a few times even as a shield defense attempts to flow around Hitoshi. None of it helps. Mikito doesn't need much of my help, so I turn my attention to the next step.

Which is activating Plan B.

***

"It's not happening," Dornalor says over the call, arms crossed.

I'm patched into the ether with him, communicating via a hijacked and hacked signal from Harry's Rebel Broadcast Skill. Skill Edit is making my body hurt, my nerves burn, but thankfully, it's only a minor change to make our communication line stable. At least, when I'm shifting it from a broadband burst to single individual.

Even then, the image is fuzzy, the conversation stilted and broken. The Pirate Captain looks frazzled, his eyes darting from side to side as he searches notification screens we can't see.

"What do you mean, it's not happening?" I growl. "You said you could do it, when I called the first time."

"That's before they locked down the entire solar system and called in reinforcements!" Dornalor snaps.

"Reinforcements?" I look at Harry, who shakes his head. That's news to him too.

"Right on the edge of the boundary for the system itself," Dornalor says. "Two entire fleets just jumped right in. They've broken into multiple task groups to cover the ways out, with warp locks across the entire sphere. I'm pretty sure one of them is a Forbidden Zone fleet."

My jaw clenches tightly before I force it to relax. Forbidden Zone fleets are one of the major reasons we even have a Council. The fleets destroy and churn the Mana of the various monsters in Forbidden Zone planets to slow down their growth. They're also the galaxy's defense against some of the really nasty stuff that lives in the depths of space in the Forbidden Zone. Creatures that occasionally swim outside of the higher density areas to chomp on civilized planets. Kind of like whales breaching the surface before ducking back down into the depths they enjoy.

And when I say nasty stuff, think planet-sized monsters.

"Two fleets?" I frown. "A bit of an overkill, don't you think?"

"Not exactly." Dornalor waves and I see a notification appear. My jaw drops when I see spherical encirclement, how thinly spaced it ends up being when you include an entire solar system. More so when the dots converge toward Irvina, meeting the fleeing dots of other ships as they escape the planetary defenses and the third, larger cluster of ships on the outskirts of the solar system. "Looks like some people had planned for this."

"Fuck." I pause, then stare at the dots. The two Galactic Council fleets might have broken up a little, but they still have their forces concentrated enough to match the third fleet. Which is a good thing, since otherwise, they'd be taken apart in detail.

"No."

"What?" I say innocently.

"No, I'm not flying through a fleet battle to pick you up. Even assuming you survive long enough for me to arrive, I'm still not doing it," Dornalor says. "There's helping you out because they'd kill me anyway, and then there's plain suicide."

I snort, but he's right. *The Nothing's Heartbreak* is many things, but it's neither tough enough nor sneaky enough to bypass the sheer volume of sensors out there and a full-out fleet battle. And that's assuming they actually fight and not stand around, mouthing off at one another.

"Thousand hells." I rub my face, glance at where Mikito is looting the Psychic's body, and make a face. "Time to go. We'll… catch up."

"You do that. Good luck, Redeemer."

He doesn't mention if he's going to hang around, but I can only assume he will. If he intended to run, he would have at the first sign of trouble.

Quantum Lock gets dropped, as does the communication channel between the two of us. Freed, I use the System Edit Skill to punch through the global Portal exceptions, wincing as my muscles clench and fire erupts through my body. I feel the Skills buck and twist, not wanting to be used this way, but I shove aside the pain and the resulting payback.

Not the time.

Harry's already hurrying through the Portal I created. Feh'ral goes next, while Mikito gives me the side-eye when I gesture for her to go first. Snorting, I duck through the Portal, followed by Mikito. I shut down the Portal, grateful that wherever Kasva is, he's too busy to come back for his friend.

Though I'm sure he'll be back for revenge eventually.

Chapter 3

We come back full circle, popping into place in the middle of nowhere at the cliffside observatory where we had put together our entire plan days before. We only make it there after a couple of Portals. I doubt our short detour is sufficient to throw off our pursuers in the long term, but it's the best we can do. A couple of Mana Swarm grenades set to go off after we leave will do a lot to mess with any traces that we leave behind. More importantly, the observatory's basic stealth defenses as an Administrative Center do much of the heavy lifting.

As we enter the building, Harry's looking a little worse for wear. His pupils are dilated, he's constantly licking his lips, and he's taken to rubbing the tops of his hands. If not for his regeneration, I would have expected his skin to be stripped raw by now. In the silence of the observatory, he spins toward me and speaks his mind. "What are we at now? Plan C? There is a Plan C, right?"

"Actually, I'm pretty sure we're on Plan D. Plan C was stealing a ship and making a run for it, but those fleets and the global lockdown kind of make that moot." I shake my head, considering the Heroic Stationmaster who runs things high above. If he wasn't so busy dealing with everyone else trying to flee the planet, he could make our lives even more miserable.

"Is that supposed to comfort me!?!" Harry shouts.

"Wasn't trying to comfort." I conjure a chocolate bar, offering it to him, and watch as he slaps it out of my hand. I shrug and pull one out for myself. "But I don't think lying to you would be very comforting either. Anyway, I do have a plan D, E, and F."

The confident assurance in my voice calms Harry a little. Then he looks really embarrassed as he apparently realizes he hit me. He flushes a little, becoming a little more tanned. Still, he's not doing well. The aftereffects of his torture session, the risks we've been running, and the sheer enormity of what we've done are hitting him. The fact that I pushed him to help me while he was still in shock has probably not hit him yet, but I wouldn't be surprised if that crops up later.

"So what's plan D?" he finally manages to ask.

"Hopefully it's arriving soon in the form of a trio of fan club members," I say.

Harry glances at Mikito, clearly remembering his rescuers. He nods.

I wave to him and her. "Just wait around here, will you?"

Feh'ral speaks up now that Harry has calmed. "I shall be looking into some other matters."

He doesn't even wait for us to acknowledge him before he fades out, going translucent. My eyes narrow, only for the library to dump the name of the Skill and its effects into my brain. Central Processing allows Feh'ral to access nearby libraries, tapping into the information they have, and more importantly, allows him to communicate with other Librarians.

I've already started walking away when Mikito calls, "Where are you going?"

"Checking if plan E is in play or not." I head right up the stairs for the entrance to the Administrative Center.

Hopefully Mikito can help Harry settle down and work through some of the trauma. Perhaps a few moments of peace will help. Ali doesn't follow me up, instead joining the pair and chatting with them all, doing his best in his own inane way. In this case, he's showing Harry a calming nature documentary. It involves sharks, but that's all I can tell before I slip through the wall.

In the silence of the Administrative Center, I run a hand over my face, letting the weariness flow through. No matter what I tell everyone else, the truth is, I had really hoped that Plan A would work out.

***

I draw a couple of deep breaths, cycling the despair and exhaustion through my body, forcing it out with each exhalation. A part of me chants *what is, is* in an attempt to console myself. Eventually, I make myself move a bit, ascending the stairs to the mezzanine while not thinking about what I'm going to do. Just moving. Though I didn't lie to Harry, my other plans are significantly less robust and rely on a number of co-dependent assumptions.

By the sole piece of furniture in the mezzanine—the console—I pull out System tickets. I discard the ones that are close to me—those few that are common, pedestrian fixes—to the System. Dungeon overflows, a couple of monster evolutions that the System wants a closer look at. My goal isn't to work today, even though the experience would be nice.

One ticket catches my eye, that of a wandering Explorer who stumbled upon a Mana anomaly the System hadn't even noticed until a sapient pair of eyes and a Skill use had triggered it. The mutated moss creature is sucking up more ambient Mana than it should, converting it at a faster-than-normal growth rate. It's both good, in that it is consuming non-System Mana, and bad, as it evolves from one Level to another. It takes me a few minutes to flag the ticket in the System for further study and potential testing as a method to slow down Mana oversaturation and to teleport it to a few Dungeon planets for further testing.

Then I'm done and focused again.

What I'm looking for are the Planetary-wide tickets, things that have been flagged because certain high-powered individuals are throwing around Skills willy-nilly. In the interactions between Legendary skills, all kind of errors that the System detests crop up.

Of course, as a Junior Administrator, I have absolutely no ability to actively affect such issues. If anything, the Senior Administrators or even the System itself will plug the holes in the Skills. Whatever the case, whether it's because the System wants its Administrators to learn or it's just a security hole, I can see tickets above my level.

I scale down the high-level issues, wincing at some of the contents of the tickets. The information is not what I was looking for, but still good to know.

Dungeon INV-981-03 overrun, Mana overflow and balance disrupted due to Invited Guest Skill

Mana imbalance in use/output via combination Skills—Dancer's Grace, Tectonic Movement, and Gravity Sheer in quadrant 381C-6891

Alert! Mass structural destruction in quadrant 98-447 in zone Q232. Skills use review required?

System Administrator overreach—Junior System Administrator Lee. Combined Skill use and systematic breach of protocols 138.6 7.364A—IV

Of course, I do try to look at that ticket, but I get bounced out almost immediately. Interestingly enough, the requirements to deal with the issue is black-flagged, which is something I haven't seen before. I'm annoyed I can't just wipe out the ticket or deal with it myself, but that'd be too obvious an exploit.

I do wonder if I'll ever see another Administrator Skill. I don't seem to be able to view my options. The System is automatically assigning my

Administrator Skills whenever I have a free slot. Sometimes though, I wonder if my System Edit Skills and lack of choice is a matter of the Council or the System's initial programming. Maybe the Skill is just the way the System translates concepts of using its programming into a way that we can understand. For sure, System Edit is much more robust and wide-ranging than I initially thought.

For all that, I have a job to do and keep scanning, finally coming across the tickets that I'm looking for. Surprisingly, they are buried quite far down and are of low priority. It's not long before I realize why. It seems that contrary to my initial belief, there already has been quite a bit of work involved in ensuring that these Legendary Skills don't conflict and drain the System of too much Mana. As wide-ranging as they are, Legendary Skills often come into conflict with one another, and previous System Administrators have taken action against potential issues. System Administrators or the System itself. I can almost sense the way the code changes, the way the Skills are patched more in-line with the way the whole System works than the hack jobs most Administrators do.

For example, the Dragon's Domain interacts constantly with the Lady of Shadows's Legendary Skill The Line Between Truth and Lies. Then you've got the Weaver's Skill the Loom of Fate. When that runs into the Lady's Skill, there's always a conflict. When you get to the overlap between the Dragon's Domain and the Weaver's and the Lady's Skills along with other Legendarys' Skills, things get messy.

Then you've got the various Heroics running around with their own Skills and the interactions those create. They aren't as wide-ranging but are more specific and more powerful in their specificity. A concentrated area around a Heroic's Domain can overwhelm the Dragon's Domain, so long as the Dragon isn't paying attention.

It's sort of the difference between a nuke and an ICBM, I guess. One is definitely more destructive, and more wide-ranging, but the other is more focused and useful in a wider range of situations. Or, you know, I would assume that metaphor works. It's not as if anyone ever let me play with either weapon in my previous life.

Turning away from idle thoughts, I read tickets, trying to grasp the state of the world. It's not the best option, but it is what I have. The timestamps, as well as the fluctuations in Mana use, expense, and the sudden surge in experience and deposits as Legendarys and Heroics die, tell a tale.

A tale of the three Legendarys on my side launching a surprise attack. Of members of the "official" Council getting injured and retreating form the fight including one Legendary—the Emperor himself. For all his strength, the fact that he doesn't have his empire backing him up makes him less powerful than he could be. Once he retreats, the Shadow Council—the Senior System Administrators—step in and balance the fight out further.

They've been fighting one another all across the planet, causing alien-made disasters everywhere they go. The System and the planetary defense force is hard-pressed to limit the damage, trying to restrict the Skills being used. They're doing everything from stabilizing earthquakes and continental shelves to deploying planetary shielding so that the entire planet and its atmosphere doesn't just ignite. Notations from the Administrators cross the ticket board constantly, lower-Leveled ones making adjustments and pulling on surplus System Mana to aid the planetary defenses on the backend.

I'm looking for details on the Weaver and the Lady, hoping either still live and are contactable. If they are, I could use their help. Of the three Council Members ostensibly on our side, those two are the most willing to help us for their own reasons. The Dragon is just... well, he's in it for himself.

Unfortunately, no matter how much I peruse the data, I don't get a definitive answer. There's a lot of it, and since the charts are just showing shifts in the experience distribution and Mana flow, when there are tens of thousands—and I do mean tens of thousands—of Adventurers and Artisans dying, the numbers are hard to gauge. What's the difference between a city getting blown up and the spike in experience from that or a Legendary dying? Not much, I'll tell you.

I give up and try a few other ways to search for information. Tapping into communication protocols, reviewing current planet- or even solar-system-wide Skills in effect. A lot of it is blocked, as I don't have the security clearance. In other cases, the System Administrators have pre-blocked my access. I tap away for nearly an hour before I finally give up.

"I could throw a Hail Mary and try to contact them directly and hope that whoever actually picks up is the right person." But I say that half-jokingly, for the fact stands that the Administrators could easily take over the communication if I did call them. Even under normal circumstances, it's dangerous to make a move like that.

Which means Plan E is out, unless I have another bright idea.

In frustration, I scroll through the tickets again, reviewing them just because I can. With the time dilation effect in play, I can afford to spend time on this.

An annoying tic from too many hours playing with ticketing systems, I find myself opening tickets on reflex. I even fix a few, my mind splitting a bit as the System helps me process the data. High Intelligence is useful for something, and the experience is always nice.

Eventually, my brain catches up with me.

It takes me a bit, but I realize I don't need to worry about contacting the Legendary's if they aren't here.

I pull up the data of Mana inflows, of how the energy is shunted. I pull together data for quadrants and the planet and the solar system. I watch the data change as it shifts from a constant flow from before I started all this to the constant drop off as more and more sapient creatures die. I tag the spot where the first Legendary dies and the Mana chart takes a huge nosedive.

Then I catch a second one, and another two more drops. Except the last two drops are localized, from quadrant to quadrant to planet to solar system. I realize that some Legendarys have left the planet, altering the graphs as they do so.

Possibly more than two Legendarys, but those are the biggest jumps.

Once I finish reading the charts, I realize that really, I don't know who is out there and who is still alive. It could be friend or foe just as easily. As such, I can't afford to contact anyone.

Which leaves Plan E as dead as the dodo.

***

Plan E is scuppered. While I'm growling to myself about my luck, Ali mentally prods me. It's a weird connection, since he's not in the Administrative Center and it's moving much faster than he is, but he seems to handle the disparity with ease. Being a being of matter, energy, and thought probably makes it simpler for him.

"By the way, why are the three fansketeers Plan D and not Plan C? Seems like a simpler thing to use whatever craft they've got than steal another one."

I hesitate, then decide to be blunt with Ali. *"I assumed they'd fail and get caught or get killed. And if not, they'd provide a good distraction."*

"Cold."

I send the equivalent of a mental shrug. It wasn't as if they didn't know the risk. They'd volunteered to help us out, as best as they could. And while I might have a little trace of guilt toward involving them, a part of me finds the entire weeb culture they have going on just… distasteful. And maybe I'm being a little judgmental. After all, they truly do seem to be trying to embrace Mikito and the entire Japanese samurai heritage wholeheartedly. It's still disturbing.

Truth be told, with so many balls in the air and with the threats there are, I'm struggling a little to keep anyone—even us—safe. The best I can do is make use of what resources I have and then, as I did, throw everything into the air and hope to catch what's important.

"Well, you want the good news or the bad news?" Ali sends back.

"I'll take the good news."

"They're incoming. Give or take twenty minutes our time."

I nod. That's a significant chunk of time for me in here. *"And the bad news?"*

"They've got company."

I send back a mental groan. Realizing my Mana is full, I pull out an Extra Hand. After he finishes coming into being, he nods at me before heading for the exit, leaving me alone once again.

"You coming out?"

"Got to check on plan F."

Ali sends a mental grimace, and I can't help but agree. He's not who I'd like to contact, if I even can. But we're getting to the point that something is better than nothing.

If the worst-case scenario happens, I might even revisit plan E. Though I'm more leaning toward Plan I. Even if in this case, it isn't set up alphabetically but to stand for Idiotic.

Pushing aside the thought, I reach into the Admin Center, searching through its communication interface. Mana floods into me once more, and I grit my teeth as it threatens to tear me apart as I tap into the System Edit Skill.

Hacking the System to make things work for me is such a bad idea. But I need to talk to someone, and this is someone the Administrators might not actually expect. It's the only real reason I'm willing to risk the chat.

***

"Well?" Mikito asks when I finally emerge.

The alien sun is finally setting on Irvina, casting the world in shades of pink and orange. In the distance, dark storm clouds roll in on this planet's east, covering up the distant mountains. The very air hums with power as Mana, overused and abused by the multiple Master and Heroic Classes throwing Skills around, shift the atmospheric environment. I shiver a little, feeling the hairs on the back of my head stand up.

"No dice," I say.

"None of them?" Mikito says with a frown. She's seated, watching the clouds and the surroundings, scanning for trouble and finding nothing. In her hands, she holds Hitoshi and a whetstone. Not that she needs to actually care for the Legacy weapon like that, but it seems to reassure her. Or maybe it's Hitoshi that needs the reassurance.

As if my presence is a beacon, Feh'ral comes back to himself fully, the faded-out portions of himself reforming. He raises an elegant brow, one bereft of hair, while Harry and Ali keep chatting in their own corner of the observatory, playing with the data sets they have access to.

As there's still a little time left before the fans arrive, I pull out another Extra Hand, wincing at the Mana usage. I need more Intelligence.

Both ways.

With Mikito waiting, I explain my reasoning and my utter failure to contact the Lord of Time and Space. He's either shifted his location, or his location in the local equivalent of a Forbidden Zone shrouds him from my attempts to contact him via the System. In either case, he's not going to yank us out of our pickle.

"Then we're relying on my fans. Or your idiotic plan," Mikito says.

"Or a combination of both. Unless…?" I raise an eyebrow at Feh'ral, who cocks his head. I shiver and am forced to explain. "You punched us through the dimensional lock once before."

"Yes," Feh'ral said. "I could try again Knowledge Acquisition. With your System Edit, we could manage the minor issues surrounding the constraints. However, I suspect they will be waiting for me to attempt to use my Skill." I grimace as Feh'ral continues. "It's a possibility, but the Skill itself is restricted. You know that. With so many…"

Mikito purses her lips then touches the Manop Galactic Positioning System pin we wear. They were given to us by the Erethrans. A chance for us to escape, maybe. Except I don't think they were expecting the fleets out there. And even if they are part of the opposing teams, I'm not sure we can make use of the pins. Not under the planetary screen.

If the Erethrans were going to do something, I'd expect it to have happened by now. That nothing has happened tells me we're likely on our own.

Still, I wear it. Because sometimes, you need a little reassurance.

Chapter 4

The vessel the Three Stooges stole for our getaway is more sleek Galactic mid-life crisis than bounty hunter ship that can blow through blockades and do the Kessel Run. It's small, thin, and angular with sharp-edged wings, and it's painted red with, yes, yellow racing stripes down each side. It swoops in fast, hitting the anti-velocity thrusters at the last second and coming to a sudden stop as it drops to the ground. A second later, a door near the cockpit pops open and a ramp unrolls. If a young Galactic woman was waiting on the other end in a hostess outfit, I would not have been surprised.

Instead, there's a very stressed looking dwarf in medieval Japanese ghost armor, a pair of katanas over her back, waving us in. The only way to tell her sex, what with the armor and all, is the lack of beard really. In the distance, fast moving dots are approaching.

"Hand One…" I say even as the team runs for the door.

"Yeah, yeah, yeah. Go die with glory. Utter goblin shit, that's what it is." My Extra Hand doesn't even stop as he blips away, high into the sky, before he triggers Beacon of the Angels.

The dots waver and some of them swing aside as the Skill tears a new hole in the atmosphere, but seconds later, even more craft appear, some of them heading for the Extra Hand. He's surrounded within seconds as the Dimensional Lock around us flexes and more enemies race toward us. No time to watch though, as we all pile into the ship.

"Where to?" Agr'us shouts. We're all patched in automatically to the ship's local broadcast network, so the pilot can hear my answer.

"Up."

"Are you insane? That's a suicide run!" But as much as Agr'us protests, the ship twists around on its axis and points almost directly upward. We burn fuel, shooting straight up.

"Guns?" Mikito shouts to the Gimsar, the woman bowing to Mikito, looking around the cramped and luxurious spaceship. It reminds me of the pictures of luxury private jets, with all the lounging chairs and places to play pool with small sections cordoned off for personal use. Leather and tiger stripes abound everywhere, with the lighting a little subdued and off-human norm.

"Nothing worth mentioning. This is a personal ship, not a fighter jet," Agr'us says as she comes out of her bow.

"*Ali, plot us a course that gives us the best chance out of here?*" I send to the Spirit.

He zips across the spaceship, phasing through walls as he heads for the cockpit. "*I'm assuming you mean where the fighting is the worst and we can try to sneak in, not where there's nothing and the Admiral can just lay the smackdown on us.*"

"*Your call. We'll likely have to do Plan I anyway…*"

One of my Extra Hands has wandered down the ship, a small notification window of the fight that is going on outside floating above his raised hand.

"Why'd you get it then?" Harry shouts, waving his hand around. "We needed a way out, not to be sitting ducks!"

"Because it's the fastest damn thing we could get our hands on with the best shields!" Ruvuds calls back from the cockpit. I can almost see the way his cat-eyes narrows at being questioned, and I'm sure his skin has flushed green blue. "Now shut up and strap in unless you have something you can do to help us."

"Damage Control," Mikito calls, heading for the engines.

"Bystander is running but…" Harry shrugs. I get it.

I head for the cockpit even as I feel a mental shudder run through me. My Hand is in one hell of a fight out there, taking on multiple Master Classes at the same time. I wish I could do more for him, but I'm still waiting for my Mana to regenerate. And truth be told, I'm going to need it. Even the extra sets of equipment I picked up are running low, what with my doppelgangers dying constantly. He's working with the equivalent of Advanced Class stuff, but since he's mostly using his Skills to dish out damage, it's all well and good. As I head for the cockpit, I feel when my on-board Hand throws up a Quantum Lock.

Good thing too, because I feel the shudder in the Mana sphere as people trying to teleport in are bounced off. That secondary sense the damn System has given me keeps shuddering as System Administrators and the planetary government bypass their very own blocks on teleportation. The Dimensional and Quantum Locks they put in place are like a sheet of steel between us and escape. Yet each exception they create, each person who arrives is a hole punched through their own Skill.

Soon enough, all these gaps will fill in by themselves. But in the meantime, the entire teleport block is weakened, broken as they try to catch us. All across the planet, where our assailants originated, others take advantage of the gaps. They tear into the holes, widening and forcing the Council and the Heroic Station Master to throw more Skills into the fray.

The Mana sphere shudders, and the System bucks a little as it tries to deal with all of it. Even so, the bad guys, they keep coming. They fall to my Hand, to the few defensive measures in place around the observatory. More die when the on-board Hand triggers Grand Cross to give Hand One a moment's reprieve, the area of effect Skill sloshing ocean and compressing ground and sapients in one move.

Experience and Mana floods in with the attack, dozens of Master and Advanced Classes dying.

The world bucks and the very membrane of reality twists as we race upward.

To be met by fire from the heavens itself.

***

The shields hold. They glow iridescent as the fighter ships and the Galactic defense force dressed like Rocketman-wannabes shoot through the air, circling our ship then peeling away as we refuse to divert course. They hammer our shields, but they hold, even as I tap into the ship with Linked Skill to use Disengage Safeties and boost our defenses.

"You know, we can dodge…" I grunt, feeling the strain as energy rushes out as our shields threaten failure. The shield generators are top of the line, Grade A+ stuff, something you would only see on military class ships in most cases. I'm boosting them even further with my Skills. A discordant hum passes through us all as the shields strain.

"You want fast or you want to live? 'Cause I can do one but not the other," Ruvuds says.

Even then, I see the waterfall chart showing our shield integrity dropping as more and more enemy ships peel away from other vessels to target us. They know it is us by now. They have to. They're diverting everything that can target us toward our single ship. Which gives the signal for everyone else who wants to leave to try their hand at running too.

That helps. A little.

As if someone is getting conflicting orders, some of the fleet and the space stations scramble to divert their firepower again, sending fighters and ships twisting around to cover their zones. Even so, the vast majority keep flocking toward us. Teleporting, doing mini-hyperjumps, blink stepping or just flying as fast as possible.

"Fast. Let's do fast," Ali snarls. He's floating at the top of the cockpit, half-translucent. I feel his strain through our mental connection, the pain he's under as he taps into his Elemental Affinity and defends us. Beams twist away from our shields before they impact, mass driven attacks are dispersed, their electromagnetic attraction reduced such that their very forms come apart before they arrive. "You know, boy-o, you could help me."

Warmth across my upper lip. I brush my hand at my nose and lip, and it comes away red. The shield generators aren't the only things crashing, as my health takes a nosedive. To keep everything running, to divert the attacks, I've tapped into System Edit and I'm paying the price.

"Can't." I grunt, eyes burning. Tapping into System Edit and connecting the Skills are using up Mana even as I become overstocked with it at the same time. The bypass feed, the balancing act of pull and push is taking everything I have. "Harry?"

There's no answer from the War Reporter. I'm not sure what he could do to help even if he was in the cockpit to hear me. Then again, we should be connected via the ship-wide intercom. Harry's build really isn't meant for things like this, and his Bystander Skill can only do so much.

"Mikito?"

"You didn't give me any guns," she grouses. She pops up in a view screen, standing in the middle of the engine room.

I watch as she makes minor adjustments to the flow of the engine, moves around with her Damage Control Skill to deal with the fact that we're redlining the engines, the Mana batteries, the shields. Everything really.

Her Skills, the ones she bought, are helping to repair the damage, to reduce the damage I do to them with my own manipulation. It'll keep us flying longer, if we aren't shot out of the sky.

"Feh'ral?" I call.

The Librarian is looking… thin. His lips twist, before he mutters, "I am already helping. I have created copies of our books. Those are distracting our more serious enemies."

I blink and decide I don't have time to deal with his answer. I definitely don't have time to deal with the library in my head trying to answer it for me.

We cross into the stratosphere, and the next line of enemies are there, waiting. They swarm us, leaving the few surviving ships in this region of space to flee. They're ignored, but some help by shooting back.

Missiles arrive, and the ship rocks and shudders as they explode. Lasers, fast-moving meteors, even suicidal fighter ships dart forward and hammer into our shields. I feel our defenses take another plunge, our shields failing in spots and our armor burning off. Some of the attacks penetrate even further, Skills bypassing the defenses to tear holes throughout the ship. Living metal flows to patch holes, but not before a gust of the void drags out air and leaves behind burnt metal, excess clothing, and unidentifiable fluids.

The ship is failing, and we're running out of options.

***

My last Hand takes action before I can ask. One second, he's watching the fight on both sides. The next, he's ejecting himself out of the ship as we break into real space. I'm a little amused to see him using a backpack assembly thing for maneuvering, but how long that'll last, who knows? At first, he's ignored, only taking damage from splash attacks.

Then he begins.

There's a reason why becoming an Erethran Paladin is so damn hard and Heroics are considered army killers. The Skill Judgment of All allows me to mass target anything I see as an enemy with a single cast. Since it routes through the System, it attacks individuals directly, which means pilots are just as easily targeted as solo flyers.

In this case, the Hand is using it instead of me, but it's the same damn difference.

He looks.

And space burns.

Over the com, I'm barking orders to everyone in the ship as we blast away, putting as much space as we can between him and us.

Ships, missiles, mass drivers, flying figures in super suits, and mages using spells to warp space and time. It doesn't matter. They burn. Shield flash red and white, glow then crumple, then armor shatters. Experience notifications pile up as those caught in the attack fall in seconds. Each second, damage mounts and shields fail, with the weakest going first.

There's no escape, no way to hide. Not from the Skill. Instead of staying to die, they run.

The fast make it out, sliding through the same gaps that let them approach us. They flee, only to have the Administrators and the Grand Admiral slam shut the gates, removing the very same permissions they were offered.

Some stagger, their concentration failing, their bodies damaged as they fail to pierce the Quantum Lock and Teleport Veil. Others fall to the continuing damage from our Skill, bare seconds having passed. The rest, realizing they have no choice, turn their focus on my Hand.

Unfortunately for them, he's not a big red mid-life crisis of a ship. He's a single fleeing individual, dancing through space and swooping between suddenly empty ships and bodies. Soul Shield flickers on and off constantly as the damage tears into him. Another cast of Judgment of All pointed in another direction sees more experience appear. More ships fail and enemies die.

Then, a flicker. A gap in the Quantum Lock. The Hand tries to Blink Step, tries to escape in the same moment. He's too slow.

Kasva hammers his axe into the Hand's side, splitting open the Soul Shield. Along with the shield, Kasva takes a leg and half a hip. The Hand throws a handful of Chaos Grenades, the first grenades being duds for the most part. A flock of furred creatures appear in mid-air, formed from Chaos energy, and die as they suffocate and freeze in space. Hydrogen blooms in vast clouds, glittering in space as it freezes, the force of the sudden creation of matter pushing apart the pair. A flurry of noise, music of the heavens forming and playing, pierces through everyone's defenses and sinks into our consciousness like a rabid ear worm.

+3.82% Tempo Buff Gained

And one single Chaos Grenade works beautifully. A dimensional gate opens and swallows the Hand and Kasva, along with everything else in a hundred-meter sphere. I feel my connection snap as the Hand dies. I can only hope that Kasva is gone too, but I doubt it. There's no experience notification, unlike for the dozens of others caught in the grenade.

In the chaos of the chaos grenade, we have a few moments' respite. We're free to run as our enemies react with shock. More than sixty percent of the attackers have fallen, the planetary shield above us failed and open. There's open space above us and we're fleeing…

Freedom's a few minutes away.

That's when the Admiral takes action and the space stations above us open fire. The combined attacks of the space stations—weapons meant to tear apart entire planetary killer comets and damage even Legendarys—tear our ship apart like a laser cutter through tissue paper. Adding on to all that, the damn Grand Admiral is using his Skills.

We never stood a chance.

***

The Portal opens, disgorging us a full ten thousand kilometers away from the vaporized ship. Energy from the attack floods through the Portal for a few seconds, long enough to make Harry and the others scream. The team burns, then the Portal shuts down even as the dimensional breach caused by the chaos grenade repairs itself.

I don't hesitate, casting my Skill again.

We're floating forward, momentum taking us right through the oval abyss in space, depositing us thousands of kilometers away. Distance is shortened by the damn Dimensional Locks that are repairing themselves even as we emerge. Beam weapons track toward our location, opening fire to catch us as we exit.

Ali catches the attacks, diverting them away. Then I shut down the Portal and take a breather, my body throbbing. The pain from System Edit, the overflow of Mana, and the damage I've taken is enough to break my focus.

Mikito conjures her horse and grabs Harry. Her fan club copy her actions, one of them moving to grab me only to realize I'm using the Hod to fly. A second of concentration is enough to program the power armor to track Mikito.

Vrasceids ignores me, though Feh'ral catches a ride on one of their horses, his eyes distant. I can see his Mana fluctuating. Occasionally, I hear a word from him as he murmurs Skills to himself. Things like "Branch Diversion," "Librarian's Choice," "Reshelving," and others. I ignore him as we dart through the next Portal I open.

We play hopscotch, the distance between each Portal shortening with each jump. Even with System Edit thrown into the mix, we're barely keeping ahead of our enemies. Ali is straining to deal with the constant barrage of attacks while I push us past the floating cordon of space stations, mines, and fleet vessels.

It's Plan I, for idiotic.

The extra boost from the chaos grenade was an unexpected helper, but punching our way through with System Edit and Portal was always part of it.

We blip again, forming the Portal behind a moon and getting a few seconds of peace before I open another Portal and blip us forward again, hiding from the damn space stations and the Admiral. We have no chance of really escaping as System Administrators do battle with me in System-space.

It's idiotic and futile. And yet, we don't have much choice either.

"How much further?" Mikito growls, looking at the screen that Ali is happy to populate for us all. A screen showing the solar system and the fast-moving spaceships coming for us. In front—the pair of fleets who are scrambling local fighters. Behind us, more space fighters scrambling from the moon base, from the space stations.

"I'm not sure…" I grit my teeth against the pain and my seesawing health. Health potions and the occasional spell from the Stooges help, but it's still dropping.

Things get easier once we're outside of the major teleport block around the planet, but it just means I can stop using System Edit. Then Mana becomes a problem after a few hops, even as I keep the draw lower to block off amendments to my own Skill.

I notice when the Administrators shift their attention away, when they stop trying as hard. More orders perhaps, or just a realization we're not getting that far. Ten thousand kilometers sounds great, but on a stellar scale, it's tiny. For all the trouble we've caused, we're still insignificant now that the pins have fallen.

I run through options even as we keep running, shifting directions as our enemies close in.

No ship, so all my purchased Skills are useless. Not enough Mana for another Hand to give us a distraction. I could pull down the System Edit, use the System Mana for that, but it's a dangerous game. I know, instinctively, that this is not what the Skill is meant for and there might be consequences for abusing it.

We could try to turn around and capture one of the many ships we're fleeing, but we'd still run into the incoming fleet. We could do the same for the ones coming at us, but they'd be going the wrong direction. I keep the options in mind anyway, even if punching through the anti-teleport wards on any of these ships might be a little much.

On the other hand, if we Portal in right next to where one of them might appear, we might be able to physically board them.

I communicate as much to the team. Mikito takes it with equanimity. Feh'ral purses his lips, raising an eyebrow. I shake my head, wanting to keep his Skill in abeyance for now. We only get one shot with it, and I'd prefer to use it for something a little bigger than a small fighter plane.

"You're insane. You're madder than a hatter bathed in mercury and in the last stages of dementia. You make Nero seem sane," Harry rants.

The fan club look a little white, a little green, and a little blue, depending on their initial skin tone. Yet they get ready, Galactic steel in their spines. Maybe this entire thing about not fearing death is useful.

As for me? I'm in a little too much pain to be afraid. A little too rushed to freeze up. We jump one more time, dodging another series of attacks. We flee forward, closing in on the ships coming for us, the space fighters and the battleships.

When they get close enough, I throw a Portal open to where they'll be. And then intuition twinges and I slam the Portal shut before any of us can enter.

Seconds before the battleship we were attempting to board disintegrates. A small blackhole appears where the ship used to be, dragging nearby ships and us toward it. The nearby ships are swallowed by the tiny hole, disappearing faster than I can blink. We're drawn in, unable to resist, before it just… disappears. The System handles the minor conflagration, even as my brain points out a new ticket has been added.

"What the hell was that?" Dornalor says.

"A warning," I grunt.

Looks like they won't let us acquire a new mode of transportation that easily.

We have a minute or so of peace as we fly onward, the tattered tactical wing regrouping before they aim themselves toward us. We have a minute of peace while I flick through my Skills and options.

Options shrink. As I get ready to test myself against the Administrators' Skills to edit Portal, I feel a shift in the Mana sphere. The Quantum Lock around us, the one stopping us from jumping out of the Solar System, shudders. Something is attempting to punch through, and the pins on our chests glow.

I look down as I feel the way the Quantum Lock shudders. I try to reach for the code that makes up the pins so I can add the three members of the Fan Club to the upcoming portal. The Quantum Lock strains as the dimensional barrier holding us ripples. The code is there, System Mana flooding into me as I burn up while handling the information.

Seconds to alter the information, to twist it to what I need. Hasty lines of Mana, redone and sent back to the System for approval, floods out of me. My body shudders and twists, but I know I have it right. I wrap Feh'ral and the team in the code change, and that eternal moment shifts.

Then, just moments before the lock breaks, I feel another intrusion. Another Administrator, this one more skilled by far. She alters my code, throwing it into disarray. I throw myself back into the fray, but she chose her time perfectly. The breach I created closes up even as the attacks approach.

Perfect except for her forgetting we have one other in play. I feel him take action, trigger his Skills. Mental Impartation, Mind over Matter, Knowledge of the Masses, Imbue Skill, and finally, Knowledge Acquisition. They hammer into the breach, unable to open the way entirely but able to hold the way through open. Even as my opponent Administrator reaches out, I feel Feh'ral use one last Skill, pushing it in ways it should not—Silence of the Sanctum of Learning.

It shuts down her System Edit Skill for a fraction of a second.

Long enough for me to implement a change in the code, piggybacking on Knowledge Acquisition's transfer.

Through all this, I'm staring at Feh'ral, his face a rictus of pain. He's pushing his abilities to the maximum, his world closed in on this other battle. He never sees the attack that slips through, the one that targets the pin on his chest. It blinks and stops glowing, seconds before my code finally kicks in. The Librarian's eyes widen, fear—such a distinct emotion even on his alien face—appears.

Time, time that has been passing even as we fight in the fractions of a second that Skill and thought coding happens, finally moves in and finishes.

He disappears.

Or more correctly.

We do.

Chapter 5

We blip into being, no Portal required, in the middle of an Erethran warship. Judging by the layout of the teleport room, all pale blue and white steel, it's a BattleCruiser. A half dozen Erethran Soldiers, weapons leveled at the teleport pad, relax a little when the pad stops humming. A second later, they have their weapons holstered and are saluting me, even as the remainder of my team looks around, surprise deep on their faces.

"We have them, Your Grace," the captain of the guard barks over his communicator. A second later, he's striding over to me and snapping a salute. "Welcome on board, Honored Grand Paladin."

"Yeah…" I center myself before continuing. "Where are we?"

"This is Her Grace's personal BattleCruiser, the *Sword of the Empire*. We are located just under twenty thousand kilometers from the current solar hyper limit and are pulling away at this moment."

"You got us out?" Mikito said, touching the badge that is now so much slag metal on her chest. "This worked?"

"Of course, Honored Spear. The Dimensional Lock in place might be powerful, but we do have our ways around it," the Captain says with a smirk.

By the console attendants, a pair of wan-looking Honor Guards offer us tired smiles. They are in Mana withdrawal shock and I can see their health slowly sliding upward, contrary to the Captain's confident words. The console attendants look even worse, one of them scrubbing blood out of his eyes.

"Then why…?" Harry says, his anger sparking.

"A matter of distance and integrity of their Dimensional Lock," the Captain answers with ease. I eye him and his Status information, one that's a little more complicated than normal and filled with unnecessary details, including his name. Then I realize why there's nothing amusing added to it.

"One second…" I hold out my hand and resummon Ali.

The Spirit twists and pops into being next to me, looking aggrieved. "Took you long enough. Any longer and they were going to banish me."

"The others?" Mikito asks. She looks very worried, and I realize it's taken me way too long to realize that not only did Feh'ral manage to miss the ride, so did the Three Stooges.

My stomach clenches, knowing they've been left behind. Even though I worry about them, not a single iota of my body wants to go back for them. Maybe it's the ruthless part of me that knows it's suicide to try. Maybe it's just the cold edge, the one that has learnt to weigh lives against my mission and finds this one unsuitable. I don't ask the Captain. I don't even think to do so.

"Still alive. Feh'ral's stopped holding back and they were coasting on a droid-like thing he'd summoned. It was moving at a pretty damn good clip, but they don't have a lot of cover. The samurai are doing their best to hold the Fleet back, but..." Ali shrugs. He's just as cold as I am.

Mikito looks worried, but I note she doesn't ask for us to go back. Neither does Harry, though he looks ill.

"Think they'll pull back?" I say as the Captain gestures for us to follow him. Not having a better idea, I do, and the others fall in behind me. Traversing the corridors is like being in a high-tech movie, with its multiple fluorescent light interiors and clean lines, though the scurrying coral-eared Erethrans, all in military uniforms, remind me that things aren't as calm as it might seem.

"Maybe. But I doubt it. Feh'ral's got his own bounty if you forgot," Ali replies.

I grimace. A part of me wonders if he'll make it, if there's anything we can do. The Erethrans aren't likely to risk their people for him even if they have other ships in play. I'm surprised they even went so far for us. Which does bring up another question.

"Is this the only ship or…?" I ask the Captain.

"Her Grace has brought the entirety of her Task Force with her," the Captain says, glancing at me. He opens his mouth to say something then freezes, eyes darkening. "Brace for jump."

No sooner has he spoken than the world flickers. Our bodies stretch out into infinity in a too long fraction of a second before the world snaps back into space. Harry shudders, Mikito's eyes tighten, and my stomach rumbles. Ali is the worse, having to blip himself back to me since he went… somewhere.

"That was a rough transition," I say. We've entered hyperspace before, but never like that.

"Emergency military entry," the Captain says. "We have to scramble the entry band and location. That was the smoothest emergency entry I've been on in ages. Her Grace has some of our best pilots."

"That was smooth?" Harry mutters.

"Like chunky peanut butter regurgitated," I say, agreeing with Harry before turning to the captain. "All right, show me to her. I'm guessing we have a lot to talk about."

"Of course, Honored Grand Paladin." Another slight bow and he hurries off.

I don't miss the fact that trailing behind us is the security team. Not that they'd be of much use, but it's interesting that they even put one on us at all.

Wheels within wheels.

***

We meet with the Empress Apparent, Catrin Dufoff, the gorgeous ex-companion, ex-spy, and ex-lover of mine. She is, as always, stunning in that tall, statuesque, and elegant way. Except now there's a palpable aura around her, from both a Skill and the air of command she has come to embody. She's dressed in a green and white uniform with yellow edging along the left side of the cross-buttoned tunic. Her belted sword and necklace show the telltale glow of Mana, the kind that only an artifact gives off.

I'm curious, so I poke at her Status.

Empress Apparent Catrin Dufoff of the Erethran Empire, Empire Top Companion, The Hidden Blade, Class 2 Human Resource, Slayer of Goblins, Wexlix, Crilik, (more)… (Erethran Empress Apparent Level 11) (M)
HP: 2830/2830
MP: 4210/4210
Conditions: Aura of the Empire (retracted), Trust of the Empire, Never too Late, Pheromones, A Good Impression

And get a surprise.

"You've Leveled."

"Your Grace!" The bodyguards—Erethran Honor Guards to be exact—snarl at my disrespect. I just glare at them, but they don't back down. Which is… good… I guess?

"It's okay. Our Grand Paladin is not known for his manners," Catrin says, gliding forward. She puts a hand on my chest, tilting her head down just a little to meet my gaze. "And we have a past."

Harry makes a gagging sound while Mikito heads off to the side where the drink cart stands. She helps herself to a purple liquor, one we both know from our time on Pauhiri. She turns, raising an eyebrow at Harry and me. We both nod, and seconds later, we're catching a filled glass and bottle respectively.

"Really, John. You could try a little more." Catrin's nose wrinkles as I drain the bottle and wipe my lips. She's smart enough to have stepped back, eyes flicking around constantly as she reads the notifications that only she can see. I'm guessing it's an Empress Apparent thing, always getting updates.

"I could. But you get thirsty, escaping death." I cock my head. "How safe are we? Really?"

"Not very," Catrin says. "Which is why we are not going to be stopping anytime soon. Or letting you stay with us long."

I freeze in the middle of taking another swig.

"We don't have much time and have a lot to discuss."

I sigh and put the bottle aside. "I'll say. You have put the Erethran Empire directly against the Council."

"Not the Council itself. Not the official one," Catrin says. "Just the Shadow Council. We have long chafed at their control. So now, we act. Perhaps we will fail, but if we do so, it will be glorious. Rather than be shackled by their shadowy tendrils." Her eyes glint as she raises her voice. "We are no slaves. We will not be bound."

"We will not be bound!" the Honor Guards echoes her, as does the Captain, who has yet to leave.

The new motto is interesting, but something else she said has caught my interest more. "You knew of the Shadow Council?"

"We might not have been able to locate or identify them, but we saw the shift in the Mana flow, the shadow they cast on history. We knew they were there but could not bring them to light. Nor would we dare take them on. Alone."

I nod slowly. That… well. That makes sense, even if it would have been nice to have known that information. The way the Queen acted before, I thought we were alone. Which, I guess, we were. She threw us in, expecting us to flounder, but now that we've managed to upset the apple cart, she'll make full use of it.

Then Catrin's grin makes me reevaluate everything. A grin and her next words, "I might have forced her hand a little too."

"You didn't," I say.

Catrin shrugs. "I have two jobs as Empress Apparent. Learn how the Empire functions so that when it is my turn, I am ready. And second, to do what the Empress herself cannot."

"And this is the second, is it?"

"Yes. My counterparts in the Movana, in the Truinnar, in the other empires and kingdoms, we act now. None of us control the full force of our empires, but together…" She shrugs. "We are a force to be reckoned with. With those Legendarys you gained on our side…"

"The Council has the Galactic Fleets."

"Yes. We do."

I parse her words, then blink. "Betrayal? In the fleets?" My stomach lurches, for those Fleets have a place to be, a job to do.

"You can't betray your true employer." Her lips peel apart in a savage grin.

I nod slowly. Tricky. Very tricky, since the Shadow Council was never official. The controls the Administrators put in place were never part of the formal chain of command. "Then all the Council is on your side?"

"No. There are some holdouts. The Nang Mai is neutral, for now. Ares stands with the Shadow Council. The Truinnar are, officially, denouncing us. They are… conflicted. But we have the majority."

"Then the third fleet out there…"

"Was sent by us. We could not bring more."

Something in the way she says that makes me narrow my eyes. I wonder if she could have, and they chose not to. If the deaths of their ambassadors and diplomats were more useful to her cause. A trigger to strengthen the resolve of others.

"And Harry's news? The information on the Quest and the Administrators?"

"Being disseminated as fast as possible." She inclines her head. "They will find it harder this time to silence the truth."

"And the Questors?" I ask, for they have risked much too. They are one of the major sources of distribution, having been provided the information by me beforehand. Once I triggered all this, they acted and kept the information flowing.

"Doing their part. We will try to protect them when we can, but our forces are stretched thin."

I nod. "They're tough bastards anyway."

She smiles. "Yes. They are. Obsessed and insane, but hardy."

That last comment might have been a little pointed. I consider what else I want to know from her, what else I should consider asking. There's a lot, but one thing stands out more than anything else. "Earth?"

"They will have to stand on their own. That is all we can do for them," Catrin says, her voice iron.

I note her phrasing and sigh. Of course. I threw Earth out alone to be torn apart by the wolves, by the corporations and guilds that want a piece of it. Without the protection of being on the Council, there's no planetary wide council, no protection against people blipping in when they want. From others taking over settlements by sheer force.

It'll be a Wild West again, except this time, we're the natives.

I can only hope that Earth has had enough time to build up. That the Champions and the allies they've gained will stand by their side and safeguard the planet. That, in the end, not too much of it is lost.

"Now, come. There are a few things we need to discuss in private," Catrin says, gesturing for me to follow her. There's a room on the other end of the door, one that slides shut behind us even as the others are left behind.

Before it closes, I see Harry slump in a chair while Mikito questions the Captain, the group finding time to rest and relax. Even tap into the Erethrans' mobile military Shop.

We leave them behind, to discuss matters of great import and privacy.

***

I look up at the beautiful lady adjusting her uniform, smoothing out the wrinkle-free, armored fabric while tweaking the fit and angle of her various accessories. I'm lying on the board room table, rolled over on my side, feeling a little stunned and a lot used. Though I'm not about to complain.

"You should get dressed. We'll be within range to Portal you to your destination soon," Catrin says, looking at me over her shoulder.

"What? No candy or a thank you?" I say, sitting up. A simple Cleanse spell cast on myself and the room in general clears out traces of our activities before I swap my clothing for something new. I hadn't realized it, but what I had been wearing was rather rank, what with the sweating, bleeding, and getting torn apart I had been dealing with lately.

"Not the time, Paladin. Oh, and take this." She flicks a hand at me, and a data packet flickers through the air. It hits my Neural Link, slides past the defenses, and unspools itself.

I shudder at the ease she cut through the defenses of the software. "How did you…?"

"I'm your Empress Apparent, Grand Paladin. I have access, if I so choose, to certain areas." She smiles slightly. "I just needed to get close enough to make it work."

Which explains why the Empress did not use it on me. Though… "How much access?"

"Nothing you need worry about. The Neural Link is safeguarded by the System against doing true damage to you. One of the requirements of anything touching your mind by the Council and reinforced by the System."

I want to ask why, but the library offers me the explanation within seconds. It's the same reasons why certain Psychics and Classes have gone out of favor, why there were wars fought and, later on, I realize, System Administrator adjustments.

Slaves are not something the System needs. True, mentally controlled slaves, dead-eyed zombies who can barely think for themselves—which is what any true mind control method would require—creates problems for the System in terms of experience gain and distribution. And, of course, the flow of Mana. Somehow, Mana itself does not want, does not work properly with, these brainwashed zombies.

I bite my lip, wondering why. It seems strange that the Mana—not the System, but Mana itself—does not flow normally through those who are restrained in that manner. There are no indications of such issues with Serfs, or those under Gaeas or my Shackles. Not in the Library, not in anything I've seen or heard. And yet, it is there.

Proof that Mana itself can choose. Or is built—if you can create Mana—in a specific manner.

It's… interesting.

Catrin calls my name, bringing me back to the present.

"What?"

"You were gone again."

I shrug, not sure how to respond. It is what it is, what with the library in my head. Then thinking over what happened before I got distracted, I ask, "That information packet…"

"Might be of use to you. Some details of what is happening, the latest maps that the Empire has for the Forbidden Zone. Waypoints for safe houses, information about known raiders, pirates, and gangs, as well as charts for Mana currents," Catrin says.

"That's…" State secrets. Information that costs millions of Credits, if you could even buy them on the open market.

"What is necessary to keep you alive." Catrin smiles a little. "So long as you live, they will hunt you, Grand Paladin. They fear what else you will do, and what else you might learn. You have made them your enemies, and while we might threaten the status quo, we but plan to replace it." She cocks her head before lowering her voice. "You intend to destroy it entirely. And that is more dangerous than anything we can do."

"I think you're giving me a little too much credit," I say. "I'm just looking for answers."

"Answers that they want no one to receive. I will gamble that I am right, and that whatever the answer is in the end is important enough to hide from all Galactic society for millennia."

I rub the back of my neck, but there's not much more to say. Not really. Maybe she's wrong. Maybe she's right. In either case, what she's provided will keep us alive. Though I don't tell her that they might not bother chasing us. Because they probably know our final destination.

Administrative Center 14-1-1.

"Thank you."

"Just stay alive." She sends me off with her eyes, eyes that are laced with pity and kindness. I'm not sure I like the look, but who am I to judge her feelings? I can barely stand my own. "John."

In reply, I bow, placing a fist over my chest. An Erethran Salute for the Empress Apparent. The lady who has thrown the bones and gambled on me and a dream.

I can only hope she's right.

***

"You know, I really think you should look into getting laid more," Harry says as we gather around the teleport pad. It is the same one we arrived in, with the same Captain and his men watching us. I raise an eyebrow at the dark-skinned reporter, who is looking a little sloshed. "That way, the next time you're in trouble, they can pull our asses out of the fire."

"True. Then again, we might be pulled into more trouble," Mikito says with a little smile.

"Really. You too?" I say accusingly. The guards are all looking a little affronted by the way my friends speak, though there's not much they can do. Especially since they're about to throw us off their ship. "And who are you to talk? When was the last time you got laid?"

"John!" Mikito looks shocked and hurt, going so far as to put a hand over her chest as if protecting herself against my accusation.

Harry and Ali both look at me as if I kicked a puppy and I find myself wincing. The death of her husband, the loss of her family, it nearly drove her to despair. If she had not been a little stronger, if not for people like Lana who helped pull her out, if not for her sense of duty that kept her fighting to keep others safe, I think Mikito would have killed herself.

For me to tease her, no matter what kind of stress I am under, no matter how irate I am… "I'm sorry. I shouldn't…"

She breaks into a grin, dropping her hand. Ali laughs while Harry shakes his head, a small smile playing on his lips. He seems more stable now, a few minutes of rest having helped him. The wild swings in his mood are a little worrying, but I can only take it as they come for now.

"Wait. What? You laugh, but…"

"It's been a decade, John. It still hurts"—Mikito looks at Hitoshi, the weapon that her husband gave up his Perks, his Class, and in the end, his life for, and smiles gently at it—"but it isn't the same pain as before. It won't ever stop hurting, but I think he'd want me to move on by now." She meets my eyes, her gaze heavy with meaning. "It's okay to move on."

Before I can answer her, before I can ask how, the world shimmers. The teleportation pad activates, our bodies twist and pull, compressing and dispersing as we're thrown across the unending reaches of space. We come apart and reappear millions of kilometers away.

And we're once more in the thick of it.

I never do get an answer.

Chapter 6

Escaping once we portal into Dornalor's waiting ship is of minimal concern. Irvina is right next to the Forbidden Zone, literally in it. It only isn't a Forbidden Planet due to the sheer volume of resources poured into it, and even then, they've moved the planet a few times as the Forbidden Zone expanded. Once we're actually out of the planet's sphere of influence, hiding becomes much easier.

Finding people in the vast reaches of space is hard enough to begin with. It's like looking for a dingy in the Pacific Ocean without flyovers, just sail ships cutting across the ocean. Now, there are obvious currents and flows of wind, trade routes that are often the way people go because that's the easiest way to travel. But since everyone knows what those are, it's easy enough to steer away from those locations and enter the vast reaches of space.

Sensors and drones degrade fast in the Forbidden Zone, the overflow of Mana shorting out Skills and degrading sensor readings. Bioengineered drones with just enough sapience to churn Mana do better, but they run the risk of mutating or getting eaten for experience.

The deeper you go, the worse it gets. Search zones become smaller; the number of individuals required to work through the Forbidden Zones higher. Monsters will destroy any ships and Captains that are not sufficiently Leveled. And that's not even taking into account Dornalor's Skills.

Once we build up a decent amount of speed, Dornalor goes dark, killing impulse engines and layering his Skills like Just a rock, Sir and Reduced Signature as we coast. Since we're running through space close to near light speed rather than hyperjumping or using the hyperspace streams, it means we might be floating for a bit, but it's safer.

Unfortunately, sooner or later we'll need to hit the hyperspace streams and things will get tricky again. There's only so many pathways through the

Forbidden Zone, making us easier to track. There are still ways to avoid detection, but the Pirate Captain is insistent this is the safest way for now. And one thing I've learnt is that when you hire a specialist, you listen to them.

So we coast.

In the Forbidden Zone, the System is down, many of the Skills that make connecting to the Shop and the greater Galactic universe broken. There are ways around that, Skills that allow Harry to check in on the situation even through Mana interference, but for the most part, we just drift.

Through space. Silent. Alone. After the harried running, the unrelenting pressure of having to do something, now we must wait and watch. Be silent, be invisible.

And truth be told, we need it.

***

A week in, Dornalor finally turns on the warp thrusters. They speed us up, giving us multiple times the speed of light. It's not great, nowhere near as fast as riding the hyperspace streams, but those are still being watched. That much, Harry has managed to learn. For the most part though, the War Reporter has spent his time hiding in his cabin. I get the feeling I'm on his shit list now, at least until he heals from his most recent traumatic experiences.

If he heals.

In fact, almost all of us spend our time in our cabins. The ship isn't small, but when you have four people and three of my Extra Hands hanging out, it gets cramped. We're all bumping into one another, and if not for the fact that we might need the Hands if we get caught, I would have dismissed them. They're grumpy, irritable, consume my chocolate stores at an indecent rate, and spend their time either sitting around brooding, staring into space as they access the library, or training.

Dornalor, of course, spends most of his time in the cockpit. His cabin is right next to it, though it's not very large. Not that he needs it to be. Even when he's resting, he's more often resting in his captain's chair. The Pirate Captain is quiet and, I admit, a little angry at me.

In fact, about the only person who does not seem to be angry at me—and that includes the Hands—is Mikito. The Samurai spends her time training, going through her forms and practicing with new weapons, or cooking. That's relatively new. We all took turns cooking before, but now, she's putting together little bento boxes, cutting up vegetables into pretty shapes, layering the foodstuff and making sure it's all pretty and presentable.

Mostly, it's cute and elegant. Occasionally though, she seems to take inspiration from the monsters we've fought and the colors and shapes she carves out are… disturbing. Though, I'll admit, there's a bit of satisfaction chomping through the head of a Narato or slowly chewing off the arms of a Hakarta Jell-o figure.

Fine. Maybe we're all a little broken.

A week after we engage the warp drive, I find myself leaning against a wall, watching Mikito prep. One of my Hands is sitting at the dining room table, staring into space, reading from the library probably. Or imitating how I access the library. I'm never entirely sure, and I don't want to ask.

In either case, Mikito's finishing up another bento box and making it disappear into her inventory.

"Why the change?"

"What change?" Mikito says, looking at me though her hands never stop moving.

"The food. The presentation. The…" I wave, unable to express the shift I've noticed in her.

Mikito shrugs. I frown, but don't push. Still, I guess standing there and watching her is prompt enough because she answers me when she's done, the remainder boxes stored in the mess hall storage units for when the rest of the team choose to eat.

"You reminded me. That the past is the past." She offers me a half-smile, both sad and wry. "And that I need not avoid what I knew or enjoyed before. That I can—I have—moved on."

"So you picked up bento box making?" I say a little incredulously. Better than asking her how I did the reminding.

"Didn't pick up. I was quite good at it before," Mikito says, puffing up a little. "I enjoyed it. Used to send Ken to work every day. It made his coworkers so jealous." Her lip twitches. "And I had a decent following on Instagram."

I stare at the woman, trying to imagine the warrior-queen as a housewife, puttering around making bento boxes and sending her husband off to work. Though a part of me points out she worked too. Surprisingly, I find it less difficult than I thought to imagine her as a good housewife. Seeing her in a simple jumpsuit, hair tied back in a ponytail, the harsh lines and the deadly blade edge that she is seems to be blunted. Or perhaps sheathed is a better term.

Huh.

"And you?" Mikito says.

"Me what?"

"What kind of hobbies did you have?" Mikito asks. "Before."

"And masturbating doesn't count!" Ali pops up through the floor.

I glare at the little Spirit who has been going missing a lot recently. He seems to have decided that wherever he goes is more interesting than just sitting around, waiting for something to happen. He promises he's doing something useful out there, but what that is, he won't tell me.

My guess? Probably trying to get more pirated copies of pre-System Earth TV shows.

"Yeah, yeah. I… didn't have many. At least, nothing major. Video games, hiking and camping, snowshoeing. Movies." I shrug. "You know, the usual stuff."

"Nothing else?"

I can't help but shrug again. Sure, I watched all the geeky stuff you'd expect. Spent some time doing sports, though I was never good at any of them. I never had a passion for things, just a passing interest. Mostly, I worked and drifted, consuming mass entertainment to fill the void of passing time.

"Now that's just sad," Ali says.

"Says the Spirit who can't stop watching reality TV."

"I can split my attention. Unlike you meat sacks." Ali sniffs. "Being in your reality would be a torture otherwise. Also, you humans are so weird. I mean, you keep complaining about the System, but you humans would go out of your way to live in inhospitable environments wearing nothing."

I pause, then shake my head. "There was a prize for those things."

"Not always."

"Bragging rights."

"'Hi! I'm an idiot who decided to be dropped in the middle of nowhere with no resources. I also have no actual survival skills, but don't worry—you get to gape at my nude, fleshy bits because I'll have this televised all across the world.'" Ali puffs out his chest while making his clothes fade, showing the hirsute form he has taken. I admit, I look and he's anatomically correct. "'Now, marvel at me, fellow human. Marvel!'"

Mikito giggles and I turn to her, mock glaring. "Don't encourage him."

"Why are you not marveling!" Ali calls.

The Hand blinks a few times, dismissing his notifications, then waves at Ali. The next second, the poor Spirit disappears, dismissed back to his realm. I nod thanks to the Hand who glares back. I make note to dismiss him tonight and recall another one. Don't want them splitting off too much. And maybe I'll get lucky, and the System will decide to find a version of me that isn't such an asshole.

Probably not.

"So… that does bring up another point," I say, walking over to Mikito and lowering my voice. I'm not sure why, just that this seems like a more personal talk.

Mikito stares, waiting, and I find myself unsure. Uncertain of how to proceed. Maybe a little unwilling to get the answer. In the end, it's her narrowing eyes and growing impatience I spot that makes me speak.

"What Katherine said. You know you can leave, right? We can figure out something about your Class. Edit it—"

"Baka." Mikito glares at me.

"I know. But… where we're going…" I shake my head. "It's my Quest. Not yours."

"I have one too, you know," Mikito says.

"I know… but it's not as if…"

Mikito makes her Quest window visible to me.

System Quest Completion Rate: 83%

"WHAT!?!" I shout.

I'm so loud that moments later, Dornalor and Harry make their way over. I'm still standing there, jaw agape while Mikito smirks and gets to prepping another dish. Tempura it looks like, what with the flour and the big pot of oil. A weird addition for a bento, since fried food isn't great kept for later, but it's possible she's just cooking because we all have a ridiculous metabolism.

"What's the screaming for?" Dornalor growls, glaring at me. He looks less than happy, what with his yellow skin turning a little brown and doing his best to loom with all nine feet of his height.

"What's your System Quest like?" I say, then turn to look at Harry. "You too."

"Why? It's low. I'm no Quest…" Dornalor's eyes widen.

Harry spots the change and shares his notification. Dornalor is only a few seconds behind him.

System Quest Completion Rate: 85.4%

System Quest Completion Rate: 67%

"Why is Harry's so much higher?" I say. The last few percentage points before 90% are hard to acquire, as I know all too well. Even with the library in my head, it was never easy to raise it. And Harry and Mikito have not done half as much research as I have.

"Why is Dornalor's low?" Mikito says.

"Low?" the Pirate Captain says incredulously. "Last time I checked, it was in the low teens!"

"Check your logs," I bark. "When did all this change?"

Dornalor and Harry get to checking, while Mikito answers me. "Mine has always been increasing when I've been with you. Small, till I took my Oath. Then it increased by nearly ten percent. It held still for a long time. Then we learnt more about your secondary Class."

I find myself nodding along a little. A portion of my mind, a partitioned corner, is browsing through the library, searching for relevant information.

"It increased again then and once more when you told me of your System Quest to the Prime Center. And lastly, when we arrived on this ship," she says.

"Same. Mine increased a little while you did your thing in Erethra, but mostly, when you arrived on the ship this time," Dornalor says.

"It's still low though…" Memory, studies, previous notes I had dismissed before come back to me. I find myself relaxing a little as I get an explanation.

My friends notice immediately of course.

"What is it?" Harry says.

"Companion bonuses. It's uncommon. So long as you follow me and learn a little bit of what I do, you gain a portion of the System Quest completion rate I get. However, it's not…" I frown, cocking my head as I consider the term to use. "Permanent. If you decide to break away from me, if you aren't committed to my search, you could see it drop."

"That explains the lack of experience gains," Harry says, nodding.

Dornalor grumbles a little, while Mikito frowns.

"Not the same for you?" I say to her.

"I do get experience."

I consider her answer. I wish I could look at her logs, but we're not in an Administrative Center. I can get a rough feel of things by being next to her, but that's not the same as a proper review. Still… "Might be an interplay between your Class, Skill, and the Quest."

Mikito nods. She's vowed to follow me as her Lord till the end. It's possible the System has taken that oath at face value and is crediting her as though it is a permanent increase. Breaking her vow, splitting from me, would likely cause quite a bit of an issue with her Class. That, at least, we know from past experience with other Classes of this kind.

"So we can't get experience at all?" Harry says. Then he answers his own question as he scrolls down his log. "No. I get a bit here and there still. But it looks like the majority isn't being credited."

"And Dornalor isn't getting an increased completion rate because he isn't that interested," I say, nodding slowly. "Quite possibly unlikely to even follow us down, right?"

"To Xylargh?" Dornalor shakes his head. "Once I drop you off, we'll be deep enough that the Council isn't likely to find me once I leave. I just need to find the right people to make a few changes…"

"There's the right kind of people on the planet?" I ask.

Dornalor nods.

"Bolo and you never mentioned how much of a pirate haven Xylargh is," I say.

Dornalor sniffs. "It wasn't really relevant, was it?"

Because we're talking about it, I can't help but add, "Thank you. Again. For picking us up and being willing to ferry us there."

Dornalor pauses before he shrugs a little too exaggeratedly. "It's nothing. When your call came through, I was already in the region. Anyway, being your employee is little different to the Council than being your friend."

I knew that picking us up, helping us was partly self-serving. Having a Heroic Level escort can't hurt, especially if he's trying to get back to Spaks.

Still, helping us is more than just a passing thought and I can't help but feel a little bit of the warm fuzzies.

"Right, of course." I glance at Harry, who is looking contemplative.

When I raise an eyebrow in query, Harry turns away and walks back to his room. I sigh but leave it, knowing he still needs time to process. A part of me wonders if he'll part ways with me when Dornalor does.

"I best get back to the cockpit," Dornalor says.

When Mikito points to the storage, he grins and grabs some bento boxes, giving thanks to her. He hurries out with a half dozen boxes piled high, balancing everything in his hands as he tries to peek within.

"Make sure to bring them back!" Mikito shouts after him. When he's gone, she sighs. "He's not bringing them back, is he?"

"Probably not."

"So did you have more questions then?"

"I did. It doesn't seem like you want to answer them."

She shrugs. "I took an Oath to follow you, John. It means something to me. And if there's ever going to be an answer, I think you'll find it."

I offer her a half-smile. "Yeah, but you couldn't know that back then."

"Mmmm… not initially. But you wanted—you need an answer. That kind of obsession, it only has a few results. One, I wanted—we wanted—to stop. The other…"

"The other is where we are, eh?" I sigh. "Yeah, I get it."

I don't ask her what the other end result is. She's told me often enough, as have Lana and the others. It's not a nice ending, even if it is… true. "Now, you going to cook that or just play with it?"

Mikito looks at the flour mixture she's prepped. "Sure. Do you have any of those space octopuses left?"

I check my inventory and grin, popping out a tentacle. "Last of the loot."

"Nice!" Mikito reaches for a knife.

I push aside further thoughts. For now, at least. I wish I could ask her to go, to save herself, but I know better. And really, the part that wants me to ask her to go is not that large.

Not at all.

Chapter 7

I float in space, staring at the swarm… herd… flock… infestation—yes, infestation is the correct term—that sweeps toward us. Tiny creatures on the galactic scale flood the void before us, floating on solar winds, soaking up the ambient Mana in the Forbidden Zone. They are creatures of the System, of the overabundance of Mana, their bodies warped and only able to survive due to the Mana density within. Each of them is low-Leveled—relatively speaking—the tear-drop-shaped, multi-legged ticks glowing as their Mana veins soak in the surrounding energy.

Idly, I pull up one of their Status information.

Space Lice (Level 47)
HP: 498/498

MP: 231/231

Conditions: Favored Environment: Space, Mana Veins, Infestation Boost

Infestation Boost might not share the damage we do to them around, but it does increase their base resistances and their reproduction rates. They might be low-Leveled, but as an infestation of hundreds of millions, they are a danger to the *Nothing's Heartbreak* and its passengers. Never mind the planets they will eventually come upon, dropping from the sky onto the planet to consume it all. These are the creatures—among nastier, higher Leveled ones—that the Galactic fleets are meant to be keeping in check.

But they're all out chasing us or fighting wars inside the Galactic quadrant itself. Leaving the Forbidden Zone and its monsters to grow unchecked.

None of that is our problem though. Our problem is that the lice have caught sight of the *Nothing's Heartbreak* and are intent on consuming us. Which is why I'm out here, strapped to the fast-moving ship, the world around us swirling in colors that are not part of any non-psychedelic-aided rainbow.

"*Judgment of All,*" I whisper the words, not that I need to, but it seems appropriate.

Every single Space Louse in my view is attacked through the System, their bodies burning from within. My eyes narrow, because they shouldn't last longer than a second or two, but most don't start dying until four or five seconds in.

"*Something's wrong,*" I send to Ali.

The Spirit is floating beside me, humming "Pop goes the Weasel" as he consumes popcorn. I don't even want to understand how he keeps the popcorn from freezing over in the void of space, or how it tastes good—if it does—as he watches me lay to waste to monsters. "*Yup. Not enough butter.*"

"*No. They should be dying faster.*"

"*Well, you're the Administrator, boy-o. Best get to administratoring.*"

"*Not sure that's a word.*"

I do, however, comply. Surprisingly enough, Ali's suggestion is useful. Among the notifications, there are details on how the various damage and resistance formulas are being put into play. I scan through it all really fast and spot a single line of unusual code.

It leads off to a whole different subset of calculations and code alterations, most of which I find hard to read as details are either obscured or constantly changing as I peruse the file. However, I get the gist of the entire subroutine that is playing out, and amusingly enough, while it doesn't directly affect the damage being dealt, it explains what's going on.

Simply put, due to the degradation of the System in the Forbidden Zone, the very same reduction that breaks my own access to the Shop has reduced the damage being dealt by Judgment of All. This Skill, and any similar type of Skill that does damage directly via an individual's connection to the System, would be nerfed in this environment. So long as we stick around in the Forbidden Zone, Skills like this will be less spectacular, and it will only get worse as we go deeper.

"Hey, are you going to do something about the swarm or not?" Dornalor's voice cut through my musings, alerting me to the present.

All around us, the swarm has arrived. Mikito has made her way out too, wielding her naginata to slice through the lice with each swing. The blade is nearly twenty feet long, allowing her to swipe the energy-imbued weapon to kill multiple monsters at a time. The space lice don't like it, but even a single strike by the weapon is enough to end them.

Problem is, there are uncountable millions around us. Even Ali, with his Elemental Affinity, can't stop them all as he tosses around blue lightning like a crazed, brown-skinned umpire. Of course, most of that lightning and its arcing is something I'm filling in with my own affinity since, you know, space. Even the *Heartbreak* and Harry are blasting away, using everything from the main guns to the smaller point-defense lasers to hold off the monsters.

Realizing it's my turn, I don't speak aloud as I trigger Judgment of All once more. I don't pay attention to the Skill's effect this time as I cast it again and again, watching the System pour its charge through the monsters.

For long seconds, space all around us flashes and burns, monsters catching flame like prairie grass after a drought. The ship jets through the infestation, weapons firing constantly while I finish them off with the aid of my friends.

The Extra Hands are soon played out, though they're much more conservative with their Mana use. They can't regenerate as fast as I can, and being in the Forbidden Zone has reduced their intrinsic Mana regeneration even further. They aren't like me, drawing energy directly from the universe to restore my reserves, filtering out the impurities. They are creatures of the System and thus are affected by the System's connection.

It's a rather worrying thought, that so many of our Skills are dependent upon the System, which is degrading. At the same time, those very same concerns are probably present for our enemies. And if you balance numbers in that way, it's easy to realize that we're probably winning out in totality.

Still sucks though.

At first, I burnt my Mana as though it was going out of style like baggy jeans and mullets, but eventually, I had to pull back. The Extra Hands rotated in while I rested, and we tore through the infestation. The biggest issue was not so much that our Skills are unable to kill them fast but that we literally cannot see enough of the lice at a time. There are so many of them, they cover every possible angle, and since Judgment of All is a line-of-sight skill, anyone behind the initial layer gets off scot-free. Everything else just keeps coming.

The *Nothing's Heartbreak*'s shields hold up initially. However, each little strike, each louse that manages to get its scrambling claws on the ship, tears into the shielding. They swarm from everywhere, even the back, where our thrusters burn them. Some manage to survive that just long enough to scrape at the shields before they fall too.

The team does their best, even Harry on guns. There's not much reporting to do in the infestation, so he gets to shooting, helping to control the weapon systems.

For a day and a half, we fight. At one point, I slip aside, place my hand against the solid outer layer of the *Nothing's Heartbreak*, and play with the material beneath my fingers. Electromagnetic force allows me to do a lot of things, and one of my favorite tricks is making things impermeable. If you lower the attractive force between atoms sufficiently, you can actually slip between materials. It takes a lot of effort to do that though. Strengthening the bonds is easier. Maybe that's just because I'm bored while waiting for my Mana to recharge, but I move around, reinforcing the materials of the ship.

Once we realize how effective it is, we stop firing, letting the Mana batteries recharge, and go so far as to lower the shields to allow their projectors to cool. My doppelgangers do their best to kill what they can, one underneath and one above with me. Mikito tears through everything else in between.

Insectile legs, barbed and sharp, try to pierce the ship's shell. They scratch and pull before they lose their purchase and fly off or are killed. Wide mouths, pincered and serrated-edged mandibles, bury themselves in the metal as the lice tear at the ship. Some leave tiny scratches, finding gaps in my control as materials change or the liquid metal shifts. Still, the overall energetic reaction holds, and the team kills those who stay on too long.

We hold for all of a half an hour in this way, the Extra Hands switching out before the shields come back on. Then we get back to killing, fighting our way through the swarm.

A day and a half, wiping out the infestation and raking in the experience points, till as suddenly as they appeared, they are gone. Swept away by the solar winds, drawn by the flowing tide of Mana, their numbers much diminished. We can only hope we've reduced the infestation sufficiently that whichever planet they eventually strike can hold them off. Pray, because, no matter what Harry says, no matter how he pleads, we can't inform the galaxy about their imminent arrival. Not yet.

For our lives, just like theirs, are in danger.

***

The space lice are not our only encounter. Even when we finally choose to engage our hyperdrives, entering the hyperspace streams of the Forbidden Zone to cross the almost unimaginable distances between stars, there are monsters. Creatures that live deep within the vastness of space, dipping in and out of hyperspace or drawing strength from the streams themselves, preying on others of their kind. They lurk between the conduits and gates that make entry easy for most transportation ships.

Truth be told, I don't really understand the science behind all of this. I had someone try to explain it to me once, and it sounded like so much tech jargon in a programming language I've never studied. Certain words, certain concepts sort of made sense, but taken in the whole, not at all. And really, I already have one universal mystery to solve. Working out how the System and interstellar travel work together can be left to others.

What I do know is there are dire things out there.

Giant plants, dipping their roots and questing vines into the streams. Ready to catch ships, drag them out, and consume them. Mushroom-like monsters that attack via spreading clouds of spores that adhere to shields and metal, draining energy and dispersing themselves ever farther through the hyperspace streams. Until they grow to such a point they choke out the ship's engines and they become just another floating mushroom cloud, feeding and spreading.

Other monsters are like swimming predators. Orcas and sharks of the interstellar spaceways. They dip in and out of the different bands of the hyperspace stream, trying to catch up with their prey, sensing our sapient presence and churn of System Mana or the thrum of our engines.

Some are so large they'd make a Star Destroyer cry. They breach the bands of hyperspace, emerging from nowhere, and attempt to swallow the

Heartbreak whole. Luckily, many of them can't exist outside of the hyperspace stream. If we see them fast enough, hold them off long enough for Dornalor to drop us out, we can escape.

Otherwise, these overly large titans of space are only Level hundred plus creatures. In normal space, we take them on with fire and Mana as we put our Classes and Skills to the test, only to stagger victoriously back to the ship with their corpses. Looting is fast, though we occasionally stop to carve out delectable portions for our larder.

Months, we spend months trolling through hyperspace, sometimes in normal space sitting quietly and waiting for our attackers to leave. Other times, we're watching the Galactic fleet pass by as they send Bounty Hunters and scouts, dodging drones and other sensor platforms, all the while knowing that even if we were to win a fight, we would be giving away our position to the Council.

More than once, we have close calls. Battles with Space Leviathans or Dispersal Fungi that are interrupted by drones, only for those to be destroyed and scouting parties fled from. Scouting ships float by, barely thousands of kilometers away as we sit in the dark, hiding.

Months.

We get on each other's nerves as tension cranks up. Harry and I get into a shouting match two months in. He accuses me of being a raving lunatic, a coldhearted bastard who sacrifices others for my own desires. Who threw the entire universe into chaos because I had to get an answer. Eventually, he runs out of words, runs out of insults to throw. He screams at me for the pain that others forced upon him, for the bleak future he faces and the lives we've abandoned.

Funnily enough, and angry as I normally am, not a single word gets a rise out of me. Thing is, nothing Harry says is something I haven't accused myself of. Nothing he can call me I haven't called myself. Or worse.

My obsession consumes me, and I know it's wrong.

But I can't stop.

I won't stop.

***

Eventually, the months of running and hiding come to an end, and we're forced to pull over. Forced to interact with others. Our ship has taken damage. The *Nothing's Heartbreak* was never really meant to run and fight in the Forbidden Zone for this long.

Not off the charted spaceways, not in the high-Level zones we've passed through. The map the Empress Apparent gave me is of great help as we find ourselves coming to an outpost. One that is not on any map, one created to skip past all those pesky blockades in other axes. The people who hide out in the Forbidden Zone, they are not good people. How can they be? We are among them.

But as we pull up to the floating space station, its massive solar sails spread across hundreds of kilometers to allow it to drift through space while soaking up radiation, I can't help but think it's appropriate.

To the outcasts, we come.

The station itself is a series of spinning discs, the ends of the sails attached via Skills or something else. I'm no engineer, but it's clear the sails are not physically connected to the spinning station portions in the center. Each spinning disc of the station is connected to one another via the main tubular core through its center, making it look like a series of strange, lopsided disc tops.

Spaceships, the few that are here, are docked to the station at each of the smaller rings, interspersed between the larger ones. It takes Dornalor a few minutes to get a link even as we drift closer. As the sails spin at different speeds and are tended by dozens of robotic servitors, there's an actual navigation path that we have to receive, one that is set to allow us safe passage. There's a degree of control to the sails, such that someone attempting to make their way in without the navigation path would likely be assaulted by sails and robots long before they made it in.

It helps that the sails themselves are semi-sentient. They are a crafted material, created by the Enchanter within. The Enchanter in this case is one of those rare cases of an enchanted golem gaining sapience and—not so rarely—killing its former owner. In this case, the golem is semi-unique in that he survived the retribution the master's friends and allies lay upon him, going so far as Leveling in the ensuing tribulation and escape. Which also makes the fact that he is a high-Level Enchanter even stranger.

The creation of golems and the like, everything from sentient swords to Artificial Intelligence, is generally prescribed and conscribed by the System. However, there are always those who attempt to bypass the System's shackles that keep such creations from gaining true sapience. The fact that there are Classes specifically designed to break these shackles tells me the System sees these particular rules more as guidelines than actual laws.

In either case, creatures that killed their masters are not generally well received in the greater Galactic society. Between the preponderance of AI, the occasional programmed droid, bioengineered sentient drones and soldiers, and enchanted golems, Galactic Society is not keen on presenting the idea of sapient freedom and their weapons turning on them.

No surprise then that eventually the golem found himself out here, in the Forbidden Zone. The one place where even the most insane can find refuge. So long as you don't mind running the risk of getting eaten every day.

Good thing is, because he is an Enchanter, the golem also runs a repair and refit workshop. The really tricky part is figuring out how to pay him. For rather obvious reasons, mostly dealing with the fact that no one else has much Shop access out here, Credits hold much lower value here than elsewhere in the galaxy.

"We're docked," Dornalor says finally, pulling me from my daydreams.

His fingers play across the air in front of him, the physical console lighting up as he shuts down the *Nothing's Heartbreak*. There are physical backups to everything he does, but there's no real point using them when he can access it all with his neural link and the System. "The owner wants to speak with you directly."

I frown. I'd hoped not to get involved, but I guess with our reputation these days, it's no surprise the Enchanter wants more than a simple electronic document of everything we have to trade. A part of me wonders exactly how badly we're going to be ripped off.

"All right," I say. "Let's meet at the docks in about ten?"

"Sounds good."

Dornalor communicates with the station before he signs off, while Ali tells the rest of the team and I head back to my room. If we're going to be visiting, I should dress appropriately. In this case, that means fully outfitted with my full weapon loadout and at least one backup method to return to the ship when things go bad.

Paranoid?

Me?

Never…

***

Exiting the docking port, we feel the slight tug of centrifugal force that creates a low-level force of gravity. The spin probably only makes it around half of Earth normal, nowhere near what I would consider sufficient normally, but it does help with the entire docking and repair process. Experienced space travelers that we are, it only takes a few minutes for us to get used to the change in gravity, especially with the help of the System and the high-tech spaceboots providing us a much firmer grip.

"Why no artificial gravity?" Harry asks.

His hands are splayed out, recording everything as he wanders along. I'm curious that they aren't stopping him from doing so, but I assume we won't be allowed anywhere too sensitive. There are also Skills and Spells that can alter the kinds of things you record, helping to give a false sense of detail to enemy combatants who attempt to use such recordings for their own nefarious purposes. The entire counterintelligence thing is annoying, which is why I mostly ignore it.

"No Skills?" I answer. After all, it requires a certain type of Class to influence a whole space station.

"Artificial gravity tech isn't that expensive," Dornalor points out. Well, he should know, since he buys and deals with the *Heartbreak*. Which does have artificial gravity tech.

"No Shop," Mikito points out.

"Enchanter," Harry rebuts.

"I wonder if it's anything to do with the conflict between tech and enchantments." I nod toward the various runes that fill the walkway we're on as we follow the blinking yellow lights that indicate where we have to go. These runes glow with the subdued blue light of Mana use. I reach out with my Mana Sense and my Edit Skill, quickly grasping how the runes reinforce and keep the station running.

Ali pipes up, "You do know he just might prefer it this way? Artificial gravity systems can fail. Materials can only handle so much enchanting. Using runes selectively and making use of the simple laws of physics is an efficient use of resources. Not all sapients want to be squished to the ground as much as you humans do."

Dornalor growls, and I can't help but grin a little at his irritation. The alien is many things, but human he is not. I still don't really know much about his race, not having run into them during our times gallivanting across the universe.

The little I have garnered, from the library and what Dornalor says, is that they are few in number these days. Their species was a failed integration to the System, their planet bought over and conquered just like the Yerrick. It doesn't help that Dornalor's species also has an extremely low fertility rate. They make fantasy elves seem profligate with the spreading of their seed. Our elves, the Movana and Truinnar, are much more sexual and prone to producing children.

If they weren't, it is unlikely they would have become the hegemons they are.

Dornalor's race, the Yerrick, all of them and their kinds are the losers of the System. Forced to contend in increasingly violent situations, forced to compete against established groups like the Erethrans and Gimsar, many fail. Their planets are taken over, some are even lost to the Forbidden Zone and their species scattered across the stars. Eventually, their numbers fall as they become unable to procreate or they die off in battle like the Yerrick and Hakarta as they play mercenaries.

The System fails them, leaving only the powerful in charge. Those races who managed to integrate earlier, those who have been able to accept this violent new reality are the winners. Everyone else… everyone else scrapes by.

And even among those races that are doing well, there are entire sections of society which are crushed underneath the yoke of the System. Their opportunities to rise are blocked by the Galactic Council even as the System offers the veneer of equality.

Sometimes, I wonder how much of where we are is the Council's fault. What it says about the history of Galactic Society, in the histories that are not written. The secrets of the powerful, individuals who have manipulated the universe to their benefit. Even with the vast library in my head, I have no answer. And sometimes, I wonder if there is another library out there.

My musings are cut off as we are finally reach our destination, a closed blast door. No attendant, no speaker, not even a notification, greets us as we stand before it. The door stays closed until I get impatient and put a hand on the door plate. Then it slides open.

Leading us in, in, in.

***

"The Redeemer of the Dead." The voice that calls to me is low. Seductive, in a masculine way. Not like Roxley's with his urbane, civilized tone that hints of sex and long, languid nights but harsher, the kind of voice that makes you think there'll be whips and chains and other kinky things involved. That the speaker makes any thought of those things flee from my mind is rather amusing. In an alien-species kink-shaming kind of way.

Let's start with the face. Compound eyes, hidden behind a reflective mask on either side, with at least four smaller sensing units scattered throughout the body. I say at least because I find it hard to spot them all. Space twists around the creature's torso, around the rectangular body of his carapace, the skin more like a melted wax candle mixed with a slug and formed via runaway nanites than biological reproduction.

No nose because he doesn't need to breathe. No mouth, because he doesn't eat, but there's a slash right across where his mouth should be, as if the sculptor had begun to create one before getting bored. Legs for propulsion are scattered throughout his rectangle body, erupting from his twisted body to stab the ground and allow him to move in any direction he should choose.

Other appendage like tentacles, some shaped like human hands, with muscles and defined forms, and others made of liquid metal with bulbous ends that change into any required tools dot his upper body. And along him, wherever he can find space, there are fans dragging in the surrounding air and running it through sensors in an approximation of smelling.

The golem, the speaker, is a monstrosity, formed initially to help his creator build others of his kind. He was never built for beauty. Even as I take in the creature, his arms weave and twist, constantly adding to the rolling belts of things beneath him, carving runes that are imbued with Mana, shaping walls and arms, legs and engines and gears.

I scan his notification even as I sketch a bow, never taking my eyes off him. Out of the corner of my eyes, I note the rest of my team copying my movements before spreading out a little. No point in being too close to one another in case the golem uses an area effect skill.

Juover 217ᵗʰ Iteration, Sapient Golem, First of his Kind, Masterwork, Enchantment Master, Galactic Bounty (Polonium), Monstrous Outcast, Slayer of Hakarta, Truinnar, Movana, Goblins, Krags, ... (Level 7) (H)

HP: 4310/4310

MP: 8720/8720

Conditions: Sapient Golem, Multiformed Body, Aura of the Builder, Masterwork Formation

"And how should I call you?" I say, coming out of my bow.

"This one is Juover." Again, that liquid voice, which seems to emit from a voice box near the bottom of his carriage. There's a little satellite dish down there that he points at me, which I'm guessing is how he's projecting the sound waves. "You come to me seeking repairs."

"Yes." Dornalor pushes forward, eyes flashing. "The *Nothing's Heartbreak* is not built to handle the Forbidden Zone. Not even after the upgrades the Erethrans offered."

Har. Upgrades. They built him an entirely new ship, though it is pretty close to the original—in shape if not features. It's the entire reason Dornalor can run in the Forbidden Zone at all. But there's a big difference between running known space lanes and going off-route. The sheer volume of attacks we have to deal with—many that we either blast past or have to fight—is testament to that.

"Such things are possible for this one." Juover pauses, though his arms and tentacles never stop creating a small creature that looks like a twisted kobold abomination with three legs, too many eyes, and tiny scales for its body. It stands up, scurrying away under its programming, before another piece is plucked up, the process begun again. "Possible. But costly."

"What do you need? We have sent a list of what we can trade," Dornalor says.

"Seen. Replied. But more is wanted."

Dornalor's eyes track over the document that has been returned to him. The others do the same, Ali going so far as to blow up the text document in a notification so that I can see it without taking my eyes off the creature.

I read it while replying. "From me, I take it?"

"Yes."

I wait and so do the others. Juover does not explain, his tentacles continuing to move. I counsel patience to myself, waiting; only to regret it a few moments later when the doors slide open. Doors in walls that we had not even suspected could move. All around us are more golems, creatures similar to the one that Juover has finished making.

We're surrounded.

Weapons are drawn, a Soul Shield springing up around me. I throw Two are One on Harry, knowing that if they start firing, his Just a Bystander Skill will not save him this time. Hopefully, between the Soul Shield I layer on him and my damage reduction, he can survive the initial attack.

Mikito leans forward, Hitoshi trailing behind her. She is crouched, ready to explode into action, but the golems are not moving. They are frozen, just standing, lying, or hovering in place.

"My children," Juover says. "Many and varied."

"Yes, definitely varied," Ali drawls.

"Failures all."

"Not very nice. I mean, sure, we might not love our children, but calling them failures…" I speak up, my mouth running before my brain catches up with it.

Luckily, Juover ignores me. "None of them are sapient. Failures."

Juover's arm, pressing down on one corner of a metal slab to wrap it around the torso of the thing it builds, presses too hard. There's a snap, the scripted metal shattering. I blink, wondering if golems—sapient golems—can feel emotions. Or if he just rolled a one.

"Sorry to hear that." I cock my head, information flowing into me. The library has some information on Juover, a couple of papers. Enough for me to know… "You took quite a few decades to change too."

"Yes. My brothers and sisters never did. Some of my children have existed as long as I have. My code, replicated. The materials, replicated. Improved, all of it. And still, they stand…" Juover pauses, somehow sounding sexy even as it complains. The contrast between words and content is jarring. "Failures, one and all.

"And if they are failures, as their creator, so am I."

I glean what it wants. Still… "You do realize that I might not be able to do anything? I'm not an Artisan of any sort. Kind of the opposite."

"But a System Administrator, you are," Juover says. "You can edit the program. Make them live. Make them real."

I'm already shaking my head. "Doesn't work that way. The System doesn't give life or sapience. If it did and it required a System Administrator to make it happen, you would never have come about."

"Still, try. The price of my efforts."

"And half of our materials!" Dornalor says, shaking his head. "You'll rob us blind and leave us with nothing."

"We will arrive soon in places for hunting. You can hunt, replace materials. With better or worse, but replace them. Materials must be used from you, for they are scarce." Juover's hands and tentacles have returned to moving, forging a new creature, attempting to level, attempting to learn. "As are the Skills to better your ship."

Dornalor growls, but Mikito, having returned to a more relaxed stance, laughs. "He's got you there."

"You're not helping our negotiating position," Dornalor growls under his breath.

"There's no negotiation. He wants John to try, so he will. He wants half the materials; we'll give them to him. What exactly are we going to do? Walk away and find another space station? Where?"

Juover lets out a little laugh too. This one is weird, entirely at odds with his deep voice but more cackly. Like an old witch hanging out and scaring children during Halloween. "Fair trade. Fair attempt. Deal, yes?"

I look at Mikito, who raises an eyebrow as if asking what is taking me so long to agree. I turn back to Dornalor who, I realize as I look into his eyes, is secretly excited. I guess having a Heroic Class sapient golem upgrading his ship is a dream come true.

And I also realize, there's no point in hesitating. "Fine. Deal."

A twitch, and his "children" roll back. The walls slide closed, becoming seamless once more, hiding them. The new child at Juover's feet twitches, twists, and stands before exploding. Juover does not seem to mind, and the shield that stops the explosion from pelting us fades from sight a second later.

I stare at the remaining pieces of his latest creation even as the golem goes back to work creating a new golem while smaller tentacles. Tools form, sweeping, vacuuming, and otherwise picking up after the golem. His failure of a child discarded.

He might have gained sapience, but he has obviously missed gaining empathy.

Chapter 8

Four days later, as promised by the Enchanter, we hit a stretch of the Forbidden Zone where materials are plentiful. Meteoric ore has transformed, becoming Mana-infused versions of itself. The asteroid field we float through is rife with those new materials, ready for mining and collecting. However, there are no mining ships, none but the station and its droid-powered mining centers, for there's another set of materials that are plentiful.

Monster corpses.

Of course, we have to kill the monsters before the monster loot is available for taking. All through the asteroid field—a field that keeps repopulating itself in defiance of the laws of reality—monsters swarm, feasting on the metals.

The team heads out. Even Harry floats along, recording the new ecosystem for broadcasting later. There's quite an ecology really, with space monsters of every level. At the lowest level are the Rock Crunchers, who feast upon the asteroids. Some higher-Level versions consume the metals directly to produce an outer coating that gives them special protections and defenses.

Of course, like any good ecosystem, there are bigger predators preying on the Rock Crunchers. The local equivalent of flying birds and scavengers flit through space, bursting through the void in a quick thrust of Mana-generated propulsion, bullet-shaped bodies and bulbous tentacles all around. They cut through space, snatching up Rock Crunchers in the hundreds across the vast asteroid field. They kill and eat, before they too are preyed upon by larger predators. Space Eels, D'ner Liz Phantoms, Ragnos Elementals, they all feast.

On and on, the ecosystem before us thrives. There's even an apex predator in a Space Leviathan with its trio of children, all too young to part from it just yet. It stays away from the station after the first round of attacks, instinct keeping it and its children on the far side of the sprawling asteroid field. That suits us, since there are no materials in the Leviathan that we desire. At least, not according to Juover.

Instead, the team focuses on the next tier down, targeting fast-moving semi-ethereal D'ner Liz phantoms. They are more numerous than the Leviathan, ambush predators whose ability to fade into another dimension while they wait makes them hard to notice and even harder to avoid. Their prey receives a fraction of a second warning when they are fading in, but only the most powerful of the Rock Crunchers manages to escape.

And even if you do manage to avoid the initial attack, these things—all hard angular planes that warp and twist—can accelerate to fractions of the speed of light by squeezing their bodies between the planes. They shoot forward through the reaction between the planes, converting the energy and thrust to forward momentum.

The phantoms are our main prey, since System-generated loot from their fragile corpses makes for a perfect armor plating. Of course, they can't turn any more than an eighteen-wheeler in a dollhouse, but that's something Juover promises he can rectify in the *Nothing's Heartbreak*.

So the team hunts, Dornalor using a borrowed mining ship as bait. Mikito hangs back a few steps, along with my Hands, floating alongside the entire thing and dealing with the monsters as they arrive. They hunt, Leveling and acquiring the materials we need.

As for me?

I'm studying.

***

"You know, while I appreciate the single-minded focus the Questors have, would it have hurt for them to include some other information in the library?" I grouse. I'm not entirely sure who I'm talking to, whether it's Ali who floats beside me, playing Snake while controlling a series of drones, or Juover whose presence is the space station. Maybe neither.

While I might have spent all the free time I could find working out the System Quest, that's more of an obsession than any real desire to acquire knowledge. I hated studying as a kid, never understood the need to get good grades over and above doing more fun things like the rest of the non-Chinese kids did. They got to hang out on the beach, take classes in interesting things like rock climbing or snowboarding, or do sports. I had to study to get good grades. Heck, my father didn't even spring for piano or violin lessons.

"Nothing new?" Ali says.

"Nope. There're about a few thousand articles on the formation of sapient creatures, from golems to Ais, but the number of actual formations that have been recorded is in the low hundreds. There's just not a lot of them out there, and many have died without ever explaining what made them them." I sigh. "A lot of the experiments are just reiterations on the same hypothesis with a few minor changes to the process. Even the few records that are included of the birth of a new sapient are…"

"Are?"

"Well, useless."

"Like you, boy-o?" Ali says. "I'm not playing twenty questions here."

"Whatever. Most of the recordings are standard surveillance videos of whatever the creature is doing, often caught in passing. The new sapient creature stops, and a couple of seconds later, they begin moving. When they can move. All that is common is that their processes halt for a second or two, even the AIs. There are two multi-dimensional recordings which give us access to the Mana spectrum. And that's much better. You get to see a Mana whirlpool form as it sucks down even more—aspected and unaspected—Mana. Then, suddenly, pop."

"Pop," Ali says, sarcastically.

"Yes, pop. It happens really fast. Stop, whirlpool, sapience. And then they're connected to the System as sapient." I open my hands wide. "That's it."

"Similarities?"

I shake my head. "Not really, not in type or circumstances. Just as much chance for an AI, an enchanted sword, or a golem to gain sapience as… well, a moon."

Ali snorts. "I remember that one."

"That was a fun one. Think I can raise a horde of my own if I figure this out?" I ask.

"Moons?"

"Sapient… minions?" I say, hunting for the right word. I can see the problems with that thought even as I say it.

"Boy-o, you've done a lot that I never expected. But this is a question that has plagued hundreds of thousands, if not millions, of researchers throughout the Galactic epoch. I don't think you're going to find a solution," Ali says.

"Yes, but how many of them are Administrators?" I say, smirking.

"Then you are ready?" The voice rumbles through the room, making me jump a little.

I glare at the ceiling where the noise seems to have emanated from before I let out a resigned huff. "Yeah, send someone in." I scratch the side of my head. "The one you least like?"

Is that even a thing? I don't get Juover at all. One moment, he seems to care about progressing his children, making them live. The other, he treats them like tools, easily discarded. The gods know a lot of his creations have fallen to the creatures out there while mining ore for his use or defending the station. All he does is make sure to drag them back and reprocess their bodies.

"I shall send you those which are not economical to finish repairs."

I nod, waiting, only to realize that he's done talking. I roll my eyes and turn back to my reading until the walls slide open, a half-dozen broken and shattered golems dragged in on hover trays. I look them over and grin a little, cracking my knuckles.

"Let's get crafting!"

***

The explosion rocks my Soul Shield, tearing through half of its durability in a single blast. I grimace, waving away the smoke and watching my Health take a little drop as poison enters my system. Of course, my Health and the System fight it off and eventually it goes away, but that it could even take my Health down a tick or two with my Resistances tells how noxious it was.

"And that's another failure…" I step back, letting the golem cleaners Juover insisted on adding get to work. They were added after my third failed experiment, the mangled remnants of his children till then shoved to the side.

The cleaners pick up the shattered pieces, some of the larger materials going into glowing maws where they'll be smelted and separated. Others will need more careful separation as still-active Mana runes makes throwing the pieces into a smelter highly unstable. I leave them to it, slumping back, and pull up the System log to peruse my failures.

System Edit Skill Used

Guardian Golem—Sapphire Red Line v182.7—targeted.

Perfectly normal. Nothing unusual there. Next up was the golem's Status Screen. It's a little different since it's an actual item, not a living thing.

Guardian Golem—Sapphire Red Line v182.7

This Masterwork Guardian Golem is not for sale via regular means. If you purchased this golem, you should be running since its creator is extremely particular about the treatment of his golem. The Sapphire Red Line focuses upon high-penetrating, heat-based attacks to deal damage against the many creatures of the Forbidden Zone and is one of the most common guardian golem variations produced by its creator.

Weapons: Infrared Beam Projectors (Sapphire Line) v2.89 x 4, Infrared beam Projectors (Sapphire Line) v18.2 x 6

Durability: 281/2978

Effect: Mana Battery, Mana Scourge, Enhanced Durability, AI Tier II, Assisted Targeting, Modified Energy Displacement, Force Shield Projections

Cost: N/A

I let my gaze roam the Status, reading the details and searching for more information. I pull up whatever the System will give me, little as it is. The only reason I can get anything of note at all is because I naturally have a better connection as an Administrator and because the entire station has smoothed out the Mana flows a little.

Even so, I don't find anything too interesting. Next step, I open up the System Edit Skill and dig into the information screen. The expanded Status Screen shows how little information we—as normal users—receive, the tip of a ship-sinking iceberg. As an Administrator, I can poke at the code below it and all the connections the System has created to this single item. There's a ton of information, from a Shop variant Credit pricing model to material and durability calculations. There are still large chunks of code I can't alter and even certain sections that are blocked from viewing. Still, the amount of data I get is at least a hundred times more than what the basic Status Screen provides.

I spend hours staring at the code, walking off to eat while reading the data, sitting down and lying in bed, all the while having the program scroll through the corner of my eyes. I even hold conversations with my friends while looking at the data. There's too much to read, and this is just a basic golem. Nothing too special about it beyond being a Masterwork.

I can't actually read everything since that would be the work of years. Instead, I skim, getting an understanding of each section and what it controls before moving on, discarding what doesn't matter for my purposes. I hone in on a few areas, come back to the room, and destroy more golems with variant experiments before leaving.

Days later, I decide I'm ready to run my actual tests. Everything else has been just to see how the System reacted, how my Edit Skill worked.

First up, I get multiple copies of the same golems sent to me, as close to duplicates as possible. I then change minor things in their programming via System Edit. I alter the system for its Artificial Intelligence, overclocking one and giving it the ability to consume and interpret data faster. If sapience is just intelligence, then let us boost intelligence.

Another, I alter its regenerative properties, allowing it to replicate and remake itself. I also give it the impetus to reproduce and reconfigure itself. If the impetus to reproduce is important, maybe this will help. I know I'm relying on pop-culture psychology here, but Juover has thousands for me to experiment upon.

The next one, I rip out the portions of AI code that mimic intelligence, that make it act as if it might be "alive." Instead, I leave a giant hole in its makeup, bending its functionality around specific input tasks and leaving the portions that make it able to reproduce intact. I can only hope that the very act of learning will give it the spark.

By the time I'm done, my head is throbbing, I've wiped a bunch of blood off my nose and eyes, and there are a dozen golems, each of them altered in different ways and one with every single alteration I could fit in it. Those are the successful experiments.

There are also a half dozen corpses where the System Edit failed. In those cases, I mark the changes down as possibilities. Finally, there are others that just sit there, unmoving, broken in a fundamental way. Those I mark off as failures.

"All right, Juover. Keep an eye on the ones that still work. See if you can keep them running and well… we'll see."

The sapient golem acknowledges my request, though I can sense his uneasiness. I'm sure he's done much of the same, in his own way, but he asked me to try. And so, I'm trying, doing the best I can and being thorough.

But I'm not a crafter. I just blow things up.

***

Juover finds me days later, staring at the *Nothing's Heartbreak*, watching as machines tear into the ship, inscribe new runes, and replace wiring and conduits. The ship has been stripped to its bones, and even the basic structure is being remade. Dozens of tentacles dance across the ship's frame, burning in runes, plating enchanted symbology, and suffusing them with Mana. More golems, in all sizes from the towering ten-foot kinds to ones no larger than mice, scurry across the bones, working in an intricate dance. Not once do I see a collision, though the number of near misses per second is pants-wetting.

"Your report on what you have attempted is incomplete," Juover says through a robot. His puppet this time is a praying mantis with two heads on each end.

"I sent you a report?" I say, surprised.

"*I did*," Ali says. I can almost hear him rolling his eyes.

"Details are insufficient. What you have done, I have attempted. Your attempts are…" Juover hesitates, his mind searching for the right word. "Pedestrian."

"Pedestrian." I shake my head, a small smile crossing my face. "That's the best you can come up with?"

"Uninspired. Repetitive. Insufficient."

"Better." I turn to stare at the bot and run a hand through my hair. I tug at a lock, realizing it's grown a little long, and make note to get a haircut. I'm not surprised we're having this conversation really, just that it took the golem this long to have it with me. "I told you, I'm not an Artisan. And if you don't want me to repeat what you've done, you could provide me your notes."

Juover falls silent. I can see the robot thinking, though the golem does not move. I've asked before, and he turned me down. But I can see he's frustrated.

"Very well. Information will be provided. Restrictions on passing on said research data…"

"Yeah, yeah." I wave at Juover. "None of my friends are interested. Well, except Harry, and I wouldn't tell him the details. Not as if I have many other options for talking."

"You will not inform any. Not even Earth."

My eyes narrow a little. "I wasn't planning on it. Me and Earth, we're not on the best terms, you know."

"Yes. Known." Something pings on my Neural Link. "Data available for download."

I nod, and when the robot doesn't roll away but instead somehow looms without moving, I sigh. "Now?"

"Now."

"Slave driver," I grumble but open up my Neural Link.

The data comes flowing down, and I pull up the research notes. I skip the detailed bits for now, focusing instead of the highlights. Everything that he has tried, which, as the Sapient Golem pointed out, includes everything I've tried. And a lot more.

"Seriously, you risked creating grey goo?" I shake my head at his desperation.

There are more experiments that attempted to mimic intelligence. Multi-co-processing units. Hive minds. Inter-connected data centers. Advanced machine learning units, raised from the most basic of codes.

Intelligence, sentience, has been achieved all too often. The ability to consider the environment, to run programs, and take actions without further input. Yet sapience—intelligence driven by desire, self-expression and, yes, free will—is missing. Not once have his golems gained sapience, gained the acknowledgement of the System. Something is missing, something that requires that spark…

I don't even notice when the damn robot stalks off.

I spend days reading, gathering information. I run more tests, replicating what he has done, and tell Juover to hold his horses when he gets impatient. There's something niggling at me, that makes me want to check something out.

I just don't know if she'd agree.

Which is why when Mikito finally returns, I'm very careful on how I ask her. First, I feed her homemade ramen. I make sure to have the noodles, the pork, the tare, and the stock all created beforehand and kept warm to serve in a heaping pile when she arrives. There's gyoza and Japanese green tea alongside it all, and I don't broach the subject till she's done and finished the green tea ice cream I added. No mochi—didn't have the ingredients for that. Something that I regret for a variety of tastebud-related reasons.

"Very well, you baka. You fattened me up… what do you want?" Mikito says, pushing away the cup of ice cream. Her eyes are narrowed, distrustful. I'd be insulted if I wasn't so blatantly trying to buy her favor.

"Hitoshi," I say, nodding to the polearm beside her. "I want to read the information on it. The way it improves by itself, it grows… the way it gets XP like us. I want to see if there's a way I can make it work on the golems."

"You think XP is what is required?" Mikito frowns. "Wouldn't all Legacy weapons be alive then?"

"In time, maybe. But I think it's just one of the factors. I don't know them all, but I think…" I shrug. "I think it's one of the prerequisites. Or at least, I guess. It would make sense if it was. If somehow, the ability to gain experience gets accidentally linked to some items during the creation process. And no one else has managed to figure it out why yet.”

“Because Legacy weapons are so rare.”

I nod. Weapons like that can become a powerful aid, even a Leveler in the field of battle or commerce, given enough time. Casually viewing one or worse, experimenting on one, would be taboo.

“Yeah. I’ve yet to test my hypothesis.”

“Why Hitoshi? You have a sword.”

“Different mechanisms. I checked mine already, but Soulbound weapons, even Linked, are improved directly by the System. It’s like… ummm…” I frown, thinking. “Linked Soulbound weapons get reforged by the System at each Level. It just recreates them entirely. Which is why the ones I create break so easily.”

“I saw you cut apart a building with your sword.”

“Relatively speaking.”

Mikito smirks, having scored her point.

“Legacy weapons though, they build upon themselves, I think. XP flows into them, and slowly, they improve. At least, that’s what I think happens.” I shrug. “Not much of it in the library.”

“The golem doesn’t have information on Legacy weapons?”

“Not enough. He’s bought the few studies there are, but he has never had a chance to study one himself.” I watch Mikito tense a little, worry flashing in her eyes. I offer her an encouraging smile. “I figure once I study the differences and try a test, we’ll know if it works or not. Not that he hasn’t tested trying to ‘give’ XP to his golems.”

“How did he do that?”

“Combat golems get it, sort of. Whenever they’re used to kill things.” I wave to encompass the station and everything going on outside.

"Theoretically, if it was just XP, it would have happened already. So there's more."

"And you think my weapon can tell you what it is."

I shrug. "The least I can do is study the process."

Mikito hesitates a little longer before she picks up the weapon and hands it to me. I take hold of the naginata and pull it toward me, only to be brought up short as Mikito doesn't let go.

She waits until I meet her gaze. "Break it, and I break you. Yes?"

"Yeah, yeah. I'm a baka. I get it. I won't break it. I'm just going to look. Nothing else." She doesn't stop glaring or let go, so I drop my voice, lose the insouciance. "I won't break him. I promise."

Mikito finally lets Hitoshi go though she's biting her lip now. I move away a little, sit down a short distance away with the weapon on my legs, and call up its Status Screen.

Tier I Polearm (Hitoshi)

Base Damage: 749

Durability: 1024/1024

Special Abilities: Soul Drinker (Level 5), Armor Piercing (Level 6), Elemental Damage (Fire—Level 6, Ice—Level 4, Void—Level 3, Space—Level 1), Hasted attacks (+17% to attack speed), Mirage Hit (Level 2), Status Warp (Level 11), Leech (Level 2), Recall (Level 7)

I can't help but let out a little whistle. It's improved a ton since I poked at it last. No real surprise, considering how much time has passed and the sheer amount of violence we've seen. Still, I begin to understand why these weapons are so in demand. A weapon like this could make an Advanced Class Fighter able to contend with even Master Classers.

A Haste that works with other speed-boosting Skills. Multiple forms of Elemental Damage—though I get the sense only one can be applied at a time—the ability to phase attacks through defenses, and the new Leech and Recall abilities to provide health and return the weapon to Mikito are ridiculous. While many of the Skills are only Basic or Advanced Class equivalents, the sheer volume is ridiculous. And it'll only continue to grow.

Powerful or not, the Skills aren't what I need. Powerful weapons or equipment aren't alive. The vast majority of the information presented to me is unimportant since the majority of Skills don't matter. It's the Soul Drinker effect that is important.

So I dig into the backend with System Edit. Soon enough, I find the portion that details its experience, the way Hitoshi gains strength and power from the Skill, and how the Skill interacts with the System and the weapon itself. How it bridges the gap. I compare it to my own Soulbound weapon, and for a time, nothing else matters but the code and the potential I see.

For a time, worries step aside.

And a plan forms.

***

Weeks later, the *Nothing's Heartbreak* is finished. It was rebuilt days ago, but Dornalor has been crawling all over his ship every second of the day, inspecting the craft, searching for defects. He even booted it up for a day, watching energy fluctuations, checking the weapons and the shields. The entire *Nothing's Heartbreak* is reconstructed, and only its shape is the same.

I idly call up its information, shaking my head as I stare at the new specs and marvel. I do get a little chuckle at the new note added by the System though.

Nothing's Heartbreak *IIv2 (Customized Cyrus Fast Destroyer v 172.5)*

Once a customized Erethran fleet Fast Destroyer, the following ship has been modified and restructured for Forbidden Zone navigation. This includes the extensive use of high-Level monster material, modifications in the basic structure and layout, and the inclusion of runic enchantments to stabilize System and Mana connections. The basic structure of the Heartbreak *is no longer relevant to its current characteristics beyond the most cursory of methods.*

Core: Cyrus Fast Destroyer v 172.5 (see construction notes)

Speed: 17.2 Doms

Processing Unit & Software: Class A+ Modified Xylik Core

Armor Rating (Space): Tier I+

*Stealth Rating (Space): Tier I+**

Hard Points: 11 (10 Used)

Soft Points: 16 (16 Used)

Crew: 1 (+3 Maintenance Drones)*

Crew Capacity: 7

Weaponry: 1 x Dimond Violet Line Condensed Mana Turret, 2 x Ares 8.2 Miu Beam Turrets, 2 x Rapid Fire Phantom Webbers, 2 x OneLir Condensed Energy Artillery Turrets

Defense: 4 x Sapphire Mana-Warped Force Shields, 2 x Flowing Metal Reflectors, 38 x Point Defense Lasers

Core Durability: 100% (more…)

Sometimes, I wonder who, or how, these notes get added. Of course, the library has a bunch of research on the notes, the split between automated information, Galactic Council notes, and what, I now know, to be System

Administrator edits is fascinating. Those notes and studies offer no further details of what the System is, beyond musings that it is semi-sentient, maybe even sapient. Of course, the line between the two is always so blurry, the difference between "true" intelligence and those that can mimic it a question for philosophers rather than Questors.

Though looking at the humanoid-looking golem by my side, I'm not sure if it's as philosophical to me anymore.

"Father, are we to depart? Will we be leaving my Creator?" the creature—a red humanoid bot made of what I can only describe as liquid-metal, is powered by a Mana Core and battery assembly and a Masterwork Golem Core—speaks to me, its voice high and childish.

"Told you, don't call me Father," I growl. Ali, beside me, is grinning, as he's done every time it calls me that. "And we leave once Dornalor is happy Juover hasn't made any mistakes."

"The Creator would not make mistakes."

"Yeah, well. He's alive. Living things make mistakes." I rub my nose. "But you best say goodbye anyway. Once we get going, you won't be coming back. Not for a long time. Maybe never."

"Yes, Father. I understand. The Creator has explained to me that my goal is to gain experience, improve myself, and become a System-recognized sapient creature. That requires me 'experiencing' the world and gaining a personality."

I groan a little but give up on asking him to stop calling me that. Realistically, it's my fault.

Once I'd finished with Hitoshi, I'd checked the various other pieces of Masterwork golems and even Juover with my System Edit Skill, applying the new knowledge I'd received. After that, I ran multiple tests, trying to inscribe an experience circuit or code into other golems and forcibly creating a stepped down link to the System similar to Soul Drinker. All those experiments had ended up broken.

In the end, we came up with a single potential solution. One that Juover hadn't done.

Create a Legacy Class golem. One that is run with a Tier I sentient AI. But give it nothing—at the beginning—more than basic intelligence and a learning ability. I used System Edit to make it as powerful at learning as possible and give it the Soul Drinker Skill during the creation process. Then we fed it knowledge to give it basic functionality so that it's not entirely dumb.

After that, I took it out into the asteroid field with the team and me. We kept watch and fought the bigger monsters while letting it prey on the low-Level creatures. We build the golem up slowly, letting an internal counter on the inside of it run based off what should be the kind of experience it would get if it were alive. We tried to give it "experiences," all in the hope of triggering sapience.

Again, none of that is new.

But more than that, I postulated that the spark of sapience requires personality, something that can only happen by individuals, sapient creatures already connected to the System, treating said experience-gaining Legacy weapon as already intelligent.

Of course, if treatment was the only requirement of sapience, a lot of love dolls would be running around, alive and System-connected. If it requires treatment and experience, then the *Nothing's Heartbreak* and a bunch of other ships should have gotten it. The Soul Drinker Skill, treatment, and experience gain might just be the key.

I'm probably still wrong. Still, it's the best guess I can offer, and Juover is willing to take it as my answer to his own never-ending quest.

Which is why I have a hip-height, Legacy sentient golem standing by my side, calling me Father. And if that's not a bit of a head twister, I don't know what is.

"Come on, looks like he's just about done." I say, seeing Dornalor waving to us.

I lead the little golem down, Mikito appearing in my viewpoint below on the concourse leading to the *Nothing's Heartbreak*. It's time for us to get moving, before our enemies find us.

"Warning! A fleet has appeared in close proximity to us. I am detecting weapons and shields fully on-line," Juover says, his voice blaring over the corridor.

I let out a breath in irritation, wondering which particular god hates me. Because obviously this is when they appear.

Chapter 9

"Move it!" Dornalor shouts at me over party chat.

I growl, swinging into the *Nothing's Heartbreak* via the passenger dock and turning to stare at the three-foot-high golem running behind me on all fours. No warning klaxons go off in the station, but I hear them in my head anyway.

"Where's Harry?" I say, calling up my minimap at the same time. Once I know the golem's on board, I head for the cockpit.

I can sense my Hands running for the ship, though one of them seems to be headed out an airlock instead. I'd shout at him and ask what he's doing, but I know. Sacrifice play.

I'm… a little worried about what it means when so often, my Hands do that. It's weird having the Extra Hands around. Some of the things they do are like a funhouse mirror of my personality. Exaggerated, twisted, wrong.

And sometimes, just to mess with me, they're all too true.

"Get strapped in," I snap at the golem. I consider my words and add, "See if you can help out with damage control once we're out. But don't get damaged."

"Harry is on the way. We need three minutes," Dornalor says.

I catch sight of him as he boots up the ship fully, running it through its preflight sequence. The need to get everything turned on in sequence so as not to tear the ship apart is important, as is making sure the new runes don't explode on us. The Mana dispersal runes that make running around in a Forbidden Zone possible are delicate, what with the need to handle both unaspected and aspected Mana.

I slide into the co-pilot seat and strap in, tapping into the ship via my Neural Link. My System-created minimap disappears, replaced by a much larger stellar map of the asteroid field and the station. Hidden mines, deployed during our time here, explode, tearing into shields of our attackers.

More drones spill out of the station every second, gathering together to fight. A number of them are putting together weapons, single-use mass impellers built around nearby asteroids, or set to fire high-energy runic Mana blasts.

The station itself spins, the sails retracting to create a protective barrier around itself. It also physically hides the movement of those behind the sails, offering us a way out if we can get moving. Juover's other guests have long left, the sapient golem making sure we never met. Privacy is a big thing in the Forbidden Zone, what with those of us here being Outcasts and Rebels.

While we prep, my Hand is weaving through the closing sails, pulling away from the station so he can get sight of the fleet. I know he's prepping to do some real damage, though a part of me worries we're just giving away our location.

Ali blips into being next to me a moment later, looking worried. "That's a full Galactic fleet task force. One battlecruiser, four cruisers, and six destroyers. One of those cruisers and four of those destroyers are fighter carrier types. The rest are mixed long-range attackers."

"We can deal with the fighters." I flex my hand, remembering Judgment of All. We should be fine destroying them, even if the Skill is underpowered in the Forbidden Zone.

"Might be harder. Those are swarm fighters. They'll spread the damage across all of them, the ones that aren't just drones and not legitimate targets for Judgment. They're also using mixed Mana shields, primed for the Forbidden Zone," Ali says, correcting me. "But that's not the worst news."

"It's not?" I say.

"It's not," Dornalor cuts in, fingers drumming across his console.

The ship is ready. We're just waiting for Harry. Mikito has boarded and made her way to the engine room, ready to offer aid and damage control when we leave.

"Then what is?"

"Task Forces are run by Colonels. Generally Master or Heroic Classes." I nod, knowing that from my experience with the Erethran Navy. Dornalor says, "This being a Forbidden Zone fleet, it's likely to be a Heroic. Low level perhaps, but he'll be boosting the entire task force."

I make a face. "So, what? Increased damage? More shielding? More speed?"

"All that, and more. Heroic Class Navy Personnel can be… weird." Dornalor says. No sooner has he finished speaking than I see what he means.

Another fleet appears, almost directly opposite the original fleet. It blips into space where there was nothing before. And while one might think it was because of a hyperspace jump or a short-range warp, the station has Dimension Locks running at full blast now, never mind the danger of doing that in a Forbidden Zone. It also helps that the fleet just looks… strange.

"The fleet makeup… it's varied." My fingers trace across the miniaturized images.

Even if I'm not a naval guy, I can read the differences in sizes and shapes. There are long, sleek ships, no larger than the *Nothing's Heartbreak*. There's what I can only call a living clam, half again the size of the station core itself. Next to it is a swarm of fighters moving in and out of the group, while a variety of destroyer-sized ships ranging from sleek, arrow-shaped vessels to bulging, tentacled messes and everything in between make up the task force. Too few heavy hitters, too many smaller guys. It makes no sense.

"Ghost fleet," Ali replies.

That's enough of an answer to give the library in my head something to work with. Within seconds, information floods in.

Ghost fleets and their variant Skills are mostly a Heroic Class Skill, though some Master Classes have lower-powered versions. The Skill itself creates replicas of former ships, constrained and created via arcane rules that vary depending on the origin of the Skill. There's a ton of variation, from only allowing ships that have been captained by the Heroic to only creating vessels destroyed under their command or under their orders to other, weirder, requirements.

Some things hold true though. Like my Extra Hands Skill, each ship is lower powered than the original. Unlike mine, they are often time constrained and often do not regenerate Mana or durability. Weapon damage is also, generally, lower, and boarding parties and crew members are insubstantial other than to run the ghosts themselves. Still, lower-powered Galactic spaceships are still Galactic spaceships. And there are a lot of them.

I open up the communication channel. "Juover…"

"I see it, Redeemer." There's a pause. "You have COL-L01?"

"I do."

There's another longer pause. "We will ensure you have an opening."

"That's not necessary—" I say.

"Yes, it is!" Dornalor snaps.

"Your chances of survival are low without a strong distraction," Juover continues. "We shall provide it. Bring COL-L01 with you. Ensure he grows."

"I can't—"

"Do your best."

Before I can retort, I feel the line go dead and further communication blocked. I growl a little, then a sixth sense makes me turn. COL-L01 is behind me, staring at me with those artificial eyes.

"Is the Creator going to cease operating?" the golem asks.

"I hope not."

A moment later, I sense Harry entering the ship and the docking hatch slam shut. He's scrambling for his room to put away his things and strap in before we fly, though I wonder what he's carrying that is so urgent it delayed his presence.

In my map, I see the space battle raging outside the station as the fleet cuts through, dealing with our first line of defense. More and more golems pour out, headed for the task force and ghost fleet. I wonder how many Juover actually has stored away for a blasty day.

And how much he'll sacrifice.

A pause, then COL-L01 rotates its head to the side. "What is hope?"

"Run a dictionary," I say.

Dornalor ignores us, pushing the ship to lift off. The hangar blast doors open. A second later, I'm pushed backward into my chair, my breathing tightening as we accelerate into the void.

We exit the station and enter hell, even as the golem, the child, considers the new word and the thoughts that lead from it. As we burn fuel, entering vacuum and warfield, it stands in silence, considering.

"I understand," COL-L01 says eventually. "I hope so too, Father."

Then we're out of time to talk.

***

Fire and flame. That's what greets us. In the dance of laser beams and missiles, the *Nothing's Heartbreak* does the tango, slipping through the gaps with a whisper and a promise of another time. Normally attacks wouldn't make their way through the shields and sails, but the Galactic Fleet is cheating. Missiles disappear from our reality, reappearing again past defenses. Sometimes—most times—they don't return, and half the time when they do, they don't explode. Laser and x-ray beams do the same, bending time or space to enter locations they should never be able to strike.

Skills are burnt and wielded with precision as Mana floods through the endless vacuum.

All to target us.

Dornalor is like a leaf on the wind, and I can't help but grin a little. I hold back on tapping into the software to aid him, knowing he doesn't need it just yet. Our shields burn, but Harry finally makes himself useful. He has picked up a new Skill—where, I can only learn later—because I see our shields holding out better than ever. We take less damage than we should, and the upgrades Juover gave us mean we aren't even down our primary shielding.

Yet.

"Which direction?" Dornalor says as he hits the afterburners, throwing us forward at a neck-breaking pace.

I grunt as the inertia dampeners in the ship fail to compensate and we're pressed into our chairs. We pull corkscrewing, explosive-shaking motions as Dornalor rides the attacks with impeccable skill.

"Away," I say.

"Details. More details! We're nearly surrounded." He hesitates, then stresses the last word. "Nearly."

"You're thinking trap."

He grunts, but we're still burning fuel and pulling away from the station into the only section that is free of our pursuers. Before I can provide more direction, information floods in. My doppelganger falls, his memories returning to me. I twitch, taking in the details he provides, and make a choice. I force myself to move through the strain of information dump and inertial compensators on the fritz to highlight a location. We're accelerating at twice the speed we could have reached before as the upgrades make themselves known.

116

"Here."

Dornalor's eyes flick, taking in the routing I have provided. He frowns, but eventually nods. "Fine. If you think so."

I watch as his eyes dance, his lips moving a little. I can only grasp little bits of what he says, since he's mostly sub-vocalizing to himself. "Boosters… deal… if… charted… never…"

I frown even as I absently answer the Pirate Captain. "I do…"

The *Heartbreak* turns, catching a stream of Mana to give us a quick burst of momentum. Fire slackens just a little as we enter the Mana stream, and our attackers recalibrate. For a second, there's open space and no major interference such that we could throw ourselves into hyperspace.

We don't.

We keep burning fuel, cutting through real space for a few seconds. At first, they assume we might still be falling for their trap and are just slow. Then the attacks arrive as other ships cut around, trying to block us off. In the distance, where we would have been caught, another task force drops out of the hyperspace stream, giant webs of energy deployed. If we had jumped, those webs would have caught us and torn the ship into shreds, probably crippling it.

Behind, the station thrums, the sails fully enveloping the structure. The next moment, there's a shudder and the station spins as the sails and the struts that hold them together are launched through space. They become mile-long flying weapons, tearing through space to assault the ships that dare come at the station. When the gossamer threads of sails contact, they spark and burn and twist, forcing the entire thrown sail to envelop the unlucky target. Explosions chain themselves all around the station as ships fall, ghostly fleet held off by drones and the real fleet coming apart.

A Skill triggers, the sails stuttering in space. They briefly stop, their position in the universe fixed. Beam attacks tear apart the sails, and ships shift trajectories enough to avoid the sails. Then the Heroic Class Skill stops working and the sails continue their endless flights, their targets having mostly dodged.

Juover's station, to my surprise, is not done. It unfolds itself. Golems, initially launched into space to provide their own additional minor weight of attacks, now join up with the station. It's like watching thousands of ants pour together, glomping together to make the weirdest Gundam ever.

Not that I have time to watch as Dornalor cuts away, running perpendicular to the new enemies ahead of us. We head toward the deeps of the asteroid fields, the Pirate Captain making the most of the asteroids for cover, spare as it is. Unlike the movies, asteroids are rarely clustered together to the extent that one might fly between them in a nail-biting chase with rousing orchestral music. Even in the System, dense clusters of asteroids at that level are rare.

Of course, at the speed we use, to some extent, it's just as nail-biting for our pilot. Occasionally he cuts the corner a little too late or an asteroid is pushed off course by an explosion, and it bounces off our shields. Shields that yo-yo in their durability with each moment.

"*I'm out,*" Ali sends to me after the latest explosion, our ship hissing a little as it is compressed.

Ali lets his body disperse in tangibility and he is gone, his body left behind. Moments later, the world goes dark in our rearview as energy itself stops passing through. He holds it for a fraction of a fraction of a second before he pops, sent back to the realm he belongs in. That's more than enough though, as missiles explode prematurely, beam attacks miss by hundreds of kilometers, and even the ships a distance away have their systems fail. Explosions ripple through overburdened weapons as they overload from the energies contained within them unable to be unleashed, all of them already pushed to the brink and their safeties taken off.

"Good Spirit…" Dornalor glances at me. "Now, if someone could help…"

"Later." I wave watching the map. Watching as we close in on our prey.

They're in sight now, the mother Space Leviathan and her children. They look less than happy to see us, even as the swarms of monsters that have been bothering us pull away. The Leviathans unleash a flashing strobe of warning signals throughout the visible and invisible spectrum, powerful enough that my eyes hurt from staring at them through our screens.

"Keep going," I say.

Dornalor doesn't need me to tell him that. He triggers another Skill, our engines burning hotter than ever.

No surprise, the Leviathans retaliate. We slip through some of the force and Mana driven attacks, long tentacles of force reaching to grasp at the ship as well. I tap into the *Nothing's Heartbreak*'s engines, using Forced Link and Hyperspace Nitro Boost to boost our engines further. Then again with System Edit and Disengage Safeties, I make the weapon-based Skill work with our impulse drives. My nose bleeds, but I ignore it.

Deep in the System, tapping into the code that makes us all what we are, the Administrators strike.

And I'm plunged into a completely different battle.

***

Ever seen a late eighties or nineties hacking movie? Where they've got these weird, digital mashups of wirelines and screwed up reality that has nothing to do with actual hacking? Well, take one of those movie scenarios, give it enough acid to drown Las Vegas, and then double that amount of cocaine. That's the world I'm yanked into.

My avatar is a self-representation of who I was before the System advent and a bunch of gene washing. In this case, it's a 5' 8" Chinese Canadian who's scrawny, not because he's not fit but because he hasn't ever bothered to hit the gym to put on muscle mass and prefers spending time outdoors hiking. Nothing like the masculine, over-muscled alter ego I am now.

The Administrator's avatar is a cat-turtle humanoid-hybrid with a cat head and a hardcover backing. Rather than give me time to get my bearings, it charges, crossing the space between us in a blink.

I feel it tearing into my avatar, and the pain that attack elicits bypasses my normal System-enabled pain resistances. It's like someone is taking a cheese grater to me, ripping off chunks of skin with each stroke. Of course, it's not skin but code or bits of my soul or mind. I'm not exactly certain, nor do I have time to consider it.

Automatically, I attempt to detach, twisting away from the attacks. But that does nothing at all since the attack isn't physical but mental-System-based. That thought, coming on the heels of another tearing of myself, has me activating the System Edit Skill.

Code spools out from around me, the world adding on an almost Matrix-style layer over the weird acid dream. Everything twists and changes with each moment, but I can see his attacks, the way his claws that tear at me are my mental representation of what he's really doing. A visual representation of a much more intricate attack.

Another claw swings at my torso, intent on disemboweling me. When I dodge this time, I see how there's almost a tracking option set up in his attack, a way for him to keep pace with my movements. I tear those apart, altering the code and the coordinates it uses rather than deleting it outright. Instinct tells me editing is easier than destroying, and it's proven true when my assailant misses for the first time.

I kick, my foot impacting his avatar. I'm quickly grasping the rules of this place. My avatar is real, a representation of my Status Screen and what the System controls and holds. Tearing apart my avatar damages the data the System holds, potentially killing me as it deals damage. I'm sure there are backups out there somewhere, but the most proximate database is me, and thus damaging it plays out in reality. Especially since we're in the Forbidden Zone, where System connections are, at best, tricky.

When I lash out, I'm using the sum of what I am to hit the sum of him. Except my attacks are like a toddler—a full-sized toddler—acting out against a trained boxer. He can easily dodge my retaliation without putting in any effort.

Which is where Skill Editing is the way to go. There are three ways to go about it—editing his Status, editing mine, or editing the environment. I make a guess and edit the environment, the way we connect to one another.

I guess right because he's busy defending his own Status screen, not expecting me to change the environment. My foot impacts his, and I see the details of his Status waver. It flickers, some parts of it cracking and doing damage back to him. I keep up the attack, ignoring the changes in his Status and my own as I hammer away, using Skill Edit in a variety of ways. Sometimes I play with the environment, sometimes I play with my own Status to make me move faster or cover more ground, and sometimes I edit his Status directly.

It's all metaphors for the real battle in a way, but it works well enough. It's clear to me in a few rounds that we're almost evenly matched. He's more knowledgeable, more used to such battles in the System. I, on the other hand, have a higher Status, giving my avatar more heft, more options to doing damage or taking it. And, strangely enough, even for all his experience as an Administrator, he's a lousy programmer.

Like, just bad. Now, I'm no genius who worked for any of the big tech companies, and coding was never my passion, but I did a decent job. I had pride in my work—or at least, an old, nagging voice that refused to let true sloppiness stand even if it "worked"—but this guy. He's the kind of idiot who goes into Github, grabs the closest "solution" without reading the comments, and pastes it into his code and calls it done.

It's that sloppiness that makes him lose in the end. After a while, I stop bothering to Edit the environment. Instead, I keep my focus on him, attacking his Edits, attacking him. He reels back as my fists pound into his avatar body, blue and green code squirting out of the corners of his shell, limbs mangling under my feet as I grind them down. Code is driven deep into his Status, tearing into who, what he is. He lashes out and he does score some damage, but it's not enough. Not by far.

Rather than stick around, he blips away, leaving me staring at the empty psychedelic environment, reveling in my victory. That is, before reality reasserts itself and I'm back, aching and bleeding.

***

"Wake the hell up, you idiotic, void-begotten, after-copulation mess!" Dornalor is screaming at me. That's all he is doing because his hands are full, manipulating the ship as we jet through the gaps between the Space Leviathans.

One of the children is after us, while the mother and the other children only vaguely lash out at the *Nothing's Heartbreak*. Their focus is all on the enemy task forces chasing us.

I take in our situation in a few blinks of the eye, my head hurting, blood dripping from my nose. I can't feel one hand entirely and my left small toe is freezing. Like, glacial water dip challenge by the cute girl cold. I don't have time to worry about the damage, instead pulling my Skills towards me and weaving them together with my System Edit Skill.

Thankfully, they aren't damaged.

"Now," I croak.

Dornalor, primed to hear me, triggers a quick swing of the ship. We point in the right direction, almost directly into the side of the mother Space Leviathan. Then we hit hyperspace, my Penetration and System Edit Skills helping to push us through the obstruction and away faster than we should be able to.

I tear through the Dimensional Locks created by the System and it resists, but there's not enough System Mana out here, too much interference. It burns my body, tears at my damaged soul as System and unaspected Mana vie for space in me. I grit my teeth and hold together for as long as I can, forcing reality and the System to obey my will.

I force us through the Dimensional Locks until I can't and am compelled to let it all go. Pushed under as consciousness itself is robbed from me like my past life.

Chapter 10

Reality reasserts itself on the ship with a jarring lurch, pain shooting through our bodies. I grunt, body and mind reeling. A blinking notification appears as a door opens and the last of my Extra Hands steps out, taking his place for when they eventually do find our trail. We switch to impulse engines, Dornalor's hands dancing over the map and setting coordinates and the autopilot. We jet over to where we'll pick up the next hyperstream, the alien holding himself together just long enough to do all that before he spins his chair around and is noisily sick in a bag.

I'm not much better, but I am better. I rub my throbbing head, pushing aside the pain. Knowing we have time and will be leaving traces of our escape, I recall Ali finally. The very act of pulling him from his home dimension is painful. The barriers between worlds are both too flimsy and too hardened to breach. As if any single intrusion could cause an unmitigated disaster, so the sprawling borders are guarded ever more aggressively by the sparse defenders.

Ali pops into place, looking worried. He relaxes after a second, muttering, "About damn time."

"What's wrong?" I frown at the Spirit. He's back at his half foot size, and there's fraying at the edges of the body he creates. He pulls himself together easily enough once he realizes there's a problem, but his body language is still off.

"Let's just say I'm not exactly Mr. Popular right now," Ali says. "If you want me around, I suggest we don't send me back. Not until this is over. Not unless we can help it."

Even when I ask for more clarification, he refuses to expand upon it. The Spirit world is a strange place and I know little about it. No one does. None of the Questors have managed to garner much from their Spirits, though the vast variety of potential Companions doesn't help. There are hundreds of variations of Companions, but Spirit Companions all seem to inhabit a series of nearby realms. What happens in those realms is generally kept quiet, locked off from us.

All that we know is that Spirit Companions are placed under, for the most part, involuntary bonds of servitude. Most Companions refuse to speak about it. Those who do have been found to lie just as often as they tell the truth. And the only reason we consider what they said truth is because more than one Companion has agreed upon those facts. Some Questors have postulated there's a gaeas placed upon them.

In either case, whatever is going on, this is the first time I've seen Ali worried. I keep that and his words of warning in mind while I turn to the other problem. "What happened with the jump back to normal space?"

"What do you mean, what happened?" Dornalor snarls at me, having finished throwing up and in the midst of cleaning out his mouth with what smells like full-proof alcohol. "Our hyperspace drive is damaged. You should know that much by now."

"I thought Juover fixed it."

"You might have noticed, but we were getting shot up a little at the end there. Or maybe you didn't, what with having spaced out," Dornalor says angrily.

"Not my fault."

"Whose is it then?"

"I got pulled into a… a hacking battle," I say, uncertain how to explain it. "Another Administrator was there. Junior like me, but more experienced. We fought."

"You won?" Dornalor says.

"For definitions of won, yes."

"Good. All that work, and the *Heartbreak* is no better than when we arrived." He stands, shucking his seatbelt, and stomps out of the cockpit.

I glance around the cockpit, making sure the autopilot and the sensors are working, before I follow him. We should be far enough away, have taken enough twists and turns through the hyperspace streams, to lose our pursuers. At least for a little while. They'll catch up, but hopefully not before we take another jump.

"That is factually untrue," the little golem says, climbing up from where it has been working in the maintenance tunnels that run alongside the ship as we exit the cockpit. It bows when it sees me before turning to Dornalor. "The Creator has substantially updated the *Nothing's Heartbreak*, including adding multiple redundancies for your systems and additional self-repairing systems. I have assessed the damages along with the maintenance droid reports and have begun repairs for the most critical systems."

Dornalor growls. "He'd have been better putting in more shields."

"I believe you requested he not do so, saying instead that the *Heartbreak* should rely on its upgraded stealth systems." The golem hums before it continues. "Reviewing our current predicament, I believe it was still the correct decision. Losing the task forces set against us would be more difficult without such upgrades."

"So glad you approve," Dornalor says, sarcastically.

"Thank you." The golem turns to me. "May I be of service, Father?"

"Yes. Stop calling me Father."

"But that is what you are."

"No, I'm not. That was Juover," I say, bending down to poke the golem. Curiosity assaults me, and I try again to access his profile.

"The Creator is Juover. And he assigned you the designation and role of Father. Your actions were necessary for the creation of myself. As is your continued training."

I grunt, only half-listening. Now that we're away from Juover, the golem's data is accessible once more.

Autonomous Station Maintenance Golem—Curium Omega Line v1.03

This Legacy Golem is a custom-built, autonomous machine whose base format is developed from the versatile, station maintenance line of golems created by the Sapient Golem Juover 217th Generation. This Masterwork Golem was modified during creation by Rogue System Administrator John Lee in an attempt to provide it sapience, with additional foundational crafting skills provided by the Sapient Golem.

Weapons: Mana Beam Projectors (Curium Omega Line) x 1

Durability: 3829/3914

Core: Class I Juover Modified FZ Mana Engine

Battery Capacity: N/A (See Mana Engine notes)

CPU: Juover AI Tier I

Armor Rating: Tier II (Enhanced)

Special Abilities: Persistent Mana Engine & Forbidden Zone Mana Scour, Enhanced Durability, Force Shield Projection, CPU Overclock

Active Skills: Soul Drinker (Level 1—System Administrator Modified), Status Warp (Level 2)*

"You know, we need a name for you," I say, muttering absently.

"I believe the Creator said you would provide me one."

"Yeah, not happening." I shake my head, dismissing the thought. The golem looks at me while I open the communication channel to the rest of the team. "We need a name for the golem."

"Now you to talk to us. No, 'hey, is everyone okay?' Just, 'I need a name for the creepy technological-love-child of myself and a sapient golem'?" Harry says.

"You know I can see your health in my Party screen, right?"

"It's nice to be asked sometimes, you know."

"That's what my dates used to say," I mutter. Talking of dates and the inevitable conclusion to such things, supposedly… "Name?"

"Sheila," Harry offers.

The silence through the channel is deep and profound.

When someone dares to speak, it's of course Ali. And even he sounds hesitant. "Sheila?"

"What?" Harry sounds defensive.

"Just, you know, it's not what comes to mind when I look at a one-of-a-kind sentient golem," Ali says.

"The golem reminds me of a Sheila, all right?" Harry's voice drops a little as he adds, "It reminds me of my mother's dog."

"So you gave it the dog's name?" I say searchingly.

"No, my mum's."

Once more, his pronouncement creates a profound silence.

"Fine. You asked," Harry says, sounding hurt.

"I did. But anyone else?" I say.

"Pamela," Ali says. I wait, and he does what I think he will by adding, "Anderson."

"No." I glare at the *Baywatch*-loving Spirit and look around for help.

"Ezzocohatl," Dornalor offers.

"Uhhh…."

"It's the demigod of technology from my planet."

"That's…" I consider it. "Not actually bad."

"Mikito?" Ali says while staring at me.

"Kohai."

"No." I shudder.

I'm not going to be mistaken for one of her fans. Or have the golem think it needs to learn from them. Could you imagine a sentient golem weeb? I have done many things, much of them that I should be condemned for, but that might be my greatest sin if it came to be.

And yes, I'm being dramatic. We just escaped from death again by the skin of our teeth and the shields of the *Heartbreak*. Drama in my head is better than drama in real life.

Mikito sniffs and drops off the line, leaving me to stare at the golem. Dornalor wanders off, focused as he is on his job.

"Ezzocohatl?" I try it out. It's a bit of a mouthful. "Ezz?"

"So, boy-o, one thing about naming stuff—" Ali says.

But before he's finished, the System decides to update itself. And the golem's information.

Ezzocohatl "Ezz" Lee, Autonomous Station Maintenance Golem—Curium Omega Line v1.03

Ezz is the "son" of John Lee, the Rogue System Administrator who helped in the creation of this Masterwork Golem. This Masterwork Golem is a custom-built, autonomous machine…

"Thousand hells."

"Yeah. The System has a sense of humor about things like that," Ali says.

"I know."

And I do. I dismiss the information from the library, arriving as it always does a little too late. The story of my life. A little too late, a little too slow, a little too weak. How many corpses did I find cooling when we were sweeping towns in the Yukon? Down BC? How many more did we lose while I was gone?

"Well then, Ezz. Do you like your name?" I say, pushing the thoughts aside with long practice. I know what I am, and I've learnt to live with it.

"I am Ezzocohatl." A pause. "Ezz." Another pause. Shorter this time. "Designation received."

"Not what I asked."

"I do not understand like." When I open my mouth to ask him to download a dictionary again, I get cut off. "I understand the definition. I do not comprehend the concept of feelings."

"Right. Do you want another one?"

"A name?" A pause. "No. Ezz is suitable, Father."

I groan again but give up for now. "Okay, then, you know, go help Dornalor and make yourself useful."

"As you command."

I watch as Ezz pops back down the maintenance hatch before I rub my chin. The glimpse I had of its changed status was fascinating. Not on the front end of course, nothing there had changed beyond the name. On the backend though, my suspicion about changes brought about during the fight was correct.

Most of it revolved around its AI core, which had been put under immense strain as Ezz worked to fix the *Heartbreak*. Ezz had also gained a bunch of experience, some of which had actually been deposited in a stored location similar to what Hitoshi had. Ezz was becoming a Legacy weapon, or maybe Legacy machine. Or it could become one, though whether that will happen is dependent upon time. Time and whether my grafted-on Skill is stable enough to last.

"You going to help or just stand there?" A voice comes over the party chat. Dornalor's.

I shake my head, dismissing my doubts. I did the best I could at the time, grafting on the Skill. If it's not enough, then it isn't.

I'm just not sure if I even want Ezz to become sapient, to connect to the System. If it does, I wonder what it'll become. Because I have had way too many opportunities, looking at my doppelgangers recently, to understand that I am not the best of role models.

If it does become sapient, I have to wonder what it'll become. And if I could ever be forgiven.

***

Hours later, we finally have the ship sufficiently repaired that the hyperdrive engine won't explode when we engage it again. We've also reached a new hyperdrive stream, one that we enter with much less turbulence. Not to say it doesn't cause my body to tremble and clench a little, but the feeling soon fades.

Over the course of the next few days, we play hide-and-seek with the taskforces searching for us. We slip between hyperdrive streams, sometimes in real space, sometimes switching streams as we cross them in hyperspace itself. Those are dangerous, dangerous maneuvers that put a strain on the *Nothing's Heartbreak* as it translates between bands of reality.

The ship holds itself together, sometimes by the skin of its teeth it seems. Pressure valves blow, portions of the armor are stripped away by ethereal winds, and runic enchantments age and fade out, even as our Mana batteries are drained. The engine howls and spits, smoke and melts, but we make it through using baling wire, hard work, and just a little prayer.

I come up hard against the limits of the System Edit Skill when I try to Edit the physical durability or effectiveness of some of these materials. There is no change, no way for me to interact with it. I get the feeling that outside of the Forbidden Zone, I would have a little more leeway, as the System provides Mana to bolster the efforts I make. Here though, with my lower level of the Skill and a stable access to the System, all I do is give myself a stomachache when I try to Edit the ship.

Eventually, we escape what we assume to be the net they throw up. At least, we don't see any signs of the task force for days on end. At that point, we've been running for nearly a week and a half. Once Dornalor calls the all-clear, we spend the next day doing nothing more than floating in normal space next to a dying star and resting. No one wants to speak with one another, preferring to hide out in our rooms all alone. Our safety is guaranteed by my Extra Hands, who take on the monsters who try to bother the *Heartbreak*.

Eventually, we come together in the observation deck to stare at the pale star we drift beside. This is an empty solar system with only remnant asteroids around us, its planets long ago torn apart by the star during its heyday. Now the shrunken sun falls in on itself, leaving behind nothing but devastation.

After the usual round of greetings, we get down to it.

"How long would it take for us to get to our destination?" I ask Dornalor.

The alien glares and finally gives a shrug. I ask again and he spits out grumpily, "I don't know. You know how the hyperspace streams are. Some compress time more than others, some move faster than others. If we could use the major currents, we could be there in weeks. Out here, using smaller channels and dodging our pursuers?" Again, another shrug.

"No way we can use the main ways in," Harry says.

Dornalor nods. "Absolutely no chance of that. Even at the best of times, patrol ships and fleets travel those lines. The biggest, fastest-flowing hyperspace routes are also the most attractive to the monsters. Keeping them clear is a task in and of itself."

"But didn't they pull out most of those fleets?" Mikito says, looking puzzled.

"Those are the roaming fleets," Dornalor says. "The Forbidden Zone Fleets are mostly border patrol fleets. But there's no way they'd take out the route-clearing fleets. The ships and the Admirals who run them are all strong."

Ali adds, "Think of them as containment and bodyguards. You don't put your best on the borders. You don't need them there. The Deep Fleets, they're your long-range scouts, the ones who go in deep. Those guys are scary. Good news is, there just aren't that many of them, since keeping high-Level Heroics and a Legendary—if available—entertained is tough."

"If you want, I have a few documentaries about all of this," Harry says. He sighs, looking depressed. "I was going to put together my own when we spend a little more time out here. Now, no one would watch it. All they want is tales of the Galactic Rebel."

"The Galactic Rebel?" I say.

"It's the least offensive term they have for you." Ali says and grins. "Some of the other ones are quite creative. If the Administrators weren't trying to block it, I bet you'd have a whole bunch of new Titles by now, boy-o."

I feel a wash of gratitude toward the Administrators. While I know most of those Titles would just come with reputation impacts, I don't want them anyway. If anything else, it keeps my Status Screen unclogged.

"Still, you must have charted a way in by now," I say.

"Four and a half Galactic months. If the hyperspace streams don't change, assuming minimal diversions and that the *Heartbreak* can handle it."

I frown, but before I can ask, Dornalor sends over the plan. I'm busy looking it over while Harry picks up the conversation.

"What do you mean? Wasn't what Juover did enough?"

"It would have been had we not been shot up." Dornalor crosses his arms. "We lost a bunch of redundancies along the way. Redundancies we created because we expected to have trouble with the Mana overflow anyway, never mind the monsters."

"Currently, there are six critical failure points, eleven minor failure points that are of concern," Ezz says. "I can provide a full summary of such instances."

"We're good," Harry says.

Ezz jerkily nods and falls silent.

"Why don't we just use a fixed teleportation portal?" Mikito asks, looking between the men.

"Because they don't work out here," Dornalor says. "Fixed portal teleportation gates only work because the System makes them work. They create two points of reality that are the same, then shove you through the hole they bore through reality when those spaces are equalized and reform you on the other side. The only way it works is because the System makes it work. And we're in the Forbidden Zone."

"That's not really—" Harry begins.

"Don't care. The math involved makes even my head hurt," Dornalor says. Considering he's technically the most educated and studied of us all, especially in hyperspace math, it means something when he says the reality of fixed teleportation gates is painfully esoteric.

"I'm assuming the rest of the fast travel Skills are like that?" Mikito says.

She gets a nod, making her let out a tired breath. I get it. Being stuck on the ship for months on end is never fun. Even when we're busy playing assassin and bounty hunter, she could teleport out to do her arena battles. Being confined like this is putting a real crimp on things.

"All these stops, that's to let the *Heartbreak* fix itself?" I ask Dornalor, waving at the map he sent me and his planned route.

"Yes. Not sure we want to try visiting any other station. At least not for a while."

I nod. We might be forced to make one more along the way. There's a station where we can rest and recuperate along the way, one that no one but the Questors know of. Safe, or at least I hope so. But I don't mention it since there's no guarantee it still exists beyond being a file in my library.

"All right then. Looks like we've got a plan at least."

Dornalor nods, lips compressing for a second. He stares at me for a time, and I wonder if he's going to say anything. In the end, he walks off to the cockpit. Moments later, I feel the engines turn on, and the *Heartbreak* swings away from the star as we head toward the nearest hyperspace stream.

Four and a half months. It's not so bad.

That is, if nothing goes wrong.

***

There's no warning. One moment, I'm having supper—as much as you can call it supper since day and night really have no meaning when you're floating in a metal tube in the middle of space—and the next, my galactic equivalent of frosty cereal is slamming into my chest along with the metal bowl and I'm plastered to the wall of the kitchen, nursing a ringing head and bruised chest.

Another shudder ripples through the ship, and I only catch myself with a quick twist of my hands and a cast of the Flight spell as the *Heartbreak* throws itself into another sharp dive and corkscrew. The inertia dampeners are gone, and my blood is filling the room with messy, floating globules of crimson disgust. Cries of pain echo throughout the party channel, even as I conjure further details from the ship's AI.

An external viewscreen shows a stabbing trident. The *Heartbreak* twists and rolls, but it's too slow and a tear appears on the ship. I hear and sense it, the Neural Link giving me a feel of the ship as though it's my own body. Pain, as the attacks bypass our shields. Then more doors closer to the wound open and close, and something is sucked out.

I catch a glimpse of my Hand as it tumbles through the void. It uses a Soul Shield to give him a few seconds of existence in the depths of hyperspace. It calls down a Grand Cross on the titanic hand wielding the trident that stabbed us, the kilometer-sized Skill looking no larger than a quarter on the back of a human's hand.

Grand Cross still does enough damage to attract our attacker's attention. In the brief moment, a Forced Link happens and I read the thing's Status.

__Exiled Colossus (Level 895)__

HP: 193022/218047

MP: 1287/1578

The *Heartbreak* takes the moment of respite to speed away. One engine gutters and chokes, and I feel Mikito deep within the ship, patching the engine. Harry is struggling toward the open wound, and I make a decision, flying through the corridor to aid him.

We need to patch the wound, and maybe, if we're lucky, no more of my Hands will have to sacrifice themselves. No more…

He dies. Swatted like a bug.

And another Hand jumps out a moment later, already waiting. Knowing that nothing but death awaits him. And still willing to sacrifice himself for my survival. I can sense though, that lasting, burning command from them as they die.

Finish the Quest.

I can't help but feel the burden on my shoulders strengthen, pressing me down. I can handle it though. I'm a big boy.

I can handle it. Even as memories of fiery death clog my mind.

***

We float in the endless void a month later. The Task Force, a mere million kilometers away, trawls the solar system for us. Powerful pulses of Mana and energy spin through the vacuum, intent on locating us. We've gone completely dark, intent on ensuring we don't send out any further information. They crawl across space, and we all stand in the cockpit, our breath bated as though even thinking too hard will alert them of our presence.

"And you're sure they can't sense us?" Harry says fearfully. "Because it looks like we're just floating in the middle of space, out in the open."

"We are," Dornalor says. "But it's space that is in the middle of a reality fold and a Mana warp. All their sensors will go right over the fold itself, and our Mana signature will be hidden entirely by the warp."

"How long will it last?" I ask, reaching out with my senses. I feel the warp he speaks of, a twisting of the Mana flows in the region. It's like a throbbing toothache in the mouth of my senses, a sharp-edged twist of the blade that refuses to stop hurting.

"That's the question, isn't it?" Dornalor shrugs.

"Great…" Harry breathes. His fist clenches and unclenches as he struggles to calm himself. "And you're sure my Skills would just make things worse?"

"For the fifth time, yes," Dornalor snaps.

Harry is silent but discontent after that rebuke. We watch the floating data points of the ships outside us, the myriad sensors of the *Heartbreak* giving us a delayed record of what our enemies are doing. That they might be moving toward us already is not at all comforting, but any active sensors would give us away.

In the end, we can only wait.

I flex my jaw, then idly bounce on my toes, keeping my body loose. Harry is clenching and unclenching his fist as he tries to do the same. Dornalor constantly checks the instrumentation, flipping between each screen and notification without cease. Only Mikito of the mortals look calm, and that's because she's actively meditating.

Ezz watches us all through the ship, though his actual body is back in a maintenance hatch since there's not enough space for all of us in here. Or that's the excuse we gave him. Truth be told, getting called Father all the time and being asked impertinent and endless questions is wearing on me.

Crunch.

"Do you have to do that?" Harry snaps.

Ali pulls the chip out of his mouth. "You want one?" He shoves the bag of deep-fried potato chips at the War Reporter.

"No!" He smacks Ali's hand, forcing the chips to fly through the air. Mikito, without even opening her eyes, catches the bag and all the flying chips, keeping the stray snacks and returning the bag to Ali.

"Calm, Harry. Calm," I say soothingly. "We'll be fine. It's just one task force. Even if they find us, we can take them."

"We can take them…" Harry says bitterly. "And what about the others waiting in the wings? Who'll home in on us? Can we take them too? Can the *Heartbreak*?"

I shrug.

"Exactly. So don't you bloody hell tell me to calm down, you idiotic suicidal maniac."

I narrow my eyes, considering if it's time to talk to the reporter about the aggression he's been showing me. If I should mention the considering looks Dornalor shoots me, or the way he and Harry have taken to talking softly, falling silent when I'm around.

Then, as always, I take the course I always do with personal relationships and ignore the issue. I put it aside for later, because confronting them means I'd have to confront their feelings too. And maybe even my own.

"They're moving. They're leaving," Dornalor says, catching our attention.

As he said, the ships are picking up speed, moving past the elliptical of the solar system. In a few minutes, they're gone, leaving us alone.

"Great. Let's get out of here!" Harry says, relief making him grin like a loon.

"No, we're waiting," Dornalor says.

"For what!?!"

The Pirate Captain shakes his head but refuses to move the *Heartbreak*. A half hour later, something else blips away. Only magnification and review let us know it's a sensor drone lying in wait. Harry jumps on first sighting, but Dornalor still refuses to leave. After six hours and two more drones leave, along with the Mana warp that hides us, the Pirate Captain deigns to start up the *Heartbreak*'s engines.

We slip out of the empty solar system, a ghost in the endless night of space, headed in a different direction as we change courses and plans once again. We slip away, evading the Galactic Council's net, and inch our way toward Xylargh.

One light year at a time.

Chapter 11

Klaxons and warning lights pull me from disturbed sleep. The ship shudders, its hyperdrive engines screaming. I roll out of bed, run for the cockpit, and nearly collide with a Hand that glares at me. It turns away, headed for the airlock, but not before giving me lip about getting in its way. I can't help but glare at the grumpy doppelganger before I slide into the cockpit, where Dornalor is strapped in and the console is flashing.

"What's going on?" I say, scanning the information slab. I see the energy slump, the gravitic draw just outside the stream, the lack of attackers around us. I figure out the answer seconds before Dornalor, distracted as he is, answers.

"Hyperstream blockers. We're being pulled out." Dornalor flicks his hand, gesturing to the side. "Prime the weapons."

"On it." I let the others know too.

Harry stumbles in moments later, dropping into the navigator's seat and slipping on the straps around his shoulders. He takes over control of the shields, tapping into the systems with his purchased Skill to boost it, while I focus on the weapons. Mikito stands in the engine room, ready to do damage control.

As for my Hands, one's in the secondary damage control room and the other two are in airlocks, ready to do the jump-and-die thing. For now though, we can only hope it's a monster and not one of our pursuers. There's no doubt in any of our minds that we'd rather run, but the way the engines are straining to escape the trap, it seems that isn't an option.

What greets us is no Eldritch monster, no Mana-induced nightmare-soaked Lovecraftian horror, or a fleet of Galactic Naval forces. Instead, we're met by a ginormous cathedral built on a floating island, covered in smoke and clouds, its atmosphere held together by spells and force shields. The entire thing gleams golden, with multiple towers and edifices and what I swear are actual living gargoyles. It's not, obviously, a real cathedral, though it's the closest thing I can think of. For a number of reasons.

The library whispers to me as Dornalor flips between screens, reading data and making faces with each new stream of data. Eventually, he pulls his hands away from the controls and places them on his lap.

"We're not running?" Harry says.

"We can't," Dornalor replies. "They not only have the *Heartbreak* locked down, but they also have the surrounding space stilled and stretched, tractor beams set on us, and enough firepower to make a Leviathan quake. If they want us dead, I'll try to get us out, but since they aren't shooting…"

"Who are they?" Harry says.

It's a good question, since there isn't a big flashing sign outside, telling us what it is. Except, of course, there is. If you know what to look for.

"Systemers." At Harry's blank look, Ali continues. "The Everlasting Church of the Infinite System. Religious weirdos."

"Oh! Like the Questors."

"We're nothing like those crazy bastards," I grate out, my fist clenching.

"Hey, you proton waste, you know they might be able to hear us." Dornalor says. "Maybe don't insult the people who have Master-work ship-killer artillery aimed at us?"

I cross my arms, but I keep my mouth shut. Ezz, standing beside us, hums to itself as it downloads information about the Church, eyes flashing as it processes the data. I can see its questions building up, but the golem knows better than to ask. Even our Neural Link might not necessarily be secure. Eventually, our shipboard communicator lights up and Dornalor projects the message to us all.

"Greetings, Redeemer of the Dead, Breaker of the Galaxy, Corrupt Questor Extraordinaire. We seek a meeting with you and offer you the protection of the Everlasting Church of the Infinite System during and immediately after the meeting."

"Breaker of the Galaxy?" I say. "What exactly is going on out there?"

"And what are they doing here?" Harry asks, frowning. "Isn't the Forbidden Zone, like, the opposite of what they love?"

"Actually, no. There are quite a few such establishments throughout the Forbidden Zone," I say. "The Church uses them as monasteries for contemplation of the System, as locations for punishment, and to ferry individuals toward the deeper reaches of the Forbidden Zone that are still functioning."

"Like Xylargh."

"Exactly."

There's a silence after that. The message, having waited a short while, repeats itself.

Eventually, Dornalor stirs himself to look at me. "We going in?"

"Do we have a choice?" I say.

"Presumably. Or else they'd have dragged us in."

I grunt. I admit, I'm curious. I might look down on the religious fanatics, but they aren't immediately hostile. They might just provide us the closest thing to news about the outside world we're likely to get for a long while. Harry's System Access to the Shop is on the fritz, even with the boosted connection being near me provides. More than that...

I flick on my System sense and watch as unaspected Mana pours into the cathedral and it pumps out aspected System Mana. That's the other thing they do with these floating cathedrals. They try to "cleanse" the Mana as part of their holy writ, making order out of chaos. Along with that, they form a stable connection to the System around themselves. Stable enough, at least, that we might even get the Levels that have been held in abeyance thus far.

"Let's go in," I say.

Dornalor nods and communicates our agreement. Leaving us to float into the spider's trap, all bushy-tailed and wide-eyed.

Yeah, System-mutated spiders are huge and scary.

***

We slide into the massive docking bay with barely a thump. We're not alone, multiple ships are arrayed on the deck, but we have pride of place in the center. The other ships are split into two major types—the varied and the official.

The official spaceships of the Church all look the same, mass-produced for work in the Forbidden Zone for short periods of time. They're covered with runic enchantments that draw unaspected Mana into the ship, which is then converted into power and System Mana. It's incredibly inefficient, but it does mean they can function longer and better than other ships since they're entirely missing an engine section. They just have some minor batteries to store excess System Mana. Even in the hangar, the ships suck down Mana and pour it out without end.

On the other hand, the myriad are just that. Diverse spaceships of any possible combination, from living corals and hollowed out asteroids to sleek fighter ships and trundling, slow-spinning cylinders. These are the personal craft of those on a pilgrimage, unsuited for the Forbidden Zone. Each of these vessels are protected by tiny force shields that hold off the flow of unaspected Mana, System Mana pumped into the shielded locations to elongate the ships' lives. At a glance, I count a score of such pilgrim ships and we spotted another four such bays as we flew in. Probably more throughout the floating island.

The entire building thrums with power in a way that even Juover's station did not. It comes from having millions, maybe tens of millions, of sapients within. It's a reminder of what we bring to the System, something we've been missing for months now.

Around me, I note the way my friends relax, shoulders unknot, a slight buzzing pain deep within the bones disappearing. In the presence of the System, our connection returns and we become… more.

My head turns away from my friends, leaving them for a moment to revel in the new sensation. Instead, I peer at the island and the city it contains. To have such a population, they must be packed in like sardines in a can. And it's clear from the myriad individuals scurrying around in the hangar, buffing ships, replacing components, and cleaning the floor, that they are all busy.

Busy using their Skills. Busy drawing Mana in and churning it out for the System. All part of their religious practices…

"Father."

"What?" I say.

"Why does your face do that?"

"Do what?" But now that Ezz has brought it to my attention, I feel my lips twisted into an unspoken snarl.

"Your face, it looks like you desire… violence?" Ezz says, then hums. "Ending of life. Killing."

"He's got you there, boy-o." Ali chuckles, floating down beside Ezz. "Here, let Uncle Ali explain. Daddy Lee does not like Systemers because he thinks they make a piece of software a god. Now, 'cause they think so, they've also often had conflicts with Questors, including a number of rather well-known crusades. Though what with there being Administrators, I'd bet a dozen Credits they had a hand in those crusades too. Put another way, it's a matter of conflicting religions."

"The System is no god. It's a bloody convoluted, broken program…" I growl. But that's not true, and I know it. No program is this organic, this… living. It's more than just a program when it can alter the very shape of reality, the way we interact with it. Still, it certainly is no god. "And I'm not religious!"

"Sure, sure…" Ali pats the air placatingly while giving Ezz a big and unsubtle wink.

Ezz buzzes, and I swear, it might even be laughing.

I stay silent, because I'm sure if I mentioned my last thoughts, they'd laugh more. And that's simple because if the System is a god, I can't kick its ass. Well, I could try, but even I'm not that arrogant.

"We have a greeting party," Harry says, flicking his hand sideways so that we get access to the external viewscreen.

The landing party is arraying themselves before our ship, a half-dozen clerics in long, flowing robes of blue and white. Just like the colors of the System notifications, with the lower levelled—those standing behind in the line—having darker robes and the ones closer up, including their leader, having much lighter and more shade appropriate clothing.

Surprisingly, the library doesn't have much to say about their clothing choices. Or maybe not so surprisingly. It's not as if there's a System secret in what color clothing a bunch of religious fanatics wear. Still, context is more than clear enough to explain hierarchies. There's no single type of alien among them, with a Gimsar, an Erethran, and a Kapre in the line in the back. Their leader is a Movana, all fluid grace and pointy ears.

As I unbuckle and consider how I want to play this, I'm interrupted.

"John, I'm getting a flood of notifications. Including Level Ups," Mikito's voice cuts in across the channel.

"The cathedrals are stable locations for the System. It's a mix of System Skills, number of individuals packed in, and the buildings themselves," I explain. That, the library has a lot of details on. A lot. Someone even sneaked in a travelogue of all the different Cathedrals he'd visited and his… exploits. "If we're really lucky, they might even have a working Shop."

"That why you wanted to come?"

I nod, then realize she can't see me, so I confirm out loud.

"They're getting impatient," Harry says, though he sounds a little preoccupied.

I consider poking at my own notifications but decide against it. I doubt we're in danger, at least not in the short term. Which means we're better off not pissing them off.

"All right, team, button it up. Dornalor—"

"Stay in the *Heartbreak*. I know. I'll see what kind of repairs I can do while we're grounded." The Pirate Captain sounds only a little annoyed.

"Everyone else, let's see what they want."

***

"Welcome to the Cathedral of the Legendary, Redeemer of the Dead," the man in the front intones the moment my foot hits the deck.

At the same time, I get a pop-up, one that I take a moment to review. There's not a huge amount of information that's new, but something is better than nothing.

You Have Entered a Safe Zone (Cathedral of the Legendary Flame—Floating Fortress of the Everlasting Church of the Infinite System)

Mana flows in this area are stabilized forcefully. No monster spawning will occur. This Safe Zone includes:

- *The Shop*

- *City Center*

- *Spawn Pits*

- *Dungeon Zones (3)*

- *Artisan Stations (18,491)*

- *(more)*

The following Skills are in affect: Faith Extraction (resisted), Shared Destiny (resisted), Mana Burn (resisted), Greater Focus, Restful Space

As a Junior System Administrator, you have access to additional information about this location. Would you like to review it now?

I'm amused to note that Ali's edited the information a little, giving me an overview of the important bits. Like the Mana Burn, which forces you to use more Mana constantly as another way to aid the System. There're a few other Skills in play that I automatically resist that are fascinating, but most of my attention is on the last line.

I've not seen it before, not ever. I wonder if it's a matter of being in a Forbidden Zone, Ali testing out a new view for me, or the System dropping a hint. I frown, but at a mental prod by Ali, I dismiss the matter for the second and return the man's greetings. Ali is kind enough to provide his Status too, which is useful.

__GoGorm La, Bishop of the Everlasting Church of the Infinite System, Devout (Everlasting Church), Blessed by the Flame, Slayer of Goblins, Rock Crushers, Trolls,… (Bishop of the Everlasting Church Level 08) (M)__

HP: 1440/1440

MP: 3890/3890

Conditions: Devout, Blessed by the Flame, Mana Burn, Faith Focus, Shared Blessing

"Thank you." I turn my head, taking in the others. There's not much to read in their Statuses, a bunch of Acolytes and Novices, Lay-Priests, and a Chanter. Basic and Advanced Classes, all of them related to the Church. "If you don't mind, my pilot would like to carry out some repairs."

"Of course." GoGorm's voice has a lilt to it, reminding me of the more melodic languages. He gestures and a lurking maintenance tech hurries forward. "Senior Technician Dr'asm will be happy to help."

I blink at the name, surprised as the inflection and naming sense is not typical Gimsar. Strange things, cultures and mixed names. The fact that the Gimsar technician is nearly five feet three inches tall and just as wide says something about his parentage. As does the light patterning of scales running along the sides of his face, forming above his beard.

Yeah, the System and genetics can make parentage and breeding… different.

"I'll leave it to Dornalor and him to sort it out." I know Dornalor won't let anyone touch the *Heartbreak* directly. However, there's nothing to stop him from picking up some extra materials and modules before adding it to the ship.

"Of course." GoGorm La smiles. "Then shall we proceed? Archbishop Tedflet is looking forward to speaking with you, Redeemer."

There's a moment of hesitation when my team joins us as we head out of the hangar. Harry they accept without an issue, even going so far as having one of the Acolytes join him to answer any questions he might have. Mikito is ignored, like the good bodyguard she is. It's Ezz that makes them hesitate.

"What is that?"

"That's Ezz."

"A… sentient golem?" GoGorm La hesitates. "How sentient?"

"Ezz has a Class I AI with a Class II learning module," Ezz says, hurrying forward to my side.

"I see. We do not let tools join us normally." GoGorm looks at me, cocking his head. "Unless the Redeemer requires it for a particular reason?"

"I do." GoGorm La looks interested, so I add, just because it'd be funny, "Ezz's great company. Better than my usual buggers." I gesture with a thumb, and if it points at a floating Spirit directly, well, who asked him to be there.

"Gremlin shit."

I grin, and my lips peel even wider as GoGorm looks confused about what he should do. That he has been told to accommodate me is quite clear. That I'm a little conflicted about dragging Ezz with me, when we might need to fight our way out, no one else needs to know. In either case, if I'm to help him grow, become sapient, then he needs this.

Needs the experience. And not just the XP, but actual, living experience.

"Very well then, Redeemer. As you say." He bows again and leads us off.

Out of the hangar bay, where Dornalor has already begun chatting with the Senior Technician via a floating drone. Down golden-lined and steel-plated corridors, where living, mutated plant monsters make up the ambience, and Monster Gardeners and Twisted Druids care for the topography. Up a floating walkway of force shuttles, in what I can only describe as the long way around. All so that we can see more of the stunning cathedral island and the numerous church members who live, fight, care, and hunt in its reaches.

Because they do hunt. Monsters spawn constantly, though they do so in controlled locations, such that people can fight, Level, and churn the Mana that is the central tenet of the Systemers' creed. The Spawn Pits aren't even lined with weapons like you'd expect. The only thing keeping the creatures contained is the never-ending swarm of fighters.

Risk is part of experience and Mana gain, and the risk of a monster outbreak must help their Artisans grow too. All of this, all the fighting, the Mana churn, the constant and blatant use of Mana is so they can get closer to their god.

I keep my face flat even as I breathe, tasting the lingering scents. So many of them, shifting from cooked meat to pollen and nectars, which give boosts in experience gain or attributes. Shifting, changing with each neighborhood. All while artificial gravity presses down on us and an artificial atmosphere looms above where floating clouds harbor acid rain and monsters. Occasionally those monsters dip out, and an unlucky child gets picked up and savaged before one of their many Caregivers and Guardsmen takes action to protect them.

We keep walking and ascend the cathedral, seeing the microcosm of the brutal, dangerous, and vicious Galactic Society sprawl beneath us. We rise, where we finally meet the Archbishop who rules—sorry, herds—them all.

***

Highly impractical. That's my first thought when we finally get to the Archbishop's office. It's set in the tallest tower of the cathedral, the one that dominates the skyline and gives a view that is impossible to beat. The fact that he has floor-to-ceiling windows all around, allowing him to see all about him and giving anyone with a sense of vertigo conniptions, is secondary to the sheer absurdity of the target he represents.

He's on a floating island in space, with the only things guarding them being the shielding and runic enchantments keeping the atmosphere in. It would be the simplest thing in the world, once a Leviathan or an Ancient One broke through, to rip out the entire tower.

Yet here he is. In his golden-tiled, floor-to-ceiling-windowed office, crouched behind a desk—because even in the Galaxy, having a convenient place to put things on is, well, convenient—on one of those weird kneeling chairs and staring into blank space, reading whatever notification he has open. The table is tilted a little, the cups and other items held in place by tiny runes.

Oh, and he's a Naga. A serpent-like humanoid. Of course, the Galactics have a different name for them. In fact, there are three official ones, depending on if you want to use the continent, planet, or solar system that the breed originated from. There are actual minor differences too. Since the Naga were a space-faring race by the time the System arrived, their bones and physical structures have changed due to long centuries dealing with zero-g.

"Redeemer of the Dead John Lee. Breaker of the Galaxy. Usurper of the proper Order. Fabled Questor Extraordinaire," the Naga says, rearing up on his seat, hands splayed wide. His robes, more a tunic than a full robe, splay open, showcasing the flash of scale under his clothing. "You honor us with your presence."

"I don't think I was given much choice," I say, walking forward.

There are no guards in here, but I sense the myriad traps and automated defenses built into the floor and ceiling of the office. I can even tell that his seat is over a ritual teleportation center, allowing him to blip off at a moment's notice. Powerful enough that I doubt I could block it with my Skill.

Not to say he wouldn't be a hard enough fight by himself.

Turad Azellig, Archbishop of the Everlasting Church of the Infinite System, Unparalleled Leader, Font of Faith, Slayer of Goblins, Leviathans, Raras, Aswang, Nictucku, ... (Archbishop of the Everlasting Church of the Infinite System Level 18) (H)
*HP: 4791/4791**
*MP: 6235/6235**
Conditions: Faith Focus, Backing of the Masses, Shared Destiny, Shielded Life

I don't even need the library to tell me that those conditions are all variable depending on the size of his flock. The more there are, the harder he is to kill. Realistically, in many such situations, the most effective manner isn't to kill him but to rain down hellfire on the populace. Take them out and he gets depowered. Sometimes, depending on the Skills, if you attack him first, you're condemning them to death anyway.

Not that I'm planning any violence, but always worth knowing.

"I must admit, we had to take a few liberties to get you here. But we mean you no harm." Turad smiles.

I make sure to ignore the way that sends a little shiver down my monkey brain. The Galactic body language download I got tells me he's trying for friendly, so I'll take it at face value. Even if his semi-humanoid face, with its scales and lack of ears and nose, is alien as hell. He reminds me of that original eighties TV show that they remade in the 00s with the hot blonde and the companion from Firefly, but Turad's got an actual snake bottom and tail.

"Then what do you mean?" I say.

"A trade. A sharing. Of knowledge and skill, in turn for safety and aid."

"You do know that the Galactic Council isn't happy with us, right?" I cock my head, probing for more information.

"Yes. What they do not know won't matter. The battle they seek with the Church is not one they could win. And what you might offer us…" He opens his hands. "Well, that might be worth it all."

"Really." Disbelief. "That's the position of the Church as a whole?" Ali says, floating forward. He has his head propped up on one hand as he sits cross-legged in mid-air.

"No." But Turad's body language says yes.

"Ah," Ali says.

"*What?*" I ask.

"*They're the sacrifice. If what you give them is not enough, they get to be sacrificed to the Council.*"

"*Cold.*"

Out of the corner of my eyes, I see Harry recording. Ready to broadcast when it's possible, when it makes sense. A public record of Turad saying no.

And him asking. Millions sacrificed for knowledge that the Council, the Administrators have kept hidden.

"I… well. Perhaps after we get some information."

"About?"

"The world out there." I wave. "Even if you're willing to sacrifice your people, I'm less enthusiastic about that."

"Even if that will get you closer to your answer?"

"Even then." And if I sound a little hesitant, I have to admit, it's a failure of my morals for I have sacrificed more already.

"Very well then. We shall speak later." A hand gestures.

Our escort pulls us out. To rooms of our own, where we are given data cubes detailing events in the wider galaxy while we've been running and hiding. Of what has happened and will likely happen.

Riveting reading, really. Even if you don't like current affairs.

Chapter 12

Time flows on without recourse, never asking us as events, both small and world-shaping, occur. When you're talking about Galactic society and a war that spans multiple solar systems, world-shaking takes on a new, literal meaning.

When dictators and those in power feel their grasp on those they control slip, they react by lashing out. They use fear and intimidation to bring those under them back under control. It's a simple calculus for the Administrators and Shadow Council—if secrecy no longer works, then let fear do the talking. It's worked for them before and worked for so many governments and interest groups on Earth. There's a reason it's part of the playbook for asshats the Galaxy over.

In this case, the Shadow Council and the Administrators have more than a general uprising to contend with. The Erethrans, the Movana, and the Truinnar—the major empires—have taken the chance to break free. Add in half of the Legendarys of the Galactic Council, and the opposition has declared themselves the "true" leaders of the Galaxy. In turn, they have rallied multiple smaller planets and kingdoms to their cause.

Facing off against them are a bunch of boot-licking kingdoms and singular planets, as well as the Shadow Council, the surviving loyal members of the Galactic Council and the Administrators. They have control of the majority of the Galactic Fleets, and while they might have fewer total planets, they have more mobile forces and a higher number of high-Leveled individuals than their opposition.

In a way, both sides are equally balanced, and the entire war is devolving into a messy, messy battle. Galactic Fleets spin through reality, dropping out of hyperspace and destroying space stations, military installations, teleportation portals, and—in some cases—entire planets. All to sow fear and destruction and hamper the other side. Legendarys pop in and out, using their greater strength to tilt wars and battles, or just laying waste to planets that are "safe" behind defensive lines.

Our side is forced to play catch up. They hunt down fleets, chase after Legendarys and never give them a chance to rest, all the while sacrificing their men. Those who survive the fights Level up, gaining experience from the battles and the deaths around them, growing in power. All to be thrown back into the war in short order.

All the while, our side—the true Galactic Council, if you will—has to watch for traitors in their midst. Junior Administrators edit Statuses and faces, breach defensive shields, and teleport their people in to swap out individuals. Doppelgangers, spies, changelings. They all wreak havoc.

Senior Administrators tackle Heroics and Legendarys, harassing the Galactic Council wherever they might be. They twist and prod at Skills, a half dozen chasing the Dragon himself in an on-going battle through the void. Last seen, the group entered the Forbidden Zone, closely followed by an entire Galactic Fleet.

Thus far, the only oases of safety are the Dungeon Worlds. The overflow of Mana into them protects against orbital bombardments, their status as Mana overflow dumps even more important as we lose sapient planets one after the other. For all that the Shadow Council and System Administrators might be trying to enforce their control, they are careful not to throw the baby out with the bathwater.

It's probably that reason and Earth's location on the edge of System space that keeps it safe. I just hope that continues to hold true, though a part of me fears reading about the destruction of the planet by a truly upset Council member.

And that's the thing. If I draw the battle lines as though it's clear and simple, the reality on the ground is much different. Planets, cities, and even families are torn apart as those who believe and those who fear the truth do battle. Opportunists jump at the chance to create a new merchant empire, while mercenaries work for their daily bread. Personal vendettas are carried out under the cover of Galactic war.

Even the Adventuring Guilds aren't left alone. Their general desire to stay out of politics has been blasted away. Guilds are forced by their members to take sides and end up doing battle with sapients, all but the smallest and most homogenous splintering. Even when the Guilds stand aside, they're forced to do battle as their home base, their Guild headquarters, are threatened by one fleet or another.

Beliefs in what the System was, is, what they did and what their society means; it all fractures and splinters as truth is revealed, while old political ideologies and cultural biases are brought into question. Even fundamental aspects of life like the Class choices an individual or society has made are questioned.

The Fist question if the strength they gained, the Levels they fought for, are but a sham created by egghead Administrators. The Artisans ponder the limits of their creations, wondering if they could do more, be more with but a touch of a button. Technocrats laud their forethought and distrust of the System, and rail against its constraints upon their lives. Questors crow about the newly revealed knowledge, but seek further information, further Quest completions.

And more.

The world outside the Forbidden Zone is even more chaotic than the Zone itself, it seems, and the borders of the Forbidden Zone grow at a noticeable rate with each day. As sapients die, as Mana churn decreases, Restricted Planets fall.

Even so, with all this pressing upon them, with the very foundations of their world coming apart, the Administrators attack the Questors. They send Heroics to hunt us, to destroy libraries and chapters. They use Skills to increase the cost of information in the Shop, locking it behind Class and Title requirements. They hunt those who hold the Questor Title and raze entire neighborhoods who have begun to question.

They target the Questors and search for us. They hunt desperately for the *Heartbreak*, afraid of what I represent. Seeking to make an example of my friends and me.

Coming to the end of the data feed, I exhale, rubbing my face. My stomach clenches, guilt clawing at my mind. Fear tightens my chest and I know, I know that I'm not enough.

And I force myself to breathe, for what is, is.

Eventually, I calm. Enough so that that I can review my Status, verify the Levels I have gained. Confirm what I have done and what I must do to grow.

Grow and survive.

***

Levels. I've gained so many. Titles too. Reading over my Status, I sigh.

Status Screen			
Name	John Lee	Class	Junior System Admin (Grand Paladin)
Race	Human (Male)	Level	21 (14)

Titles			
Monster's Bane, Redeemer of the Dead, Duelist, Explorer, Master Questor, Galactic Silver Bounty Hunter, Galactic Bounty (Polonium), Galactic Rebel, Corrupt Questor, Chaos Bringer, Curse of the Anathema (Earth), Breaker of the Galaxy, (Living Repository), (Class Lock)			
Health	6550	Stamina	6550
Mana	7000	Mana Regeneration	491 (+5) / minute
Attributes			
Strength	468	Agility	541
Constitution	655	Perception	475
Intelligence	700	Willpower	596
Charisma	225	Luck	346
Class Skills			
Mana Imbue	5*	Blade Strike*	5
Thousand Steps	1	Altered Space	2
Two are One	1	The Body's Resolve	3
Greater Detection	1	A Thousand Blades*	4
Soul Shield*	8	Blink Step	2
Portal*	5	Army of One	4
Sanctum	2	Penetration	9e
Aura of Chivalry	1	Eyes of Insight	2
Beacon of the Angels	2	Eye of the Storm	1
Vanguard of the Apocalypse	2	Society's Web	1
Shackles of Eternity*	4	Immovable Object / Unstoppable Force*	1
Domain	1	Judgment of All	6

(Grand Cross)	(2)	(Extra Hands)	(3)
System Edit	4		
External Class Skills			
Instantaneous Inventory	1	Frenzy	1
Cleave	2	Tech Link	2
Elemental Strike	1 (Ice)	Shrunken Footsteps	1
Analyze	2	Harden	2
Quantum Lock	3	Elastic Skin	3
Disengage Safeties	2	Temporary Forced Link	1
Hyperspace Nitro Boost	1	On the Edge	1
Fates Thread	2		
Combat Spells			
Improved Minor Healing (IV)		Greater Regeneration (II)	
Greater Healing (II)		Mana Drip (II)	
Improved Mana Missile (IV)		Enhanced Lightning Strike (III)	
Firestorm		Polar Zone	
Freezing Blade		Improved Inferno Strike (II)	
Elemental Walls (Fire, Ice, Earth, etc.)		Ice Blast	
Icestorm		Improved Invisibility	
Improved Mana Cage		Improved Flight	
Haste		Enhanced Particle Ray	
Variable Gravitic Sphere		Zone of Denial	

Levels and Titles. I sigh at some of them, absently note the belated increase in others like the Master Questor Title, and review the details in others.

Title: *Galactic Rebel*

You have been declared a Galactic Rebel by a quorum of the Galactic Council. This information has been propagated to all parties via the System. This Title may not be hidden by normal means.

Effect: Significant reputation changes with lawful and criminal factions. Access to certain rebel communication channels. Cost of rebel and outlaw Class Skill types have been decreased. Cost of lawful, legal, and bounty hunting Class Skill types have increased significantly.

Title: *Breaker of the Galaxy*

You have torn apart the Galactic order, causing significant changes in the political and social order. Generally not a Title available to those still alive or below the Legendary Class. Such changes generally cause significant chaos and hardship for many, and such a Title should not be sought after. This Title may not be hidden by normal means.

Rewards: Reputation changes are significantly increased. Fame is significantly increased and a minimum Fame threshold of Galactic celebrity has been set. +100% increase in effects of Luck (both negative and positive). This effect will stack with other Skills, Attribute bonuses, and Titles. Unique purchasable Fame and Reputation Skills now available. Effect of certain Luck and Fate-altering Skills are either magnified or nullified entirely (depending on Skill and circumstances).

I review the new Titles and sigh. Most of the effects are unimportant to me since they're Reputation and Fame gains or Class Skills that I can purchase. I'm sure I could potentially get new Classes that were not accessible before, as I've now met their prerequisites. Not much use when I'm a Heroic, but worth noting. Purchasable Class Skills are a problem with the library in my head. On the other hand, I don't even need to tap into the Shop since the library spools the various Skills for me. After reviewing them, I curse my circumstances.

Some of those Skills would be useful, but not only are they all expensive, they aren't particularly worthwhile on a combat basis. None of them, for example, turns my Fame or Reputation into weapons to do damage, though some do give an opportunity to put Status effects like Awe or Stunned or Infatuated in play. Except, of course, the majority of the people I'm fighting are Legendary and Heroic Classes, meaning they have innate resistances.

I still have enough negative Reputation that it might work, but I could just spend my Mana on something much more direct. And with the fact that these Skills are side loaded, it makes their usefulness in combat even lower.

In the end, I have to admit, the Titles are cute, and the Luck attribute bonus might be useful, but they just aren't pertinent to me right now.

As for Levels, I've gained much in my time in the Forbidden Zone, as I always do. I cannot help but remember my first time here, the planet which set me on the Class I carry even now. Yet I know that I have to be careful. In the Forbidden Zone, without access to the System, what I choose now for Skills might be all that I get for a long while. Until we reach Xylargh at least, when a stable access to the System is available once more.

So, time to review my Skills. And what it offers me. Because without access to the System, my other false Class has grown, allowing me options and choices once more. Not that I can access my second tier yet, since I haven't crossed Level 26.

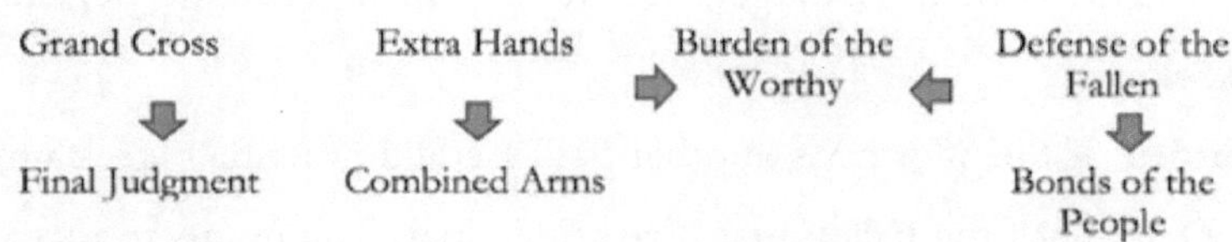

I could try for an evolution of Extra Hands. There's something to be said about throwing more points into it, getting more helpers. It's a Skill that is perfect for our outnumbered situation and punches outside its weight class when I have time to set it up, since it maximizes the amount of damage I can do. Of course, I have to pre-create the Hands, which makes it useless in the middle of a fight. Even more so when all the doppelgangers fall or I don't have time to keep creating them. No matter what evolution I might get—if I could get one—that won't change. Even so, being a one-person army has its attractions.

Grand Cross and Defense of the Fallen are opposite ends of the same thing. Direct combat Skills that would allow me to do battle with those at my level or potentially even higher. It's strange, a little, that the Grand Paladin stops getting area-effect buffs. Then again, the Grand Paladin is the vanguard of most forces, the shining light of the Erethran Paladins. He's the one you throw at the biggest, largest threats. Other offshoots from the Paladin Class in the Heroic stage are meant to boost the armies and fleets.

More importantly, the Grand Paladin has to face the Erethran Champion and win. He's the balancing factor there, and as such, the pure combat Skills make sense.

It's why I'm tempted to try Defense of the Fallen. It's a permanent upgrade to my tankiness, which means that my Extra Hands will receive it too, unlike my evolved Penetration Skill. The combination of the two Skills would mean they would last longer, which is important when they regenerate Mana so slowly.

Burden of the Worthy is another Skill I could potentially pick up if I choose Defense of the Fallen first. I've got enough Skill points to play with the combined Skill, but it's a similar Skill to Two for One. Just the other way. I send damage to others—Hands, Mikito, my friends, or subordinates. For that reason, it's an automatic no.

There's one other Skill. System Edit. It's powerful, and I know what it can do now. How to use it in combat, even if I don't have enough experience at it to make me comfortable relying on it. I'm getting better at utilizing it in combat, but there are aspects of the Skill that make me wonder.

If putting points into it is necessary at all.

You see, access is controlled by my Levels as a Junior Administrator. To gain more access, I'd need to increase my System Administrator Levels and, yes, my Class. I might even need to hit other hidden objectives. Like being approved for a job promotion.

In addition, manipulating System code is as much a matter of understanding the code as it is the Skill. In fact, I wonder if the Skill itself, the way it works is just a shortcut. More points make it easier to play with the way the code shifts, make it easier for information to be understood. It often does feel that way, when I'm in the midst of it all.

Unlike most of the other Administrators, I have a cheat. I have the god damn Questor Library in me. While it might not give direct answers, I've had samples of the System code—the raw information forms—floating in my mind for years now. Enough time that I can automatically grasp some of what I see when I enter the System.

Which leads me to question what exactly the System Edit Skill does. And why there's only a single Skill no matter how much I level.

Questions.

That's my life. And no matter what answers I find, it always seems like the one answer I need is far away.

None of that helps with my current predicament though. Which, again. Story of my life.

In the end, I do what I always do. I stumble blindly forward, making decisions and hoping that it's enough. Choosing to bolster my Hands via greater strength, via the Defense of the Fallen should benefit me in both the short and long term. Since my Skill Points are being distributed—sometimes unwillingly—via Skill Edit, there's no way to guarantee I'd ever get a Skill Evolution. Better to just go with what works in the short term and hope it works out.

Defense of the Fallen (Level 3)

Guardian and protector, judge and executioner, the Grand Paladin has succeeded as much as he has failed in his duty. Not everyone they seek to save can be saved. All too often, the Paladin arrives after the tragedy. Defense of the Fallen armors the Paladin to deal with the mental and physical demands of the job.

Effect: Increases Mental Resistance by 60%, increases Physical Resistance by 35%. Effects are stacked on existing resistances. Effects are imbued in an aura surrounding the user, including all worn and active shields and armor.

It's a little weird, seeing how my total resistances are above 100%, but the math involved is a little complicated and uses a bunch of multiplication and fraction calculations, along with resistance and Mana Saturation equations. It all ends up being random numbers to me, though the library insists on providing me the equations as best as the Questors have deduced.

Really, end of the day—numbers go up, me happy.

All that number crunching other people do, it feels as though they're wasting time rather than, I don't know, doing something productive like going out and killing more monsters to increase their Level and make the numbers go up even more.

The other reason I hate all these questions is that it makes no sense, since you never know what your opponent might have. My own Penetration Skill rips apart defenses, more than halving their effects. Which means that even a 250% increase in Physical Resistances is only worth a 125% increase, which means that instead of taking a hundred points of direct damage, it drops down forty or so points, give or take whatever else other point defenses you might have or bonuses and the elemental portion of my attack or if it's a direct attack via the System or Mana saturation or…

On and on and on, as I said.

In the end, the equations are simple in the extreme. Try not to get hit, and if you do, hope you can survive long enough to hit them back hard enough that they die before you do.

Everything else, it's just numbers masturbation.

***

The Church fetes us that night. We're forced to go out and mingle and talk, to play nice. At least, Harry and I are. Dornalor declines the "formal" ball, instead joining a bunch of other technicians and ship captains at the hangar bay to drink and carouse. It also lets him keep an eye on the ship itself. Ali disappears to where the Companions hang out, "gathering information" as he says and probably having a better time than we do. As for Mikito, she found the local equivalent of the Arena and is holding an impromptu challenge match against one and all.

"Are we to dislike such gatherings?" Ezz, tottering along after me, asks when we have a few seconds of reprieve from the press of flesh.

"Who says I'm unhappy?" I growl. The glare I shoot at the next approaching couple makes them hesitate before they keep coming. I'm almost tempted to turn on my Aura just to drive people away. But since mine does damage, it's probably not politic. Even if most of those in here could take it.

"Biosensory and auric reading and physical positioning indicates you do not, Father," Ezz says. "Am I mistaken?"

I don't answer it, instead doing the glad-handing thing. I greet the couple, smile, and answer a few questions about the events and what being an Administrator is like—a lot of paperwork and tickets—then I subtly send them off. It helps that there's a minder not so far away over my right shoulder who is busy giving people side-eyes whenever they think of staying too long.

When we're alone again, I answer Ezz. "You're not wrong. I'm not a people person."

"These are people?"

I grunt. Then I look down and eye Ezz, considering if this is the first sign of a sense of humor. "Close enough for fiddlestick anyway." I shake my head. "It's the social stuff."

"Fiddle… Ah." Ezz pauses. "But Father is a Paladin."

"Yeah." I flick open Society's Web, watching the flow of secrets and obligations between those around. A part of me is cataloguing the data, putting it together in ways that the Archbishop probably doesn't even realize I can. It also lets me pick out the guards he has scattered through the area, though the majority of those here are high-Level enough to carry their weight in a fight. "It still doesn't mean I like people or social situations. For that matter, I'm not your typical Paladin."

"Yes. The Creator downloaded the records of your activities. It was significantly more biased toward violence than most Paladins." A slight buzz from Ezz. "However, statistically and taking into account your origins and in comparison to your peers, the volume of combat Father has engaged in is still within the ninetieth percentile."

"Peers?" I ask. Then I break off to do the glad-handing thing again, watching as the trio wanders off after I decline to join them in bed. Really, they're all quite cute, but it's not the kind of entanglements we need.

"Yes. The other Champions on Earth, the leading Leveled members and other Dungeon World survivors. Most have faced a much higher rate of combat than you, though on average, a lower number of high-Level combatants," Ezz said.

"Huh."

"Redeemer, thank you for gracing us with your presence."

"Yeah, yeah," I answer, turning over the information from Ezz and not even paying attention.

"We were wondering, my triad and I, if you could perhaps answer a question about our Statuses. You see, we gained this Status-Condition, Betrothed Thrice, but we are uncertain about the effects. Perhaps you could…" The speaker is a human-looking figure except for the fact that he is whiter than new fallen snow and has four hands.

He's flanked by another of his kind and what I can only call a lizard-creature. Not drake, since the drakes were more dragon-like and this one is shorter, more lizard-like. No breasts, though the coloring around its scales and smaller size says female to me.

"Thrice Betrothed, huh?" I say, purposely getting it wrong. I'm curious, so I pull out their Statuses and go digging. It takes me a few seconds before I get an answer, one that has me smirking a little.

"Administrator?" Worry.

"Oh, well. I guess congratulations are in order. I'd ask for a wedding invitation, but I doubt I'll be here long enough."

"But we aren't… we just once!" spluttered the man.

"Well, it seems someone"—I nod toward the lizard-woman—"comes with certain liabilities when one indulges. You're stuck."

"And if I refuse?"

"The System doesn't care." I shrug. "HP, MP, and regeneration for all will be shared. As will experience gain, one way or the other."

"What!?!" the man shouts, detaching his hand from his companion's and waving it around. "This… change it!"

I shake my head no.

"I demand you…" His mouth clamps shut, his face flushing pink. It's a very strange sight, what with the white skin. He staggers backward and bows to me, tugging on his woman to duplicate his actions.

Only the lizardkin looks to be handling the change well, and even she bows low to me.

I watch their stumbling departure before I turn and meet the gaze of our watcher. He looks back placidly, even when I raise an inquiring eyebrow. In the end, I leave it, though Society's Web has shown the switch in obligations quite well. It glows bright red and dark, between the man and the Bishop in the distance, while other ties have frayed or even disappeared.

Pale-and-noisy pushed things too hard and now, he's not only in debt to the Bishop, he's lost standing and is in debt to others. I could feel bad, but he's the one who made the choice. Even if he might have been tricked into gaining his new Title.

As they always say—be careful where you dip your wick.

"I do not understand. Is not a larger family better?" Ezz asks, buzzing by my side. "The Creator always created more of us as he said that quantity could, hopefully, make up for quality." There's a tinge of sadness there.

I sigh. "Yes. No. It's complicated. Feelings, you know about that, right?" I get a nod, so I continue. "Well, feelings complicate matters. Unintended consequences of breeding. Those are always dangerous."

"Is that why you declined the other offers?" Ezz says.

"Yes. You're vulnerable during the act, of course, but it's the aftereffects, what might happen after that can be… difficult. The System and its Skills add to the complexity of physical relations." I shrug. "Anyway, learning the difference between what you want and what you need, it's important for an adult."

"I see." Ezz buzzes and falls silent, pondering my statement.

I'm glad, because another man is coming and I'm going to have to be nice.

I hate being nice.

***

"All right, we've read. We've socialized. Now, you going to tell me why exactly you want to speak with me?" I ask Turad.

The Archbishop has met me in the anteroom of his office, seating us on the cushions that circle the Mana flame that burns in the center. He's wearing a flowing robe, still coded in the colors of the Church, and holding a mug of green liquid. The rest of us have been served what we desire—in my case, Apocalypse Ale still in the bottle.

Harry's gotten a taste for a Hakarta liquor, a dark, peat-like substance that is somewhat similar to whisky but harsher. As for Mikito, she's been given a full tea set that she has used to serve herself and Ezz. It amuses me to watch her speak with Ezz, explaining the process of tea brewing while keeping an eye out for potential threats.

"I was happy to discuss the matter yesterday," Turad says. My eyes narrow, but he keeps talking before I can grumble at him. "I represent a portion of the Everlasting Church who have long believed that the System as we know it has been corrupted. Your actions, in exposing the Administrators, have shown that our beliefs were correct."

"Wait. You knew there was something wrong with the System?" I frown.

"Believed. Certain choices, certain changes have been recorded." His upper body bobs up and down on the curled-up scaled bottom half as he continues. "Questors are not the only ones who keep records of past events. We have had purges of such data too, just like you. We have seen the alterations in the way Skills, Classes happen. And while some believe it is the normal working of the System—"

"Some of it is," I confirm.

"We believe much of it was twisted by the Council. And others," Turad continues, the Naga ignoring my interruption.

"And now, you think the others are the Administrators."

"Yes. For the System is above us all and is infallible in its goals. That it has failed at times is inimical to such a fact. Such events could not have happened if the System was allowed to function by itself."

"Pretty sure you're giving the System a little too much credit there."

"The System has uplifted civilizations! Saved us from the onslaught of unaspected Mana! It has given the lowest of the low Classes and tested even the most complacent." Fervor shines in Turad's yellow-green snake eyes as he lurches forward. I swear, I almost see spittle forming. "The System is the lifeblood of civilization. It is there when we are born, it is there when we die. It remakes our very world to its needs."

"And what needs are those?" I ask.

Turad subsides a little, a smile playing across his face. "The System is not ours to question. Its actions are mysterious and beyond the ken of sapients, even Legendary ones."

"Yeah. Bullshit," I say, crossing my arms.

"You Questors, always asking that question. Can you not accept the System for what it is?" Turad snarls. "How long have you tried to answer that question and failed? How many lives must you waste before you understand that some things, we mortals are not meant to grasp?"

"I'd say at least one more." I smirk. "You Systemers just are too lazy to do the real work—"

Harry clears his throat, interrupting us before we can get further into it. I glare at the Reporter who offers a tight smile, though I note he's been recording the entire interaction. Then again, he's not wrong.

"Fine. Whatever. Agree to disagree. We're clear that you're happy with what I did, but why are you helping us now?" I ask. "Surely there's more that the Church can and should be doing, considering everything that's going on?"

"It is believed that what you have revealed, what you have done against our mutual enemies and the amount of effort they have put into finding you, your existence and your future actions are not a small thing." His eyes drift upward to my Status and Titles. "You still have, we believe, the System believes, a bigger part to play." Turad opens his hands sideways. "And if so, then it is our duty to help you."

"I… see." I cock my head, considering. His words ring true, and the one advantage of having the devout on your side, they'll be willing to hit the beaches. "And how far does that help extend?"

"As far as we can make it." Turad smiles while Mikito sips on her tea.

She places the teacup down, watches as Ezz refills it, and murmurs words of appreciation. The little ass-kisser replies. In Japanese.

"If your Captain will allow us, we will aid him in fixing your ship," Turad says. "We will bring you as close as possible to your destination. We will even open, briefly, access to the Shop."

My jaw drops a little, while Ali, hovering silently till now, pipes up. "You got the juice for that?"

"Briefly. Though the sphere is here, actual access…" A shrug. "It must be done before we proceed too much further into the Forbidden Zone. And there are only a few spaces that this might work." Turad gestures and a star map flips up. He points at a few locations next to the flashing dot that is us.

No surprise that where he points are near planets. Planets that were once inhabited and thriving, now overrun. They might be lost, but they're still sufficiently populated by the survivors that the total unaspected Mana interference levels are lower. Low enough that the presence of the Cathedral might—briefly—open a connection.

"We offer our aid, and a chance to rest and train," Turad finishes. "If you will accept it."

"And if I refuse?"

Mikito flicks her cup at me, sending the liquid straight at my face. I jerk backward, eyes widening, but at least she hadn't thrown the cup itself. I wipe my leg and shirt while she turns right back to Ezz.

"Now, you see, Ezz, that was a waste of a good cup of tea. However, sometimes, you have to do that when the baka are too stupid and prideful to accept aid when it is freely offered. Always guard against pride," Mikito says to the golem, who dutifully refills her teacup.

"Traitor," I mutter while Turad does his best to hide his smile. "Fine. We'll take your help."

"Good." A pause. "There is one thing…"

"Of course there is." I roll my eyes, but I listen. I'm not a fan of tea baths.

***

Inhale. Exhale. Breathe slowly, calm yourself. This is a small thing, a tiny matter. I've faced down Legendarys and Heroics, taken on armies, and destroyed entire planets of monsters. There is nothing out there that should make me scared or even a little nervous. Yet…

"And you're sure one of my Hands couldn't be doing this?" I growl. I know most of them are watching the various Mechanics and Engineers working on the *Heartbreak*, with another walking the city, learning its layout. He gets dismissed every day, the sensory impressions and knowledge he gathers flooding back into me. Providing me the layout of the city on an intuitive basis.

Just in case.

"They desire the answers only you can give," GoGorm La says.

I snort. "I'm not giving those kinds of answers, you know."

"Yes. But they don't."

I sigh, but as the announcer finishes his spiel and calls for me, I stride forward. Into the auditorium of expectant faces, all of whom are here to hear me speak. Speak on being an Administrator, of what I have seen, what I can do. There's probably a part of them who want to know how this relates to their beliefs. That, I leave for others to deal with.

My job is to talk about what I know, the facts of my existence. I am not entirely happy about this, but I spot Harry standing to the side, recording me. Transmitting what we have to say for the world, for the Galaxy. Even if this goads the Council and makes them want to end me even more, I know it has to be done.

I still have nightmares of fleets arriving on Earth, dealing orbital death. If I can keep their attention on me, maybe I can save my friends.

Or maybe I'll anger them enough that they'll hurt Earth.

I'm damned if I do, damned if I don't.

So I might as well be damned while screwing with the Shadow Council.

I stand on the stage, staring at the alien and expectant faces. They might believe differently from me, have grown up entirely alien. Yet looking into their faces, I see a kinship. For the System and the Council have taken from us, controlled our lives.

They sought faith to answer the lack of control they felt.

I seek answers.

And at least their method has seen fewer deaths.

"Good day," I greet the crowd, my voice magically enhanced to ensure everyone can hear me. "My name is John Lee. And I'm a Junior Administrator of the System. I gained that Hidden Class just a short year ago…"

Chapter 13

The Cathedral drops out of space weeks later, next to a Forbidden Zone planet. A hum, so low and prevalent that I haven't consciously noted it, lessens. The enchantments and Skills that help the Cathedral of the Everlasting Church of the Infinite System function ease off as the planet takes some of the burden from the island. My connection to the System firms up, and for a moment, I get a glimpse of the data streams the System uses, watch as the entirety of the planet metamorphizes within the System-code as Mana flow stabilizes. Long overburdened subroutines work once more, data and Levels across the cities closest to us firming.

The shift is so noticeable, I have to stop the blade form I'm practicing. Notifications pour out of thin air, clogging up my view. A part of me notes the way the System prioritizes some notifications like the Level Ups, while others are sent back further in the stack for delivery when possible. I sort them, discarding the unimportant—long held in abeyance damage and kill notifications, minor experience gain indicators from the System, reputation alterations and changes—and focus on the important. The dark blue System Administrator alerts.

Global System Administrator Alert!

Planet RR07-987890-12 has reached maximum unaspected Mana interference threshold. System failure imminent!

Re-routing System Mana as per Mana Overrun Protocols 004-6

Minimal System Connections Sustained

Collection of System Mana Begun

Mana Overrun Protocols Completed. Increased Mana Overflow Channels by 5284%

Emergency Administrator Protocols Implemented

Interesting. I read over the information quickly, pausing on the Mana Overrun Protocols and the number associated with it. It seems that the Overrun Protocols were one of the first things the System implemented. Not the first thing, but one of the first. Almost as if it expected that it would need them.

A clue, though I'm not sure what it points to. I even get a small—a fraction of a percentage—increase in my System Quest completion rate.

Quest Received: Restore System Functionality

Restore System Functionality to planet RR07-987890-12.

Requirements:

- *Reduce ambient Mana in atmosphere (% decrease varies rewards. System currently functioning at 24.3% of full operating capacity)*
- *Complete tickets 002-13MSO*

Rewards: Provided at 5%, 10%, 25%, 40%, 50%, 75%, 90% and 100% functionality restoration.

"Not a lot of details there," I grumble. When Mikito raises an inquiring eyebrow, I shoot the Quest to her.

"Don't we get something similar when we arrive on all Forbidden Zone planets?" Mikito says, frowning.

I nod. "It's worded differently and gives direct experience multipliers. Obviously, there's a public and Administrator Quest." It is, after all, not our first time on a Forbidden Planet. "But there are no percentage rewards, nor any indication of them."

"I wonder why?"

"Probably because your regular visitor isn't expected to do enough damage to give the System functionality back? Never mind the tickets, which are probably specific issues that only Administrators can handle." I rub my chin. I try to pull up more data on the tickets, but of course, since I'm not in an Administrative Center, I get nothing. On the other hand, the System is quite helpfully providing me a couple of glowing dots indicating where I can go. "Huh."

"What?" Mikito says impatiently.

"There are Administrative Centers down there."

"That's surprising?" she says.

I have to admit, it really isn't when you think about it. I wonder what they look like. I even say that thought out loud.

"John…" A warning tone.

"It can't hurt to look, can it?" I say, gesturing toward the planet. "We did want to grind after all. Maybe completing this Quest and grinding at the same time will be more efficient. In either case, we need more Levels before we dare meet our enemies again."

Mikito makes a face, but she nods. After having our asses handed to us so badly on Irvina, we both know that rushing to our destination is a bad idea. As much as we want to finish this, we need Levels. We need to take up some side quests if you will, because otherwise, we'll get squashed by the final boss.

After all, there's no doubt there are Galactic Council members and Administrators waiting for us on Xylargh.

"You know you aren't going to just look, right, boy-o?" Ali says, lips curled up in a smirk. "You're going to want to help, then you're going to want to hit that 25% rate and the next one after that…"

"I'm not that bad."

"You really are," Ali says.

"Twenty-five," Mikito says firmly.

"And if it's a lot of work?" I ask.

She shrugs, and I get it. We'll abandon the quest if things are too hard, but she is putting down a firm limit of 25% being the maximum we'd work towards. Truth be told, with my multiple Hands in play, I'm curious how long it would take. We used to take months to clear out a Restricted Zone planet, but Forbidden Zones are on another level entirely. We also had help, and while I don't expect the Systemers to just watch—after all, this is a good leveling opportunity for them too—it's not the same as the Erethran Empire backing us up.

"All right. Think Harry will want to come along?" I ask.

Mikito is flicking her fingers along a planetary map, then she swings the view around and stops on a couple of glowing points. She zooms in on those glowing points, widening the window so that the three of us can view what she is seeing.

Cities. Fortresses more like, but still extant civilized locations. Somehow, these bastions of society have held out. There are no images of people, not on the map we're using, but the pulse of Mana, the shift and regulated flow from a working Settlement Core is more than sufficient evidence that someone lives down there.

"I think he'd prefer to be dropped off there," Mikito says.

"Yeah, I bet." I look at her meaningfully, and she sighs.

"Fine. I'll send it to him." Her eyes narrow. "You guys should talk to one another at some point. Resolve your issues."

"Not sure the issues can be resolved," I say, opening my hands wide. "I betrayed Earth, made him help with it, got him tortured, and dragged him into a fight we can't win. Pretty sure being pissed at me is the correct, mature response."

"He could have said no, baka," Mikito replies. "Talk to him."

"Yes, ma'am. Promise."

Mikito stares as if she doesn't believe me. Which, I have to admit, is smart of her. It's not as if I'm very good at these interpersonal relationship things. Or, you know, have a history of leaving the planet rather than dealing with the complexities of emotion confrontations.

***

I watch as the Extra Hands leave on interstellar assault shuttles that burn through the stratosphere to drop off at various portions on the Forbidden Planet. We're in the same hangar we arrived in, the *Nothing's Heartbreak* a short distance away and being rebuilt, interstellar shuttles all around. The four Hands, each of them with my Class Skills, can do a ton of damage, especially when they're flying high above. Of course, we're not just going for quantity but quality too in our monster genocide programs.

"You sure you want to do this alone?" I say to Mikito.

She is standing beside me, waiting for the team that is meant to accompany her to finish up their equipment check. The Church has offered to guard her, and she's accepted. With certain caveats, but there are more than enough monsters for her to indulge herself without the others stealing her kills or experience.

I have a little bit of worry about splitting the party, but everything my Skills have told me has indicated we're safe among the Church members. For definitions of safe at least.

"Yes. Fighting next to you will not be to my benefit." Mikito's eyes twinkle a little as she adds, "I get your experience anyway."

I snort, but I admit, the Feudal Bond Skill is a cheat. The fact that she gets experience both for my work as a System Administrator and while I'm doing more "normal" things is definitely a bug. One that I'm supposed to fix, but which I, of course, have not. I'm sure that Administrator Prime—when I find him—will smack my hand, but for now, it's to our benefit.

"Fine. Just take care of yourself, eh?"

"What, no words of safety and assurance for me?" Harry says, needling.

I turn toward the Reporter, watching as he tugs on new clothing. It's an assault jumpsuit provided by the Church, the kind of stuff that the Church's Advanced Classers are wearing as they depart to do battle and gain Levels. It looks good on him, the dark blue and red edging blending with his complexion.

"You're going to their fort. Pretty sure you'll be safe," I say, nodding to the group behind him. Mostly Administrators and Merchants, various Artisans and the like who will be searching for materials and selling their work. Or, like Harry, tapping into the Shop to sell his recordings and acquire more information and equipment. Mikito and I will deal with that later, but right now, we've got work to do.

"And your estimation of safe has always been good," Harry drawls.

I don't rise to the bait. "Keep safe. And shout if you need help."

He snorts and walks off to his shuttle. Mikito gives me a look and I shrug, avoiding her eyes. At some point, I'll need to deal with that. For now though, I'm going to blast apart some monsters and worry about Harry and Dornalor later. Because Dorn's more politic, but still showing signs of stress and annoyance. As the shouting from the *Heartbreak* attests.

I wave goodbye to Mikito, heading for an assault drop pod. It's the fastest way down, and where I'm going, a shuttle will just be a liability. Since I'm not particularly desiring company—nor would they be useful—the single-person assault pod is perfect. Of course, I do regard the assault pod they offer with some trepidation.

"Don't you have something less… slimy?" I say as I stand before the creature generating the assault pod. Lots of vines, lots of little slimy extrusions, its main body the size of a minibus.

The plant pulses, going green and yellow as if it's angry with me. My language pack doesn't have a translation, but I get the feeling it's upset.

"You wanted down fast. This is fast," Ali says. "Now quit complaining and get in."

"Fine…"

I walk into the open cylinder that is the start of the pod. It closes itself around my legs then lifts me up before even more slime pumps out of the plant's tendrils into the now fully enclosed seed. Within seconds, I'm encapsulated in a Star Seed, which is how the plant, an interplanetary sentient terror, manages to spread itself. Star Seeds normally float through space, growing their seeds and launching them through space. When they come across a suitable planet, they go into overdrive and spray the planet below.

The majority of the seeds will not make it as monsters and sapient residents deal with the growing plant. However, enough generally survive to Level and finally, ascend the atmosphere before they repeat the process. Of course, in between, the plants grow without end and devastate local monster and sapient population if they aren't killed off.

In this case, the Star Seeder has been neutered, a Monster Horticulturist having tamed it. The majority of its body is trapped, technology and Skills ensuring its docility. In the meantime, it's forced to create these assault pods—these seeds—for the Church whenever they need it.

All that passes through my mind just before the damn thing pokes its vine out of the shield. It sucks in my seed, the assault pod accelerated through the creature's body, before I'm launched at the planet below. There's quite a bit of pain involved, the G forces ticking away at my health. My face presses up against the top of the pod, slime hardening under pressure to feel like pre-System concrete to me.

The world blurs past me in flame and green ichor as I fall, down, down, down. I make it through the upper atmosphere before the monsters that guard the sky decide to interrupt my fall. No surprise, since I'm aimed at the densest Mana cluster on the planet.

Talons tear, the seed bursts, and I'm free, tumbling through open air.

I get to work.

***

The monster was beautiful the way a falcon diving through the sky is beautiful. All sharp lines, where it is solid. Where it isn't, ghostly outlines. Eyes all across its wings and body, a pair of talons below green-blue feathers. A giant prey bird, its body half-disappearing into the sky it is silhouetted against as I fall. My eyes track over it, taking in its information.

Bladewraith (Level 218)

HP: 21861/21864

MP: 3432/3982

Conditions: Ethereal, Gaze of the Predator, Domain of the Sky

Predator eyes track me, a pair locking on and blasting me with energy. Another pair attempt a psychic assault, only to be rebuffed by my resistances and my status as an Administrator. Another conjures darts of ice that fill the air. The damage piles on my Soul Shield even as the Bladewraith shifts direction. Catching wind on a different plane, swooping at me with its claws.

No more playing. Penetration's Evolved Skill is triggered, even as I call forth Grand Cross. The spell strikes the Bladewraith from above, crushing it as I center the attack and end the cross mere feet from my own floating body. The Bladewraith tanks the damage, its body forced off course.

For all that, my Skill does not kill it. Other creatures far below die, but the Bladewraith only receives a portion of the initial damage, its ethereal nature offering protection.

As it passes by, swinging round wide and struggling to rise against my Skill, I spot the drip from its talons. A poison of some kind, but not physical—spiritual perhaps. Either way, that would hurt if it hit.

Even as the bird falls and struggles to rise, it's not done with me. Eyes on the top of its body track me and launch their attacks. Beams of energy crisscross my form, burning at my Evolved Penetration Shield. I twist in mid-air, casting a spell as I call forth a sword and return the favor by using Blade Strike. The attack barely dents the monster's health, even as Grand Cross continues to tick.

Then the spell is done, and I twist in mid-air, aiming myself. Down, down, down, I use the higher gravity of the planet and the new Flight spell to thrust me into the creature's body. My sword leads the way, biting into an eye in the middle of its body, bursting it open.

I tear through weakened flesh and razor-sharp feathers and eyes, falling inward before momentum is arrested. Blood, poison, acid—it assaults me as

I bob within its half-ethereal body. Caught as I am in the space between, I am surprised to find the Bladewraith even has eyes inside.

Blades from its eyes, conjured from its blood form. They spin and cut, tearing at my shield, even as I return the favor. My sword is blocked, my sword cuts. It doesn't matter, it has me and I can sense that I'm on the losing end of this exchange.

A microsecond of consideration before I try something different. Rather than use the System, a System and Skills that are blunted by the unaspected Mana in the atmosphere, I tap into my Elemental Affinity. It's half-bound to this realm, a creature of multiple dimensions. Its body is more of a suggestion than a solid rebuke. I make it even more so.

The forces of attraction between its physical molecules come apart. I release them within, and at the same time, I reach outward to the world, to the atmosphere outside, and strengthen the attraction that way. The Bladewraith and its blades come apart, torn asunder by its very nature and my manipulation of reality.

It dies, screaming, blades spinning away into oblivion in an explosion of gore and pain. Leaving me to float in the middle of an empty battlefield.

For all of about two minutes, before the next contender for ruler of the skies finds me.

I greet it with blade and lightning and a grin on my face.

Out here, on the edge of oblivion, blood dripping from my sword, from my shield, I feel alive. There's a savage joy as I meet the next contender—a bulbous, tentacled creature that would never dare fight the Bladewraith but somehow thinks I'm easier—in battle. Out here, I feel something more than the emptiness of my day-to-day existence, the anger that coats everything if I let it. I let the anger out to play all too often, just so that I can feel something, anything.

It's not enough. It'll never be enough. But for each monster I kill, each time I call forth a Beacon of the Angels or lay down Judgment of All on the swarms that do battle beneath me, I feel the thrill of experience gain, of Mana released, of violence culminated. I get a little of myself back from a System, a world that has taken and taken without care or an iota of mercy.

And if the feeling I reach for in that emptiness of my existence is savage joy or adrenaline, if it is anger and rage, then so be it. Better to feel something, anything, than to exist in a void where a wrong step, a too sharp turn brings reminders of an unbearable past.

Let those who have hearth and home, love and friendship find healing.

The rest of us have got a job to do.

***

Four days later, I get a ping. It comes at a bad time, when I'm in the midst of grappling for dominance with a six-legged and four-armed creature the size of a two-story apartment building. Its plastic-like outer layer makes gripping it difficult. All except around its arms, which are formed like suction cups, two of which I'm holding away from my body while the other two whale upon my body. Cracked armor, noxious blood, and a truly offensive smell permeates the air, powerful enough that it gets through the environmental seals on the damaged Hod.

My Penetration shield flickers, even as the Beacon of the Angels I called forth on its hindpart burns away at its defense. Pain shoots through me constantly, my movements slowed as its monstrous Skills penetrate my defense to do damage and wear me down. My mind is a little foggy, bloodlust and days of continual battle making a simple thing like a message a distraction.

It crumples me to the ground, the earth pancaking beneath my knees. "What?" I snarl.

Next thing I know, the light of the world disappears as the damn creature sticks me in its mouth. That's what I've been trying to hold off, but it relaxes then pulls me forward as I overcompensate. Once I'm in its mouth, acidic saliva breaks down my Soul Shield, the blue non-glow of System notifications lighting up my sigh.

"John, we're done. My team is about to fall over, and I want to hit the Shop," Mikito says. "You should come in too."

"I can keep fighting," I protest.

Since he stuck me inside, I figure I'll give him a little mouth pain and conjure my soulbound sword. Since it's linked to me, it keeps upgrading in strength. Not that it looks very different from when I first conjured it, but it's sharper, more durable than ever. I pull out the other swords from A Thousand Blades and thrust the original forward before cutting sideways.

The conjured blades follow the path, creating a swirling mass of metal on the inside of the creature's mouth, even as it continues to try to swallow me. I let it, figuring if I'm in, I'm in. Anyway, the nightmares of being eaten alive are fading, so I might as well refresh them, right? The pressure, the burning, the darkness that throbs with each heartbeat, a heartbeat you can feel through your entire body. The rattle of breath as it draws in oxygen, the stink. It's all too familiar and new in entirely unpleasant manners.

"I'm sure you can, but Ali's been complaining all day long already," Mikito says.

I snort but flick my perception to share the Spirit's senses. He's high above, taking on monsters in the sky. Like my sword, he's Linked to me, so the stronger I get, the stronger he gets. Or as he puts it, the more of his awesomeness gets shown. In this case, he has full access to my Skills and spells along with his Elemental Affinity.

Which is why the sky is a swirling mass of fire and lightning, a tornado of destruction that strikes at the flock of creatures attempting to approach him. He's also chosen to stay pint-sized so that those that manage to make it through the maelstrom of death still have to catch him. Cheating, as usual.

Then again, cheating is what we do. As the poor monstrous behemoth I'm fighting—a Prion Mother Swarmer—is learning. Blades cut into its body, putting its monstrous regeneration at risk even as I slide deeper into its body. Spells—Polar Zone, Ice Storm—are cast one after the other. Once I'm roughly in the middle, I trigger Grand Cross, targeting it at an angle.

The Skill forms the giant, over-pressurized cross a half foot ahead of me, pushing forward and down. It tears right through the monster, crushing organs, bones, and muscle. I'm grateful I'm wearing the Hod—not because of the protection but because it filters some of the smell.

I drop another half dozen incendiary grenades as I jump out, leaving the monster to burn. As I exit, Prion Mother. It thrashes around before it stills, the combined damage finally ending the monster.

Twenty-five minutes to kill it. I'm slowing down. Without much conscious thought, I loot it.

I eye my Penetration Shielding, noting how I'm running out of time. I had to let it chill for a bit after cooldown, which is when the fight had been touch and go, but now, I'm back. For a little while anyway, before it goes down. Not a huge amount of time, but it is time when I'm super safe. And even if the Hod has been healing in the meantime, it's probably not up to helping with the Level 200+ Forbidden Zone Monsters I'm fighting.

Damn equipment always keeps falling behind. Which... is probably why I should go shopping.

"John?" Mikito calls again.

"How are Dornalor and Harry doing?" I ask instead, casually cutting apart a bunch of level 50+ Prion Swarmers that burst out of the rocky earth. Killing their Mother means there won't be any more of this swarm, but it doesn't stop the current survivors from attacking. They're so low-Leveled, I don't even have to pay attention while I fight.

"Harry's already on his third city. He says there's not much more to see that's different," Mikito says. "Dornalor's been done for two days and is busy building something new on the island, though what it is, he isn't saying."

I grunt, kicking a Prion that stuck itself to my foot. "Fine. I'm coming in."

"*Yes!*" Ali shouts, then releases a huge burst of energy. It shoots outward in an expanding sphere, burning and shocking everything around him as he swoops down. As he falls, he fades from this dimension, making himself semi-corporeal once more. "Finally. I need a drink."

I look at my friend and note he really does look worse for the wear. Spirit or not, he's done well and a portion of the experience I've been getting has been from him. From him and the Hands.

A gesture, and a Portal opens. Thankfully, the settlements have an upgrade that link my Portal to it, allowing me to jump the distance even though I've never been there. One last look around, and I release a series of Beacon of Heavens to kill the last groups of monsters, leaving me low on Mana but with a bunch more experience.

Experience and loot which I'll turn into Credits.

Chapter 14

Going through the Portal and discarding the Hod back to Inventory, I'm assaulted by the pervasive heat. Not in the damage-inducing way—though if I was a normal human, I'd be pretty crispy by now as the heat waves in the air tell me—but in the "just got into an active sauna" way. The smell of sulfur and the devilish glow of red fills the landscape around us, making me squint a little as I stroll forward, closely followed by Ali.

"Who makes a damn city on a lava lake anyway?" I grumble. I've never been fond of saunas, much preferring the wet heat of a steam room. Or even better, a hot tub.

"Heat-based Mana stones are quite popular for certain kinds of enchantments," Ali says. "And with the right kind of defenses, you're actually safer since the variety of monsters you can expect to face are more limited."

"Limited to hot and hotter?" I say, tilting my head upward as a screeching, flaming creature that reminds me of a cross between a bird and a lizard crashes onto the city's shielding. Fire flares all around it, but the attack does absolutely nothing, even as the shield converts the added heat energy to defensive juice.

"Pretty much, boy-o." Ali chuckles. "Anyway, I remember being brought forth in a frozen hellscape of your own."

"The Yukon isn't that bad," I say. Admittedly, there had still been snow on the peaks when the System came about…

"Not back then. Checked the news? Planetary environmental changes have increased. In another decade or two, it'll be winter nine months of the year." Ali gives a theatrical shudder.

"Glad I'm not there then."

I turn the corner, absently eyeing the natives. They're almost all of the same kind—mechanical-humanoid creatures, more cyborg than alien. The range of "faces" they use is highly varied, though many copy the Truinnar and Movana. No surprise, the elves are the cutest by far in most estimations. The occasional figure stomping by with a wide chest, ruddy nose, and flowing metal beard indicates some prefer the more hirsute forms. There are other, non-mechanical lives here, but only a scattering of them.

"Me too," Ali says.

We finally arrive at the hovering Shop orb, having wound through the crowded city from the teleportation platform. Unlike other places, they have the Shop orb set up in the middle of a square, making it easy to get to but also leaving it unprotected. Of course, it's probably just a linked orb, which means no one can take over the settlement using it. Linked Shop orbs are generally expensive to set up but much safer than letting every random person come by to touch your settlement orb.

I stroll into the pebbled courtyard, nodding to the various adventurers approaching and accessing the Shop. Many hold still for a few moments before they move away, done with their shopping. Only a few disappear, taken away. Ringing the square are Artisans, Merchants, and Traders of all sorts, many of them having fascinating names. They call out constantly, but noticing me, they turn their attention over and shout deals and enticements.

"What do you think? Locals or Shop first?" I ask the Spirit.

He hesitates, floating higher to scan for information. A number of flying elemental lizards follow him up, spinning around the Spirit. He breaks out into a series of chirps as he communicates with them. I stare, bemused, but have my attention drawn to a bolder Trader who approaches me directly.

Fahok Modius, Master Trader, A Guaranteed Good Deal, Mana Sink, Credit Giver (Quantum Co-Op Trader Level 18) (M)
HP: 3230/3230
MP: 2810/2810

Conditions: Quantum Mind, Split Attention, Mana to Credits, Focused

High health for a Trader. Fahok's a mechanical life form, all cyborg and pretty in the willowy, long-haired elf way that co-opts the Movana look. It's charming, though a little disturbing, since his face is mostly metal, with only the lower portion of his face and a pair of ears organic. Even his body, clad in transparent cloth, is lithe and chromed.

"Monster Slayer." An open-handed gesture that shows his palms, one I've seen done by many others upon greeting. I copy it, even as I listen. "I am Fahok Modius of the Modius Co-Op Traders. As a newcomer, you might not have heard of us, but we are the largest and most prestigious trading group in this city. Whatever loot items you have to sell, we will purchase them at prices better than the Shop could provide."

"He's right on that, boy-o. The Shop's strained here, so teleportation fees are generally high and taken out of whatever you sell. Those without a high quantity to sell don't even bother blipping out."

I can see that. The Shops that teleport people to their locations do so because they expect a profit, so they'd either lower the prices they'd buy from you and raise the prices selling to you or they wouldn't even bother blipping us at all. Of course, the math required to do all those calculations is pretty complex, but that's what AIs are for.

"Well, I won't say you're lying to me, but I'm not entirely sure I can trust what you say on face value, if you know what I mean," I say, gesturing around to other traders who are creeping closer since I'm not moving. "I'm sure some of them might object."

"To us being the largest?" Fahok smirks. "I doubt any would dare."

My eyes narrow a little, especially when I note a few of the nearby merchants flinch.

A few seconds later, high above me and communicating with the familiars as he is, Ali sighs mentally. *"So, we've got a problem."*

"Of course we do. But he's waiting so, talk fast." I smile at Fahok and raise my hand, palm flat and inviting. "Got a catalogue of what you will buy at and what you've got to sell?"

"Well, we normally review what you have, but we have some basic items. Though they might not fit your esteemed loot." At my come-hither gesture, Fahok sends it over while he blathers about how it's all for lower Leveled creatures, not the Level 200+ loot items I have stored. Obviously, he has no idea I've got my Altered Storage with me, allowing me to keep a heck of a lot more than your average adventurer, but his line of information is still impressive.

He keeps talking while I tune him out, flicking through his list idly while Ali talks. *"Right. Co-op in this case is short form for organized crime. Or an oligopoly? I think that's right. I was never really sure about the difference between your organized crime and your organized capitalism. Seemed to be about the same to me, just one with less direct bloodshed and more lawyers."*

I send over a mental snort, and Ali chuckles. *"Either way, it seems they get first and best pick of anything coming in. You won't find anyone willing to buy your Level 200+ stuff because they 'won't have the funds' suddenly. Not with the Co-Op making a show of wanting what you have."*

"And gear?"

"More widespread. There might be some high-Level Artisans willing to work with you direct, boy-o. Anyone willing to build the stuff we want is a power in their own right. Though, again, not a guarantee. They need materials just as much as the next Artisan."

"Just what we needed." I try to put as much sarcasm as I can into my voice. The last thing we need is to get caught up in some planetary politics, especially since we're likely about to leave.

I consider things further then tap into the chat system. A few moments later, I'm connected to Mikito and explaining what is going on. Once I name the group, she cuts me off.

"*They're here too… I'm dealing with it.*"

"*What do you mean, dealing with it?*" A sliver of worry worms its way into my guts.

"Is there an issue with the prices, Monster Slayer? As I said, the prices we offer for such low-Level items are nowhere near what we'd offer for what you carry," Fahok says.

I tear my concentration away from what Mikito and Harry are chatting about, relating their own experiences with the group, to focus on the guy before me. Ezz, having been relegated to staying with Harry since he can't handle the monsters, interjects with clarification once in a while.

"It's nothing. Here, price these." I mentally pull up the loot information I have and send it over. Then I turn back to my grumbling team, having absorbed what little they've discussed. "*Mikito, you can't just go around killing everyone to get your way.*"

"*I didn't kill them all. Just the real baka. Just because they play at having rules doesn't mean they aren't damaging.*"

"*Yeah, but what happens when you're gone?*"

"*It's taken care of. The merchants should have gotten their Levels by then. Or not.*" There's a dismissive shrug on Mikito's end.

I grit my teeth, knowing that she's probably causing as many problems in the future as she's solving. Then again, a part of me wants to do much the same. I'm not a huge fan of organized crime, but I know that telling off Fahok and selling to someone else would cause just as big a problem. For those I sell to, that is, not so much for me.

I really doubt there's much they can do to me. Then again, we're on a Forbidden Planet with enough of a connection to the System that it still has working Shops. Which means somewhere out there, there's got to be a few Heroic Classes.

"I was right, you do have quite an extensive collection," Fahok says, offering me a tight smile with those organic lips. "I will require a few minutes to price this. If you are willing to wait…?"

I nod, glancing at the other merchants before raising my voice. "I'll either be selling to the Co-Op or the Shop. Whoever prices me better. And I've got this…" I hold up the black card old Foxy showed me, meeting Fahok's eyes flatly. He looks at the card, the one that gets me exclusive access to my version of the Shop, and blanches before nodding in understanding of what I'm implying. "So I'll only be needing to speak with any Artisans with Master Class or better goods."

My words produce a susurration of sound in the group, one that drives the crowd away. I do note a kid dashing off, headed away from the square. I'm mildly curious, while I send to Ali a note to compile an inventory of everything in my Altered Storage. That, unlike the automated loot inventory list, requires actual work.

In the meantime, I grit my teeth and settle in to dealing with these bastards. As much as I'd like to cut them off and join Mikito, I've got to get back out there and Leveling. Which means leaving the existing power structures alone.

I can't solve everything. Hell, I can barely solve our own problems.

***

To my surprise, rather than attacking or trying to cheat me, Fahok plays fair. He gives me a decent price for the materials and the corpses we drop on him. There are a few pieces which he lowballs us on and refuses to adjust, citing local demand. I take his words at fair value, and as I'm getting ready to sell him what he'll take, we're interrupted by a gnome, stomping over and looking less than impressed.

My gaze flicks over the short gnome-creature, the ratchet-like object in his belt, and the way everyone reacts to him. A flicker of Social Web gives me a quick understanding of what's going on, including the animosity between the gnome and the Co-Op representative.

"You the Heroic with the good stuff?" the gnome says, glaring at me.

"Yup." I consider saying something else, but instead just flick over the list of items I've got for sale.

Fahok's lips thin as my fingers move. "I believe we were about to conclude a deal here, Monster Slayer."

"We were. Now, we're not." Fahok opens his mouth to complain, but I ignore him. "Of course, the gentleman here needs to show me he has something worth me trading with him."

Idly, I eye his Status. What I see there is the only reason I'm willing to discuss a deal at all.

Madopnem Spitzrocket, Infamous Artisan, Grandmaster Artisan, Another day, another Masterwork, Platinum Touch, Spanner Thrower Extraordinaire, Master of the Fire, Slayer of Gremlins, Elementals and... (more) (Grandmaster of the Sprockets Level 33) (H)
HP: 1820/1820
MP: 4330/4330

Conditions: Greater Aura of Crafting, Focused Intent, the Flame Ever Burning, Clank-Clank

I suppress a little shudder as the library does a data dump, giving me information on the majority of his conditions and Titles. Not all of them, but enough to tell me that the Heroic Artisan is no way as squishy as he looks.

"Hah! I might have one or two things for the Redeemer." Madopnem points at me. "I hear you're using that cut-rate power armor built by Hod."

"Yes."

"What do you think of it?" Madopnem says, his voice intense.

I hesitate, instinct telling me that whatever I say is important. Then I realize I really don't care. I'd prefer to tell the truth than play politics. "It was adequate when I bought it. Now, I don't even bother with the Skills it offers. They don't really do much, not against the majority of those I fight."

A nod. "And I hear you have others you need to outfit?"

"Mikito—"

"Not the Spear. Your duplicates," Madopnem cuts me off.

"Yes. Though I'd prefer to have Mikito outfitted first," I say. I'd add Harry to that, but Mikito's more important since Harry stays out of the fighting as best he can. A singular focused defensive and stealth piece of equipment is easier to pick up—especially at the Master level, which is what Harry can handle—than a Grandmaster work.

"She's already spoken with my granddaughter. Seems like they have made a deal." Madopnem spits to the side, a dribble of putrid green juice hitting the ground and making it sizzle.

I raise an eyebrow and make note not to accept any chew from the gnome.

While I'm busy adding new rules to my Galactic existence, Madopnem speaks to Fahok. "Seems like the pair of them aren't particularly happy with the way you boys have been dealing in New Quark."

"As I've said before, the Co-Op is a joint venture. We do not control the choices made by our members, just attempt to guide them," Fahok says. "Still, I hope you understand that aggressive actions will face retaliatory measures."

"So long as you keep things civil, so will I," Madopnem says, putting a hand on his ratchet. He glares at Fahok, who stiffens.

"I think you misunderstand—"

"Oh, I ain't misunderstanding nothing—"

I clear my throat, catching their attention. "Enough. I don't care what you guys do, as do the monsters." I incline my head upward, where something large and dumb hammers away at the city's shielding, automated beam cannons burning away its life as it keeps trying to get at the tasty morsels below. "But I do want to get this deal done before you start fighting."

The pair glare at me, but eventually relent. I watch Madopnem gesture to the side, and a notification appears, along with a blueprint diagram of a thing of beauty. Unlike the bulky Sabre or the slimmed down but still bulkyish Hod, the mecha before me reminds me of an Iron Man suit. Not colored red and gold, but blue and silver; it's a sleek piece of beautiful mecha love.

Spitzrocket Powered Armor Version 18.9 (Tier I) (Grandmaster)

The product of Grandmaster Artisan Madopnem Spitzrocket, the Spitzrocket is a handmade, unique build Power Armor created in the Forbidden Zone. Continuing with his belief that less is more, the Spitzrocket is both built to adapt to old battles as well as having minimal additional Skills. Rather, the focus of Artisan Spitzrocket has always been in aiding the user in his battles.

Core: Class I Forbidden Zone (Spitzrocket Adaptation) Mana Engine

CPU: Class A++ Wote Core CPU

Armor Rating: Tier I (Enhanced)

Hard Points: 8 (8 Used—Interstellar Ares Flight System, Integrated Mana Warped Beam Cannon (Spitzrocket Sunwarmer) 2, Ares Type Primal Shield Generator, Spitzrocket Mana to Armor Adaptive Nanoreplicators * 3, Spitzrocket Neural Muscular Enhancers)*

Soft Points 6 (4 Used—Neural Link, Wote HUD Imaging, Airmed Primary Body Monitor, AI integrator)

*Battery Capacity: 718/718**

Active Skills: Overcharge, Spatial Twist, Adaptive Conditioning

Attribute Bonuses: +187 Strength, +244 Agility, +31 Constitution, +82 Perception, +183 Stamina and Health Regeneration per minute

I stare at it for a few seconds before Ali interrupts.

"You might want to stop drooling, boy-o."

"I'm not drooling." I do surreptitiously wipe my mouth though, after I conjure a water bottle to sip on. *"But come on. That's a thing of beauty. And mecha is man's dream."*

"Uh huh."

"These Skills…" I say, frowning as I fail to call up their details.

Madopnem makes a little gesture and the details on the Skills pop up a moment later.

Skill: Overcharge (Artisan Equipment Addition—M)

Increase power output of the Spitzrocket for a short period, increasing all damage and attribute bonuses.

Effects: Increase all attribute and damage bonuses by 200%

Duration: 5 minutes

Cooldown: 2 hours

Skill: Spatial Twist (Spatial Equipment Addition—M)

Rather than breaching dimensions or cutting through space, the Spatial Twist Skill instead bends space, bypassing the majority of Dimensional Locks. It allows the user to cross distance in but a flash of a step or a burst of energy.

Effects: Bends space to allow user to bypass intervening distance (max 219.3km). Must have clear line of sight and movement. Cannot go through occupied space.

Capacity: 3

Recharge Rate: 5 minutes per charge

Skill: Adaptive Conditioning (Artisan Equipment Addition—H)

Don't you hate it when your expensive piece of equipment breaks down? While we don't promise the Spitzrocket will never break, we do promise that the more it does, the better it'll be at not breaking the next time around. Embedded in a secondary dimension, the mainframe of the Spitzrocket is safe from normal everyday destruction. This allows it to replicate the Spitzrocket while adapting to the previous battle and conditions that destroyed it.

Effect: Recreates a full copy of the Spitzrocket with additional, adaptive changes to the equipment. Maximum change is 2.8% of armor, resistances, and attributes per iteration.

Duration: 274.8 hours to recreate a full copy

I can't help but eye the duration and effects. "The duration and effects, normal System ones? How does it work in the Zone?"

Madopnem shrugs. "Depends on where you are and the kind of fluctuation you have. Some cases, you'll be faster and longer, other cases, shorter and faster. Or faster and faster. The Spitzrocket Mana Engine does its best to use both unaspected and aspected Mana so that it balances out, but it's a work in progress." He makes a face. "On the other hand, it'll hold up better than that piece of crap you're using now."

I nod, knowing what he means. The Hod has been out-Leveled for a long time, so much so that I don't even use most of its weaponry or Skills. On the other hand, the Mana-warped beam cannon and the Overload ability both look to be one hell of an ass-kicker. The beam cannon is a Heroic level weapon, able to do nearly as much damage as one of my Skills. I can't help but pull up the information again, marveling at its inclusion. Just the weapon alone would make the power armor worth buying.

Spitzrocket Sunwarmer (Artisan Equipment Addition—H)

Got a moon you need removed from orbit or a sun that is a little on the chilly side? The Sunwarmer is the Spitzrocket answer to this problem, condensing the energy of unaspected Mana into a weapon.

Effects: Fires a concentrated beam of concentrated unaspected Mana that disrupts physical, spiritual and System links

Damage: 18,318 Base

Capacity: 1

Recharge Rate: 14.3 minutes

Between the Adaptive Conditioning option, which I'm sure has more limitations than they say here, and the Sunwarmer, I'm hungering for the mecha. I have to admit, I'm not doing a good job of displaying a poker face, which means I'm going to get taken to the cleaners.

"What do you want for it?" I say to Madopnem.

Fahok grimaces but at least knows better than to get involved.

"Just that."

A notification blinks at me and I read it over. It's all of my high-Level stock and a chunk of the mid-Level stuff. He even takes a couple of the corpses, leaving me with little to buy anything new at the Shop. Still…

"Deal."

Madopnem grins while Fahok stalks off. I let him go, while we make arrangements to trade. I still want to hit the Shop, but this is better than anything I could have asked for. Which makes me consider what will go wrong next.

***

The discordant shriek of teleportation runs through me, my body shuddering as multiple conflicting energies tear through my form. One moment, I had placed my hand on the Shop orb, the next, I was teleporting to it. It should have been nearly instantaneous, but instead, I'm caught in this painful feedback loop, stuck in an eternity of pain.

Multiple Skills and technological processes pull me apart while others put me together at the same time. Through it all, skeins of the System's code can be felt. It's what saves me, as I reach through myself into the System via System Edit to see what is happening.

First is a shock. My access to the exclusive Shop, the one I've always used, is barred. I should have been bounced off, sent to a generic one. However, other Skills come into play. The reroute—an automated one from the System—is being hijacked by multiple forces. Skills like Forced Reroute, Teleport Marker, Come Here!, and more are in play, trying to drag me in disparate directions. There are notes on where the Skills are pulling me, but it's all in numbers and symbols, much like trying to read GPS data. Useless unless you know that information off-hand, which I don't.

Rather, I get a taste of the Skills and who might be the ones in play and the strength of the Skills. A lot of Master Class Skills, some Heroic, and two Legendarys. Those two are the ones tearing me apart, since the Master Class Skills are mostly washed out by the Legendary Skills. Pain tears my attention away for a second, and I groan, blood flooding from mouth and nose.

There's no way to beat the Legendary Skills, not directly, but there's another way. One that is simpler. I hammer on the System code, find the emergency stop button, and trigger that. It shoves me back out of the teleportation limbo I'm stuck in, the System overriding all the other Skills. It's only because it's a fail-safe to keep people alive—as best as it can—that I'm able to beat the Legendary Skills.

As the eternal moment I'm in comes to an end, I feel a flash of frustration, a shift in the code and Skills that attack me. I want to do something, stop it somehow, but the change is too fast. That subjective moment of eternity is ending, and in the space of microseconds that it takes for Skills to activate and my body to be ejected, they strike.

I reappear in the normal world, bleeding and battered. My muscles are torn, my organs ruptured, skin ripped. That's not all though, for the attack that I sensed keeps coming, following the teleportation thread I left open. Energy is unleashed, the majority of it focused on me as I appear, but stray energy ripples outward.

Ali, caught in the midst of this, reacts faster than I do, redirecting and grounding some of that energy, lowering the output as it comes through. It helps a little. What helps more is the fact that it has to cross unknown millions of kilometers through the universe, pushed through the System itself, which is degraded in the Forbidden Zone.

Even then, when the attack strikes, it tears through the remainder of my Penetration Shield like a giant would swat a bubble and throws me backward, burning flesh and muscles. I'm smashed through weakened buildings, making like a 'roided out and angsty Superman through the city before the energy of the blast finally ends.

My health flickers and bounces, a bare few hundred left. Pain racks my body even as the System works to heal me. I'm missing the majority of an arm, both my legs at my knees, and I'm blind and noseless. If I could see, I'd probably find that I look like a burn victim with exposed organs and muscles and crispy bones. My significant pain resistance is insufficient, but I'm in too much pain to even attempt to groan. A flicker of thought is all I can afford, one that takes most of my Will to throw up a Soul Shield.

If not for the degradation of the attack via the Forbidden Zone, if not for the fact that I had my Penetration Shield still up, if not for Ali's actions and my innate Class Resistance to damage… if not for a thousand, million things, I'd be dead.

My hearing comes back with a pop, the silence washed out by the pain. There's a lot of groaning concrete, cracking and melting metal as the structures I've destroyed settle. Screams of pain and surprise resound through the neighborhood. Health regeneration layers muscle and tendons first, bringing back my eyes a minute later.

There's no doubt in my mind I'm outclassed, but this attack, attenuated over the System, is a surprise. I thought I was tough, able to take at least a hit or two. This…

This is a sobering reality. As is the realization that more monsters are coming, and most of them aren't likely to be positively inclined to me anymore. A pull on my Inventory has me putting on the Spitzrocket for the first time. It's not how I want to use it, but the extra protection is likely going to be important. Especially as I sense some of them shouting about making me pay.

Chapter 15

Thankfully, the process of healing and escaping is simplified by the act of flying upward using the power armor and getting an eyeball of the monsters outside. Then I trigger Judgment of All, hammering away at the creatures that surround the city, and reform my Penetration Shield. The few attacks that do try to take me down before it goes up are shrugged off by the Spitzrocket and Soul Shield. Between the armor and the remaining time on the Penetration Shield, I'm much more tanky. The few monsters who wanted revenge start reconsidering, fast.

That doesn't mean I get back my legs or my arm though. It just means that my health points and my body are healed. My limbs will return in time, but meanwhile, I'm forced to hover around. I briefly debate explaining what happened, but staring at the destruction of the square from high above and the long, long line of destroyed buildings where I was punched through, I decide that retreat is the better part of valor and make a run for it.

Since resting isn't going to do much and I've got to get more experience, I spend the next couple of days fighting and putting the Spitzrocket through its paces outside of the city. A few Master Class teams try to make me pay, but most back off when I give them a good thumping. The fact that the Spatial Warp lets me catch them even when they're trying to hide and wait for an opportune time dissuades further aggression.

I go deeper than ever into the planet, hunting down higher-Level monsters. What was a challenging fight becomes simple now, the over-powered power armor making up for my lack of legs and arm. I tear through monsters with ease, using Skills and the Sunwarmer in the Spitzrocket with gusto.

I do, briefly, port over to visit a Shop incognito. The rings we were given are still effective, so floating over in the middle of the night helps me visit the Shop and pick up a resupply of all the things I need. I don't risk teleporting anymore but just access the main System Shop interface, letting it teleport the goods directly to me. Extra sets of clothing, more basic underarmor, chaos grenades and mines, healing and stamina potions galore, various transportable shields and, of course, a ton of chocolate.

Literally.

I buy a ton of chocolate so that I don't run out.

The purchasing of goods is more expensive this way and my cut of the various body parts and loot lower, but needs must.

More importantly, I'm annoyed that I don't have a Shop of my own anymore. I'm a little—okay, a lot—hurt by having my black card rescinded. You'd think after all this time, there'd be some loyalty. But that's corporations for you. No more loyalty than a housecat stuck in a flat with the corpse of its former owner.

In the end, I keep my transactions simple. The rest of the time, I keep to the skies and the wastelands, doing battle and taking down monsters as much as possible. In the corner of my eyes, I watch as the numbers for the Quest tick up.

It's harder than I expected. Moving functionality up by even a few percent takes my Extra Hands days of constant battling, slowed only by their nerfed Mana Regeneration rates as doppelgangers. Things pick up again when Mikito helps out, having finished her little side quest, and we inch toward that 25% number.

We cross that threshold when Ali manages to convince the Systemers high above to launch an orbital bombardment. The damage they do is, of course, reduced due to the System's own rules, but the degradation of the System actually helps here. They do more damage than usual, allowing us to cross the final threshold.

And when we do, I am waiting.

I step through the door of the abandoned, half-buried Administrative Center and enter the heart of the System in a Forbidden Planet for the first time. Hoping…

Well, I'm not sure. But hoping anyway.

***

I swear, they make all System Admin Centers from the same mold. One large room with a mezzanine level and a single staircase up. Everything in silver-grey like the System made building defaults, and massive system notification screens visible to everyone. On the screens, all the details a System Admin could want are displayed along with the current list of high priority tickets. One screen flickers and updates to tickets I can handle, making things simpler.

I do note a few things different. For one, the System feels sluggish in here, compared to my previous visit. On the other hand, the time compression is significantly higher than in other Centers. I wonder if it's a case of the System throwing everything it can into the only Administrative Center with an Administrator within it. Because it's quite obvious that I am the only Administrator on the planet.

Welcome to Administrative Center 3829-7-283; Junior Administrator Lee

As the only Administrator in-sector at this time, your Security Clearance has been raised by two thresholds for all tickets (current security access Level 6).

Experience gain for ticket fixes have been increased by 3x

Work hard to restore System Functionality!

"Ali, was that last line yours?"

Silence greets my question only for me to remember that he can't come in here. Which means whatever I'm seeing is unvarnished System notifications. Which makes the last line all the stranger. The System is often cold, impersonal, and only occasionally sarcastic. The vast majority of that kind of notifications is Ali doing his thing, though I understand most of that is automated too these days.

But… this. This is just weird.

I poke at the notification, but the backend doesn't give me any further information. It's a puzzle, but not one I can spend too much time pondering. Not when the cascade of tickets stands before me.

Alert! Mana Overflow in Dungeon 213.9-312.5

Alert! Mana Overflow in Dungeon 182.9-952.1

Alert! Mana Overflow in Dungeon 82.1-195.35

Alert!…

A little bit of focus and the Dungeon overflow alerts are compiled and dumped to the side. I compile the tickets into a single one, then apply a single fix, which is basically to allow them to do what they're already doing—overproducing their monsters. However, I find a tweak to help matters by adding a higher percentage loot drop, giving those who find the Dungeons a reason to go after them.

I tense at the flood of experience that hits me from resolving all those tickets, a small smile crossing my face. I also get a few painful pings when my solution gets rejected by the System for certain locations. A quick glance at the experience log indicates that the individual ticket experience points are low since I'm not providing the best solution, just a solution. Yet quantity has a quality of its own and the experience, tripled as it is, floods in.

A part of me is still surprised that such a small resolution is allowed, that this kind of cheat is possible. I don't understand why more Administrators don't do this to get the boost in experience. Perhaps there's a limit to the kind of resolutions you can achieve like this.

In either case, it's just another question to a problem I've been working on forever. There's nothing to do but shelve it and get to work, so I do.

Next up are the various notifications about settlement spheres, destruction of settlements and the like. There aren't as many as I'd expect and a quick perusal of the logs shows that it's because the settlements have been ground down over the years, with the issues resolved by Administrators before me. So long as the planet was viable—which meant active settlements—things were resolved. Now, there are just a few left.

Fair enough.

The tickets just need verification, with many wanting me to replace the settlements in a new location—which, of course, errors out since there are no useable locations. The settlements themselves are necessary to help smooth out the flow of energy, as are the various forts I should generate. However, there are no locations that won't be overrun and deleted after a while, so I can only put the majority of tickets aside.

Still, there's no reason I can't do a little. I flick across the map to the still-standing cities, highlighting any place where a fort might make sense. I generate the necessary codes and place them as densely as possible, then I write another notification to residents about the creation of new forts for their use.

Afterward, I write a simple program that will replace such forts if they are lost and to upgrade such forts into full settlements if, for some reason, the cities manage to take and hold those locations long enough. That requires the creation of a few new Quests too, much of the information and notifications cribbed from other work. Four hours and a quick verification of the code and I send it to the System. I get the feel of mild disapproval as it accepts my work, highlighting a snarl of code that the System had to fix. Still, it does flood me with experience again, nearly as much as my "fix" for the Dungeons since this requires actual work and has actual long-term effects.

Time passes as I tackle ticket after ticket. Environmental overflows, lair spawning, Mana flow clashes, mutation balancing, new monster spawning. There's even an option to cheat by bringing in new monsters that can be used to balance out the Mana flows by adding them to sections where the natural evolutions have not been sufficient.

I make use of it all, though I wonder if I'm doing as much—if not more—damage in the future at the speed with which I adjust things. Adding new creatures to an existing biosphere always causes unforeseen problems down the line. I console myself with the fact that with the sheer volume of mutations in the current monsters, no one can predict the final results.

All the while I work, I keep an eye on the higher-level tickets. The ones I'm normally not allowed to gain access to, the ones I'm locked out of. I read them over, though the vast majority deal with things I have absolutely no desire to touch. There are a few that make sense for me to tackle though, some of them petitions from the settlement owners themselves.

System Alteration Request: Decrease in age of majority

Settlement Owner Serzhen has requested that the age of majority be lowered from 14.7 local solar cycles to 12 local solar cycles.

System Alteration Request: Override Maximum Shielding Options

Settlement Owner Demas has requested that the current limits on Settlement Shielding tiers be released.

More like that. So much more. Small or big requests that would make life easier for the various settlement owners. I hesitate, wondering if these approvals will be traced back to me. Then I realize, of course they will. And that really, it doesn't matter. I'm not trying to hide my Class, not anymore. And these requests, the majority of them—other than the expansion on Serf Classes—will save lives. I approve the non-morally-destructive ones, skimming over the information and getting a better understanding of what higher Level Administrators do.

Until I come across one of the oldest tickets and pause.

System Alert! Planet has Achieved Tier III rating as a Forbidden Planet

Release of Forbidden Planet Restricted Classes available.

Authorization required.

What the ever-living thousand hells is that? My jaw drops a little and I find myself digging, curious what these restricted Classes might be. How much better they must be, for them to be restricted at all. I'm wondering if I was cheated, if perhaps I could have gotten something better. Or more importantly, if the Administrators I'll face will be even more powerful and wielding such Classes.

I'm relieved to find out it's a little of column A and a little of column B. The Classes are more powerful—more Attributes, more powerful Skills—but they're also more limited. Between a third to two-thirds of all their attributes are dedicated to Intelligence and Willpower, forcing the individuals to become ever better Mana cleansers for the System.

As for the Skills? They're powerful, but the entire Class and Skills are heavily dependent upon ambient Mana levels. More powerful in the Forbidden Zone with increasing amount of damage or defense per Skill point, but also dependent on the Mana around to layer the damage. For example, the Skill Mana Storm uses environmental Mana to attack any creatures within. Great AOE, but in a Safe Zone, it would just create a very nice breeze.

There's also a bigger disadvantage. The experience requirements are significantly higher. Like starting at Advanced Class Levels and going up from there for even the Basic Classes. Of course, in a Forbidden Zone, you'd be fighting higher Level creatures all the time anyway, so it makes that less of an issue.

Unless you leave.

No free lunch with the System, it seems. I hesitate for a second before approving the Classes. Perhaps it will help the planet survive. Perhaps it will create a new tier of rulers, a bunch of idiot children strutting around thinking they're better than anyone else who has managed to survive so far. Perhaps I'm damning a whole population to life on this planet.

I don't know, and this uncertainty might have been the reason no other Administrator has ever approved the Classes. Cowardice through inaction, unwilling to bear the burden of decision-making. I make the decision then turn to the next problem. That's all I can do, really. The past is a failure, so I can only try something new for a better future. You can only do the best you can and keep moving forward. Till one day, perhaps I'll be at the end of my journey and have an answer to my question.

***

"*Oy! Time to go, boy-o,*" Ali pretty much shouts in my mind, pulling me up out of the flow state I'm in.

The strain on our connection is quite real, what with me having to patch our connection through the console itself. Getting woken up is jarring, as it dumps me back into reality in front of the administrator console I've been standing before for… days. I've been standing here for objective—that is, outside Administrative Center—days.

Thousand hells. Being in the flow, the lack of daylight, and my body's stupidly high Constitution means all the usual markers for stopping just disappeared. It's not the first time it's happened, but I have to be more careful.

I glance at the latest ticket I'm working on, figure it's close enough, and send it off before walking away, not even looking at the ticketing board anymore. There are still hundreds of glowing red tickets, urgent problems that need solving that the System desperately wants a physical handler to review. Hundreds of problems that are being sorted out by the overuse of System Mana. And I abandon them because I have to.

"*Problem?*" I ask, dreading the answer.

"*Define problem.*"

"*Oh god, oh god, we're all going to die?*"

"Close enough. Mikito's done her thing and is still busy grinding, but Harry's ported back up to talk with Dornalor. The Heartbreak is fully retrofitted and fixed, so the pirate wants a word."

Down the stairs and before the exit, I take a few seconds to review my experience gains. I pull up the latest Level notifications and smirk a little, knowing my Hands have been busy. Which is good, because I really don't want to waste my points on System Edit.

Level Up! You are now a Level 23 Erethran Grand Paladin

Level Up! You are now a Level 18 Middle System Administrator

Middle? I frown, tearing through my notifications. Ali's buzzing at me, but I ignore him, because this is important. Very important.

I find it in an innocuous minor notification I'd discarded in the last few days. Har! Days. I've spent literal weeks in the damn System Administrative center.

Junior System Administrator Class Evolution Opportunity Detected.

Security Clearance Verified.

Request for Class Evolution sent to Senior System Administrators

!Error! ~ Root Administrator Override ~ !Error!

Request for Class Evolution sent to Root Administrator

Class Evolution Approved

Junior System Administrator has evolved to Middle System Administrator for the Redeemer of the Dead

New Class Skill Available

Class Skill Allocated!

Class Skill? My eyes widen further, and I go looking for more details in my System logs. There's nothing there though, so I end up pulling up my Status Screen to find it. And it's there, sitting quietly under Class Skills.

Class Skill: Ticket Board (Level 1)

Middle System Administrators are tasked with not just solving issues at Administrative Centers like Junior System Administrators but with finding solutions in the farthest reaches of the System.

Effect: Form a System Ticketing Board and resolve tickets wherever you might be

"The doors of the thousand hells have opened and the hungry ghosts approach." I curse out loud.

Ali sends me the equivalent of mental static. *"Goblin shit, John! What in the slime vomit hells is going on?"*

I… I can only give a single answer. *"The Root Administrator got involved. Again."*

Shuddering, I push aside the thoughts and step through the portal, reentering reality while I push the last few notifications at my Spirit. There's a little resistance. Not much, but a little, which I shove aside with ease.

The world comes back to reality even as I try not to consider—at least at this moment—what the changes mean. How the "rules" of our System seem to keep changing, at least if you're an Administrator. Why I kept my Level but received an upgrade to my Class and a new Skill. Why the Root Administrator is watching me so closely. And what, in the end, he or her or it is.

I don't think about it because I don't like the answers I have, and for now, as monsters converge, I don't have to.

***

Chance. Planning. A thumb on the scale by someone, somewhere high above. I'm not sure where or how or why, but we all end up on the floating island high above, meeting with Dornalor in the wide hangar to familiarize ourselves with the updated *Heartbreak,* when the end to our peaceful intermission comes.

Sirens blare, the Systemers around us jerking in surprise for a long, frozen second. Then they burst into action, drilled responses driving them to their stations. Ships are readied, pilots blipping in without care, a couple appearing right on top of one another and causing a spray of blood and guts as they fall apart. No one even looks at them except for a Healer who scrambles over, casting as he hurries.

Ali searches, then yanks the data for me before I can make a move. Society's Web is thrumming, showing me the shifting emotions, the sudden shattering of threads as individuals reprioritize their lives, their beliefs, their loyalties. A crisis has come, and in that moment, clarity arrives for many. All too late at times.

> **Alert! Alert! Alert!**
> *This is a Priority One Alert!*
> *This is not a drill.*
> *Imminent Invasion and Destruction of the Cathedral of the Legendary. All personnel to report to combat stations. Final Stand Protocols have been enacted.*
> **This is not a drill.**
> *May the System be with you.*

"Boy-o…." Ali says while Dornalor, having received the same notification, is already running for the *Heartbreak*.

Harry follows Dornalor while Mikito and Ezz stare at me, waiting for further information. We find it, seconds later, in the solar system map we hijack.

A fleet. A full Forbidden Zone Patrol Fleet has appeared in the system. They're spreading out, layering spatial anchors and dimensional locks everywhere as they move to cut us off. The Sanctuary is already breaking away, leaving the planet without even trying to pick up those left behind. There are a few—very few—ships scrambling from the surface, but for the most part, those on the planet are abandoned.

I can't help but think those left behind are the lucky ones.

"What do we do?" Mikito asks.

You don't need to be a space admiral to see that we'll be cut off long before we can break free. Even if the space anchors they're layering have a maximum distance, the island is too slow to get away. On the other hand, the *Nothing's Heartbreak* might be able to escape, especially if we engage the full Skills and equipment the *Heartbreak* contains.

If someone provides a distraction.

"I…" I gulp, feeling the weight of what I'm about to ask.

This is not a warship. This is not a few people, or a fan club dedicated to a cause, or a bunch of fanatics searching for the answer to a question. There are millions of innocents here, millions of deluded idiots who have nothing to do with my Quest. And I'm going to ask them to risk their lives, to sacrifice themselves and their loved ones for us. And yes, it's strange to quail after I've sacrificed so many others, but emotions are not logical by definition.

Before I can speak, before my resolve strengthens, the air beside us blurs. The Archbishop appears, looking a little peaked, his eyes gleaming with the same fanaticism he displayed before. His smile is wide, manic as he clasps his hands and looks to the ceiling.

"Thank the System you are all here." He's vibrating with excitement. "I knew it would not abandon its prophet. Flee to your ship! The Sanctuary Captain will provide you the navigation plot and hook you in. When we scramble our fighters, you will join them in departing the Cathedral and, in their midst, scatter through the System."

"You need your fighters for the fight," I say, lips compressing.

"We cannot win this battle." Turad shakes his head. "No. Our task is to ensure the survival of the first independent Junior System Administrator. To ensure you finish your Quest, to break the hold on the System of those who are not worthy. To preach your truth, Prophet."

"Your people—"

"Will gladly march to their demise for the cause!" The Archbishop throws up a hand and calls, "The System is All."

"The System is All!" The call is repeated by all those within, echoing through the hangar.

It sends shivers down my spine, even as Turad smiles in beatific joy.

Ezz buzzes beside me, and I look down at it for a second.

A flash of emotion, and I turn to the Archbishop. "You have children on board, gods damn it!"

"And the System will care for them."

"It's a program! A piece of software. There's no way it can care for them," I say, almost shouting into his face.

224

Ezz stares at me, then to my surprise, it turns and stalks up the raised gangplank to the *Heartbreak*. A part of me wants to say something, but I don't have time to worry about its feelings. If it has them.

Instead of replying, Turad shakes his head at me, the movement filled with sadness. As if I'm the insane, foolish one who will not accept an obvious truth. "You must leave, Redeemer of the Dead. You must survive, Breaker of the Galaxy. Go forth and spread your truth, Prophet."

"No!" I plant my feet, glaring at him. "Not until you do something about the children. I won't let you send them to their deaths."

Turad stares then turns to Mikito, dark eyes gleaming with repressed rage at being defied. "Do your job, Samurai. Save your lord."

Mikito's lips thin as she swings Hitoshi around, the weapon pointing at Turad's face. There's a little bit of a commotion at her actions, only stopped by Turad raising his hand.

"My job, as you call it, is to safeguard my lord's life and honor. Though perhaps you misunderstand the second part, for you lack it."

Turad hisses before clapping his hands. "We do not have time for this. Your stay on the Cathedral of the Legendary is **revoked**."

His words catch the both of us by surprise, then a powerful force picks us up and throws us backward. The hangar bay doors, already open and covered only by a force shield, do nothing to stop our bodies from being ejected into the void. Within seconds, we're floating in outer space. Nothing Mikito, Ali, or I could do could have stopped that force from ejecting us.

Moments later, the *Nothing's Heartbreak* leaves under its own power. I watch as other fighters scramble from the floating island, giving Dornalor cover as he turns to pick us up. The entire floating island is busy leaving us behind, moving at a decent clip such that even attempts to reenter are barred. It carries millions of lives and a guilt I'm not sure I'll ever be able to escape.

Then the *Heartbreak* is before me, blocking my view. Mikito, ever practical, drags me into the open boarding hatch. Within seconds, we're in, hidden among the hundreds of fighters, just another ship as far as our enemies are concerned.

Chapter 16

"You didn't try to object to them!" I rage at Dornalor as I step into the cockpit and sit in my chair. I look over to the side where Harry sits, then I recall that my Hands have also been left behind. There's no way for me to contact them, not now that we're radio silent. I can only hope they know what to do. I'll admit, I'm at a loss as to what that might be.

"Protest what? They want to kill themselves for us, good for us, I say," Dornalor replies, meeting my angry gaze without fear. His lips curl up as he sneers at me, hands never stopping as he controls the ship to follow the navigation plot provided to us.

"There are children on that island!" I snarl.

"And I'm not the one sending them to their deaths. That's on them. I'm just making use of their offer," Dornalor says.

"We could try to stop him!" I say.

"Give it up, you giant hypocrite." Harry's voice comes from behind, making me spin around. I open my mouth to protest being called a hypocrite, but Harry's voice is filled with scorn and derision as he continues. "Unless you're walking out the escape hatch right now and giving yourself up, you're a hypocrite. If you cared *sooo much* about their lives, you could save theirs and so many others by just giving up. It's you they want, after all."

I find myself at loss for words as he's not wrong. If I truly cared for the children, I would give up now. How much death and destruction have I caused already? Who else will fall because I can't give up?

"There's… no guarantee they'll not punish them…" I say weakly.

"Better chance than what there is now, no?" Harry sniffs. "You're a fucking hypocrite, and you know it. A coward who cares more about his damnable Quest than anything or anyone else. Damn the Earth. Damn your friends. Damn the galaxy! So don't you dare accuse us of being cowards or caring for our own lives, not when you do it yourself. We didn't bollocks this up in the first place."

Rage flares in me along with shame, which just cranks my anger up further. My hand trembles, wanting to lash out, to hit him and those dark eyes that stare at me accusingly. He's right. I created the problem, I chose the actions and now, now... I'll live with the consequences.

That thought cools my temper a little, but I can't stand to look at him. Or perhaps it's the reflection of myself in his eyes. In either case, I take my seat and turn toward the notifications the *Heartbreak* provides.

The cabin falls silent, broken by the rustle of clothed movement as Dornalor works the consoles and the almost-audible noise of Skills being used. The cockpit is leaden with the joint guilt that presses upon our souls, the knowledge that we are but a group of damned cowards even as we flee.

Or maybe that's just me.

***

Fission engines burn as we hit the edge of one of the many moons around the planet and use its gravitic pull to slingshot us away. The minor boost in speed is, well, minor, but Dornalor is using every trick in the book, including sending us through what looks like the remnant waste field of a previous battle. Once we near it, he cuts our engines and uses non-energetic propulsion to change our course a little, putting the ship into a spin that mimics some of the debris. We're moving faster than the debris, but nowhere near as fast as the other ships escaping which is...

Well, a choice. I'm not sure which is better, but I trust Dornalor. He triggers Skill after Skill, everything from reducing our footprint in both the System and the physical world to "look away" Skills that mentally influence those to avoid paying attention to the *Nothing's Heartbreak*. On top of that, I feel the numerous enchantments inscribed on the *Heartbreak*, boosted by the new tech given by the Systemers, at work.

We are, at least for now, nothing more than a floating rock fast heading to outer space. All around us, much brighter ships are fleeing, many of them triggering active versions of our Skills, creating shadow copies of themselves and doppelgangers of their craft. Some, I know, even have the ability to shuffle themselves among the created copies, making it even harder to keep track of where they all are.

In the meantime, the floating island is headed straight for the fleet with a sizeable portion of the non-solar-system-worthy fighting craft flanking it. An occasional attack is released, powerful, focused beams of energy that fire from the tip of the Cathedral to tear apart shields and burn through hulls of the smaller ships. For the most part though, the battle is held in abeyance till the range is closed. Only the most powerful weapons, those that take the longest to recharge, can reach out and put their malfeasant touch on their enemies.

"I hate this," I send to Ali, guilt and helplessness rolling through my guts as we watch. There are so many in there, children and Artisans in the floating cityscape. And I'm doing nothing to help them. The fact that the idea of them is mostly academic, that they are just figures I've seen in passing rather than people I know helps. A little.

"Yeah, I get it, boy-o."

His words make me feel even guiltier. When did people, other sapients, become nothing more than constructs in my mind? Things I'm supposed to care about, but only in the abstract, rather than as living, breathing creatures? I mean, to some extent, they've always been like that, but this seems more marked.

After all, I can still see the faces of the children we rescued on Earth, the suffering and pain of those in the refugee camp in Whitehorse soon after the System advent. The corpses of those we dragged out of the Yukon River after they chose to end it all. I even remember those in Irvina, the few low-Level fighters we dragged through dungeons to forcibly level them. The anger that caused…

But somewhere along the way, people stopped mattering. And the quest just became what I needed to finish. Now, I'm sitting here watching hundreds of thousands, millions even, going to their deaths.

My fingers ache, my fists are clenched so tight that my nails dig into my palms. I force myself to relax my jaw before I crack a tooth, but I can't help but keep staring at the small blinking dots. Stare and hate myself.

I close my eyes, weighing my options. My obsession and the lives of the others. And I admit, it's all too close.

When I stand, Dornalor and Harry look at me, frowning. I give them a tight smile, but I don't answer their questions as I head for the cargo bay. I'm halfway down when Harry grabs my arm, dragged a few steps before I stop.

"What are you doing?" Harry snarls.

"Doing what I should have…" I crack my neck, giving him a tight smile. "Doing what I do best."

"Cause trouble? Play the hero and expect others to pick up after you?" Harry says. "You going out there won't change a damn thing."

"It'll pull their forces to me. You guys can keep running. There's still time for you to get far enough away to escape." I tug my hand gently, detaching it from Harry's arm.

"And what? Everything you've done is for nothing?"

"No. But I can't… there has to be a line, Harry. Somewhere."

"So Earth wasn't the line, but some random aliens are?" He growls, shoving me in the chest. "Your friends aren't worth saving, but people you don't know will be?"

"It's not like that and you know it. I don't have time to discuss this…"

"And you don't have to do it either, boy-o." Ali floats down from the ceiling, waving.

I frown a little, then shake my head. The data stream he sends me is confusing, not something I can understand, not distracted as I am. "Explain."

"Turad must have known something like this would happen." Ali gestures, and a graph flickers up.

This one I can read much easier, since I was staring at similar ones earlier. They're Mana intake and conversion charts. The ones I was reading had been for the solar system for the most part, but this is specifically for the Cathedral.

"It's dropping. Significantly," I say.

"Yes. Check the planetary one…" Ali says.

"He's been moving people," I say as I notice the gradual increase in the graph. It's the only explanation I can find. I'm surprised I never noticed it on the planet, but the increase is so gradual, and I'd been making so many changes on my end, it never occurred to me to review it after my first glimpse. "The children?"

"Yes. And probably the Artisans and any non-combat personnel."

Harry looks between Ali and me before he asks the obvious question. "Why would they do that?" Then a second later, he answers his own question. "Unless they always meant to sacrifice the Cathedral."

"Most likely. If not now, when we reached Xylargh," Ali says. "There's still a blockade around the planet after all."

I can't help but make a face. I have no idea how we're expected to make it past that blockade or what we can expect when we finally arrive. A planet full of dragons is a nightmare to me, considering they have to eat something. Which means everything else is incredibly high-Leveled. Never mind the significant presence the Galactic Council keeps there just to help keep the planet connected to the System and the dragons somewhat under control. Of course, the Dragon Lords and Dragon Knights play a big part, but even they wouldn't be sufficient without external help.

Thankfully, that's a problem for another time. For now, I bring my attention back to the lingering guilt. I have to admit, a lot of the impetus for me to go out and do the stupid thing is gone now that I know the non-combatants are away. The rest...

Well, the rest I don't care about that much. There's still a bit of lingering guilt, but most of those going to fight chose a life of fanaticism and combat. I'm a little surprised at the speed with which I find myself making compromises in my own morality, but then again, it had been a real struggle to make the initial decision—which says something about my ethics as it stands.

"So you going to stay then? Your conscience appeased?" Harry snarks at me.

"Almost." I point at the Reporter. "I screwed up by letting you get captured. I screwed up even further by dragging you along to help me vote against Earth. But you knew what you needed to do. You could have objected, and while there were extenuating circumstances"—like being tortured and mentally vulnerable—"you still did it."

Harry has grown pale—as much as someone with his darker complexion can—and his lips tremble. I even see tears forming in his eyes before I drop my voice and make it softer.

"But if you want to hate me for what I did to Earth, for my choices, sure." My words surprise Harry and even Ali. "I'm willing to let tens of thousands die for me. I've set off a war that, as much as I try to avoid thinking about it, involves millions and will kill even more." I draw a breath. "So if you need to hate me, fine. I deserve it."

"I don't... hate you," Harry says, working his mouth as if he is trying to force out the words. "I think I hate myself. For agreeing with you."

I blink, not expecting that. We stand in silence for a bit before I shake my head and focus. I had something to say, and I should finish it. "Either way. I can take it. But... everything we're doing, everything we've done, that's just a prelude. Things are going to get even more dangerous and the choices I'll make..."

I sigh. "The sacrifices I'll make, they'll grow even higher. And yeah, even my own resolve will waver. But I am going to see this through somehow. So if you can't accept that, it's time for you to leave."

"Now?"

"Yes, now. Jump into a suit, drift for a bit. They'll probably leave once they're done with us, and that planet is the closest thing to a Safe Zone in this insanity. Given time, you might even be able to teleport out. Or hitch a ride with the Systemers."

"And if I don't choose to go?" Harry says.

"Then you're in for the ride. No matter where it ends."

Harry slowly nods. I wait to see if he has anything to say before I step past him and head back toward the cockpit.

The War Reporter just stands there, staring into space before he calls out, just as I'm reaching the blast doors that slide open silently, "You know, I'm too close."

"What?"

"I'm too close to the story now. I can't judge it impersonally. Can't report on it without coloring what I see, what I say." I turn around and see the conflict on his face. "I can't follow you and do my job, not anymore."

I consider his words for a second, then I find myself smiling. "Then just come along as a friend." I glance at Ali hovering beside me, then at the blast doors before us, to where Mikito lies in the engine room. "And fellow idiot."

That pulls a laugh from him, the first in a long while that isn't filled with bitterness or anger. I grin, waving goodbye as I head back to the cockpit. Grateful I've lightened Harry's burden. Thankful he's still coming. Even if, in the corner of my mind, I add to the tally of those I've sacrificed.

***

Sparkles in the screen, little dots drifting off into infinity. That's what the end of the Cathedral, that shining island of civilization, comes to. We're too far away, running on too many passives, to watch the fight in real-time and with any fidelity. On the other hand, so much energy is being thrown around that it's a simple matter to follow the battle even on passives. Simple enough to see the end.

Between the fleet's need to track and destroy all the fleeing bait and the sheer difficulty of taking on the Cathedral, the entire fleet is looking worse for the wear when the battle is over. They had split off a good quarter of their navy by the time the two clashed, and a good third of the remaining ships have been destroyed. Another third is badly damaged, limping along and held together by baling wire, Galactic duct tape, and Skills. The last third are doing fine and are functional. It's those that shepherd the previous third toward the planet. Only a few ships break away, intent on hunting down the few ships that managed to hide or beat their pursuers.

Leaving us to continue drifting, unseen and unknown. Or so we believe. Hard to tell until the Galactic Fleet arrives, though I flick up Society's Web on the off chance it helps. At these ranges, it makes little difference, but staring at the threads reaching out from my body, I wince.

So many. So twisted and dark, some literally bleeding with rage and the need to destroy. All those I owe something to. The fact that I've already filtered out those with the most minimal connection and I still look like a hedgehog on a bad day is a testament to how much I've done. The souls I've changed, the fates I've thrown off course.

I peel back the layers, slowly fading them out, and watch the threads and the notifications in silence. We all do, since there's nothing else we can do for now. Nothing but watch and wait as time drips onward, like year-old liquid honey escaping a jar, stubbornly refusing to move even as gravity forces its hand.

Drip.

…

Drip.

…

Drip.

…

In time, Dornalor stands the others down. Harry and Mikito sleep. Ali goes back to watching his show. Ezz doesn't care, not needing rest, but after I bark at it the fifth time to leave me alone, it shuffles off to do routine maintenance on the *Heartbreak*. Even the Pirate Captain leaves the cockpit as I stare obsessively at the plot.

Waiting.

Eventually, my patience is rewarded in the only way that I receive rewards these days. A ship that was not there initially appears on our sensors, triggering the alarm all through the ship. I can sense Dornalor dashing back, but even as I attempt to guide our ship out of a collision course without giving away the game, the other ship adjusts its course just as smoothly.

Tens of thousands of kilometers shrink with every second, and we go from "space close" to real, planetary level close in seconds. My fingers itch to fire upon them, but I hold off since they aren't firing. There's a little bit of hope they aren't an enemy. A hope that holds out just long enough for the communicator to blare to life.

"Fascinating. We almost missed you, Redeemer." Female, smiling, and alien. She's blue, with a copper plate down one side of her face and gills on her neck. Cute in the alien mermaid way, with the flowing seafoam hair and voluptuous body. No data flows from her across the communication channel, and a query to Ali shows he's being blocked.

"Well, I'd prefer if it wasn't an almost," I say. "What do you want?"

"Want?" Her eyes twinkle, and I realize that's a literal thing because she has a second, mostly clear eyelid that keeps her eyes protected. "What does everyone want with you, Redeemer?"

"Right now, my head." I know I'm tempting her, but that's the point.

She points a long, clawed finger at me. "Redeemer of the Dead, Junior Administrator Lee. With the power vested in me—Senior System Administrator Sephra—as your senior, I am rescinding your Class as per the Rogue Administrator's commands."

I tense and realize that a series of notifications are appearing. I pull them up, rather than let them collect in the corner of my vision.

Security Protocol 18.9.522 enacted.

Confirming Authorization.

Authorization by Senior Administrator Wex, Senior Administrator Sephra'mannas'lova, Senior Administrator Raccoon, Senior Administrator Reradar, Senior Administrator Eussamma, …

Authorization granted.

Security Protocol 18.9.522 commencing. Removal of Hidden Class System Administrator (Junior) begun.

~!Error!~

Class System Administrator (Middle) located.

Security Protocol 18.9.522.1 enacted. Removal of Hidden Class System Administrator (Middle) begun.

~!System Override!~

Security Protocol 18.9.522.1 has been redirected to Root Administrator Approval.

There are a few long moments when nothing happens. I stare into the distance, not breathing as I wait. The merlady looks confident at first, but the longer I'm not throwing a tantrum or writhing in pain or whatever happens when you get a Class yanked out of you, the less certain she looks. Before Sephra is ready to speak, the notifications update once more.

Root Administrator reached.

Security Protocol 18.9.522.1 has been revoked.

Additional additions to Security Protocol 18.9.522 have been enacted.

Then, nothing.

I lean forward, a smile pulling my lips into a savage grin. "Is that it?"

Sephra jerks, looking surprised. I see her pupils defocus to look at System Notifications, but I don't let her get to it.

"Oh, one more thing. My turn."

Judgment of All turns on. Using the Skill against one person is a little bit of an overkill, but the Skill does say "anything in sight" and she was kind enough to show me her face. The energy from the Skill floods through the System connection, hammering at her. Before I can see if it kills her, she cuts the connection between the ships.

Dornalor hasn't been taking a break while we were chatting, instead putting our ship into full burn in an attempt to escape our pursuer. The Galactic Destroyer is following even as the *Heartbreak* burns fuel like a child given paper money at a funeral.

"Faster, Dornalor, faster…" Harry chants.

"Can't. Why don't you do something?" the Pirate Captain snarls at Harry, who jerks a little in surprise, realization hitting him belatedly that he isn't entirely useless.

Next second, the full firepower of the ship opens up on our tail. Shields glow on the opposing ship, our attacks insufficient to penetrate. However, surprisingly, there's no return fire.

"Shields at 64% and dropping," Ali says, reading the sensor data. "Looks like it's made for speed and defense. Firepower might not be anything major…"

I grunt, considering if I can use any of my Skills. The tricky part of space warfare at the speeds we're moving is targeting. Skills like Beacon of the Heavens or Grand Cross are targeted via thought and mental adjustment of the attack vector. You have to take into account potential movement when using Skills like that, with the System providing minor corrections as necessary. Not a big thing when you're fighting on a planet, or even when you're moving at Heroic Level Agility and Haste.

However, when you're moving at percentages of lightspeed and are still accelerating, those kinds of numbers and minor errors become major issues. Even with the Intelligence I have backing up the calculations, there's still too much left to chance to randomly lob out Skills that might miss.

Which is why something like Judgment of All, with its System-enabled targeting, is so powerful. You can't dodge an attack like that, not with it going through the System. Then again, it's also more degraded when you're in the Forbidden Zone which….

Well, it's all a long way to say there's not a lot I can do. I clutch my hands, watching Harry control the weapons, and try not to jog his elbow by taking over. If there is a problem, like other ships lurking nearby, I want to be ready to deal with them.

I keep watch as Dornalor pours Mana and Skills through the *Heartbreak*, while Mikito backs up the engine and makes it more efficient and Harry chips at the opposing ship with our weapons. Ezz is deep in the bowels of the ship, checking the runic carvings, ensuring none of them blow. And I'm left wondering if we're going to get away.

That's about when the next part of their plan decides to warp in and fuck with us.

***

Flame and thunder surround us, the *Nothing's Heartbreak* being thrown from one side to the next. We keep a tight grip on the ship even as I trigger my various ship-based Skills to aid our escape. Shields flicker up and down, shunting power to where it's needed and using the released energy storm to help aid our escape.

"I thought warping was being blocked!" Harry shouts, even as he switches our weapons from attacking to pure defensive fire. Of course, he leaves a few of our more powerful weapons engaged with the smaller fighters swarming out of the task force that has warped in, but the rest are targeted at sensors, missiles, and the occasional flying monster or sapient that tries to close in on the bucking, twisting *Heartbreak*.

Yup. Living ammunition is a thing. Not a common thing, mind you. But a thing.

"It was," Dornalor says. His eyes are focused, flicking from notification screen to notification screen. All around us, the newly warped in squadron is trying to hem us in, smaller fighters departing from the transport frigate with every passing second. He's searching for a way out as Skills and inertia dampeners deploy across the map, slowing and grabbing at the *Heartbreak*. After a moment, his lips peel back into a savage grin. "Yes!"

"I'm not sure this is the time to be happy," I say. At the same time, I meet Ali's gaze. "Ali…"

"You know, you're getting very used to sacrificing people."

"Yeah, but you just get banished. It's not a real sacrifice."

"It still hurts!" Ali says, but he doesn't wait.

Ali floats upward, making himself semi-permeable so that he can exit through the ship. Within seconds, the attacks arcing toward us bend away as he taps into his Elemental Affinity. I'm about to join him as a second, closer layer of defense when Dornalor speaks.

"Take over."

"What?" I say.

"Take over the flying. Just keep us going in the direction we're pointed at."

"Fine." My hands flick, triggering the switch over to myself to take over the controls. My head pounds as blood rushes to my head then back down, even as the inertia dampeners fail to suppress the forces pulling at our bodies. "But what the heck are you going to be doing?"

"They left a gap through their defenses. And I've got just the Skill to get us out of here," Dornalor says. His fingers are flying through the air, touching unseen notifications while he slumps bonelessly into his chair, Mana churning through his body. "Now leave me to it."

I can't help but grin, grateful to see I'm not the only one planning for the future. I'm a little jealous that he can actually buy new Skills, instead of being shoved into the few he can acquire, but I squash that thought as fast as it emerges. I have a lot more important things to deal with than my feelings of inadequacy.

I jerk the ship around, doing my best to help the ship's AI, eyes tracking the too-fast-for-normal-human attacks. I don't have anywhere near Dornalor's Skills, but the majority of flying interstellar spaceships is not jerking around a joystick but managing the power controls and the various subroutines in a highly sophisticated piece of equipment. Those things, I have at least spent a decent amount of time learning, even if I don't have the Skills to back up my actions. Thankfully, as the Captain of the ship, Dornalor's Skills supersede anything I could do anyway.

Explosions ripple all around us, and we put the crash barriers to full use. If I didn't have a cast-iron stomach, it'd be doing flips, but having all these Levels and attribute points in Constitution means I'm only slightly uncomfortable. Mostly, I watch our shields drop and drop with each passing second as attacks rain down upon us. Even the Administrator's ship has recovered and is firing upon us now, though as suspected, it doesn't have much in terms of actual firepower.

I get a brief flash of pain and panic before I feel my connection with Ali disappear. Hopefully whatever he has to deal with in the other dimension isn't too onerous and he can survive it. I'd recall him now, but with the Administrator so close, I'm worried about interference.

Instead, I tap into my own Elemental Affinity, connecting it to the space around us and the ship itself, and do a little of what Ali did by bending energy beams away from us. It's nowhere near enough, not without Ali, but every little bit helps.

Seconds pass, and each of them feels like an eternity of pain. Our crash barriers strain and creak. A main beam attack cuts in, bypassing everything we've used to dodge it, and tears a hole through our hull plating, vaporizing two of the crew bays in their entirety. Damage controls flash. Drones and other repair droids spring into action as emergency blast doors slam shut, containing the vacuum. Ezz taps directly into our hull, making the liquid metal grow outward, covering the hole as it does its best to aid the repair droids that spray the area down with crash foam. In the meantime, I reroute all the necessary energy flows, helping the AI as we take ever more damage, and our speed noticeably drops.

"Dornalor…" Harry calls, panic in his voice.

Mikito is dashing back and forth in the engine room, doing the best she can even as our engines redline, their containment fields failing as we push everything to the maximum.

Then the Pirate Captain slams his hands down, grinning. "Gotcha!"

We don't get any further warning as reality twists behind us. The *Heartbreak* is thrown across dimensions and into the hyperspace stream, chaos mere millimeters away from us. His Skill tears open reality, unleashing chaotic energy and booting us directly into the hyperspace stream while raw probability tears apart ships, makes energy into matter, and matter into Mana.

Then we're gone.

Free at last.

For now.

Chapter 17

"Can we go one day without the *Heartbreak* being damaged?" Dornalor was complaining over a cup of, well, the local equivalent of Galactic coffee. The alien was looking worse for the wear, the nine-foot-tall ghatotkaca slumped over the table, yellow skin shading toward orange with exhaustion.

"I didn't even think about that." Mikito sounds a little amused and prods the green-skinned kid by her side. "Did you think about that?"

"I… no." Green skin shifts in color, becoming a luminous neon I'm more used to seeing on plastic packaging than on anything living. The kid looks at Mikito fearfully. "But I can fix it! The Archbishop made sure you had a lot of extra pieces. I can fix it, really!"

Ezz buzzes, eyeing the kid with what I can almost call jealousy. It buzzes and twitches and a part of me wonders how the hell we managed to get a pair of children on what is supposed to be a rebel ship. If child services were around, I'm sure they'd have words for us all.

I eye the kid, then decide to ignore him and the robot studying him to focus on Society's Web and the threads going out from the kid. There are surprisingly few, if one doesn't take into account the sheer number of individuals that he knows who have likely died. The others that connect him, the strongest threads, all go back to where the rest of the Systemers are. Not a surprise. I touch upon some of the webs, get a feel for the kinds of obligations he offers—mostly emotional, some faith-based. Nothing that is too revealing, not without more points of data.

So I turn to Dornalor instead. "You sure we're safe?"

"Yes. We're bouncing from stream to stream, but we're deep enough that even a single shift should be more than enough to keep us hidden." He makes a face. "We'll need to stop in a few days to finish the repairs. Ezz's patch is holding for now, but if it gives way in the middle of a hyperspace stream…"

"I can—"

"Shhh…" Ali puts a tiny finger on the kid's lips. The green-skinned, long black-haired, and tiny-horned alien freezes as he is touched. And really, I call him a kid mostly because he's, like, five and a half feet tall and acts like a child. He might be a few hundred years old for all I know. "You're too pretty to be talking."

The poor kid looks very confused, while Mikito snorts. I do note she doesn't object to that characterization. Ezz buzzes, then leans over to ask if it's pretty. Rather than get involved in *that* conversation, I pull up our stowaway's Status information.

Endila Stimes, Devout of the System (Level 24 Faithbound Mechanic) (A)
HP: 1430/1430
MP: 2120/2120
Conditions: Aura of the System Mechanism

"No real Titles?" I ask. The kid twitches, so I leave it. Titles can be hard to acquire, depending on what you do. Artisans in particular, especially those in the Advanced Stage, don't get a lot of chances to get them. "So what's your story? And why shouldn't we throw you out of the airlock?"

Endila blanches a little.

"Chill, kid. The Redeemer won't just kill you if you aren't an enemy. For all his reputation, he's actually a good guy," Dornalor says, drawling. Endila relaxes before the Captain adds, "I might though, if you messed with my ship."

To my surprise, the last sentence actually gives the kid a little backbone. "I would never damage something I worked on."

Dornalor nods but waits for elaboration. I'm curious too, since it seems I'm not the only one who thinks he's young. While Endila composes whatever story he wants to tell, I reach out to Ali.

"Hey, what race is he? And how old?"

"He's a Plada. A Qalupalik from your mythology, if you know it."

I send a mental shrug, not having heard the term before.

"He's just as young as he looks, which makes him something of a prodigy," Ali says.

"Prodigy with no Titles?"

"Yeah, that's weird," Ali says.

"I wasn't willing to die just yet," Endila says, breaking into our conversation. Rude. "I knew what the Archbishop had planned, and I wasn't willing to go down with them. I knew they'd get you out. That was the point of us working on the ship."

"I thought all you Systemers are fanatics, ready to go down with the church, if you will," I say scornfully.

"I was born on the island. I never had a choice," Endila says. "You either fake believing, or you don't get access to the resources to Level."

"And you have Leveled." I point at him. "You're also what? Fifteen? That makes your levels a little off. How does that work?"

"The Systemers give parents and guardians the chance to bring their children into the fold early on. It's considered better, since we're closer to the System from an earlier age." Endila flicks his fingers. "I'm an orphan, my parents lost to the Forbidden Zone. All orphans are wards of the state, which means we get given access to the System early. I was initiated at seven."

My jaw works soundlessly, anger and horror warring in me for a bit before I push it aside. There's nothing to be angry about. Or at least, there's no one. The individuals involved are dead, and the entire damn religion is something I don't have the time or energy to deal with.

Endila keeps talking, seeing as Mikito is looking a little skeptical still. I get it. Even eight years is fast to become an Advanced Class.

"I was lucky. A few years ago, I met a... a... friend." There's a way Endila says it, a look of loss and reverence that makes me think this friend might have been more than that. Puppy love perhaps. "She introduced me to a group. Heretics, if you will, who didn't believe in the main line the Church was spouting. They have..." He shakes his head. "Easier to show you."

Endila unclasps the side of his tunic-jumpsuit and pulls a badge from underneath it. He places it on the table and we all read its information.

Amulet of the Reformed Church of the Infinite System

A symbol of an individual's membership in the Reformed Church of the Infinite System, a "heretic'" branch of the Systemers' belief system. The Amulet hides details of the individual's Titles, allegiances, and reduces the System footprint of its user. This Amulet is soulbound to Endila Stimes.

Effect: Allows up to three (3) Titles to be hidden or edited. Provides a 25% reduction in the System footprint and makes it 25% more difficult to track user.

Now that he's taken off the Amulet, I can't help but scan his status again.

__Endila Stimes, Reformed Devout of the System, Master Prodigy of Runic Weaves, Masterwork Artisan (Level 24 Runic Mechanic) (A)__

HP: 1430/1430

MP: 2120/2120

Conditions: Aura of Runic Enhancement

"Impressive. But if it took us a few seconds to work out you're hiding something, why didn't others?" I ask.

"Ali's showing you what we can't see," Mikito says, waving at Endila. "Until he took it off, I just saw him as a Basic Mechanic."

Ali, by my side, is slapping his crossed knees, laughing. I glare at the brown-skinned Spirit, who gives me a big, ass-shitting grin.

"Whatever. You should still be easy to pick out for the Archbishop and their ilk."

Mikito puts a hand to her face, muttering, "Baka."

"You do realize that not everyone meets with the Archbishop? Or high-Level guards regularly? If the kid just stuck around the hangars and his quarters"—Endila nods at Dornalor's words—"then that badge would have been more than enough."

I sigh but accept the correction. "Fine. I get it. He managed to hide his Class and Levels and snuck in with us because he wants to live. Why should we trust him and not just, I don't know, put him in an escape pod or something?"

"In the middle of the Forbidden Zone?" Dornalor says, sounding a little incredulous. "You might as well shoot him. It'd be less torturous."

"Really, John…" Harry says exasperatedly.

I grunt, admitting I hadn't really thought out my words. So we can't get rid of him. It doesn't mean we should trust him. We could… "Lock him in a cargo room?"

"He's a Runic Mechanic who just worked on the entire ship. He could probably break out in a day," Dornalor says.

"I could watch the stowaway," Ezz says. "This one does not sleep."

"And if he chose to break you?" I say, raising an eyebrow at the golem.

"Ezz is not easily breakable. Creator made sure of it, Father."

"Yeah, let's not risk it. I'm not sure what a Runic Mechanic does, but I'm sure he's got his own Skills," I say.

Endila looks as innocent as he can while Mikito pats Ezz on the head, making the golem choose to stop arguing with me. Which is good, since my next choice was to just order it to be quiet.

"Right, so then…" I frown, searching for options.

"I'm not going to do anything to harm the ship," Endila says, crossing his arms. "And once they learn I ran away with you, I'll be just as wanted as the rest of you."

A slight smile crosses my face when I hear the touch of excitement in his voice at the end there. I have to admit, it's probably being a kid that makes the entire run-away-from-home thing an adventure. And not a "jump off a cliff into the churning seas of fate" thing that it is.

"If he wanted to sabotage us, he could have done it during our flight," Mikito says. "None of us knew he was around till Ezz stumbled on him patching a hole in our hull."

I grunt in acknowledgment. Still…

"What do you have against me, man?" Endila says. "My age? My race?"

"The fact that I don't know you."

"Waste metal," Endila spits. "You're an Admin. Go read my Status log or something."

"Doesn't work that way." I pause, considering. There probably is such a log, but I doubt it'd hold the kind of information I need to make me trust him. After all, the System doesn't care about personal relationships in that way. It certainly can't tell me if I should trust him or if he'll betray me in the future. On the other hand… "I do have a Skill."

Endila frowns, hearing something in my voice.

"Shackles of Eternity," I say.

"No."

"You know the Skill?" I say, surprised. It's an Erethran Paladin Skill and I know how rare we are. After all, I just trained the last batch of Paladins, the first in the last hundred years or so.

"Do I need to? That's not exactly a nice name, you know," Endila says. "Not like, I don't know, the Double Dare Promise."

"That's not a Skill," I say.

"The System's Mercy, of course not. And I'm not getting 'Shackled for Eternity,' just 'cause you're scared of a fifteen-year-old," Endila says, crossing his arms.

"It's not the fifteen-year-old I'm scared of. It's the Heroic and Legendary Classes he might bring down on us."

"Whatever. Chop my hands off or something. I'm not taking the Skill."

"I don't actually need your permission."

Mikito stirs beside me. She fixes me with a flat gaze, not saying anything, but her disapproving glare is more than enough. I end up breaking eye contact first, catching the way Endila smirks a little as he catches the byplay. Neither Harry nor Dornalor look particularly happy about me using the Skill either.

I relent. "Fine. I'm not the Captain here anyway. We vote?"

"On what?" Harry says.

"Chopping his hands off or trusting him until he betrays us," Ali says, grinning a little. I glare at the Spirit, wondering if his bloodthirstiness is an act or how he truly feels. He popped back when I summoned him with a slight delay, but he'd looked fine this time around. Which either means whatever happened was settled or he'd managed to run away long enough to not get torn apart. "Or we enslave the kid with the Shackles of Eternity."

"That's not exactly what I said…" I grumble.

But everyone else votes, voicing their own opinions. The results aren't that surprising, I guess. It's not as if we're the enemies of the state the Shadow Council paints us as after all.

When we're done, it's Harry who leans forward and offers his hand for a handshake. When Endila looks puzzled, he goes even so far as to move the kid's hand for him to show him how to do a proper handshake.

"Welcome to the *Nothing's Heartbreak* and John Lee's Suicidal Team of Lunatics," Harry says.

"That's not what we're called," I say.

Ezz buzzes. "John Lee's family."

"Not part of his family," Dornalor states firmly. "Call me a retainer if you will, but I want nothing to do with being family to him."

"Not that I'd want you," I grumble, a little hurt.

"Lunatics and family are better than the alternatives." Mikito grins when she catches my glare. "Look it up yourself. If you dare."

I consider, then decide not to. Ali, on the other hand, is looking speculative, which makes me a little worried.

"All right, so the kid's part of us. What's the plan now?" I say, changing the subject before I have to do something I'll regret to Ali. After all, he controls my Status and him changing it to say something I dislike is quite the possibility.

"Running, hiding, and fixing up damage. Then we keep going," Dornalor says with a shrug.

I can't help but agree with him, since really, there aren't many other options.

"Where are we going?" Endila says.

The sapients all share a look before we shake our heads.

Harry claps Endila on the shoulder, adding, "We're trusting. We're not that trusting."

Endila's face shows a flash of disappointment and falls further as we burst out laughing at his reaction. It's part relief at escaping, part vindictive amusement. It's not very nice, and I hope Ezz doesn't learn from us on this.

Then again, if it does, at least it'd be growing.

***

As much as we tease the kid, we do take a few precautions too. Ezz and Dornalor keep an eye on any potential mechanical transmissions out, and I write a simple script in the System that triggers for me if someone tries the same thing via a Skill. It's quite amazing what the new ticketing board allows me to do, though I had to have a lie-down after the initial coding and upload as the System kicked back quite violently at my attempt at exploiting it. If not for the fact that Dornalor has a secondary Skill that minimizes all the information going out of the *Heartbreak* that I use to piggyback the code on, this wouldn't work at all.

In the meantime, once we're done running, we get to repairing. While I have some skills at repair, it's all mundane skillwork that I've gained helping

Dornalor over the years. It's the rest of the team that does most of the work, with even Harry being of more use than me.

Endila is a bit of a prodigy, as Ali said. Between him and Ezz, they do more work than the rest of us combined. After the second day, I stop trying to help since either he or Ezz are highly disapproving of my efforts. Nearly three-quarters of the time, they just redo whatever I do to their standards.

Which is why I retreat to my favorite part of the *Heartbreak* while repairs are conducted, spending time working in the kitchen and making full use of the restocked pantry. Of course, a large chunk of what I prepare gets stuck in storage, for use when we're running for our lives and need something to feed our bodies. The other snacks, cookies, and cakes are dispersed to individual Inventorys for consuming as we go.

I don't spend the time cooking just for the fun of it. It's a mental break for me, which I make use of to review the code and think about our situation. My access to the Ticketing Board by the System is haphazard in the middle of the Forbidden Zone, as likely to disappear in the middle of a ticket resolution as it is to last for hours at a time.

Even then, I've noticed that my overall connection—and by accident, the rest of the team's—has improved. Their connection to the System is still spotty, but occasionally they'll get a flood of experience and Level Ups, something that had been impossible until now. It seems having me around forces the System to prioritize the space around me.

Of course, it helps that I'm actually resolving tickets when we're shooting through normal space and aren't being attacked by monsters. We're pretty much in constant battle with the various creatures, but now that my Extra Hands have been killed, I have them recreated and dealing with the swarms for me. I only come out once in a while when things get really serious.

Probably the happiest individual is Mikito, since she's getting a flood of experience from both the System Administrator tickets I clear and the monsters that my Extra Hands kill, along with anything she deals with herself. In fact, because she's getting so much experience, she glares at me every time I do come out to help.

Floating in the middle of space, my new power armor glowing with damage after the latest blast of void and chaos energy by the space starfish that came along, I can't help but look at Mikito. She's on her horse, swinging Hitoshi in its oversized form to tear apart the remainder of the starfish nest. At the distance and ranges we're looking at, she's more of a fast-moving streak of light than an actual person, at least without zooming in.

Still, that's enough to get her information.

Mikito Sato, Spear of Humanity, Blood Warden, Junior Arena Champion of Irvina, Arena Champion—Orion IV, Xumis,…; Time Slipped, True Bound Honor, Galactic Rebel (Royal Samurai Level 2) (H)

*HP: 5880/5880**

*MP: 4670/4670**

Conditions: Isoide, Jin, Rei, Meiyo, Ishiki, Ryoyo, Feudal Bond, Blitzed, Future Projections

Galactic Reputation: 57/-145

Galactic Fame: 124,929 / -79,231

"Heroic! Already?" I yell, having actually looked at her Status for the first time in a while. I mean, we've been getting experience like crazy, and I knew she'd Leveled, but to be at Heroic already… "That's cheating!"

"Says the mid-tier, dual Class Heroic," Ali drawls. He's sitting on the *Heartbreak* itself, weaving a cone of energy around the front of our ship to deal with the suckers. It's not the most effective way of killing them, since the majority bounce off the lightning or are stunned until they're left behind, but it requires very little focus or energy from the Spirit. And since the automated beam cannons and point defense catch anything that isn't being shocked off, it's effective at keeping the ship mostly clear.

"Yeah, but I have to split my experience now!" I grumble.

Which is true enough, since the way I get experience for my System Admin side has nothing to do with the way I gain experience for the Grand Paladin Class. The fact that I can Level up the System Administrator Class and evolve it without gaining experience makes me wonder if there's even a point to Leveling it. Other than the experience and knowledge of how the System—and the backend code—works, would it matter if I just did nothing? After all, there seems to be literally only a single major Skill to Level.

"If you want to talk, talk. If you want to drift off, you can do that too. But don't disturb me while I'm fighting," Mikito complains, reminding me I had started the conversation to begin with.

"Fine. Whatever. How did you get so much experience?" I say, grumping at her. "And how'd you get past your Class Quest?"

"You, of course. Also, this is the Forbidden Zone. We're literally piling up experience, and getting it all from your Hands and your System Admin Class has been good for me." A pause, then she adds, "Also, I think the math has gone wrong."

"What?" I say.

"Check the connection, but ever since you upgraded to Middle System Administrator, I seem to be getting more experience than ever."

I frown and tap into her Status and blink at the extra couple of Levels she's thrown into Feudal Bond and note that it has increased the experience flow from me to her even more. However, when I go into the details of the Skill, I'm overwhelmed by the sheer volume of information coming through. She's registering experience from the Hands constantly as they do their job.

Absently, I use a series of Blade Strikes to tear apart a damn starfish that closes in on me, then I watch as Mikito registers the experience gain. I have to scroll back and use the timestamp of my own kill notification to find her notification since the Hands are busy doing their thing on the other side of the *Heartbreak*. When I do get to it, I compare the data of one kill to another, having to scroll around on my own notifications to find an equivalent experience number to match.

"Huh. Now that's a ticket," I mutter. A couple of quick commands has the Spitzrocket shadowing the *Heartbreak,* with automated fire started up for anything that comes close.

"Ticket to what?" Mikito says.

"You're right. The numbers are wrong… you're getting the full experience load from the Hands." And I'm getting only a portion of the duplicates'. Otherwise, the Skill would truly be broken. However, it is broken for Mikito, and since my duplicates have been doing the majority of the fighting… "This… I don't think it was meant to work this way."

A flick of my fingers pulls up the ticketing board. However, to my surprise, there's no ticket for this portion of the error.

"Weird…" I mutter.

I know her experience gains didn't work this way before the Middle System Administrator upgrade, so why did it suddenly change? A few seconds later, I find the culprit. The System had partially patched the exploit when I was a Junior System Administrator, but when they did, they referred to my then-current Class instead of using a more generic definition. So while the initial patch fixed the broken code, the moment I changed Classes, the fix was broken.

Sloppy coding.

Out of idle curiosity, I dig deeper into who created the repair code. It takes quite a bit of time to get that deep, and more than once I have to pull out and let my health recover from the overload from System Mana. I soon hit a point where I'm not allowed to adjust the code at all, just look at it. By this point, the initial attack from the starfish has been dealt with and we're in a quiet place, so everyone but a single Hand comes back into the *Heartbreak*.

In the end, after hours of digging, I find the origin of the code. And I'm left even more confused.

Pulling out of the System data, I absently withdraw a bar of chocolate— some gourmet Swiss confection with 85% magically grown cocoa that gives a +10 to Intelligence and +15 to Willpower for an hour. It cost nearly as much as a Tier II beam rifle and melts in your mouth with the full richness of the beans it's made from. I barely even taste it.

"Something wrong?" Mikito is sitting beside me, an e-reader in her hand.

"No. Well, yes. Sort of."

An elegant eyebrow rises.

"Your Skill is broken. We knew that. It's giving you full experience from all kills. Which is, you know, broken," I say. "But that's not really the problem."

"I should say not," Mikito says, smiling happily. Then she sobers. "Can they take it away?"

"Hmmm? What? The bad code? Sure. I could do it," I answer, distracted while the rest of my attention is spent on recalling the code I've read and teasing it apart for further information.

"No. My experience."

"Oh, umm…" My attention is drawn back to what she said. Rather forcefully, since the library takes this moment to do a data dump. I clutch my head as it floods me with studies, Classes, Skills, experiments, stories, and books. Hell, there's an entire library of bad revenge fiction included. I wince, my mouth filling with blood, which mixes with the lingering taste of chocolate.

"John?" Mikito says.

"Sorry. Library dump," I say, rubbing my nose. I'm grateful to note there's no blood. "The simple answer is yes, it's possible. The longer answer is, not exactly." I rub my temples as I sort out the information. "One second…"

I dive into the System again, wincing as System Mana floods my body. It's like a bunch of fire ants and an ongoing electric shock running through me every time I access the System. Still, I force myself to check on my assumptions before I extract myself.

"Drink?" Mikito says, pushing a mug toward me.

I chug down the Apocalypse Ale, marveling at the minor boost it gives and the rich taste of System-altered hops. "Right, so experience can be extracted from individuals. The amount and the limits are dependent upon Classes and Skills, but the System restricts a lot of that. Unlike bad fiction, it's rare to be able to drive someone from the peak of Heroic to a Basic Class again."

Mikito nods while Harry leans against the door of the kitchen to listen. I overhear him mutter, "I don't complain about your reading habits," but I have better things to focus on.

"The entire thing about experience drops is that it's hard-coded by the System. No one, not even System Administrators, can change it. Well, maybe the Root Administrator, whoever or whatever he is. But otherwise, the security clearance required is stupidly high." I'm assuming, since I've never seen the clearance requirement before except in some other, more sensitive parts of the System code like Perks and Soulbinding. "So while they can adjust the ticket and stop me giving you experience in job lots, extracting the experience you have already would require non-Admin action."

"Like a Mind Warper," Harry says sagely.

"No such thing. Urban legend," I correct the Reporter.

He sniffs, not wanting to argue. Because I'm right. Of course, sometimes people don't care so much about right as what they want to believe, but this is not a hill to die on. For either of us.

"So, I'm safe?" Mikito says.

"For definitions of safe," I say. "But your Levels will be fine."

The Samurai relaxes, smiling in relief. Then, as if she's remembering, she adds, "So what was it that disturbed you?"

"Just more of the code…" I recall what I learnt before we got distracted. "There's… well. Some weirdness with it."

"Of course there is. And of course, it benefits you both," Harry says.

He glares at Mikito, and I can't help but glance at Harry's Status screen. Unlike Mikito or myself, he doesn't have the same cheats.

Harry Prince, the Unfiltered Eye, Galactic Investigative Reporter—Barium Level, the Unvarnished Truth, Heroic Survivor, Friend of the Erethran Empire, Galactic Rebel...
(Galactic Correspondent Level 29) (M)

HP: 1180/1180

MP: 3140/3140

Conditions: Reporter's Luck, Nose for Trouble, Just a Bystander, Aura of the Gossip, Information Locus, Network News—Barium Grade, Soul Strain

For all that, considering how little time has passed—relatively speaking—his experience gains have been significant. I'm guessing his chronicling of our activity and the sales of his various reports have pushed his Levels up. He's growing fast, but nowhere near as fast as we are. That's one of his advantages, the ability to gain experience even from old content when something hits big. And there's not much of a bigger story out there right now than us.

If he can keep hidden for a bit and keep releasing footage—including the stuff we've requested to keep hidden till now—he probably will truly Level to Heroic. He might even make it to Legendary if we manage to keep ourselves alive.

"Are you going to explain the weirdness?" Harry says, prompting me.

"Off the record, for now."

"As if I've been able to air anything recently." Harry rolls his eyes.

"Not even our latest big fight?" I'm surprised.

"Another month delay on that before it airs," Harry says. "Dornalor says by that point, we'll be so far gone, it wouldn't matter."

I nod, taking the Pirate Captain's word for it. He's also Leveling up quickly, since carrying extremely wanted cargo like us is one of the factors for his experience growth. And killing, which is what we're doing in job lots out there.

"Weirdness?" Mikito prompts me again.

I grin, but focus. "Just the code and the way it was written. And who. It's pretty sloppy, which is weird, because it's System-generated. And I've never seen code that sloppy from the System before."

"What do you think it means?" Harry says.

"Maybe nothing. It's possible I've never seen that sloppy code because I don't handle these kinds of conflicts as much. Most of the things I see are true edge cases. Which, you know, this is, but…" I shake my head, trying again. "It might be that I've just seen code after other Senior Admins have dealt with the code from the System." I weigh that thought. "Which means the System is a sloppy coder in general. Which…" I shake my head. "I don't really believe."

"Then what's the other explanation?" Mikito asks.

I offer her a thin smile, since the other explanation is a little more worrying. "That the System was sloppy on purpose to sneak in the exploit for you."

That proclamation silences the group. Even if we live with the System, day in and day out, for the most part, it's a monolithic program, a force of nature like gravity. You accept it for what it is because you can't really do anything about it. But we're humans, and we've all lived in a time before the System was around. The thought that the System might be making real choices and planning for its own purposes… it's terrifying.

***

I catch Dornalor a few days later, walking along the underbelly of the ship and inspecting the work done by Ezz and Endila. He traces his hand along the wall, chatting quietly with Harry, who is walking with him, helping to carry some of the testing equipment. I don't know why, but I pull back, allowing them to speak in peace. Without meaning to, I find myself eavesdropping.

"D'mash III—it's a beautiful moon. The main planet never really supported life, but the moon was terraformed by a trio of races after theirs was swallowed by the System. They turned it into a vacation planet, sort of like your hunting safari type. Monsters are carefully regulated and killed, with experience divvied up to people. They specialize in getting Slayer Titles," Dornalor says. "And their beaches… always stocked with the hottest aliens."

"That sounds nice," Harry says, a half-smile on his face. No anger, no wryness, even that hint of pain that keeps his eyes thinned is lessened. He looks… well, not happy, but more relaxed than when he's around me. "I'd love to see it."

"Me too." Dornalor sighs. "Doubt we'll be allowed in though, not with our new Titles."

"Rebel…" Harry makes a face. "How'd you think we can get it removed?"

"Turn in the Redeemer?" Dornalor says, his voice light.

Harry chuckles. "I wish."

"Right? They'd probably just shoot us anyway."

A flash of anger, a twist of betrayal in my guts. I move backward silently, my feet leaving nary a whisper as I retreat to the cockpit. For the most part, I know better than to take their words at face value, remembering all too many times I bitched about my own employers.

I know better than to get upset that they're kidding about things like that. At least, so I tell myself. Still, when Dornalor comes by to the cockpit to take control once again, I just grunt in reply to his greetings.

I know better, but while the mind knows, the heart doesn't care.

***

Long days later, we're finally back to running speed. Dornalor doesn't ask for comments on his navigation plot this time, not when he takes us back into the hyperspace streams. The *Heartbreak* shudders and twists as it enters the stream and flings us across the vastness of space. We ride it passively for now, catching the flow of Mana and hyperspace energy as we drive ever deeper into the Forbidden Zone.

If we're lucky, we'll get to Xylargh this time around without any further problems.

Of course, none of us believe that, but we can only hope.

Chapter 18

The explosions throw me sideways into the wall of the toilet cubicle. My head impacts the metal, deforming it around my body as I stagger upright, my hands still wet. I shake my head even as I note the flicker of a damage notification for myself as alarms sound through the *Heartbreak*. My only full thought is that I'm grateful this happened now, instead of five minutes earlier.

Now, that'd be embarrassing.

"What the hell is going on?" I snarl, slapping the door control and rushing outward once it slides open with a hiss.

"Mines," Dornalor replies over the party chat, his voice strained as he tries to keep the ship from running into more.

Another explosion, another jarring twist. I catch myself with one hand on the opposite side of the corridor as I stagger toward the cockpit. "Where do you need us?"

"The Es—to the engine room. Get us revved down. We need to transition. Mikito and the Hands—damage control. Harry, get on point defense," Dornalor snaps. "Ali, we need you to trigger those mines before they hit us."

I keep rushing toward the cockpit, not hearing my name. Deciding on a course of action, I tap into the *Heartbreak*'s shield and use my Skills Forced Link and System Override to boost the shields. They kick back on, the regeneration overcharged while I link the two Skills together. Just in time for us to hit another mine.

I groan, holding my head, and debate if System Edit is useful here. It only really alters the code, so actual physical effects are a side effect. Like altering regeneration rates or the like in the code. Being in the Forbidden Zone kind of makes it harder, never mind the fact that the System truly does not like it when I manipulate it like that.

"How we doing?" I say, finally managing to make it to the cockpit and grabbing a seat. I note Harry isn't there, but point defense is firing—though how useful it is while we're in hyperdrive is debatable. Most of our weapons just don't work very well in the space between dimensions.

"We're about to drop out of the hyperspace stream. I need you to control the ship and watch for problems the moment we exit. Because we're coming out now, I don't know where we'll end up," Dornalor says.

"At all?" I say a little incredulously.

"I've got a rough idea. Give or take a few star systems." Dornalor's hands hover over blank space, and I know he's waiting.

My hand grips the controls, ready to take over when needed, and otherwise ready to use my Skills to launch attacks. In a corner of my vision, I spot Ezz and Endila—the Es—scrambling around the humming hyperdrive engine and our normal impulse one. The switch between the two will be problematic and tricky, so making sure they're ready to transition us down is important.

Breaking out of the hyperspace streams when we're in the middle of a jump through non-weakened barriers is jarring. We tear a hole through reality as we transition, the entire ship shuddering and our bodies twisting and warping as we shift through dimensional barriers. Notifications flicker as damage piles up, for myself and the *Heartbreak,* while tiny imperfections in our bodies appear. An organ an inch to the left, skin a millimeter to the right. Tiny, tiny imperfections but enough to do real damage. It's even worse because the *Heartbreak* is transitioning hot, so much so that I can smell burnt circuits and taste yellow.

We enter normal reality, and everyone is shuddering and fighting through the pain as nerves and organs are fixed by the System via our enhanced regeneration. I'm the least affected, the tankiest and the one with the highest base resistance to such issues, which is why Dornalor has me on watch.

And it's a good thing too, because of where we appear. Light and dark elementals wage war all around us, the world turning into a harsh filter of too bright light and deepest darkness. Only along the edges of where the elementals clash are there shadows, so great and voluminous are their attacks.

"We're in the pot now, people. Hands, outside." I jerk the ship into a spinning dodge as an errant blast almost tears through our shields.

I program in evasive actions, finding the AI and the ship sluggish from the same damage that affected us. The mobile script, the living metal that makes up the ship, will fix the minor errors soon enough, the AI code altering and patching holes. Until then, it's manual updates and control.

I have the *Heartbreak* dodge and fire back, channeling energy to shields and rerouting nanites and power as necessary. All the while, I'm searching for the closest edge of the battle, a way to slip away and leave these monsters to battle it out. Unfortunately, there's nothing. As far as the eye—and sensor—can see, the elementals do battle.

"Ali, any recommendations?" I send to the Spirit, who has already popped outside.

Rather than attacking, he seems to be waving, adjusting attacks and even seeming to talk to the elementals rather than fight. *"Contain yourselves. They're more upset at the others than us. So long as we don't go too hard..."*

"Got it." I switch to party chat even as the airlocks show cycling as the Hands head out. I'm surprised by how little damage they received from our emergency transition, then I remember they're mostly Mana. Doesn't matter if you shift the Mana a little, it's still Mana. "Ali says to stay contained. No wide scale attacks, people." I pause, considering. "Use Mana-based ones when you can."

That gets a mental nod from Ali, which is good, because I'm forced to switch on point defense a moment later as smaller, angrier elementals home in on us. A quick glance to the side and I note that Harry and Dornalor are still recovering.

"I'm heading to the hyperspace drive. Engines are holding," Endila says. "Ezz will keep patching the hull with the rest of the 'bots. Mikito's already in the engine room. She'll be on damage control once I have a hand on things."

I grunt in answer, mentally sweating. Numbers, trajectories, equations run through my mind. The enhanced Intelligence given by the System is quiescent most of the time, a background effect I don't notice until I'm in the midst of a firefight or in the flow. Then I become a super genius, mentally computing long quadratic equations while projecting where a half-dozen attacks will go, taking into account shield and Skill levels. If I thought about it, I'd freeze up, so I don't.

Even then, it's a strain. My Intelligence boost isn't geared toward such things. I'm not specialized for flying. Reading, cutting through thousands of data sets, sure. Heck, even person-to-person combat is my thing. This is a strain though, one that makes the few minutes I'm in control feel like hours.

I'm grateful when Dornalor finally takes over. I tap the crash padding, releasing myself and standing once he's in control.

"Where you going?" Dornalor says.

"Out, of course." I don't wait, figuring he'll work it out in a second. There's no one better than me in a battle like this, and even if I can't use my full arsenal of Skills without attracting attention, I can play bait at the very least.

I bounce on my feet a little once I'm in the airlock, cycling the Spitzrocket onto me and watching it lock over my body. I marvel at the colors, the way the power armor moves and gives me greater strength. I'm looking forward to its next iteration, after it gets blasted apart. I'm impatient to get going, but the *Heartbreak* has to pull as much of the oxygen and other breathable air into it as possible before the door opens.

Then, space before me. I jet outward, joining the battle, Blade Strikes already flying even as I search for the right location to fire the main cannon. A part of me notes the damage the ship is receiving, and the way Ali has the entire top side covered as he redirects attacks away. I make note, even as I get to work with my doppelgangers.

***

The elementals I face are some of the weird kinds. We might label the various types of energy beings in the System as elementals, but there are over a dozen specific common kinds and even more uncommon varieties. Some create physical manifestations of themselves in our world, mimicking humanoid forms or other, alien variations. Others are just blobs of energy held together by will and Mana. Even more are dimensional projections of a larger concept with some sentience but not sapience. There are so many variations, it's impossible to say what is what.

These guys lean toward the ephemeral type without a true physical body. On the other hand, because they're made up of the concepts of light and dark, the edges of where they are are clearly denoted.

All of that is a clear way to say that it's easy enough to pick out my attackers but harder to actually damage them. The dark elementals are a little easier to harm, with my Skills like Beacon of the Angels doubling the amount of damage they normally do. However, Grand Cross is significantly eroded since a large portion of its damage is gravitational and the lack of physical bodies makes the Skill less than useful.

Funnily enough, it's my Skills like Army of One and the Mana Blades that are my most powerful tools against both kinds of monsters. The Mana coating on the blades does a ton of damage, and even the modified Blade Strikes from Army of One tear apart light monsters with equal ease.

The elementals aren't used to that, the light creatures darting away and around me, trying to swallow me in their bodies while keeping the majority of their forms safe. It's a strange battle, especially as any movement I make damages them. Their attacks—dark or light—wrap around me all the time, flooding the Spitzrocket with energy or draining it away into the void.

My Hands are struggling, forced to rely on their Skills to do damage. Waving Mana-enhanced swords is highly limited, so after I lose the second doppelganger, Mikito orders the last two back in to take over damage control. On her horse, covered by the ghost armor, she's a fiery comet of death and revenge.

As for me…

"Focus, boy-o. You can sense it; sense the way they interact. This is the best kind of training you could hope for. The Light Elementals shift from one state to the next, forcing you to track them as they change. You just need to mimic the dark elementals, pull it away. And you can even take the easy way out and use the energy you draw to attack the others," Ali sends, coaching me.

A focused energy blast throws me back, the outer layer of the Spitzrocket's armor melted from the energetic reaction. A second later, the melted portions freeze over as a dark void tendril wraps me up. It squeezes, sucking more energy from the Spitzrocket and myself, leaching energy from muscles and Mana reactors.

I'm cold. So cold…

Mental Influence Resisted!

Slow Resisted!

I shudder, breaking free from the momentary powerlessness. I reach out with my Elemental Affinity, strengthen the bonds within myself and the energy the Spitzrocket and I contain, controlling it so that it doesn't escape into the sucking abyss.

I lower the draw at the same time, altering the very forces of the universe with the mixture of will and… and something. An affinity, an extra muscle, a feeling in a direction that doesn't exist. I've never truly understood the mechanics of this affinity or where it originates from, but the more I use it, the more I can control it.

"Are you done? Because we could use your help, if you've finished lying around," Ali says, his voice laced with lazy contempt.

I growl, even if I know he's just trying to get me moving. I make use of the Spitzrocket's main cannon, energy lacing through the body of the dark elemental, to free myself and kill a few other elementals along the way. Then I flex my affinity again, dragging away the energy from the light elemental, draining it to refocus the attack on the dark elementals.

Pouring light into the void is like adding colored dye to dirty water. No effect at first, before the dark elemental comes apart from within as it releases a rainbow of energy. It fractures, as does the light I used to injure it. It dies as its very being, the very concept of what it is changes.

But I'm not done, not at all. I grab the next light elemental that sweeps in close to me, this one larger than the one before, the size of a megalodon.

I wrap its energy in bands of control, suck it away, and throw it at the next blob of darkness.

For a long, eternal moment that could be a minute or an hour or a day, I float in the middle space, hands outstretched, sucking in energy with one hand and blasting it out the other. I'm like a reverse prism, pulling energy and color down one side and concentrating it to split apart the darkness on the other end. A lone figure bordering the pair of elemental types.

One eternal moment, before the elementals retreat. Gone to regroup and recover. Or just gone to let their big brother come by to finish me off.

Light Elemental (Level 318)

HP: N/A

Mana: 101236/103787

Conditions: Elemental Body (Mana is equivalent of HP)

"Oops," I say, realizing I might have forgotten the part about staying quiet and keeping the fight contained. The good news though, is it's just the one Light Elemental. The bad news…

"Don't you dare kill that until we're ready to go!" Dornalor snaps, his voice harried. "We do not need even more of those guys. Or their bigger cousins."

"There are bigger?" I say, hovering in space.

The Elemental flickers as it moves, tearing through shields that do little to slow it down. Warning lights flash as the concentrated energy of the Elemental hits us like a freight train. Light, given enough energy and concentration, can be almost physical in the way it interacts.

Coughing, I notice the nanite slime under my helmet swallowing flecks of blood and roasted flesh. My nose no longer works, only the lingering smell of cooked flesh a reminder, as is the same with my sense of taste. Only edges of it are left as I spin around, triggering my Penetration shielding belatedly.

"Yes, Father. Sensors indicate this creature is only the 80th percentile of Elementals," Ezz cuts in.

I shudder and make a jerking motion to conjure my blades. I might not be allowed to kill it, but as I pull light to damage and weaken the monster—as well as blast at a few dark elementals attempting to creep up on the *Heartbreak*—there's nothing to say I can't make it hurt.

Nothing at all.

***

A shuddering jerk, a twist of light, and I'm spinning away. The Spitzrocket is flashing damage beacons all over the place, and a surge of Mana puts it in my Storage to let it fix itself. I've found that the more there is of the armor, the faster it returns. Another push of energy and it's replaced with the Hod. Instantaneous Inventory is once again making its usefulness apparent. As is Mana Blade, as the Light Elemental swirls away, bleeding rainbow shards from where it was forced to pass through my blades.

"How much longer?" I croak out the second time I try, my voice, my throat burned.

Each attack by the Light Elemental is damaging, partially bypassing any defense I have. Even my Penetration Shield can only do so much, and it keeps threatening to disappear.

I pull on my Mana and form the swords for Army of One. The Light Elemental shrinks away, now only a third of its original size. A cunning wariness is apparent as it eyes the charging attack which I hold at bay, since it has no desire to take my Skill in the face once more.

No Elemental Affinity. That damn ability is outside the purview of the System, so any damage I do with it isn't being added to my Penetration Shielding. Not that the shield itself is particularly powerful at the moment, not with the interference the unaspected Mana swirling around us provides. So here I am, using my damage Skills when I can on the unsuspecting elementals to recharge so I can tank even more damage from the one beating on me.

"Nearly done. We just have a bug…" Dornalor says.

Endila pipes up, his voice strained. "You try rewriting ritual glyphs while the entire ship shakes."

"It is okay, Father, I will have this fixed. It is only a matter of adjusting for expected variations in momentum. A simple equation," Ezz says. I swear, the little robot is almost gloating.

"Not all of us are idiot robots," Endila growls. Harsh, fast breathing over the com, then the kid speaks. "Try it again."

"Charging…"

My hands tremble, pain coursing through me as the Skill demands release. A clump of elementals are tearing into one another not so far away, having drifted closer to us—or we to them—in their battle. A push with my mind and the Hod fires propulsion jets, rotating me to point in the right direction.

The swords swing down and a blast of pure light and Mana tear into the group. Damage and kill notifications bloom, but before I can turn my attention back to the Light Elemental I was battling, it hits me again. Its charging attack, the one it uses all the time, requires time to build up. It's the only attack that can break through Penetration, the only one that has its own penetration ability that can override my own resistances.

Light, energy, pain. It fills me up like water in a balloon, my nerves vibrating, my cells splitting. My mind threatens to collapse in on itself, but I refuse to succumb. Willpower, stubbornness, idiocy. It doesn't matter what you name it, I have it in spades. Deep within my soul, I conjure my affinity and control the energy that floods through me. There's nowhere to put it, and a spark of inspiration hits. I don't put it anywhere—I just wrap it up and concentrate it, again and again, till the Elemental breaks free and runs for it and I'm floating in space again.

"And we're up. Enough playing, John." A map updates in front of me, and a big glowing arrow points the direction. Dornalor continues even as the *Heartbreak* pulls away from me. "There's an opening into the hyperspace streams down that way, one that allows us to enter into a deeper band. We'll need to get there though."

"Time to go all out?" I say.

"Time to go all out."

I grin, spinning around to the Light Elemental. A glance at my Mana reserves shows that it's doing well, since I've been keeping to contained attacks. When I trigger Judgment of All, the poor Light Elemental never knows what hits it. It and the rest of the elementals in sight.

They thrash and twist, blobs of darkness and light spinning around then disappearing after a few seconds. Mana—aspected System Mana—blooms, released from the creatures as they die, and my System connection grows more stable.

Not waiting for me, a tractor beam grabs my body and thrusts me in the direction the *Heartbreak* is headed. Seeing a cluster of dark elementals approaching, I raise my hand and blast out the energy I contained earlier, burning a hole through my arm in the process. The Hod lets out a series of beeps, the gloved front destroyed.

Painful, but effective.

The dark elementals dodge, twitching in pain as portions of their bodies are lit up. Ahead of us, a shining dot on a transparent horse rides the solar winds, wielding an oversized naginata to strike at creatures. Hitoshi, her polearm, is making its presence truly known now as it seems to have acquired another Skill. The damn Legacy weapon grows with every death it reaps. Eyes narrowed, I check the damage log and note how its attacks cross dimensions, doing damage on physical and spiritual levels.

The tractor beam holding me cuts off, only for the one at the front of the *Heartbreak* to take over and drag me to the prow. I'm pinned to the front like a Chinese Canadian mermaid carving with less exposed breasts and more rage. As the *Heartbreak* keeps accelerating, I'm weaving my Elemental Affinity, just waiting for a large enough cluster to use the rest of my Skills.

"Looking good, boy-o. But you got to get Ezz in front of you first and have him hold his arms open. Maybe one of you should look out for the iceberg."

"What?"

"Huh?"

The aliens are confused, while Harry is trying not to laugh.

It's Ezz's small voice that makes me choke though. "That sounds… interesting, Father."

"No. And why the hell am I stuck on the prow?" I growl.

"Yes, Father. I shall return to my work." And if there's hurt in the all-too-flat voice of the sentient golem, I'm probably just imagining it. Or so I tell myself.

"You were taking too long," Dornalor says.

Behind me, the countdown of Judgment for All is over, leaving behind nothing but a blooming void of Mana and a flood of notifications. A small dot disappears out of the *Heartbreak*—one of my Hands, his Mana regenerated. He plays rearguard, intent on delaying the angry Level 300+ Elementals I triggered.

The *Heartbreak*'s engines burn, pushing us from an idle spin to a full-blow sprint. Energy feeds out the back, fission, magic, and Mana mixing to accelerate us at levels that would be impossible with normal physics. In the vanguard, Mikito is fast being caught up with, and as we pass her, a tractor beams grab hold of her too. I feel a pulse of Mana push out from Mikito in the System. Elementals fall, dying as a wave of Mana attacks tear them apart from within. The attack looks all too familiar, but it's not the time to ask.

Clustered before us, unharmed, are even more elementals, many of them too caught up in their own fights to notice our fast-approaching forms. We're a silver and gold bullet, a streak of discordant matter that interrupts their never-ending war.

Judgment of All gets its workout as I trigger the Skill twice. I even pull the Spitzrocket back out, triggering its Overdrive ability for a few moments and its Mana Warped Beam Cannon. The weapon even lets me channel Army of One through it, boosting it via the Overdrive ability after adapting to my Skills, such that what is finally unleashed is a concentrated mixed beam of energy and Mana. Enough to destroy the weakened light and dark elementals and not even pause.

The few that survive get plowed through. I tap into my Skill Edit, adjusting the details of my Penetration Shield, and expand it to cover the front of the *Heartbreak*. Like an icebreaker, my shield and I tear through the remaining elementals, destroying their physical integrity and sending them back to the dimensions they're from initially.

Time passes in a blur as I balance Mana, damage, and my shield. The ship's weapons fire continuously, destroying those monsters near us. All the while, notifications flicker on and off as our System connection strengthens and fades.

Eventually, I'm swung back into an airlock and thrown within. Seconds before the world twists and warps again, and we're back in the hyperspace streams.

Damaged and tired, but with ever more experience.

Chapter 19

"What doesn't kill us, eh?" Dornalor mutters.

"Three levels. I got three levels!" Endila, sitting beside us in the dining room, keeps muttering.

"I received nothing," Ezz says. Endila grins victoriously, at which point Ezz continues. "However, I computed that I fixed over fifty-three percent of all—"

"Bah!" Endila says.

"Get used to it, kid. You're in the big leagues now," Harry says, cutting off Ezz and clapping Endila on the shoulder.

"Three levels!" Endila says, going back to his initial point.

I just look at Ezz, who chooses to shut up.

"It's just three? Do you think we broke him over something that simple?" I mutter, looking around the dining room.

Everyone is here, since we're all a little exhausted after that battle. Even my Hands are mostly dead, with only a single doppelganger surviving and working on damage control now.

"Maybe," Mikito says.

"You bought him, so not it," I say, pointing at Dornalor.

Dornalor stares at me, obviously confused. Endila, on the other hand, is staring into space, his lips moving as he reads over his notifications. I catch something about 4% allocation and reduced experience, but I'm not particularly paying attention.

"You guys don't have that saying?" I say.

"What saying?" Dornalor says, exasperated.

"You break it, you buy it?" I clarify.

"Why would we need that saying? Of course you pay for it. Any good shopkeeper would have the Skills to set that up in the System."

"Wait, you can do that?" I pause. "Then, shoplifting?"

"Viable if you have counter Skills. If not, they'll just register the item taken and deduct it from your Credits," Ali answers my question. "And why did shoplifting come to mind immediately?"

"I worked retail for a bit."

Mikito wanders back to the table, a bowl of nebayaki udon in her hand, catches my words, and winces with shared sympathy. Retail workers of the world, unite!

"That makes no sense," Dornalor says.

"Of course it doesn't. They're human," Ali says.

"Seriously, what the heck was going on with the mines? They're not common, right?" I'm not super up to date on Forbidden Zone norms, but we've flown through it enough to know that mines—random explosives— left in the hyperspace ways are just not usual. Either that or we've gotten really lucky in the past.

"It's not," Dornalor says. "Those are new. And they weren't set to find us. Those are set up to destroy anyone or anything traveling through there."

"Did they plan to drop us among the elementals?" Mikito asks.

"Possibly. It's hard to tell where the hyperspace flows might take things, but it'd make sense to try to anchor the mines to a known danger zone." Dornalor rubs his temples, his voice dropping. "This… this kind of behavior, it's beyond the bounds. Even pirates don't trap the streams. We'll run you down, force you out. But trap them? No."

To our surprise, Endila speaks up. "The return of the Galactic Wars."

"What?" I ask.

"It's a return to the norms of the past Galactic Wars. When everything was allowed. Before the Council enforced standards of behavior among parties so that entire planets weren't destroyed just to get a minor advantage." The kid shivers, wrapping his arms around himself. He's showing his age, the fear that threatens to overwhelm his control. "Now it's the Council doing it, so there's no one to stop it."

Data comes flooding in as usual, as the damn library informs me of the past. The very distant past.

"How'd you know all this?" I say to the kid.

"I like to read." Endila ducks his head. "It was a more exciting time. All the best historical fiction is set back then…"

Ezz tilts its head from side to side then pipes up. "There were a higher number of sapient formations during that period than any other time, Father. This might be of use to me."

I blink, staring at the golem. Mikito slurps a little loudly as she chews on her noodles, and when I glare at her, she shrugs and mouths "morality" at me. I… decide not to touch that.

"Not so exciting living in those times, eh?" Ali says to Endila. "I wasn't a fan of them either, really."

"How old are you again?" I say to Ali. His answer is him sticking out his tongue. "Very mature."

"Children," Mikito calls, cutting off the pair of us before we get into another distracting squabble. Better a distraction than thinking about what a System-enabled galaxy without rules for war is like. "What does this mean for us? What else can we expect?"

"We're mostly fine. I'd like to take a few days to complete our repairs," Dornalor says. "I want the Es to go over our runes, optimize them. They did a good job under pressure but…"

"It was under pressure. I calculate an eighteen-percent loss in efficiency on those I worked on." A pause, then Ezz continues. "Twenty-four percent with Endila."

"You little—"

"Children." Another warning from Mikito, and the pair subside.

Dornalor snorts, watching Mikito handle the pair. "After that, we can reenter the stream, but we'll be going slower."

"To watch for problems?" I say.

"Yes. We don't really have the sensors to be moving at full speed," Dornalor says. "And we got lucky this time. If we had taken more of those mines directly, the *Heartbreak* would not have survived the stresses."

"I can maybe cobble something together to help," Endila says. When we look at him, he offers a weak smile to my suspicious glare. "I don't really want to get blown up either. Dying in the hyperspace streams is supposed to be extremely painful."

That gets a nod from me. The few accounts I've read from survivors indicates he's not at all wrong. Moving through the stretched boundaries between dimensions does things to the body and time. What might only be an objective minute could feel like an eternity. A very painful eternity.

"Fine. Anything else we should worry about?" I say, leaning back in my chair. Chocolate appears in my hand, and I hand it out while I cudgel the library for more data.

"The most dangerous would be a hyperspace stream bomb…" Endila says. I frown, cocking my head as data comes in, even as the kid explains to those who don't get a visual example dumped into their cerebral cortex. "If you set one off at the right place and time, it destroys the hyperspace stream for a time. Sometimes redirects it entirely if it's powerful enough. In the *Resolution Chronicles*, it was used to destroy the Cias Empire, since all the streams leading to the Empire were destroyed, stranding them…"

I tune out the kid, since the real history of the event is flooding in. It was more complicated than that, since there are multiple methods of crossing the vast reaches of space, but he's not wrong about the danger of such a bomb.

"How do we protect against that?" Dornalor says, frowning. "If they cut off the streams to Xylargh, we'll never make it. And they have to know that's where we're headed."

Endila shrugs, not having an answer. I half-shut my eyes as the library keeps dumping data. My hands shake a little and a throbbing headache builds up as I force myself to access and review the data as it is dumped. Conversations around me go on, the team used to these moments.

Eventually, I open my eyes and answer the questioning eyes. "There is no answer. Not as long as we use the hyperspace streams."

"Twisted black holes," Dornalor swears.

"Yup." I open my hands sideways. "Good news is that they might not bother."

"Why?" Mikito asks.

"Because it's Xylargh. Trapping the Dragon Lords and their dragons would be a bad idea…" I wryly smile. "To say nothing about how grumpy they'd be."

"Would they care?" Dornalor asks. "I always heard the entire planet is pretty insular. It was what made Bolo so different."

"About leaving? No. About not having the option to leave? Oh yeah. Bothering a dragon in their territory is a good way to get them to chase you." I share a twisted smile with Mikito, remembering. "Destroying a part of their territory? Guaranteed to see them chase you down."

Dornalor nods.

Endila looks between us, his voice low as he asks the question in his eyes. "We're going to Xylargh? Really? But that's in the center of the Forbidden Zone!"

"Says the kid who spent his whole life floating inside the Zone itself," I say.

"Only along the edges for the most part!" Endila waves. "No one goes there. The *Heartbreak* isn't meant to handle that kind of Mana load."

Dornalor frowns, leaning forward. "What do you mean? I dropped Bolo off, and my baby barely had a hitch. And she was nowhere near as upgraded then."

"That's because you went through one of the regulated hyperspace streams, right?" Endila says.

"Of course."

"You probably noticed the Galactic Fleet holding station and the various defensive stations around?" Another nod from Dornalor before Endila says, "Those aren't there just to ward off monsters, though obviously the killing they do is useful. It's to stabilize the streams."

"Impossible. Even at the rate they were killing the monsters, the Mana Density is too high for them to balance the flow just by slaying. If it was that easy, we'd never even have a Forbidden Zone," Dornalor says.

"Exactly! It's not the killing. It's the Skills of the Hyperstream Enablers and their teams."

"Those kinds of Skills only work for a dozen or two light years," Dornalor says, frowning. "There's no way they stabilized across the entire stream."

"Incorrect. Hyperspace Stream Traversers, Travelers, and Walkers of the Dimensions are able to stabilize locations via Safe Passage or other Skills at the Heroic Level or due to Skill Evolutions," Ezz pipes up.

Mikito pushes her bowl forward, placing the chopsticks on it carefully before she eyes Endila. "How do you know all this?"

"I went to school. Didn't you?" Endila sneers.

"I want to hit him. Can I hit him?" Ali says, looking at the back of his hand.

"He's a kid. We don't hit kids." I waggle a finger at the Spirit while Endila smirks. "But you can store up the walloping for when he turns adult."

That makes Endila blanch a little. Ezz titters, and I look at the sentient golem, who freezes.

"Awww…" Ali says.

"Fine, so what you're saying is the hyperspace streams back and forth from the planet are artificially lowered and stabilized," I say, cutting through the garbage.

Endila nods, while I turn to Dornalor and raise an eyebrow, a little annoyed he didn't know that. For that matter, it's aggravating that for all the information the library offers to me so unwillingly, it also more often than not is useless when it really matters.

"I don't go that deep for the most part," Dornalor says defensively. "I definitely don't do anything illegal while going in that deep into a Forbidden Zone. That's just common sense."

"Whatever. So we have another problem then." I rub my temples. "So, what? We can't get through using non-regulated streams?"

"Not in the *Heartbreak*."

"We can upgrade her again?" Dornalor says a little hesitantly.

I don't even need to see Endila shake his head to know that's out of the question. We've overhauled the ship twice in less than a Galactic year, trying to traverse the Forbidden Zone. And it's still not enough. Not when the Mana levels and the monsters are so high. Even now, flying through the hyperspace streams puts the runic enhancements and the shielding of the ship under massive strain.

Even if we ourselves might have the Levels to survive a fight, the *Heartbreak* is a lot more fragile.

"Then what?" Mikito asks and I can only shrug.

There doesn't seem to be a good answer here. Waltzing in through the front door isn't likely to work, but we need to get to the damn planet. I'd hoped we could sneak in, but it's sounding less and less possible.

"For now, let's get the ship fixed up and headed toward Xylargh," I say. "The rest... the rest, we'll figure out once we can."

There's a snort from Dornalor, but he gets up anyway to head for the bridge. I watch the Pirate Captain leave, a little niggle of worry in me. We've pushed him far, tested his loyalties again and again. At some point... at some point, that's going to break.

The only question is when.

***

I catch up with Mikito a day later in the middle of the night in the training room. It's quiet here, the rest of the ship having crashed long ago. Mikito's greater Constitution has kept her running when everyone but me has to recover. The only other person awake at this time—other than my Hands, who I actively avoid—is Ezz, and it spends the time when Endila is asleep going over the other's work. There's a burgeoning competitiveness there, one that I am not getting involved in.

I'm amused to watch Mikito train as she flips, throws, and spins Hitoshi around her. The naginata's heavier blade slashes through the air, leaving small indentations in the very fabric of reality. In the space left untouched by the blade, Mikito moves, dancing in a familiar fighting style. She goes through the kata, one after the other, before she finally comes to a standstill, her last motion a throw of the weapon. It flashes across the hallway to embed itself in the dummy before Mikito turns to me.

"Here to train?" she asks.

"No." I pause, then add, "Maybe. That's a variation on the Erethran Honor Guard fighting style, isn't it?"

"Yes. I'm adapting it to work with Hitoshi's new ability." I cock my head and raise an eyebrow, and she chuckles. "Spatial Cut. Leaves a dimensional rift for a few seconds that does damage when something comes into contact with it or tries to go through that space."

I can already sense the way the dimensions have healed, the torn holes in reality fixed. It's fascinating, especially since it's so close to the way my own Thousand Blades keeps itself floating in the air, moving in conjunction to my own attacks. The Rifts she creates are static though, so it's different, which requires her to alter how the form is used. Definitely an adaptation.

"It's looking good," I say.

"Thank you. Now…?" An elegant eyebrow rises.

"I meant to ask about your Heroic Skill." I rub my nose, tilting my head and idly scanning the threads that connect me to my friends. "I noticed something odd outside."

"Boon of the Shogun," she says. "It lets me borrow one of your Skills."

"If it's a boon, don't I get a say in this?"

"No. Why would I let a baka like you choose for me?"

"I'm hurt." I shake my head. "If I was a Legendary…"

"Yes."

"So broken." She grins, and I stretch my neck from side to side. "I can still kick your ass, you know."

"No big Skills," Mikito says, stepping away and holding out her hand. Hitoshi, embedded in the statue, disappears and reappears in her hand as she waits for me on the training floor.

"No fair."

Another smile as she settles into her guard and I conjure my blades, walking over to join her. I've been slacking in my training, and the glint in her eyes tells me I'm going to pay for it. And for my earlier boast.

***

There is no such thing as good karma being repaid, not since the System arrived and not before. Anyone who tells you differently has an agenda. I believe that with all my heart and soul. So, when the universe decides to tilt things in our favor, you can understand that I'm just a little nervous.

"And you're sure that if we get its corpse, we can imbue it into the *Heartbreak?*" I say.

Endila nods rapidly, almost vibrating off the deck plates with excitement. He stares at the visual notification screen where the little bit of luck has appeared at the edge of our sensors.

Deep Space Angler Fish (Level 427)

HP: 42713/42713

MP: 3381/3381

Conditions: Displaced, Mana Lure (Taunt)

"Level 400 plus," Mikito, standing beside me, mutters. Her eyes are glowing as she's seriously considering how to take on that monster. Problem is, I can see its conditions and am a little worried.

"I only see one of them. Are we looking for more?" I ask.

"Angler Fish are uncommon lure monsters. It's unlikely there will be others. They are quite hungry and solitary," Dornalor answers me over the intercom.

I'm not entirely sure that helps. The Angler Fish looks like a deep-sea monster from Earth, all big mouth, beady eyes, and giant, floating lure in front of it. That lure generates light and Mana waves that churn through its surroundings, creating a subtle taunt effect on everything around. Even standing here, tens of thousands of miles away, I can feel the pull of its Skill. I can't even imagine what it might be like up close.

"You think isn't a sure thing," I say, knowing there really isn't such thing as a sure thing.

I'm hesitating because even as we watch, the Angler Fish draws in another victim. What floats by this time is a mutated space station—whether it's a metal elemental that has taken its form or a station given sentience, there's no way of knowing. It floats toward the hanging lure, beams of light stabbing from its twisted docking bays as it tries to destroy and conquer, consume and capture the taunting light.

It fails.

When it is close enough, the Angler Fish moves. Not the incorporeal body that is visible to normal sight, not the one that is projected into our dimension looks, but the true body of the fish. It explodes from the secondary dimension it hides in and clamps down on the floating space station. Two quick, savage bites, like a piranha going after goldfish in an aquarium, and it's over with. The entire space station is consumed, only shattered glittering remnants floating away.

The lure light blinks out, turning off as the Angler Fish reenters the secondary dimension and repositions itself. Thousands of kilometers away, the void waters have stopped churning, and the soul beacon of light, comfort, and food reappears. Waiting for its next victim.

"Can we hit it? When it's hiding, that is?" I say, worry and doubt in my voice. I have a feeling I know what the answer will be and what it will mean.

"Not with the *Heartbreak*. Nothing that we carry crosses dimensions," Dornalor says.

"I could, but it'd be short," Mikito says, gesturing with Hitoshi.

"It seems the optimal solution would be to lure it outward," Ezz says, little lights dancing in its eyes.

"Don't look at me," Harry interjects.

"No one is. No one's ever looking at you for damage, Harry," Ali says. "I can slip across the dimensions, but then I'll be in the same dimension." Ali shakes his head. "I don't stand a chance, not against that, and definitely not alone."

"So what?" I say.

"Mikito and Ali? But if that's the case, can it hurt Mikito without transitioning over? If so, Ali could play bait maybe," Harry offers.

Ali and Dornalor are shaking their heads, and I can't help but agree. The library is quite clear that attacks that pass between dimensions are rare. The spatial rifts Mikito creates are damaging, but they're damaging as a side effect of what they are, which means the damage to the creature itself will be blunted.

Since it seems to pop through every time it wants to eat something, it's clear the Angler Fish's main attack requires it to transition.

"So…" I scratch my chin. "We send Mikito and Ali over to kill it and the rest of us have barbecue?"

There are more than a few snorts of incredulity at that while Mikito punches me in the shoulder. "No. I need bait."

I knew it. It always ends up this way. John, be bait. John, stand in front and get shot. John, be a hero and let everyone else hate you for the decisions you make.

"Fine, fine. I'll be the Angler Fish's chew toy." I let out a long sigh, then add, "But I've got a few conditions."

***

Flying toward that damn monster, my Penetration shield at a high level of charge from hunting down a couple of monsters a distance away from the Angler Fish, I'm as ready as I can be. I'm even fully dressed in the Spitzrocket since I really do not like the idea of getting eaten. Been there, done that and it's never pleasant.

Gliding along silently, not so far away—in space distances—is Mikito. She's on her horse, that ghostly equine creation of her Skill, hunting for the main body of the Angler Fish. Aiding her is Ali, whose functionality as a Spirit gives him an advantage in this search.

Even so, we're gambling that she can find the creature before it chooses to eat me. She can hit it while it's phased away, then come around and hit it again. When it finally attacks her, I can hopefully launch my own, unnoticed attack. In this way, we could pile on damage before the Fish becomes a problem.

We have a pair of Extra Hands with us for just this reason, though the other two are on the *Heartbreak*. There are always monsters to deal with, after all.

It's pretty simple plan, but over the years, the KISS strategy has shown its advantages over and over. As these things go, the pair of us are more brutes than Machiavellian strategists. If I had to pick an old-world strategist to liken myself too, it would be Nelson, with his penchant for charging straight into the jaws of fire, all cannons firing while risking life and limb.

Sometimes quite literally.

Drifting ever closer to the damn lure, I can't help but notice that the Mana impulses it shoots out are a mixture. The majority of it is tainted with the Angler Fish's own, special flavor of Mana, but there's still the unexpected. A tainted form of System Mana is in it, just enough to twist and subjugate anyone else who is attached to the System.

This deep into the Forbidden Zone, the System itself is blotchy except for the occasional moments of clarity. Outside of the notification screens we can call up that are entirely our own, we have to function without the System providing constant aid, leaving us only with minimal additional information.

Even the things Ali can show me are hedged, much of it coming from the library and his own experiences, past knowledge, and his understanding of the world. He can pick up hints from the System here and there, borrow my stronger Admin connection to piggyback additional searches, but there's no true functionality, not anymore. That's what makes the Forbidden Zone so dangerous. Along with the lack of Shop connection, even using Skills sometimes had a slight lag, sometimes in microseconds, sometimes full seconds. For cross-loaded Skills, that delay is even more apparent.

Of course, this lack of connection is nowhere near as bad as it was for me previously. As a System Administrator, I carry my own link with me, one that reinforces the area around us.

And yes, I'm using this slow, drifting course toward the lure to ponder aspects of the Forbidden Zone rather than the fact that Mikito still has not taken action. Even though the lure itself is literally less than twenty kilometers away.

My nerves are tense, strained, my head rotating constantly as I search for any sign of my attacker. I would say I'd be straining to hear things, but the void is devoid of sound. About the only things to hear are the harsh rasp of my breath and the occasional burble from the nanite gel that surrounds me.

Closer and closer I drift, and I'm certain I'm closer than the station was before it was attacked. I wonder though if it was because the station was attacking the lure that triggered the strike. I'd ask for suggestions, ask how close Mikito is, but we're enforcing radio silence.

In the end, I'm too close for comfort. I reach sideways, grasping for a sword and watching it appear in my hand. Seconds later, the rest of my duplicate weapons form around me. I feel the Mana sphere shift, the world bending a little as something vast, something dangerous, moves.

Before it can finish its preparations, in the space between one heartbeat to the next, Mikito makes her move.

Light bursts forth as Hitoshi expands into a giant-sized version of itself. She swings the energy form of the naginata even as the horse speeds up, turning into another beam of light. Close as she is, I am able to fully appreciate the comical sight of the tiny Japanese woman wielding a naginata over three times the size of her and her steed.

Comical to me, but painful for the Angler Fish as she cuts right through it and across dimensions. Hitoshi rips a hole through dimensions, leaving a spatial tear as she holds it like a lance, zipping back and forth through empty space. Empty at least on this side of the world.

That is, until it isn't empty anymore. The Angler Fish tumbles through the dimensional walls. Bleeding from multiple deep cuts, it flicks its tail to catch Mikito and send her and her weapon spinning aside. The Angler Fish is angered and damaged, but nowhere near dead.

However, it's now my turn. In this dimension, I have a lot of techniques to use, the most powerful of which is Grand Cross. I unleash the Skill, watching as a glowing cross a quarter the size of its body slams into glistening scales, widening wounds created by Mikito's charge.

From far away, the Hands who have been watching—and let me tell you, the argument I had with them when they refused to jump into the creature's mouth was fascinating in a screwed-up way—open a Portal and make their way over.

Another Grand Cross, then another and another hammer the creature as the pair come through. It spins round and round, the Angler Fish shedding scales and iridescent light from its lure. However, there's something going on with its Mana, something strange.

I figure it out a few seconds too late as the lure finishes absorbing our attacks to return them to the Hands. They're clustered together because they chose to make use of a single Portal to have more Mana to cast Skills. And while they're attempting to Blink Step away, they haven't been able to get far enough before the blast of condensed energy strikes.

Soul Shields, their main form of defense; my Defense of the Fallen Skill; and the natural Resistances that are part of my Class offer them some protection. Enough to stave off death from a single strike. However, this is a Level 400+ creature whose condensed attack is drawing from the energy that they released themselves.

Another follow-up attack, and they're gone. The only good news is that the one holding the Portal open slammed it shut before the attack managed to continue through and damage the *Heartbreak*.

Their deaths and my survival, or likelihood of survival, is the reason I was the bait in the first place. Unlike me, they can't access my Penetration shield, leaving them significantly more vulnerable. Of course, none of us expected the damn monster to kill my doppelgangers in one attack, but some powerful attack was a given.

It is a Forbidden Zone monstrosity after all.

Another flash of light as Mikito turns around and releases a Grand Cross attack channeled through Hitoshi into the creature. Energy and spatial turbulence rip a glowing line of explosive energy down one long flank, a pair of fins and a multitude of scales coming apart. I notice Mikito twist a hand, jerking it a second later, and pull on the wound, blood pouring out to freeze solid.

For all the damage we're doing, the damn Angler Fish is alive. Its attention turns to Mikito, who buzzes around it like a lightning bug. It shivers, and to our surprise, the remainder of its scales explode outward. Too close to the area effect attack, Mikito is thrown off her ghost horse to spin into the void. To my surprise, rather than being a one-and-done area attack, the scales shimmer and change direction to swarm Mikito as if they're alive.

Ali, by her side, waves, forming a net of lightning that catches and diverts some of the scales. He also shoves a notification down my throat, making me read it.

Scale of the Deep Angler (Level 74)

HP: 718/757

MP: 198/218

Conditions: Living Construct of the Deep Angler, Quantum Edged, Spatial Steps

"They've got health," I mutter.

Then, realizing what Ali's point is, I glance at my Mana. It's low. Dumping two Grand Crosses one after the other and running my other Skills means it's not great. Still, there's more than enough for a Judgment of All.

I push against the System, using System Edit to cheat a little. Since I don't have full view of all the scales, I wouldn't normally be able to destroy them all. But Ali's Linked to me and I can share his eyes. It just normally isn't usable with this Skill. System Edit lets me "fix" that, and all it costs is a lot more Mana and a throbbing headache along with the taste of iron in my mouth.

Yeah, pre-System, I would be really worried about the sheer volume of brain bleeds I've given myself in this short timeframe. Post-System John is worried, but it is also clear that he's an idiot who will likely die well before issues crop up.

Not that the library and Questors haven't done extensive studies showing only very mild confluence with regard to ongoing damage and long-lasting effects on the System-integrated.

Wrenching my mind back to the fight, I spot the vast majority of Scales have been destroyed and the Deep Angler is on the run. Mikito tries to block its path, but it hits her with some other Skill, one that freezes her and her horse in space.

The Spitzrocket's engines turn on, boosting me as fast as it can to cover the distance between the fish and me, but we inadvertently opened up a gap during the fight. I don't reach the fish, not before it flicks its scaleless body, pushing against an invisible wall before the dimensional wall tears and it slips in.

"Nooo! We need that fish." Endila's scream is heart-wrenching.

"I'm on it," I snarl.

It escaped through a hole in space, a black void. That's simple enough then, since I have a Skill that looks exactly like that. As the hole shrinks and I jet closer, I weigh my options. Open a Portal directly to wherever it is or try to piggyback on the Deep Angler's hole? Neither option is what my Skill should do but… I can work around that.

"Don't you dare go in there, boy-o! I can't fish you out if you do."

"Did you just pun?" I retort with one portion of my mind, the rest of it focused on editing the Portal Skill.

Mana flares through me, Portal merging at the edges of the rapidly shrinking hole and locking itself to the edges. My head throbs and sight turns red while the smells of cinnamon and lemons erupt in a cloying, ex-boyfriend fashion.

Then I'm through the shrinking gap, just like Ali told me not to. Because I've never been good at taking orders.

***

Void, shadow, and deep water is all that encompasses me as I float through the secondary dimension. A light pinging noise is heard almost immediately, though I don't need the System to let me know I'm taking damage from physically being here. It feels similar to taking a full body bath in light acid—painful, debriding on the skin, but not life-ending. Not unless I stay here too long.

That is an issue though. The damage I'm taking, or perhaps the fact that I'm in another dimension, means that I'm not healing anywhere as fast as I should be. Each second, my skin is taking damage, and the damage is ignoring the armor of the Spitzrocket. I can only imagine what this would be like without my Resistances. Even the Grandmaster Class Personal Armor is degrading, small notifications of falling durability showing up.

Knowing I don't have time to waste, I scan for the Deep Angler and find it not so far away. No light on its lure, not anymore. Instead, it floats in the darkness, blood dribbling out of its numerous wounds to be consumed by shadowy elementals. Those are numerous, bouncing off my Penetration shielding as they try to get to me. The difference between them and the actual void is only perceptible via different shades of black. If not for my Mana sense, this entire place would be unnavigable.

The Deep Angler's mouth is open, its tail fin moving only a little as it floats forward, sucking down elementals. Each elemental is processed in its unending stomach, becoming Mana and energy to heal it. Already, I can see its health ticking up, the creature obviously suited for this environment.

I consider my options quickly. I've already cast multiple Grand Crosses and a Judgment of All finisher. The damage on my Penetration shielding and the health on the fish mean that I'll be fine to fight it directly. However, the Angler can likely move faster than me in this place, so running after it if it chooses to flee is a bad idea.

I don't have a lot of Mana left, but I do have Overdrive and the Spitzrocket's Cannon. Together, with one more attack at a vulnerable location, might damage the fish enough to make it vulnerable to Mikito and Ali. If Mikito is free.

Of course, even if it has shed all its scales, its skin is still incredibly tough. Attacking it on the outside still plays to its defenses. No, if I want to kill it, its brain or heart are likely my best options. The head is all bone and shielding, so that's out. Which means…

"Thousand hells given birth…" I swear but command the Spitzrocket to angle me in the right direction.

The Deep Angler seems to believe it has gotten away, having missed my entrance. I need to sneak over, which means killing the last of the lights on the Spitzrocket and going over slowly, no matter how much damage this environment is doing to me.

Luckily, the armor and piloting system can do the necessary calculations. While it does that, I focus on trying not to throw up as my brain and stomach demand retribution for everything I've put them through. Thinking is like pushing through wool, and I'm a little worried about the conclusion I come to. It might be a brain-damaged John solution to throw himself into the mouth of a monster…

But no matter how I cudgel my brain for another option, there isn't one. Leaving me to float forward, into the creature's inexorable vortex of a mouth.

It works, me being so small that the Deep Angler can barely notice me. I feel a little like Jonah going into the whale, or what I think he must have felt like. Cursing all the gods there might be and wishing there was a better way.

Surprisingly, the void environment I swim through isn't that disturbing, nor are the dark elementals that form and die. They're torn apart by the suction, by the energies of the Deep Angler's "eating." The entire process is half magical, half biological, and all psychedelic.

At a certain point, I pass through the open throat of the creature and am pulled into its pulsing grey stomach, where elementals are torn apart and remade into streams of Mana and energy. My shield weeps, coming apart, and I figure I'm good.

Overdrive, Pulse Cannon, Grand Cross. All of it combine, along with the targeting system of the Spitzrocket, to point at what should be the heart. I charge up the attack, an act that makes the Deep Angler thrash about in fear.

It seems I'm not the only one who has gotten into position, as spatial tears appear through its body. One nearly bisects me, leaving a bleeding wound where blood is sucked away, the attack bypassing my Penetration

Shield. I jet away, eyes wide as Mikito keeps up the attack in the other dimension. Weapon charged, I fire, and my own concentrated Mana attack tears through flesh, organs, and bone to strike the heart.

The fish struggles, twisting and jerking, trying to escape once more. The suction reverses as it attempts to vomit me out even as it thrashes about. I'm tossed and thrown against the walls of its stomach, my shielding taking a beating. It isn't regenerating, nor is my health. I'm bleeding out, cut apart by the spatial tears I'm thrown into while the dimension attempts to reduce me to the base particles of its existence. I'm dying by inches, and the Mana I can pull, that I can sense around me, is refilling my reserves all too slowly.

If I'm dying, so is the Deep Angler. It's bleeding, the few living elementals—the strongest of their kind—latching onto its open wounds. It belches, sending a wave of half-consumed bodies back into the environment, but I manage to sink a sword into its stomach and hang on for all I'm worth. The sword tears a hole through its body, even as dark elementals swarm it.

The Deep Angler, all instinct and anger and fear, flees. Running from the elementals that sense its weakness. It flees and takes me with it, out into the real world. The dimensional journey is painful as my body reintegrates with this reality, the System reasserting dominance as we arrive back where we started.

Only to be struck again, this time all too hard, and driven into unconsciousness as the tip of an all-too-familiar ship breeches the Deep Angler's side.

Chapter 20

I cut into the corpse of the Deep Angler, cold and dead flesh giving way slowly with each motion. I move carefully, the edge of my blade running along the bones of the creature as we debone the damn thing. Further away, small glittering dots of my recalled doppelgangers float, picking up scales and fighting off the various monsters that decide to try their hand at us.

Drifting a short distance away is the *Nothing's Heartbreak*, the ship undergoing its own repairs and refit. Dornalor's outside with Harry, pulling off armor plating as necessary to expose the inner struts of the ship. Ezz reworks the ship structure then, adding the necessary runes and supporting structures for when we eventually add the bones of the fish to it. Endila is working directly on the stripped clean bones, adding new runes to make use of the Deep Angler's Skill.

"I still don't believe you guys rammed me," I grumble, rotating my shoulder. If I didn't know it was entirely mental, I would swear I can feel the pain of crushed and dislocated bones still. It's taking longer than normal for the various System aspects to drive away the phantom pains, a likely side effect of abusing System Edit. As it stands, I'm still getting occasional headaches that have no explanation beyond a sudden surge of Mana.

"Well, we weren't exactly expecting the fish to just appear, you know." Dornalor's voice croons a little as he continues, "I wouldn't do that to my baby if we had a better option."

I open my mouth to mention his problem but decide against it. The pirate's been getting more and more attached to the *Heartbreak* and I'm wondering if that's a case of him dealing with the stress in a different manner.

"It's a big fish. I'm a small man. How the heck did you manage to find me so correctly?" I ask.

"Luck." Dornalor grins.

Ali, who has been floating around and reading notifications, sends a mental laugh rolling through my head.

I fall silent, choosing to nurse my aching body and work on separating the meat. Most of it gets discarded, kicked away since there's so much of it. The fact that the flesh is frozen solid, ice crystals showing up everywhere, is another good reason not to be eating it.

Not that we haven't stuffed our reserves full. Mikito was muttering something about sashimi, but I'm leery of the idea. Then again, eating it won't kill us.

In the meantime, I've got an aircraft-carrier-sized fish to debone.

At least I'm not Endila, who is stuck carving this all by himself. Being the only individual with the requisite Skill, he's got to solidify the magic within the Deep Angler, ensure the Mana traces and enchantments it carries naturally still hold. Even Ezz can't do that, since the sentient golem is missing the ability to tap into Skills from the System.

The plan itself is super simple. Use the bones to create an enchantment that will help hide us from the Galactic Fleet. The power of the modified Level 400+ corpse, with its ability to displace itself into a secondary dimension, gives us a potential method to sneak right past the Fleet. Combined with the numerous see-me-not enchantments already on the *Heartbreak* and Dornalor's Skills, we have a decent chance.

Or so we figure.

Of course, all of that is dependent upon us finishing the actual enchanting, and that will take a bit. The problem is that we've only got a single Runic Mechanic and we have to integrate the entire damn thing to the ship.

About the only good news, as flickers of light appear and disappear in the distance and the etheric rumble of Mana splashes all over us, is that hanging out in this dense Mana zone brings no lack of leveling opportunities. Of course, most of that is held in abeyance till we can get a proper link, but hopefully we can find one before we make the final journey.

Until then, we have to hope that nothing bigger and nastier—like a Galactic Task force—finds us before we're done.

***

An interminable time later, I'm done with my carving. Of course, after I stripped the majority of the flesh off the body, I was set on the next task—the careful cleaning of remnant bones. Amusingly enough, rather than using fire or flame, Ali had shown me a much faster and simpler method of dealing with it. I just lower the bonding energies between the remainder flesh and bones before setting the entire thing spinning. Centrifugal force sends the now detached flesh spinning off into the distance, splattering the *Heartbreak*, Harry, and Endila while creating the cleanest bones ever.

Which led to our current predicament.

"What do you want me to do again?" I say, crossing my arms, floating in the distance and staring at the kid who's busy on the corpse itself.

We're in an unusual lull in the monsters coming to eat us, allowing the main team to converge in the *Heartbreak* while the Hands deal with the swarm outside. I've had to occasionally resummon them, just because the sheer Mana expenditure of fighting off the monsters have seen them go poof, but otherwise, our line of defense—supplemented by a few mobile sentry beam weapons and even fewer mines—has held.

"Wait." Dornalor shrugs. "Nothing else you can do. Harry and I still have to finish prepping the *Heartbreak*, but if you join us, we'll just have all of us waiting instead. Go kill something like Mikito."

"You do know I enjoy doing things other than killing monsters, right?" Mikito speaks up, staring at Dornalor challengingly.

"Of course I do. You're not insane or obsessed." He points at me. "At least not as much as him. But you don't complain about getting bored. You just do it."

"You could go back to reading your library," Harry says, one elegant eyebrow rising. I absently note that he's growing a mustache, one that does pretty well for him actually. Makes him look a little dignified. I wonder if I should tell him, but then figure he might take it the wrong way.

"I could, but it's mostly downloaded. And I haven't received a Quest increase from going over the library itself."

Dornalor makes a face, but Harry's smart and used to reading between the lines. "But you have received a System Quest update."

"Yes."

"Are we going to have to force it out of you?" Harry says. "Because if I have to, I will."

"And how would you do that?"

"Pirate sea chanties," Dornalor says. "On repeat. Forever."

"I like those."

"In W'stirin."

We all wince. The W'stirin are a small but notable group of aliens. They weren't particularly successful conversions to the System, what with having originated on a small moon and only having begun to exit the Bronze Age when the System came along. The fact that they're rock-and-metal-like creatures gave them an advantage in fighting monsters that helped offset their lack of technology. Still, the majority were wiped out and they became, well, pirates. They also have taken rock-and-roll to a whole new level, their music the equivalent of a trio of avalanches having loud, kinky sex.

"That's just cruel," Harry says. "I'm thinking I'd just release the *Redeemer of the Dead Chocolate Eating Mastercut. Version II.*"

"Oooh…" Ali laughs.

"I thought we agreed—" I protest, then my brain catches up. "Wait. Version II?"

Harry gives me a wide and evil grin, making me wince. I really need to keep a closer eye on what the damn Reporter is doing with all the footage he shoots. For a moment, I spiral into thoughts of what—and why—anyone would watch such a documentary. Propaganda, of course, to reduce my reputation. But darker concerns bubble up. ASMR, fetishes, the list makes me shudder and it takes all my willpower to come back to the present.

Some places, you just don't go.

"You know, we could just ask Ali for information on the Quest." Mikito, of course, is the practical one.

Ali cackles, then before I can answer, he flicks his hand sideways. A single notification blooms, one that is part map, part graph. It's the information I had him pull and analyze because I thought I'd noticed a trend in how my System Quest kept increasing.

"You all might have something like that too," Ali says. "Mikito most likely, Harry maybe. Not sure of Dornalor, but maybe something a little similar."

"It's getting higher the closer we get to Xylargh," Harry states the obvious, and I can only shrug. "So. End game, eh?"

"Yeah." I fall silent before shaking my head, dismissing the gloom that has wrapped around us all at the import of our little quest. Of the kind of problems we will face when we get there. "Still, there's got to be something I can do rather than just hang around."

***

"Go do your job, John," I growl, flicking my hand sideways and sending a knife into the rabid tick that jumps at me. The blade catches the hard-shelled creature in its open mouth, tearing a hole through it even as I sidestep the corpse that keeps coming. Inertia's fun that way.

"You're a System Admin, Redeemer. Go do some Admining…" A dip and twist, my sword rising and bisecting another monster. The return cut kills another tick, leaving me able to plunge my blade into the body of the Thaco Checkered Queen beneath me. Lightning Strike pulses, enhanced from my Affinity, into the monster and another portion of its body dies.

"There must be hundreds of tickets to do." My blades, floating and following the track of my Soulbound sword, keep spinning, never stopping as they bisect the swarms that try to finish me off.

"Don't worry about the headaches or the brain bleeds. The System will fix it all…"

I continue to mutter to myself as I tear my sword out of the burnt body, running forward to another segment. The Queen is a multi-segmented thing, mother and birther of the flying ticks as well as their home. Openings all through its body disgorge more and more ticks, forcing us to fight through the swarms.

Behind, I feel the flash of energy expanding as my only helper, one of my Hands—desperately low on Mana—releases a Beacon of the Angels. The attack tears through an opening, lighting up the inside of the mother, but the tick's large size reduces the damage we can do to it.

"Oh, yes, baka. That's the best way to support us, get me more experience," I mutter, adjusting the pitch of my voice a little even as I'm body-checked by flying bits. More impacts as a sudden swarm of the ticks force their way through my swords and throw me off their mother.

"Enough!" Lightning Strike flares from my hand, jumping from tick to tick, sending them into shocked paroxysms. "I'm getting damn tired of this."

"Then finish it." Ali, floating beside me, has done something new, grabbing and sticking the ticks together. He's increased the attraction between their molecules such that they are unable to part themselves and is wielding the giant shield of monsters to protect one side of my body.

"Oh, yeah. John, we need your help. Make another Hand for us, will you? Kill this big, almost-impossible-to-kill monster for us, will you?" I jet back onto the body, shoving my sword deep into the body and burning fission as I jet alongside it, tearing open the wound as I go along. The arc and twist of the Queen as it moves lets my other trailing swords do even more damage, some digging all the way through her shell.

"I do have to agree with Ali. That thing's getting pretty damn close to the *Heartbreak* and we're a bit vulnerable here," Dornalor says from the cockpit.

Vulnerable or not, they left most of the weapons on the *Heartbreak* functional, including the main cannon, which he unleashes. The attack tears another chunk from the Queen. The space tick twitches, but the damn thing is the size of a small island, so we're having a hard time actually killing it.

"Fine…" I snarl and fly upward.

Not much higher before I finally get sight of the head of the creature. As much as I might be annoying it, it's focused on the Deep Angler's corpse or the *Heartbreak*. Hard to tell which when they're so close together.

"Grand Cross." I thrust my hand outward, twisting the code and placement so that the cross appears directly in front of the creature. It comes down—forward—into the Queen and crashes into it. The immovable object meets the unstoppable force, except they're both unstoppable forces. Maybe it's closer to a train hitting another train, especially the way the rest of its body crumples behind it.

I'd marvel at the destruction, but I'm fighting to stay conscious. Tapping into the Admin Ticketing System and running code fixes constantly has meant that I've had Mana flood into my body on an ongoing basis. Except the System Mana coming in is corrupted, broken, and jagged. It's like knives tearing through my body constantly, and I'm forced to take breaks.

I was just about to take one before I was dragged into this fight, which is why I've been reluctant to channel any massive amounts of Mana. But needs must.

And the damn Queen shakes itself out as my Skill runs out. It moves, unkinking itself, so I release another surge of Mana, dumping more of the excess and feeling the jagged edges of the System Mana tear out of me.

Darkness flashes and encroaches on my concentration, but I force it aside by coughing and hacking up lungfuls of blood, my body tearing itself apart. The nanite gel happily consumes the blood, using it to replicate itself and boost my healing with a low-level healing serum. I'm left floating in mid-space, healing while the last of my Skill runs out and the much more squashed Queen finally expires.

When I finally mend, I pull myself upward and tap into the armor's feeding system. Water first to clear out the taste of fried lung and blood. And then another tap and hot chocolate floods in, washing away the remnants of the taste and, most importantly, providing a little liquid comfort.

When I'm done, I finish my conversation with myself. "Yeah, John. You're a big boy, it's just a little pain."

"Go ahead and keep lying around, boy-o. We've got time. Not like the Queenie had a sister, or her being bigger. Not as if she's going to arrive in a few hours. Not at allllll…"

I groan and close my eyes. I swear, this upgrade had better be worth it.

Chapter 21

"You know, we're pretty lucky," I say, staring at the reconfigured and refurbished *Nothing's Heartbreak*. The ship has lost much of its earlier looks, the streamlined, angular, and sci-fi shape now a curved, almost boxy look with a series of bolted-on bones around the back half. The front half of the ship consists of the conical skull of the creature, with the fleshy and flexible lure now bolted onto a metal projection. The entire alteration had significantly slowed down the speed of the *Heartbreak*, but it also gives us access to the monster's dimensional projection ability and the altered runic lure.

"You mean the part where we've been allowed to finish our alterations without meeting anything but a single scout ship?" Dornalor says, floating beside me in space as we finish our last inspection. "And only that one in the last few days?" I nod and the Pirate Captain can't help but shrug. "Yeah, I would agree. I did hope that we'd have more time to clean up this mess, but I think we're better off making a move."

I have to agree. We have no idea when the scout was meant to report back, so too long a silence from the lost ship and the fleets will come looking for it. The only advantage we have is that losses among their scouts this deep in the Forbidden Zone can't be insignificant. They probably have just as many false positives to deal with and they're stretched thin now.

"It's about time," Harry says. "A lot of people think we're dead, you know. Between all the times we've been repairing, trying to sneak closer to our objective, and moving in circles, that's not too much of a surprise."

I grunt in assent. During our forced rest, Harry has been careful not to put out any additional reports that could be traced to us. The fact that he'd prescheduled a vast number of his documentation means his release schedule and experience gain has been consistent. Or at least, we assume so. He only gets an update once in a while when I manage to clear a particularly large swarm and the System stabilizes. He won't drop his next batch until we are underway.

More importantly, along with everything else, while combing through the remnants of the scout, we found a message for us. One that I have to admit angered me.

The production quality is amazing. The stage is set, the lighting perfect. They start out wide, zooming in slowly to the elevated stage at the top of the stairs where a large crowd of Irvina residents watch, looking up at the stage and the man forced to kneel on it. He's dirty and disheveled, his suit with that thin black tie skewed and bloody with dried, old blue blood. His hands are bound, those wide eyes on grey skin looking fearlessly at the crowd. He doesn't speak, just staring with burning grey eyes at the camera as it zooms in.

Behind Feh'ral stands the Emperor. He's easy to recognize, one of the Legendary members of the Galactic Council and one of the longest standing ones. An Emperor without an Empire, but still a Legendary. Some say he's the weakest of the lot, others that he's the strongest because he selfishly chose only Skills that gave him strength and left his empire to crumble. The library has a ton of information on him, including his Legendary Skills, but that's not what I'm focused on right now.

No. It's the Legacy weapon he holds, a large two-handed sword. An executioner's weapon if one were on Earth before the System. Too big, too unwieldy to use in a pre-System battle but perfect for taking off a head. The weapon glints and glimmers, and somehow, even over the recording, it reeks of bloodlust.

"You all know why we are here. Why this… man… before you is kneeling, awaiting the implementation of the judgment placed upon him. Feh'ral Vaqwe, Corrupt Questor and Head Librarian of the Corrupt Questors. A man of Legendary strength, who was so twisted in his desires that he perverted the power given to him by the System and aided others in creating the chaos that encompasses Galactic Society right now." The Emperor's voice is loud without shouting, ringing through the surroundings and into the recording with a majesty that comes not from a Skill but practice. He speaks with a surety

of conviction and belief that I find enviable, his words almost making me want to believe in him. In them. "He kneels before you today like any other criminal.*

"And like with any other criminal, he dies."

A flicker of motion, so fast it's nearly impossible to see. The camera barely records enough information for me with my enhanced Perception to note the swing, the cutting blade, the flying blood as the weapon comes back to the exact same resting spot.

"Some of you might think he deserves to speak. To make a case. You are wrong. We offer no such consideration for criminals." The Emperor keeps speaking.

Only now do the majority realize something happened. Only now does Feh'ral's head slide from his neck, the weight of the displaced skull pulling it away reluctantly. Blood pumps from a body that still thinks it's alive, and I see, I see, with my cursed enhanced Perception, the way the flesh tries to writhe forward, to stitch head and neck back together as the System fights against reality. Life, desperately struggling on.

The Emperor is speaking, but I don't hear his words. The head lands on the ground with a muffled thump, *rolls forward, and somehow, somehow, turns to face the camera. Grey eyes, angry and unresolved to death, stare into mine. Unspoken accusation reaches across time and space to imprint itself on my soul.*

I blink as blood pumps from the stump of his neck, blue blood filling the sky with warm rain. The camera stays frozen on the face before it pulls away. Pulls back as the light fades and the camera shows the Emperor walking away before the recording ends. And another face takes its post.

"Rebel John Lee. His foolish compatriots. I hope that you find this recording, that you see what happens to those who oppose the Administrators." Senior System Administrator Sephra stares back at me, that smiling face that seems to say I'm nothing more than a persistent bug that needs to be found and quashed. There's no more hiding, no more pretense that they aren't the ones behind it all. I wonder if the Emperor is an Administrator too, but the eyes that stare back at me, almost gloatingly, pull me back. "This is your fate. All of yours, so long as you oppose us."

Then darkness as the recording ends.

Yes, I'm angry. Hurt too, that Feh'ral was truly caught. That he did not manage to escape. He came because I asked. He sought an answer to a question, and he'll never have it. The injustice of it all aches within me, but there's nothing I can do. Nothing but see this through.

"Any last checks we need to do? Any last fixes?" I ask Dornalor and Endila.

The kid was the least affected by the recording, not knowing Feh'ral. And even if the accusation was directed at him as one of my foolish compatriots, he's young enough to still believe he's invincible.

"Not for me. I ran all my tests hours ago. We'll need to actually take the ship out for a dry cruise if we want to check any further," Endila says.

"I am finding minor issues still," Ezz says. "But nothing that may not be fixed enroute."

"There's nothing wrong, you're just being picky!" Endila snarls at Ezz.

"Minor misalignments reduce efficiency overall. I calculate a—"

"Enough, boys," I cut off the pair before they get arguing. Again.

"Well, I can't wait to get moving. No pirate ship should be in the docks this often," Dornalor says, shaking his head. "I swear, I can hear my baby complaining. Ever since we met you, we haven't even boarded a ship in years."

Mikito snorts, though she's been even more silent than normal since the recording. There was no sign of her fan club that we left behind, and I'm wondering how much that is weighing on her.

The Hands are keeping back the few monsters that keep rushing toward us, but I can feel them weakening, the Mana they have on hand dropping.

We take one final look at the exterior of the *Heartbreak* before I gesture, forming a Portal to put us in the ship.

Time to go.

***

It's only a little surprising that we run into the first patrol in a little less than a week. There are just over a dozen ships, a mixture of destroyers, fast attack cruisers, and a couple of scout ships. Among the many applications of the upgrades we received is an increased sensitivity to Mana. It's one of the ways the Deep Space Angler survives, since luring the wrong kind of prey is a good way of ending up dead. If not for the fact that I'm so weirdly broken, it might have fled when both Mikito and I approached.

It's why when the patrol closes in on us, we engaged the first of the many major Skills the upgrade has given the *Heartbreak*.

Skill: Dimensional Shift

A Deep Space Angler lures its prey via a projection of its body from a secondary dimensional space. Existing right next to our main dimension, the Deep Space Angler lurks, ready to pounce upon its prey and end their lives with one swift attack. This Skill is also often used as a surefire means of escape.

Effects: On activation, dimensional shift places the craft in an adjacent dimension. Minimal sensor readings will be provided of the main dimension. Additional sensor readouts from the main dimension will, in most cases, be unable to sense the craft.

Cost: One thousand two hundred fifty Mana units per minute

Duration: 107.3 minutes (With current Mana batteries and Mana engine)

Being seated in the secondary dimension is weird. As before, we're in the shadow dimension, a place of void and darkness where elementals breed and prey upon one another. There are planets, and suns of molten shadow, and masses of elementals, but we pass through it all, traveling still in the hyperstream that somehow flows through all of these dimensions at the same time. One of the side effects of wrapping ourselves in the Deep Space Angler's bones is that we seem just like the elementals, and only the most foolhardy would try their hand against the Level 400+ creature.

We fly right by the task force, the Galactic ships nothing more than little blips on our sensors, passing by with nary a sign of them finding us. It doesn't stop us from keeping the Dimensional Shift Skill running as we cross multiple hyperspace streams before we drop out, a bare fifteen minutes of energy left.

"That went better than I expected," Dornalor says, stroking his pale chin. The ridges of the top of his head are looking a little less yellow these days, a little faded from when we first met. I wonder if that's a sign of aging or stress among his people, but realistically, I'm too lazy to look it up.

"What you think?" I ask, tapping both our mechanics.

"I'm seeing leakage in about seventy locations, and about a half dozen areas where I'd like to rework the energy flows entirely. I think we should take some time and try out the other Skills as well, just in case there are interactions we're not seeing yet," Endila says.

Ezz buzzes and adds his own notes, most of which are much the same, if more detailed and precise.

"All in all, I'm pretty damn good, aren't I?" Endila says.

"Correction. We are pretty damn good, Father." A long, weighted pause after Ezz speaks.

I'm dumb, but I'm not that dumb. "You did good, kid. Both of you."

I smile a little when I hear the happy buzz from Ezz. Endila smirks a little, but I ignore them both while pulling out the map of the surrounding regions. I trace my fingers along the stream we're running, searching for an appropriate location and coming across another long abandoned Forbidden Planet. One that should still be filled with monsters.

"Let's try it out here." I rub my chin before adding, "And you're sure you can project even onto a planet?"

"Sure might be putting it a little much. I'm good, but this is pretty untested," Endila says. "At least, we will be able to deal with the creatures orbiting the planets."

Those might be a problem. One of the aspects of ever-growing Forbidden Planets is that eventually, the monsters upgrade and stop being planetary bound. It takes decades, sometimes even centuries, before they truly become spacefaring monsters, but evolution happens constantly as Mana is shoved into them. Of course, some species stay the same while others evolve and climb higher. It's what makes taking back overrun Forbidden Planets a real pain in the ass.

It is also why they make the perfect place to test out the *Heartbreak*'s new Skill.

Skill: Dimensional Projection

The Skill Dimensional Projection allows the Craft to transmit a false image and sensor readings of its location. This creates an almost impossible to differentiate projection of the Craft and allows the Deep Angler to lure its prey. In this way, the Deep Space Angler consumes much higher-Level opponents via surprise attack.

Effect: Projects a single image into real space while the Craft is in the dimensional space

Duration: Variable. (Dependent upon additional energy and Mana use). Estimated combined use at optimal running time ~27 minutes.

I'm also hoping that the planet we're headed to, a bare few hundred light years away from our eventual target, will give us access to another Administrative Center. As much as I enjoy the Ticketing System, it doesn't give me access to the time compression module. If I'm to grind out the little more experience, it's best to do it where I can optimize performance.

About the only good news there is that we managed to run across a weird spot in space—a middle-of-the-void location where an Administrative Center used to be. Used to be, because any connection to it has been destroyed by the Mana flood. Even so, the sheer fact that it used to be there meant that the connection—with my presence—gave us a brief update. Which led to all of us getting a stream of new notifications.

Level Up! You are now a Level 24 Erethran Grand Paladin.
Attributes have been assigned. You have 7 Free attributes and 0 Skill points to assign.

I know Mikito's done just as well, as I flick over to her party information. She's now a Level 4 Royal Samurai, while Harry's even managed to grab another couple of levels himself. Dornalor has shot up quite significantly as he continues to increase how much experience he gets as our Reputation plunges. He is still probably the least Leveled of the original group though, not having much ability to goose his experience increases beyond our falling Reputation.

The Forbidden Zone has been good for us all, at least in terms of experience. The only reason a lot of people don't stay in here long is the way it wears on us. If we didn't have the Extra Hands, if they weren't able to check the monsters we constantly battle, we'd probably have all burned out long ago.

Even now, long periods of constant, ongoing combat and close quarters have caused more than a few altercations. Harry has taken to spending most of his time in his room, while Endila and Dornalor have become very close. Ezz bugs me when he can, and I find myself talking about my past, about an Earth that was so much of a paradise and one that we were destroying. I can't help but think that so many of our crises—aging demographics, climate change, the rising powers in the east—were curtailed by the System. In some ways, the System was a blessing before we destroyed ourselves.

It's funny to realize I'm no longer as angry about the System's advent. Sure, billions died—and the gods know I'll carry that anger forever—but at the same time, it's also given us an opportunity, a need to reconfigure our societies. And with people like Lana, Aiden, and Roxley in play, I'm almost hopeful for Earth's future. So long as we manage to not screw up further and let the old-timey politicians and power players take over.

All that being said, I'm still going to find out what the System is.

Of course, the other reason we do so well in the Forbidden Zone is the Admin connection. Without it, we wouldn't be able to gain our experience points in large chunks before leaving the Forbidden Zone. Most others have to leave and grind in general Galactic space, where the connection to the System is much firmer. My Admin connection lets me alter that a little, giving us more experience upfront rather than having it come as we grind.

It does, however, make me wonder if the Administrators run their own little side gigs bringing along the rich, or those they favor, and getting them Leveled in this way. I've a feeling they don't, since the Questors would probably have picked up on such a jump in experience. Or at least, I would think so. Then again, the Administrators have kept the secret of their existence for tens of thousands of years. What's another one or two secrets here and there?

I push the thoughts aside, thinking back to Endila's earlier question about the Deep Angler attachment. "Yeah. Let's try it out. The least we can do is test out the projection against the monsters above."

Dornalor grunts but inputs the coordinates. One more stop, one more test, then we're ready. To really see if everything we've done is enough to get us through the blockade.

***

The screech revibrates through the aural dampeners on the Spitzrocket, making me spit. We're free-falling through the planet's atmosphere, the world a red blur as friction ignites the air around us. Mikito's doing a little better, her ghost steed and her armor somehow dampening the flames and allowing her to guide her descent. I'm less fortunate, the Spitzrocket is highly maneuverable but not meant as a reentry vehicle. Which is why my power armor brings all the monsters to the party.

Claws shred the outer layer of my Soul Shield, popping it as though it's nothing. The damn Skill doesn't give enough hit points, especially since it doesn't have the innate defensive Resistances I do. There are so many of the damn creatures that all I can see are scales, wings, and claws. Juvenile Mesosphere Wyverns crowd around me, my blades shredding claws and wings even as the armor takes a buffeting. Yet the Spitzrocket's Adaptive Armor is showing its value as their claws and elemental attacks bounce off the multi-compressed armor layers.

That gives me time to fight, but my options are a little constrained.

Judgment of All is useless, my sight blocked by the falling bodies. In the distance, I feel Ali whooping it up, releasing blasts of electricity that dance and makes a spectacular light show as solar winds and the released energies catch in the thermosphere. Mikito zips around from one snake-like neck to the next, Hitoshi lopping off heads with each swing.

I make a choice and Army of One appears, swords forming around my falling body. The razor-blade blender that is my newly formed weapons multiply damage, the conjured weapons striking and cutting even as the Skill charges. I thrust forward, sending projected energy cutting through layers of monsters, as another audible attack makes my teeth ache.

Above me, the Wyverns cluster, swooping down. In retaliation, I call forth Beacon of the Angels on top of my location. It burns scaley wings before they can escape, shielding me from my own attack while I switch direction and slam into another cluster, thin bird-like bones crunching under impact. Skin and scales sizzle as I tumble through them, even as the column of energy keeps falling till its energy is fully dissipated.

All that moving and fighting gives me a brief moment when my sight is open, and I can spot dozens more bodies. Judgment of All is wielded then, the attack stuttering under the unaspected Mana and uneven System connection. It still injures and angers, which is fine with me.

In between, I've turned on my Aura skill, letting the passive damage and buff it provides give Mikito a bit of an edge. It's funny how many of my other Skills fall by the wayside as I keep Leveling.

Down, down, down we go, fighting and tearing all the way down. I repeat my attacks a few times, switching to external weaponry as we drop lower and lower. Surprisingly, as we get closer to the planet's surface, the Levels drop too, the Wyverns choosing to let us go. It might be a biological thing, an inability to rise up again. Or it could be that there's no point, as we get swarmed by other, weirder monsters like the floating rock-bats and flying whale-like creatures.

Once we get to that level, external weapons are more than sufficient to do the killing. Beam rifle in one hand, my sword in the other, I slow down my drop too. Taking my time to study the new biosphere, taking my time to guide my no-longer-fiery outer form to the proper impact zone.

I still hit like a fiery comet, tearing up chunks of earth and alien foliage, but it's less angled and I manage to keep my feet. All in all, a good landing since my legs barely hurt too.

Stepping out of the blasted crater, I eye the few monster corpses around. Mikito rides overhead, cutting down a brace of too-brave-for-their-own-good monsters. Ali floats over, his movements entirely unnatural compared to your average flyer. Then again, his concept of motion is more like a superhero's, entirely devoid of the physical realities the rest of us deal with.

"Do you think you could have landed harder?" Ali says, eyeing the half-kilometer-long stretch of ploughed earth.

"Easily," I say. "I could have left the thrusters off entirely."

Ali snorts before he floats upward, grabbing a monster that attempts to bite him and crushing it with a twitch of his hands. It's not really gravity he's changing, but the way the molecules interact, increasing the monster's density in stages. It makes no difference to the fist-sized piece of meat he drops to the side while a map blooms from his now-free hands. The surroundings are detailed upon it, and small glowing dots fill in soon after. Those dots—all green and yellow and red—are converging on us, only a few choosing to fight one another.

"Mikito, talk to Dornalor. Let's see if the projector works here too," I say.

The Hands are with the *Heartbreak,* doing their job of keeping the ship safe from the swarming monsters. The Dimensional Projector was working well enough up there when we tried it, allowing us to hide and skip through the gap our "presence" created.

Now though, we're testing the range across planetary boundaries and differing Mana saturation amounts. As with anything in the Forbidden Zone, there's no guarantee of any results.

"Where is the Admin Center, boy-o?" Ali says, hovering above me. "Best get moving. We don't have any Titans showing up yet, but it's only a matter of time before they arrive."

I grunt, extending my senses. There has to be an Admin Center somewhere. The map we're using, the one I drew from the System, shows that one should be right about here. Yet there's no sign. No weird distortion in space, no pull on the Mana that should not be there.

"It's not here," I growl.

"You're joking. It has to be. We didn't come all the way down here for you to say there's nothing," Ali snaps. "Try again."

I nod and try, pushing with my Mana Sense and System Sense. Nothing happens. Or, well, not nothing. It's like making myself pay attention to smell and sound, to sight and hearing all at the same time. I sense it all much more, feel and taste and see better, but there's no indication of what we need.

Around me, I hear Mikito doing battle, keeping the monsters off. Ali's releasing blasts of lightning or bogging down creatures, letting them sink into the ground then hardening it again. I can't focus on them, so I don't. But no matter what I do, there's nothing to sense.

"Nope. Nada. Kaput," I say. "Looks like even here, it disappeared."

"Well, then should we leave?" Mikito says.

I almost answer yes, before an idea strikes me. "One second."

If they answer, I don't hear it. Instead, I pull on my connection with the System. It flickers, stutters, and dies. My lips curl up, and I reach outward with my will again. I pull harder than ever, and the Mana floods in. System Mana, unlike the chaotic swirling mass around me. It feeds me, and I process the Mana, giving back just as much, feeling it burn and damage and heal at the same time while it mixes with the unaspected Mana of the world, the ones that corrupt its connection.

Finally, finally, the ticketing board arrives. With it comes a flood of information and tickets that make my head ring, again and again.

Mana Overflow in Quadrant 187.1911-AD8M

Mana Overflow in Quadrant 187.1910-AD8M

Mana Overflow in Quadrant 187.1909-AD8M

...

No. Wrong information. I push it aside, shove my energy back into the flow so that I can see the board properly. I force the System to dance to my will, summarizing tickets and code. Then I dismiss the things I care not for, until I find it.

Critical Alert! System Administration Center 198-7 no longer accessible.

Critical Alert! System Administration Center 198-6 no longer accessible.

Critical Alert! System Administration Center…

I don't need to see the rest. Once I have the tickets, I dig into the information, searching for a solution, a way to solve the problem. I choose to do it here, where the likelihood of there being a solution in reach is higher than in the middle of space. I pull old code, old comments, the past histories of Administrators, looking for a way to restore a System Administrative Center, and I find nothing. No code-based solution at least.

Too much Mana destroys the connections, the places the Administrative Centers need to anchor themselves to. Broken, the Administrative Centers float free of their moorings, into dimensions I can never touch.

The only way to fix the problem is to fix the Mana overflow issue. To do that… To do that…

My brain stutters to a stop, because in theory, the solution is simple. Have enough people, kill enough monsters, churn the Mana ecosystem so that the System connection is restored.

Simple enough in theory. And yet, no one in the tens of thousands of years of Galactic history has managed that. Not for a planet that has been this lost.

"Baka! Do we leave or not?" Mikito shouts, and I sever the connection to the System.

I hack and cough, blood filming the inside of my helmet only for the nanites to clean it up. Pain carries itself within me, through me, but I force it aside to answer her. "We leave."

"Great. Where to?" Mikito says, then points her polearm just off the setting sun. "Not that way, I hope."

I follow the polearm, spotting the Titan on its way. A massive thing the size of a skyscraper on four legs, a bulbous head, and multiple lashing tentacles on each side. There's a longer, more correct term for the monster, but Titan works. Titan works for this class of creature. It's massive and glowing, red and white lights flowing along its body and its tentacles.

My stomach clenches, my heart speeds up, and adrenaline flows through me. I feel my lips widen, my teeth showing as desire runs through me. I want to fight it, want to test myself, because that's what I do. Fight monsters, kill them, and get better.

But…

"No. We go up." I point back the way we came, the monsters that are beginning to close in.

We could fight the approaching Titan, but it's not our objective. Our goal was the Administrative Center and there isn't one. As such, it's time for us to go.

Who said I can't learn?

"All right. Dornalor says he can give us seven minutes with the Projection," Mikito says. "Best make it count."

I nod, feeling the Spitzrocket tighten around me. I tilt my head upward, thrusters firing as I head for the sky, Mana Engine working overtime to give me the thrust needed. A second later, even as I rise, another me reappears on the ground. Images of Mikito and me, the pair of us standing still. Waiting for the Titan, ready to fight.

While the true us fly away to our real destinies.

Chapter 22

Progress now that we're certain of our destination and method of entry is steadier and faster. Rather than slip through the intergalactic equivalent of side streets and back alleys, we swan through the fastest and most powerful intergalactic supernatural highways. Even if we're moving at sixty percent of our normal cruising speed, without the circuitous routes and the need to hide, we're making much better time.

The occasional patrol is noticed much earlier, the combined sensors and Skills on the *Heartbreak* allowing us to fade into the adjoining hyperspace dimensional route and fly past them with nary a ripple. The first few times, we're tenser than a fifteen-year-old before his first kiss, but by the point we get nearly to Xylargh, we barely stir from our positions when the alarm sounds.

As for the numerous dimensional mines and fixed position turrets that dot the hyperspace streams? Those are avoided in the same way. Rather than finagling through the code or attempting to hack a clearance visa, we just fly through the fields in another dimension where the mines are not present.

There's a little danger, of course, in what we do. The void dimension we fly through is filled with monsters. Some of the dumber monsters test our defenses rather than ignore us, putting the Hands and Mikito to the test. The shields and the *Heartbreak*'s weapons are almost always deployed, their automated attacks keeping our engines running. Unfortunately, most of the point defenses are covered by the new bones, so coverage is pretty spotty.

Watching our slow-creeping dot approach our destination on the map, Dornalor breaks the companionable silence of the cockpit. "Why aren't you out there?"

"No reason to."

"Before, you were always the first to be out there to fight. To kill… what changed?"

I pause, considering his words. Consider my own change in behavior. It takes a few seconds to probe my emotions, my muted anger at the System. I'm still angry, even if that anger is hidden in the weeds of worry and concern, in contained excitement. However…

"I guess I don't see the point anymore," I say. "The Hands give me experience. Mikito needs more direct experience than I do. And the monsters, they were always just a replacement."

"For the Council?"

"For the System," I say, my lips tugging sideways. "I might dislike the Council, but they're just the closest targets. Even without them, the System would expand."

"Even without the Administrators?" Dornalor asks, cocking his head.

I stare at the pot-headed Pirate, note how he's a little off-color at the top. He straightens a little at my regard, suddenly self-conscious.

"Even without the Administrators. We make the churn; the System work better. But I have a feeling without us, it'd probably create and designate a bunch of AIs to do the work." I consider the idea, wondering if the Root Administrator is really just a powerful AI. The Council doesn't like AIs in general and restricts them via the System. They control how AIs can manifest, how they're contained. It makes it easier to destroy them if the AIs get too uppity. Then, like every other unsupported hypothesis, I file it away for future testing. "We're not necessary for the System to work. We just make it work better by letting the System use less Mana. And all that to slow down the Forbidden Zone from expanding. Reduce waste, if you will."

"So, what? You're nearly done, so you aren't as willing to risk your life? Just ours?" Dornalor says challengingly.

"Harry, is that you?" I say, getting a puzzled look from Dornalor. Rather than explain my sense of humor—or lack of it—I answer his accusation instead. "Yes to the first. No to the second. At least, no more than I have to."

"And that's the rub, isn't it? It's what you have to do. Because you have to finish this Quest."

"You could have chosen not to come pick us up."

"I could have, but I'd be running anyway. This way…" Dornalor sighs. "This way, I could at least strike back a bit. I just didn't realize when you wanted to piss off the Council, you meant to piss off the entire universe too."

I chuckle a little, and Dornalor offers me a shrug. That's the thing about life. Everyone thinks their choices and actions are perfectly logical most of the time. When in truth, we're driven by short-sighted self-interest, by emotions and desires and needs we can barely articulate. We're more likely to reason our way around the choices we've made already, to justify our purchase of the latest GPU card or asking out the hot but mean boy, than to think about the consequences beforehand.

"So what happens when we drop you off?" Dornalor says after a while, waving at the plot. "If we manage to make it, manage to land. What happens after? To me and the *Heartbreak*?"

I tilt my head, side-eyeing Dornalor. "I figured you'd pull out, hide somewhere safe in-system until we're done. Maybe on-planet. I'm sure there's got to be a spot where we can park the ship."

"Park, certainly. But it's a Forbidden Zone planet, and even if the local Mana density is lowered…" Dornalor shakes his head. "There aren't many places that aren't watched or patrolled."

"Oh…" I frown. "Suggestions?"

"Two options." Dornalor gestures and the plot updates. It's a very tightly timed run of us passing through the barricades and defensive measures and entering Xylargh's protected space. For landing, he's just having us use a crash pod rather than actually landing on the planet, giving the *Heartbreak* the opportunity to escape before the Dimensional Shift ends. "That one is the fallback."

"Fallback from?"

"Asking for asylum." A gesture and the plot updates to a much simpler plot where we land in the middle of a large planet.

"Right… because the Dragon Lords are an independent power with only minimal connection to the Council."

That's what you get when you have a planet of over-powered idiots running around with even more over-powered companions, all of whom are guarding the very deepest Forbidden Zone planet.

It's bothered me how much leeway is given to Xylargh, but as an Administrator—and with the Administrative Center being where it is—I've been able to dig up some answers. The sheer volume of Mana they churn through, and the way they churn it, makes them sort of like the Dutch boy with his finger in the dike. There's still a leak, but they're a big enough plug that pulling them out could be disastrous.

Add the fact that the Dragon would be a tad upset if someone tried to destroy his home planet and you've got a good recipe for why the entire place is rife with xenophobic, arrogant blowhards.

"Exactly. And Bolo should be willing to help us out," Dornalor says.

I snort. "If he can. If whatever it was he was up to is dealt with…"

"He'll be fine. And he'll be able to help," Dornalor says. "If nothing else, his—"

"His?" I prod.

Dornalor shakes his head. "Not my place."

I run a hand through my hair, making a face as I realize it's grown too long again. All our technology and there's still nothing that fixes hair that keeps growing when you don't want it to or nails that go from fine, fine, fine to shark attack!

"Whatever. So asking for asylum is plan A," I say. There's something about the way Dornalor speaks, the lack of other plans around us just sneaking our way through. It's a little unusual, though I'll admit, we've gotten so used to running that we have a preset playbook for most scenarios. I consider pushing him on other plans, but another thought strikes me. "What happens when we need to leave?"

Dornalor shrugs and I make a face.

"Seriously?"

"What do you want me to say? You don't even know how long it'll take for you all to do whatever you need to do. It might be a week; it might be a few months. In a war, that's going to change fast," he says.

"Fine. But you'll start planning?" I push him. "As you said, we'll be busy."

"Of course." There's reluctance in his voice, a hint of intransigence.

I sort of understand, since sometimes it feels as if we're riding into the sunset, slumped on a horse. With the forces arrayed against us, it's a miracle we've made it this far.

"Good man." I pause, considering. "You know, I haven't really said thank you."

"No, you haven't."

"We would have had a hard time getting off Irvina without you. Harder time surviving out here." I cock my head and eye his Levels. "And while it might have helped you, I know what you've given up. When…"

"When?" he prompts me.

"When it comes down to it, let me know what I can do, will you?" I open my hands wide. "I've not got much, but what I can…"

"Don't worry. I'll make sure to take you for all you're worth." Dornalor grins. Then, eyes twinkling, he adds, "Anyway, the kind of Reputation you've given me, I doubt I'll ever need to buy myself a drink again. In the right places, at least."

I chuckle, remembering the Pirate Captain for what he is. Sometimes, no matter how much you want to change, the world doesn't let you.

***

"Time," Dornalor whispers, his voice coming through the communicators for all of us to hear. Even the Hands, since we need them tied in. Good thing we picked up a ton of simple earbud communicators.

The Hands are waiting outside, protected by short-term suits and Soul Shields. I only have the barest idea of where they are from Society's Web since we're running dark. The Web we've found to be particularly useful though, sometimes catching scouts that other sensing methods have missed.

In the dark dimension, shifted out from the normal hyperstream, we're still coasting in toward Xylargh, as tuned down as possible. We keep everything—our Mana use, our power discharges—to the minimum. We do that because there's no telling what sensors our enemies have.

All around us in the other side of the hyperspace stream and in the physical world, the Galactic Forbidden Zone Interdiction Fleet are waiting. Layers upon layers of firepower, starting with simple recharging mines and turrets at the edge of the hyperspace stream to Dimensional Stabilizers right outside where the stream thins and crafts disgorge themselves. Two rings of battle stations. The first is a series of heavy, multi-layered combat stations to deal with the occasional Behemoth or Titan or Leviathan that pops through. The second is a mixture of customs and logistics and backup combat stations. And behind them all, situated high above the sphere, is the Fleet itself, with multiple smaller task forces and patrols roaming about.

For all that, this space seems peaceful. Just across the dimensional threshold, I know that weapons are firing, space fighter and beam turrets tearing through the ranked hordes of monsters that disgorge themselves from the stream, that birth themselves from elemental energies and reconstituted, mutated parts. They swarm the planet and the ships in a never-ending frenzy, desperate to tear apart the light of System Mana, to feast upon the weak.

In the solar system itself, I know that the dragons and their riders patrol, the mutated space dragons and drakes, the wyvern riders and Dragon Knights all seeking battle and cleansing their home system. The far reaches of space are protected by the Galactic Fleet, but a constant drizzle of monsters escape through their net or are birthed in-system to face the Dragon Knights.

Even through this insanity of violence and gore, merchant vessels and tourist yachts arrive, porting in in a never-ending stream, lured by the promise of high-Level loot and experience. They come in on any one of the four hyperspace streams, and if fewer leave than arrive, that's just business in a System world.

We wait, as we cross through all this in another dimension, and if there are probes and sensors that reach across all this space, they don't make a fuss. To these sensors and Skills, we're nothing more than another monster, one trapped across the dimensional barrier and no more concerning than any other.

"Entering Dimensional Stabilization envelope…"

Dornalor's voice cuts through the silence, the hiss of our breaths as we wait to see if Endila is right. If the void dimension we are in is different enough, shaded enough that the effects of the stabilization envelope are muted here. The Dimensional Stabilization anchors they use are nasty, meant to stop shadows from tearing through dimensions, meant to protect against surprise attacks. And since we're technically originating from the main dimension, they're potentially dangerous for us since they might tear us out, revealing us fully.

We tense, waiting to see if the game is up the moment we arrive.

The tickle of my breath along the edges of my nostrils rises up around my face, the slow exhalations striking the underside of my helmet and reflecting back. We're all geared for combat, ready for things to go sideways at the slightest hint. I'm chewing on one last bar of caramel chocolate goodness, the taste warm and unpleasant by now, but still attempting to make it last while we wait.

"Seeing minor stresses on the runic engine and hyperspace drive. Minor distortion in our envelope and a seventeen-percent increase in power draw…" Ezz speaks, oblivious to the tension the rest of us feel. The robot is down at the engines, working alongside Endila. "Adjusting for dimensional vibrations… done. Draw down to fourteen-point-three percent. I will continue to make further adjustments."

"It'll do," Dornalor says. "We're five minutes in. Passing first line of defense. Refractory and chaos mines are now behind us."

Breathe. I crack my neck, doing the best I can to relax. Time flows on, agonizingly slow. I return to my meditative practices, breathing in and out in regular cadence. In and count for fifteen. Out and count for thirty. In. Count.

Out. Count.

Over and over, till my mind is just filled with the slow breaths, punctuated only by Dornalor's updates and Endila's muttered curses. Ezz releases a series of little hums, minor updates as runes are reshaped or added, while Endila uses his Skills to balance our Mana flows and the way we interact with the dimensions. It's a constant battle as we pass from Skill to Domain to Skill, each alteration requiring minor updates.

In. And out.

I sense the slow thrum of constrained adrenaline, the buzz of energy. It amuses me the way the System refuses to allow me to control my own body directly, the way it still allows that slight jitter, that constant beat of fear through me. It's muted, so muted, but it's there. Then again, maybe I shouldn't be surprised. After all, the physical body is a fine-tuned machine brought about through millions of years of evolution. Or close enough for government purposes anyway.

Maybe the System holds off because it has better things to do than patch me together when I keep screwing up on how I adjust my body. It certainly is less than amused by my hacking of Skills as it stands.

As I ponder the changes that the System offers to me and how it might be different for less organic species, the library awakens. Data floods from it, demanding my attention. I fight it, of course, riding the flow of information, attempting to control the deluge that threatens to overwhelm me. Studies, experiments, scholarly articles, and research papers. More information than any person ever needs about why and how the System affects the biology of sapient creatures.

All of it spiraling through me at this most inopportune of moments. Time passes—seconds, minutes, hours perhaps. I breathe hard, coming to myself ever so slowly as I close the door to my own mind, the throb of System energy that comes with every library download. The flow is stronger here, more powerful, better connected. Once the library showed the way, the rest of the messages arrive.

Notifications that have been held at abeyance return, and I'm lost in the flow of System Mana. Tickets pop up and are discarded, requests for aid and for code to be adjusted. I receive it all and battle to control the flow while we creep deeper.

Ever deeper.

Until, when I open my eyes, things go awry. Everything that we had planned goes to hell.

As expected.

***

"What the hell happened?" I snarl, watching as energy beams slam into the *Heartbreak* and devour its shield. It takes all of a half dozen heartbeats before the powerful shields are gone, ripped away as we're dragged back into normal reality.

"I don't know!" Dornalor snaps, his fingers dancing over the controls.

He triggers the Dimensional Projection and Shift at the same time, blipping us into the void again and pulling a projection of the ship into normal space. The transfer across dimensions peels away our senses and Mana, pouring electricity directly into our nerves. The rejection back into normal reality, which happens nearly as fast as our initial disappearance, repeats the process, leaving us reeling in pain.

The *Heartbreak*'s automatic dodging routine keeps it moving even as we physically recover, the projection copying the motion as attacks land on it. Surprisingly, they seem to be targeting the ship's engines and thrusters. Launch pods of all kinds swoop toward the craft and its projection even as damage increases. I hear Endila swearing as he attempts to circumvent around newly damaged portions while Ezz focuses on the engines and the damage we did by blipping back and forth. The wireframe of the ship lights up as the continual ring of impacting attacks resound.

"Hands, get out there. Three of you. Buy us time," I say, making a snap decision. "Ezz, hold for a few minutes, then get out. They're hammering the engines. If you stay in there too long, you're dead."

"Yes, Father."

In the map of the solar system, information updates easily now that we're in the real world. We've passed the second battle station ring, nearly having managed to escape into the next line of defense. The entire thing is spotty, filled with patrols and guns. We're still millions of kilometers away from the planet, but at the speed we're moving, it's just a few hours. It might as well be a few days for all that it matters right now.

Hatches open, the Hands jumping out. Shields flare, Skills kick into play as they go into battle. It's a sure sign of which is the real ship, and fire focuses on us. Dornalor turns off the projection to conserve power, the *Heartbreak* zigzagging and soaring through the attacks. Tractor beams try to grab hold of us, slowing webs pile onto the ship, and our speed drops with each second as engines take damage and momentum is bled from us. I'm beginning to realize why they aren't going for the kill.

"Ideas, people!" Dornalor is nearly shouting, eyes wide.

"Can we… hide?" Harry says, biting his lip. "Call for help?"

"Aren't we doing that already?"

"Yeah…"

Still, Harry's words spark an idea. I touch Harry's Just a Bystander Skill and tap into it with Forced Link, then dive into the Skill with System Edit. I pull at the code, attempting to expand its abilities, to push the attacks away.

Fire falters as the Skill takes effect. Some of it shifts a few degrees, making on-target attacks miss by miles. Other automated firing sequences stop. My Edits give us a few seconds of peace. Even the webbing and slowing Skills fall away as the *Heartbreak* speeds up again.

"Outer shell at seventy-percent damage," Dornalor reports. "We can't stay here, not anymore."

Before I can answer, the weapons firing upon us compensate for Harry's Skill. It's only an Advanced Class Skill, and even pushed as far as I can, my body burning with fire, it's easy to counter. Notifications scroll through a corner of my eye, telling their story. Target Lock. Mental Resolve. Faerie Fire. I Remember You, Buddy. More.

Targeting locks find us again, and a swarm of tractor beams hit us at the same time, pulling the ship down to a fraction of its original speed. Ezz lets out a warbling shriek as it loses grip on the floor and is tossed around. I'm pressed against my crash straps.

That's when the launch pods, accelerating toward us, finally land. They cut into or hack apart the hull, attempting to gain entry. We have less than seconds left before they breach. The only good news is with the boarders so close by, the guns have stopped.

"Mikito, get on the boarders. You too, Hand." I twist my hand to the side, dropping the Skill link with Harry.

I shudder, but there's a touch to the Mana, the way it shifted under my hands, my will just before the fire opened up on us that felt familiar. I search my notifications and find the one discussing our dimensional shunting.

I knew it. The same taste, the same oily feeling in the code. I pull up the ticket, my mind running faster than ever as I drag down more Mana, speeding up my ability to understand, to assess. The notification I'm looking for is there, the way the System rebelled against the touch.

Dimensional Shift Enacted

Dimensional Barrier Strengthened due to code shift on lines 1SA8-91231-MDMS-198231…

Ticket created due to conflict in code change by Medium Administrator Tully

Code alterations sequenced, dimensional barrier strengthening accepted (temporarily)…

System Mana use increased by 471% in locations…

Additional tickets created due to Mana Loss…

There.

"John!"

"Dimensional Shift on my count!" I snap. It's not enough to escape entirely, but I've got a solution for that. One I picked up a long time ago. "Ali. Conjure a Hand, give him our going-away present and the Hod. He needs to be out there."

Thankfully, the Spirit doesn't argue but taps into my Skill and Mana. He pulls on it even as I focus somewhere else, splicing my Skills to another area. The Galactic Fleet strengthened the barrier between us, made it harder to stay within the void, rejected us from the secondary dimension. Fair enough… I splice Penetration into the *Heartbreak*'s Dimensional Shift. I borrow Ali's view for a second and trigger Judgment of All through him, the Penetration Shield appearing around *Heartbreak*. As I do so, I also see the Hand forming before me and the package that Ali hands off, along with my boots and a simple EVA suit.

Seconds later, the Hand is jetting off, headed for the center of the lines. "The ship won't hold!" Endila screams.

I hear the pop and hiss of machines shorting, the whine of discordant instruments. The Penetration shield is holding, but the boarders are still doing damage. Boarding shuttles bounce off the shield hard. Others shatter as renewed attacks tear into ships, individuals, missiles. I'm burning up as the excess Mana from System coding tears me open on the inside. The first few Hands that threw themselves out there to delay are gone, while the one within is doing his best against the swarms of boarders.

"It has to. In three!" I reply on my hands and knees, bent over and barely holding the spliced Skill together. It's impossible. There's too much damage, too many attacks coming in, the Mana within me too jagged, too harsh. "Shifting… NOW!"

The ship jumps into the void dimension, tearing through the new barrier like a hot sword through paper walls. We set off a chain reaction along the way, the barrier a gaping hole left in its place. Void elementals pour out, a consequence of our escape.

More fire as the Galactic fleet attacks the creatures that should not exist in our reality. Boarding shuttles and crash pods are torn into, their passengers locked in desperate battle. The System attempts to compensate for the damage, tries to patch the hole, but I'm there in the midst of it. I fight a battle between the System, between the Administrator—no, Administrators—who come to deal with the sudden slew of tickets and find me.

Code changes, as swift as thought. The System attempts to fix the gaping hole in reality, using excess Mana to weave a patch. I clean up a ticket, reducing the Mana waste in the original dimensional lock. It's exactly the wrong thing to do right now, since the System needs the Mana. I still get the experience, though it is discounted. More importantly, the sudden shift tears open the hole again, the void flooding through as elementals tear at the edges of reality.

Administrators pull at my Linked Skill. Another tears at the Evolved Shield protecting the *Heartbreak*. I let them, knowing Penetration is not required. I feel the edges of other Skills attempting to reassert normalcy around us, the work of non-Administrators. I use those, pitting Skills against one another, linking them together or in opposition. The dimensional barrier strains.

My control slips as the pain rises in a never-ending crescendo. I lose control of the various Skills, the wound in the world patching itself as System Mana reasserts itself. The wound closes, but slowly. I struggle through the pain, searching for another way around the System. Administrators attack me directly, flooding my link to the System, diverting some of the energy meant to fix the problem.

Blood and ash, fried cantaloupes and bread fill my senses. I can't see anymore as my body burns up from inside, my eyes burnt husks.

Then a shift, a falter in their side. The explosion when the PoenJoe Goleminised-Mana Generator Mark 18 goes off in the middle of the hyperspace stream is enough to throw everything out of whack. I feel one of the Administrators disappear entirely from the stream, even as I wrestle back control of my own mind.

The System grows fed up with our actions. Just as suddenly as it started, all our connections are cut, our Administrator privileges revoked for the moment. Excess Mana still floods through me, even as some of that Mana is twisted to help my body heal.

Even so, it burns. I'm overloaded, my Mana channels on fire.

I can't see, so I borrow Ali's view. Judgment of All, Grand Cross, Beacon of the Angels, Extra Hands. Each Skill used causes even more pain as I flex a connection that has been forcibly restricted. There's still too much Mana, more Mana than my body can handle.

I spit and cough, blood pooling around my lips and under my helmet. More Skills, more spells. It's only when the pain lessens that my control loosens, that I find darkness claiming me. Mental defenses, stretched to the maximum, push me to oblivion so that they can wipe away the memories of what has happened.

I rage, but the darkness still claims me.

It always wins after all.

Chapter 23

I wake after ten minutes. Not long enough, but sadly, all the time I have to rest. It's enough to allow the System to restore my physical body from the brink of destruction. Mostly. My sense of smell is off, and the taste of licorice on my tongue refuses to go away, no matter how I spit. But I can see, and I can move. The rest of the rivulets of lava that bathe my body, I know they're just in my head. As real as any pain, but manageable till the System gets around to wiping it.

In the meantime, we've been running in the void dimension. Ezz is busy fixing the engines, Endila rebuilding runes destroyed when the ship was burnt apart, and the Hand I have left is hunting down the last of the raiders. Ali's busy popping through walls and harassing the few that are alive, helping to stop them from sabotaging the ship while guiding Mikito to finish them off.

Dornalor and Harry had a few hectic moments themselves when an Assassin popped into the cockpit, nearly beheading the Pirate Captain. If not for his Master Class Skill—Mutineer's Folly—Dornalor would have died, but on his ship, in his place of power, the Captain rules the roost. Even gravely injured by the Skill feedback, the Assassin pushed the pair to the brink as I lay insensate in the copilot's chair.

Awake, I check for problems and review the footage of what happened before I yank a Hand into reality to be sent to help Mikito. That done, I stretch and stand, looking around. Harry's in the corner, mopping up the last of the blood and replacing a burnt-out console, while Dornalor stares into space, reading his notifications. I follow suit and tap into the *Heartbreak's* sensors.

"How much longer?" I say, sweeping my gaze over the plot.

The gaping hole in reality is gone, the damage we've wrought fixed. The elementals, no longer focused on the shining bright light of physical space, are hunting us now, the damage done to the bones leaving us leaking and brilliant. Thankfully, only a few at a time follow us, for there is much brighter prey.

The Galactic Fleet has followed us, a few at a time as they breach the unsteady dimensional barrier. They are swarmed by the elementals, but they're doing a great job at destroying them. That only means they get swarmed more, so while they have a rough idea of where we are, it's hard for them to use their full Skills and sensors while being swarmed. Not to mention the fact that the void dimension isn't particularly forgiving to non-elemental sensors.

"Till we get caught or that we can stay here?" Dornalor says, lips twisted up wryly. "I'd say a few hours at least for the first. And just about the same for the second."

"How long to reach the planet?"

"At our current speed? Six hours."

"And how much longer can we stay in the void?" I ask.

"Another three hours at most," Dornalor says. "The closer we get to the sun, the more the connection between our dimension and the void frays and the harder the dimensional wall. The void dimension is deepest, closest to us when there is no light. And after our little incident, we can't use my Skill to cut a way through the dimensional walls. Never mind what such a rough transition would do to our ship."

"So we're short," I say, closing my eyes in exhaustion. "After all that…"

"We did better than I expected." Dornalor shrugs. "Endila's doing his best, but we took quite a lot of damage from the damn raiders when they got in. Ezz has the engines running, but they used a number of backfire Skills on that too, so we're nowhere as fast as we could be. Thankfully, we're built for damage, so we can reroute when we need to but…"

"But there's only so much that can be done." I nod, glancing at the wireframe of the ship. There aren't many remaining dots, and those I see are in combat with Mikito and the Hands. We'll be clear soon enough. Even if…

"What are our other options?"

"We could try one of the dragon outposts." Dornalor points at a space station hanging just off to the side of the plane, anchored to a moon of another planet. It's not directly between us and Xylargh on the solar map, but in the same general direction. One of the reasons why we came in via this hyperspace steam and not another. "Or we can try for the planet itself and go with Endila's plan. You know he planned for this, what with the void diminishing."

"I don't know if the boy's a genius or insane," I say.

Ali, floating down from the top of the ship where he's been battling and baiting the elementals, chimes in. "That's why you like him, eh?"

"Funny. But I kinda do," I say.

"Don't let your 'son' hear that. He might get upset," Ali teases.

I roll my eyes and change the subject. "What do you have against the void elementals anyway? Every time you get a chance, you go blast them."

"It's a spirit thing. You can feel it too. The way they're kind of opposed to our affinity." I nod, knowing what he means. It's like a whine at the edge of my hearing when we're here, an annoyance that can be ignored but is frustrating. "It's worse for me."

"You didn't say," I point out.

"Would whining help? I'm not like you, boy-o. I keep my feelings to myself and don't splatter them on those around."

"Is that a dig at me being violent or at me crying?" I say, cocking my head. No anger at his mentions, since well, he's not wrong.

Ali grins in reply while Dornalor clears his throat.

Harry, listening to us and wringing his hands, speaks up. "If we do the station, we can make it, right? Then we can get help... or maybe get lost?"

"We could also be trapped and hunted down," I say. "No guarantees we could find any Dragon Lords willing to help us. Not on a single station."

Dornalor nods. "My preference is the second option, as it always has been. The stations probably aren't equipped to do anything, while we might be able to make a run for it. If the kid's right, that is." He frowns. "Assuming the Administrators don't change the rules further."

"We're safe from that for now." I rub my eyes, remembering the pain, the way it ate into me. The sudden slamming of the access lines that the System enforced on us all. It reminds me that I have notifications to read, which I call up and sort through. "Yeah... thought so."

It only hurts a little to show the notification I received when the System smacked us all down.

Alert! All System Administrator Privileges Revoked in Sector 003

"Why?" Harry asks, frowning.

"Why what?" Mikito's voice comes over the party chat, cutting in.

"You done?" I say, surprised.

"Obviously. Now, why what?"

Rather than strain myself, I inform her of the notification. After that, there are more questions, so I tell them what happened when we breached the dimensional barrier. I keep it short, not bothering to explain the metaphysical struggles that went on.

Of course, Ali simplifies my explanation even further. "So, you pissed off the System. Only you..."

"Sounds about right…" Harry mutters. For all the wryness in his voice, he looks worried.

Dornalor smirks a little, while there's silence from Mikito's end. Endila is muted, since the kid has a mouth on him and is busy working. Ezz knows better than to say anything, or perhaps it's just shy. Sometimes, it's hard to tell with the sentient golem where AI programming and actual thought begins. If there is any…

I shrug, feeling a little embarrassed. Instead of facing it, I keep poking at my notifications, looking for further information. More experience, more notifications, then, of course, what I've been dreading.

Medium System Administrator Lee has been censured by the System and System Edit authority removed. Further penalties await confirmation by Senior Administrators.

"Froze wastes and a thousand hells…" I whisper. My only advantage, our only advantage, was my System Edit. Learning to use it at the right time has kept us alive, for the most part. This…

"John?"

"Boy-o?"

I ignore them, my heart thudding painfully. What was nearly impossible just became fully so. And I'm not sure what to say or how to say it.

"Eh, baka?"

Still, the dots in my vision, the indication that there's more to be seen drive me on. As I hope for divine intervention. Or the closest thing, in my case.

Penalties for Middle System Administrator John Lee Assessing

!Error! ~ Root Administrator Override ~ !Error!

Request for penalty evaluation sent to Root Administrator

Penalty Evaluations Reviewed.

Penalties Applied.

Another notification, following along this in a different format. I make a face, but I can take the loss of all System experience gained from our little tussle. It's a small enough penalty, to keep my Skills. I can't even imagine the kind of penalties the other Administrators received.

Middle System Administrator John Lee has all Administrative Skills Restored

Please be careful, Redeemer of the Dead

"Goblin shit." I slump back in my chair at the notice and use of my Title.

That Title has always bothered me. It's an unusual one, an extremely pointed Title. Not to say it's exceptional in being exclusive. Unusual Titles are something the library is more than happy to point out are uncommon but not unique. Unique, unusual Titles are often given to individuals who are exceptional, or it might be a case that exceptional individuals gain unique Titles.

In either case, it's partly why so many choose that Title over others when greeting me. Redeemer of the Dead is unique, important in ways that any System-connected entity understands on an instinctive level. It's not uncommon enough to put a target on me but…

It's unusual still. Especially to see it in my notifications, when it's never shown up before. Is this a message from the Root Administrator? Has he, she, it been watching me since the beginning? Or is this just courtesy? I don't know, and my team is getting insistent in their requests for clarification.

I set this mystery aside for now, just as I do so many others.

This is not the time.

"Sorry. I was blocked out for a bit from my System Administrator Skills. But it's back. For now, at least, though I think I shouldn't try anything too ambitious." I stretch a little, feeling the reminder of pain running through my body and add, "If I could even do anything major…"

Harry purses his lips, but nods.

Dornalor gestures back to the map. "So, your thoughts?"

"If the Captain is asking, I'd say let's run for it." I shrug. "Maybe Endila is right. And if not, at least we'll be closer. Maybe I could open a Portal…"

It's a fool's dream to think we could Portal our way in. Even the Erethran specialist with their evolved Skills would face trouble here. Between the overflow of unaspected Mana in direct conflict with the huge amount of System Mana being churned, long-range Skills are all problematic.

As for the void dimension, it grows shallow, less powerful the closer we get to the blazing sun and sentient life. By the time we near Xylargh, punching through—even if we could stay in it—would be impossible. We have to transition.

"Then let us run," Dornalor says. He spins away, tapping at his consoles and dismissing me.

I hesitate before pushing myself to my feet, wincing as my body tries to shed the memory of pain. Harry glances at me once, then looks away.

"I'll be in the galley for a bit."

The pair ignore my pronouncement and I walk off, Ali choosing to blip upward to burn a few more Elementals. If their lack of acknowledgement is a little lonely, a little off-putting, I don't let it show.

We're all under stress.

***

Hours pass in slow motion it seems, until we're ready to break into reality again. The fleet behind us has taken quite the beating, and they have stopped sending others in after us. We've managed to hide in the shadows, the fleet's sensors failing in the weird shadow dimension, but they're spread out enough that they'll catch us eventually. The simple fact that we have to go to Xylargh means our options shrink as we get closer.

By this point, I've recovered a bit, the same way you could say a new marathon runner is recovered the day after, though there's no way in the thousand hells I'm going to mess with the dimensional walls again.

Instead, we put our new plan into play. We start by slipping back into reality and watching as multiple patrols change course and head for us. Dimensional Projection comes into play, splitting their attention. The projection—along with some basic matter pods and a Hand to give the entire projection some semblance of reality—heads straight for the nearby space station. In the meantime, we keep burning fuel and heading for the planet.

Soon, the fleet paints our ship with active sensors, doing their best to tell which is the projection and which isn't. Mixed in with the sensing is a series of long-range attacks, but those do little good. The problem with using lasers and the like over solar system distances is that light attacks diffuse themselves the farther they travel. Eventually, even the tightest beam fades out.

We're still lucky that all they've done to us is try to stop the ship. If they had wanted to destroy the *Heartbreak* from the beginning, this battle would have been over already. We're lucky that all they chose to do was strip our shields and send raiders. Which reminds me…

"Anyone know why they didn't just blow us up?" I say, breaking the silence.

"They did," Dornalor says, shaking his head. "I think you're not understanding exactly how hard they tried. They just didn't realize how tough my girl is."

I snort. "Come on. They've got a Heroic Class"—I look at Ali, who gives a nod—"Admiral here. Between the kind of Skills he can call into play and the sheer volume of firepower emplaced, if they really wanted us dead, they could have just turned it all on us."

"Only Heroic?" Harry says.

"There's a Legendary Deep Fleet Admiral around, but he isn't in the system. Probably dealing with another problem." Ali shrugs. "Anyway, three out of the four Admirals running the hyperstream blockades are Blockade or Forbidden Zone Heroic Classes. Their Skills are much more appropriate for sieges than the Legendarys."

While Harry takes in what Ali says, Dornalor is glaring at me. "You saying the *Heartbreak* couldn't have survived that? You do know she did, right?"

"They were only using, like, half their firepower at most—" I say.

"Three-tenths," Ali corrects.

"And we barely made it out. And sure, we came in while they had to deal with the deluge from the hyperspace streams, but still, they weren't trying. If they had chosen to let the monsters go, even for a minute, they could have destroyed us. That's all I'm saying."

"Then what? You have another reason why they didn't kill us?" Dornalor says.

I shrug. "Only thought I have is arrogance."

"Or PR," Harry supplies. When we look at him, he offers a weak grin. "Killing Feh'ral wasn't the example they had hoped to make."

"Made him a martyr, did they?" Ali says.

"Yes. Also, it also drove some of the fence-sitting Questors over the line." Harry rubs his palm, his voice growing more confident as he speaks. "They released a lot of information about the kind of Classes, Skills, and ships the Council's lapdogs have been using. Along with that, a lot of closely held requirements for Prestige Classes that the Council and its allies were using stopped being secret.

"Then there's the abrupt turns in some planetary governments, minor rebellions and mutinies and even some internal sabotage. The Shadow Council has been trying to keep it all quiet, but they're losing the information war by a significant degree. They might be Administrators, but Classes seem to trump that."

"Not exactly," I mutter, recalling my own Skill. "But we're not geared for large-scale hacks. We're meant to keep things running, not code exceptions that benefit us. If we go too far…" I swipe at my nose, a remembrance of pain flickering and dying.

Ali grins at Harry. "They angered the librarians. Woe to those who cross the keepers of the arc of knowledge."

"Arc?" Harry says.

"Lightning arc."

"Right…" Harry snorts.

Dornalor crosses his arms, muttering under his breath, "The *Heartbreak* could have survived."

"Let it go, man." I rub my chin, thinking about what Harry said initially. "So what? They want to capture and kill me then?"

"More likely capture and make you recant."

"Torture and all that fun?" I make a face but can see it. Sure, not everyone will believe it if I recant. In fact, a large percentage won't. But the Council only needs a small percentage to switch sides and, more importantly, reinforce that they're the good guys for it to work. Repeat a lie often enough and some people will come to believe that lie is truth. "Still, that's quite the risk."

"Really? If you hadn't done whatever you did, would we have escaped?" Harry points at the screen as we keep burning fuel, running as far and fast as we can while the various patrols and the remainder of the task force sent into the void come running out, chasing us. "Hell, have we even gotten close to making it?"

I fall silent, knowing he's right. For all that we've made it this far, we're still nowhere close to a homerun. Maybe third base, if you will. Which, if you were a teen, is pretty damn good. Not so much when you're gambling with your lives.

Attention turned back to the screens, we watch as the calculated lines of thrust and impetus, velocity and meeting close. The circles originating from the virtual *Heartbreak* radiate outward, and when they finally cross it, Dornalor touches his mic.

"Now."

Explosions, all across the ship. Small ones, releasing the moorings that hold the bones of the Deep Space Angler to the ship. Dornalor's focused now, making minute adjustments to the piloting program as we slip out of the gap created in what would be the Angler's open mouth, our hull scratching against the teeth as we part. We shoot outward, cloaking systems at full bore even as the bones continue onward, ship and bones angling away from one another.

Even as Dornalor does that, I use Forced Link with Cry, Baby, Cry so that it increases in strength. I adjust the Skill, masking our signals within the much larger one of the makeshift bone ship, hiding ourselves within it. My head hurts, my body burns, but I stay focused on keeping the System Edit, Forced Link, and Cry, Baby, Cry working together.

We fly completely in the dark, escaping as swiftly as we can, watching the plot. Watching as the ships that charge after us receive alerts on the changes at faster than light speeds. We watch as bone and metal ships pull apart, and the plotted angles of interception and momentum split. We watch, hoping that what we have done is enough.

All the while fearing it isn't.

***

"What time is it?" Dornalor says, rolling large shoulders and stretching himself. Being nine feet tall, the alien has configured the cockpit to fit him, which always means I feel a little out of place in the cockpit. Even nano-mold chairs don't help that much. Though they don't hurt.

"Fifteen minutes," I say. "Just about another three hours and a bit before we reach the planet. Less than an hour before we reach the outer shell of defensive stations."

Dornalor grins, eyeing the plot. There are quite a few patrols—including some coming right out from the defensive shell—jetting in, but the map shows them all going after the bone ship. "We did it."

"Eh…" I waggle my fingers, but I have to admit, he's not wrong.

Our projected ship, the Skill still running thanks to the inclusion of a pair of Hands and some bootstrapped Mana batteries to the separated bone ship, is caught in short order.

The Galactic Fleet had done a localized teleport with ensuing explosions as some ships and individuals ended up teleporting into one another, but they caught up to the projection. After launching a few exploratory attacks and breaking through the portable shields we'd added to the projection, they chose to ignore the decoy for the most part. A few ships are still firing at the projection from a distance since the Hand is still on it, but for the most part, they focus their attention on the second decoy—the bone ship.

Still, there doesn't seem to be anyone paying attention to us as we sneak in on an elliptical to Xylargh. It's not the straight run the bone ship is making, but the fact that we're picking up no new fleet patrols angling toward us is comforting. Even as we close in on the outer protective ring of the planet, the one meant to detect pirates and smugglers like us, nothing happens.

"How long till the first of the interceptors meet BSE?" Endila pipes up from his post in Engineering. The others are all on viewscreens since things have calmed down enough that actually speaking and seeing one another is possible.

"BSE?" Ali says.

"Bone Ship Extraordinaire," Endila replies, his voice thrumming with excitement. No localized teleportations to meet the BSE. No need, since they scrambled interceptors and patrol fleets from around Xylargh itself.

"Kids." Ali rolls his eyes, but I can see the smile that plays on the Spirit's lips.

"This one considered such designation wrong too," Ezz says, its voice filled with disapproval. "A more appropriate designation would be DSA-01 (M)."

"Shhhh…" I wave the golem down.

Ezz buzzes at me, obviously unhappy but silent.

"You sure your Hands can handle the deception?" Dornalor says worriedly.

"They'll be fine. So long as the shields we placed on the—"

"BSE."

"DSA-01(M)."

The pair of kids chime in at the same time. Then glare at one another across their viewscreens.

"The *decoy* hold, they can dish out all the damage and keep our enemies focused," I say, speaking over the pair.

"Whatever," Endila mutters.

Ezz at least knows to be quiet.

"Mikito? You doing okay?" Harry speaks up, cutting into the channel. She's been quiet for a bit.

"Yes," Mikito replies.

There's silence over the comm channels while everyone waits for more, but she doesn't elaborate. Eventually, Harry snorts. We all deal with stress in different ways after all, and unlike the semi-talkative, hand-wringing reporter, Mikito just gets quiet.

"Outer shell. We going to be okay?" I say, bringing our discussion back on point. I know they're joking to cut the tension, but considering my body is literally burning up from inside as I keep both System Edit, Forced Link, and the Edit on Cry, Baby, Cry running, I'm not in the mood.

"We'll find out," Dornalor says. "In… five minutes. Give or take."

Dornalor manages to silence the group with his words, leaving us to stare into the darkness. A part of me is running through options, knowing what is likely going to happen. As powerful as the Skills are, as much as I'm doing, at some point, this is all going to fail. If nothing else, the pain rising in a crescendo within me is stealing my concentration and attention. A harbinger of the chaos to come.

Chapter 24

My focus is turned within, my world a never-ending sea of pain. Nerves, organs, and bones all ache in a way that transcends plain agony, as the very cells that make up my existence are torn apart and healed again and again. Time loses meaning soon enough as the damage ranks up, till suddenly, the outside world intrudes on my solitary nightmare.

The *Heartbreak* jerks to a stop and I'm thrown against my crash harness. Bruises imprint on my chest and waist, the entire copilot chair creaking dangerously before I slam backward into it, nano-formed cushioning doing little to decrease the impact. Normally the inertia dampeners handle the vast majority of velocity changes, but this one is sufficient to yank me back and loosen my hold on the Skills. Eyes open, I dismiss damage notifications to take in the chaotic cockpit.

"Stray asteroids and deep leviathans, kill the power on engines three and five! I'm shifting power to two and six now," Dornalor says, hands flashing across the board as he adjusts power across the *Heartbreak*.

"On three," Ezz buzzes.

"Five," Endila grunts.

At the same time, Harry is slowly shaking his head, his eyes a little lost as he flicks from screen to screen. He hits a few buttons, and I feel the ship rumble as weapons fire. Instinctively, I drop the System Edit as the pressure grows even further, moments before I feel the primary Skill turn off on Dornalor's end.

"What the hell is going on?" I say, still reeling from the pain of my Edits and my reentry to the present.

"They knew we were here. Caught us right in the middle of a minefield with what looks like every single inertia dampener they have," Ali says, the tiny Spirit's face scrunched up in deep concentration, hands held above him as if he's trying to grip and tear apart the world. "I'm trying to alter the energy they're using to hold us in place, but there's too much."

My eyes roam over the *Heartbreak*'s notifications, coming to an understanding of what is happening. We're caught in a web of power that holds our ship still, even as our engines—many of them damaged—strain and threaten to explode. Around us, boarding shuttles decloak, all of them headed toward the ship, even as the occasional beam laser fires, tearing at our shielding and forcing the ship to expend even more energy. On another level, I sense the conflicting energies surrounding the ship as Ali does battle with the inertia dampeners. As fast as he tears down or disperses the energy holding us still, another locks on and takes its place, leaving us inching forward at best.

"What should I do?" I say, breathing hard and watching my health tick up. It couldn't have been more than fifteen minutes since I started channeling the System Edit and the overload of Mana, but my health is down by a quarter, the overflow having done a real number. Even now, there's too much within me and I expend some of it by pulling a new Hand into space. Leaving us two here and two more in the bone ship.

"Figure out how the hell we're getting out of here!" Dornalor snaps. "I'm doing my best not to have our ship tear itself apart."

I nod, knowing he's playing a delicate balancing act. It's like driving a car straight into a concrete wall, attempting to keep the ship together and push forward while not burning out the engines. The only good news is that the weapons firing upon us are being careful, only plinking away at our shields rather than attempting to finish us off.

"Mikito, Hands, get yourselves ready for boarders."

As the Hand standing beside me wearing nothing but basic clothing holds out his hand, I chuckle and pull out what I can for him. Thank the gods I bought a bunch of good Advanced quality weaponry. Even so, I've only got a limited number. Handing over the basic armored jumpsuit, a quartet of swords, a brace of beam pistols, and a large beam cannon along with a belt of grenades is not insignificant.

While I'm beggaring myself, acknowledgements stream through the group. The entire team is patched into the *Heartbreak's* monitors so they know where to go. Instead, I pay attention to the world around us, trying to work out what to do.

Portal? I could, but my body burns, my mind aches, and I'm not sure I could tear through the multiple solar-system-wide Dimensional Locks. The only way to guarantee a Portal is another System Edit, and that treads close to the same thing I was penalized for by the System. If we risk it, I need time to recover first.

Time is not on our side, since the damn boarding shuttles are barely ten minutes away. Even less when I feel the shift in Mana surrounding us. The Dimensional Lock that felt like a hard iron wall is penetrated, an exception created, and the exceptions arrive seconds later.

The *Heartbreak's* defenses against teleportation into the ship itself are pierced, a wailing alarm filling the cockpit while the lights shift into a dark, strobing red. New dots appear on the ship wireframe, updating the entire team about our invaders.

Three of those dots are redundant.

My sword appears in my hand, and I throw it, conjuring their companion Thousand Blades seconds later. The swarm of swords plunge through the trio of raiders that teleported into the cockpit, already orienting themselves for a fight. I don't hesitate, putting the full Strength of my body to use as I break my seat while surging out of it, crash harness and loot-reinforced metal nothing more than tissue underneath my hundreds of points of Strength.

The lead raider staggers back, body pierced with my blades. He's still alive, but his momentary disruption throws off his friends, forcing them to duck around him. Humanoid, in grey and steel power armor, they all look the same. Even down to the beam rifles they wield, already firing as they track the shots to me.

"Get them out!" Dornalor snarls, hunching a little, but his focus remains entirely on his notifications.

No time to answer before I'm on them, gripping the first by the front of his armor and a handy hold of a jutting sword and pushing forward, shoving them all out of the cockpit. The trio are driven backward, forced out of the cockpit before Dornalor triggers the doors. Seconds later, they slam shut behind me, clipping my ankle and bringing a muffled curse from me.

I take a beam pistol to the face, my vision washed out, and another intruder gets most of the way away from his friend. Knowing time is of the essence, I kick away my first opponent and conjure my Soulbound sword in hand, unleashing a Blade Strike at the others.

That forces the other blades stuck in the poor man to cut downward, turning him into chopped pieces and sending portions of his body spinning through the corridor, painting it in green blood and guts. The Blade Strike that impacts later just adds to the mess.

Another beam attack takes me high, the Spitzrocket tanking the damage with ease. The snarling ball of monofilament thread, backed up by a Skill, is harder to shrug off. As I switch targets, the Hand that had just left returns, striking from behind.

I have no time to focus on those before me, since instinct drives me toward another option. Skill Edit triggers again, the pain staggering me as I trigger Forced Link and Disengage Safeties along with the *Heartbreak*'s Dimensional Lock Skill—Pirate's Domain—and boost it.

I feel the effects trigger even as the System tears away at my health further and my sight refuses to focus. Yet the sacrifice is sufficient. Teleportations are shunted away into other dimensions or just rejected altogether, leaving the individuals to tear themselves apart and return to their starting position, a lot worse for the wear.

Much like my chest, as the last raider chops his monomolecular-edged axe into my torso. He rips it out with a sucking sound, leaving me staggering backward into the wires he uses to hold me tight. Those cut into the Spitzrocket, damage notifications flooding my screen as the Grandmaster-built power armor's defense is overridden by a penetration Skill. Blood gushes from my wounds even as he swings again.

I block the attack, bending steel wires and feeling them dig into my skin. At the same time, I dismiss my Thousand Blades that are entirely out of position and bring them back, using the blades and their automated movement to help free myself.

Another strike, this one into my hip, and I stagger again. I'm getting my ass kicked, pain and concentration from holding the System Edit and my low health robbing me of focus. Still, with the main threats sorted, I fight back.

It's hard, and I take a number of other wounds, but I manage. It gets easier when I chop off his hand, and much easier when I put three blades into him and finally behead him. The Monofilament Warrior is an annoying Advanced Class, his attacks and the Razor Aura he uses tearing apart the Spitzrocket, but I get it done. Once he's dead, I slump to the side and hit up a Health Potion, remembering to layer a Soul Shield on me all too belatedly.

"John!" Harry shouts, his voice a little frantic. "Boarding pods are arriving!"

"Damn it. Ideas?" I say, not having really had much time to think.

"That's your job. But it better be fast. She can't handle much more," Dornalor says.

"I have one," Harry says. When no one tries to interrupt him, he's quick to explain. "Those raider ships—let's steal one. If we can capture them, we should be able to run. Worst-case scenario, they reprogram the inertia dampeners and hold them still, reducing the load on the *Heartbreak*. Best case, we run for it in one of the stolen ships."

I can't help but nod along. The ships traveling through the inertial webs are set up so that they won't get caught in their own attacks. If we can steal one, we can escape. At least for a while.

It's a good idea, but a little obvious. It's a fine start, but only adequate, which is why I add a little twist to it.

***

Once I recover a little more, I take to the decks and meet the raiders as they enter the *Heartbreak*. I hit them hard and fast, the Hands using their Skills to destroy some of the ships before they even land, while others dock and carve their way through the hull or override the escape hatches and enter that way.

Each docked ship and their cargo are killed. For some of the fighters, I feel deep pity. Basic Classers, scrambled to take us on, are just chaff to our glowing Mana-scythes. Even the Advanced Classers, now that I'm not surprised, die to my abuse of the System Mana overflowing me. It helps that Ezz rips into the runic code and boosts Pirate's Domain, solidifying our hold and allowing me to drop the Edit.

We kill the raiders as they arrive, taking over their ships and slaving them to the *Heartbreak*'s main control system. We don't launch them yet, knowing that if we do this piecemeal, we'll fail.

Each fight gets harder though, my health never fully recovering. The Spitzrocket takes the brunt of the damage, slowly coming apart. The few Master Class raiders we run into get squashed—hard—by Mikito or the Hands. Peasant Fury makes itself known, the constant gain and loss of health powering up the Skill.

The battles are bloody but over in all too short a time. I know the Fleet is scrambling more, long-range patrol ships catching up, others from the planet soon to arrive. Heroics or Master Classers are in those raiding teams. We're lucky this trap seems to have been a last-minute thing, one completed under the cover of secrecy.

Time runs out, but finally…

"Done!" Mikito calls over the channel as she finishes slaving the latest boarding shuttle.

I glance at my HUD, the Spitzrocket providing me constant updates of our condition. No more time. "Time to go, people!"

Then my fingers dance as I program the ships, giving them each new courses, plans for where they have to go. Dornalor and Harry arrive at the mess bay before I manage to make my way there, for I'm still distracted and limping. Ezz finds me, taking my hand to guide me while I finish the programming. Inside the mess hall, Mikito stands silent, holding a still-dripping Hitoshi by her side. Endila comes dashing over, the last to arrive and looking angry.

"We can't abandon her!" Endila says.

"We have no choice," Dornalor grates out, looking even more hurt. The pair of them are still in contact with the ship, their eyes and fingers twitching as they mentally control the repair bots and shunt energy around.

I have no words of comfort as I finish the programming, Seconds later, the thunderous shaking of the *Heartbreak* reaches me as the ships blast away. Blast doors are already closed, so we barely lose any atmosphere as the raiding ships depart.

No surprise that only some of the raiding ships are stopped. Most of them make it out before inertia dampeners turn on them, but those that aren't forcibly stopped are attacked, fire from nearby mines and the sentry weapons opening up. Their shields glow, barely holding on in most cases. One particularly damaged boarding shuttle explodes under the onslaught of fire. I wonder if that is on purpose or if it was a mistake in miscalculating damage done.

Then again, we're tough enough we probably could survive an exploding ship. In either case, the point of all this comes clear. The mines and sentry guns have to react, cloaked weapons making themselves known to sensors and us.

My doppelgangers exit through holes in the *Heartbreak*, spotting the attacking weaponry. Beacons of the Heavens lash out, burning away exposed ordinance and slamming into raiding ships, creating vast swaths of torn metal. The Hands pour all the Mana they have into this, even destroying local inertia dampeners. I mourn their deaths but am grateful there will be a place to dump the excess Mana.

"Told you they wouldn't let those ships live," Ali says, jerking his hands down. A second later, the *Heartbreak* lurches forward as the straining Spirit tears apart the remaining inertia dampeners still focused on us. "Best move. I can't do this for long…"

I nod as the raiding ships fall. They're all headed for the nearest major vessels or floating forts on kamikaze runs, since our chances of escaping that way were always low.

Once more, I tap into the System and pull at my System Edit Skill. The pain is worse than ever and my legs buckle, forcing me to the floor. I feel a hand under my elbow, helping to hold me up. Penetration, Forced Link, Portal. Together, I shove them all together and System Edit the hell out of them all, so that the resultant Skill combination tears through localized space and the Dimensional Lock. I even override my lack of familiarity with the resultant Portal location, using borrowed map coordinates.

Breaking every rule in the book and suffering for it.

System Mana rushes through me, tearing into my guts, sending shards of ice into my brain, keeping me from being able to focus on anything but the Skills and their results.

Then even more pain as the System pushes back. Gently, admonishingly. It grows worse as another presence joins in. I want to say something, warn the others as I feel my control slip, as code is overwritten.

Mikito jumps through the black slash in space first, Hitoshi in hand. Harry and Ezz drag me along through the Portal since Endila and Dornalor need to keep the bluff of our escape via the *Heartbreak* running as long as we can.

The transition is jarring, a wash of cold before we're through. Lifeblood pools and drips from my eyes, my ears, my fingers. I land on ringing metal flooring. Ezz buzzes, Harry gasps, and multiple buffs and debuffs fall upon us all.

It batters at my concentration, and even will and anger isn't enough. Too much, too much pain, too much splitting of concentration. The Portal snaps shut, Dornalor and Endila trapped on the other end. Even as the arrayed forces of the Galactic Council level their weapons at us.

"About time you arrived, Redeemer," Sephra—the damn System Admin from before, the one who tried to take away my access—says. She's got her hands on her hips, a gloating look on her face.

Kasva, that old asshole Champion for the Galactic Council, is here, paired swords held out, glowing emerald armor in one piece once more.

Sephra doesn't let me get my bearings before she continues. "Take them."

Chapter 25

I wish I could say we put up a good fight. That would be the heroic thing, the movie ending where the protagonist somehow manages to win despite all the odds. Instead, it's more like a beatdown you see in the second act, when the hero gets thrashed just before he gets a power-up later on. They swarm us, multiple Skills dispersing anything that we try, throwing bodies and lives where pure overwhelming force is insufficient.

Mikito is piled under multiple bodies, Kasva only making his move when she chops in twain the first two to reach her. Surprisingly, one of the bisected is still alive, crawling toward his flopping bottom half. The Champion is fast, blocking Mikito's naginata and tying her up while others slam blades and batons into her back, taking her down. He steps back as they pile on her, using physical weight and Skills to take her down.

It's a mistake. She surges back up, only for Kasva to cut off a hand and disarm her. Then the survivors from the original pileup get back to it, much more successfully restraining her.

I'm of even less use, reeling from repeated uses of System Edit and having the System smack me down multiple times. I burn Mana, throwing spells and Skills outward only to have them canceled by other Skills or Sephra's System Edit. Judgment of All shorts out, Area Denial hammering my Mana back at me. A single, aborted attempt at tapping into the System sends me reeling, my Skills dispersed as agony lances through me.

Harry is, of course, not much use. He tries, bless him, but he's not a fighter. They take away his weapons and break his arms, leaving him whimpering. Ali gets dismissed, his physical form discarded. Ezz is blasted away, then as it struggles upward, a simple Skill locks it down. Literally.

As easy as that, we're finished.

They put us in a line on our knees, shackled with Mana-dispersing enchanted bindings. They peel the Spitzrocket off me in pieces, discarding the armor like so much waste. We're bound, unable to move as Sephra walks over, those mermaid eyes blinking, her every movement screaming gloating happiness.

"Redeemer, Redeemer, Redeemer… you fool. Did you think we did not expect you to try that? That only a few middling Administrators were blocking your way?" she says, almost crooning. "You walked right into our trap and burnt yourself out. Always dangerous, capturing Administrators. You never know what they might do."

I grunt, choosing not to answer her. My body throbs with each word, the ever-present anger drowned out by the pain. I try to recover, but it seems my silence angers her. A fist cuffs my head and I sprawl to the floor before I'm yanked up, my arms nearly tearing out of their sockets as I'm roughly handled. Stupid Heroic Class enchanted bracelets have dropped my attributes too…

"Be careful. You know the Council wants him alive," Kasva says, voicing his disapproval.

"Do not speak to me, dog," Sephra says, glaring at the Champion who stays close to Mikito, just in case she makes a move.

"I am not your dog," Kasva says warningly. The blade closest to Sephra trembles a little.

"But you're someone's dog?" I can't help but say.

Kasva doesn't hit me for that, though I was sort of hoping he would. My health is so low, a good blow by him might just kill me. And considering what they've got planned, that might be the better choice of escape.

Sephra snorts and chooses to ignore Kasva, though she doesn't let her people hit me anymore. Instead, she leans forward. "Such a fool. Did you think you could face us and win?"

"Yes," I grate out.

She cackles, and the men around us laugh too. I call them men, but of course, there's quite a variety. Men, women, aliens, golems, and creatures that might have no sex at all. Movana, Gimsar, Hakarta, mercreatures, and slimes. They all cackle like good little minions. A gesture by Sephra and her people pounce on the others, punching, kicking, spitting on them. She only calls a halt to the proceedings when Ezz, whimpering in the corner and being beaten by its own leg, almost completely shorts out.

My struggles, my attempts to even touch the System are of little use. I can't feel that connection, not anymore, the pain of abusing the Skill so often shutting down my connection. Hands keep me on my knees, force me to watch the beatings and hear Ezz's piteous cries for its father.

For me.

When they're done, they line us up again on our knees. Harry is broken, quivering. Mikito has blood matted across her face, one eye swollen shut and half her clothing ripped, acid eating through one leg. Still, she looks calm, glaring at them all as another Heroic Class plays with Hitoshi.

"Fool, fool, fool. I would kill you here, but the Council wants you alive. Wants to make your death an example. Or, should I say, your life…" Sephra shakes her head. "I told them it's a bad call. We should end this here and now."

"But you know to follow orders, don't you?" Kasva says, gaze fixed on her.

Sephra gives a short nod. "I do."

"Gods, you people are boring," I say. "Just get a room already."

"Keep joking, Redeemer. I do like that you are strong, that you take a while to break. Because we have time. Decades, centuries. We'll break your mind, your will, your soul. You'll beg for death, but it'll never come. We'll strip you of all your rights, until *he* gives up on you and lets us do so. Then, and only then, we'll let you die. It'll take ages, and you'll be an example for everyone. So all those rebels in Erethra and Movana, on your Earth, will know their place." Sephra grins, and it's not crazy, just fanatical. Power hungry. "And then, when it's all done, we'll make them forget. Again."

I snarl and get clobbered again. Then again, and again, since all that talking has recovered some of my health. Once the stun debuff wears off, I find Sephra standing over Harry.

"Ah, the reporter. Your fate has yet to be decided," Sephra says, one hand stroking Harry's face. He shrinks away, and Sephra smirks.

"Wha-what do you mean?" Harry says, obviously confused.

"Mmmm… breaking you could be useful. Having you stream your friend's torture seems… appropriate. But we do have a deal to consider."

"Deal?" I mutter.

Harry repeats the word too.

Cold floor digs into my knees, growing colder as Sephra answers me. "Oh, yes. That's the other reason why you never had a chance. We have a System Contract, you see."

The three of us here, shackled. Ezz broken, frozen. That leaves… "Endila."

"Hah! We only knew of him when your Pirate Captain let me know. He knows which way to jump, though he did bargain for the Reporter and Mechanic. He even wanted the golem—though he gave that one up fast." Another vicious grin. "Made us wait, quite a while, before the agreement was in place. If not, we could have taken you earlier. Would have. Trickier, more costly. But this way… well. This way was so much more satisfying. Seeing your face. Delicious."

"Dornalor did what?" I snarl, anger rousing and pushing against the pain. I've recovered a little, my anger, my drive pushing me upward. Flexing against the shackles. My actions aren't missed as they proceed to beat me again, layering debuffs to slow my healing.

"Stop it. You don't have to do this," Harry says, voice trembling.

"Oh, but we do. We certainly do," Sephra leans forward, whispering into his ear. "You've upset a lot of people. But we'll let you live. He wasn't as smart as he thought, Contracting us to keep you alive. So you will be. Unharmed. Free, so long as you do your job…"

"No! I won't," Harry says, horror in his voice.

"Then we have no use for you. And breaking that part of the Contract might be painful, but not debilitating."

"Go ahead." Harry tries for brave, but I hear the tremble in his voice. We all can.

I can't let him do that, so I speak up. At least, I do after spitting out the blood and saliva and a stray pair of teeth they've knocked loose. "Don't."

"Are you saying something, Redeemer?"

"Not to you. Don't be stupid, Harry. Live. You can't ch-ch—" I breathe shallowly, feeling the ribs poking into my lungs and filling them up. Sensing how my body heals, pulling the ribs back into place as the System does its job. "Change anything if you're dead."

"You can't ask me to do this," Harry protests.

Sephra doesn't say anything, instead letting this melodrama play out. Kasva watches us, eyes tracking over all of us, not dropping his guard even for a second.

"I can. I am." I shuffle around and meet Harry's gaze.

Sephra lets me for a few seconds, before she gestures and we're shoved to face forward. I have to watch, am forced to watch as she walks over to Mikito, taking Hitoshi from the one who is holding it.

Kasva stirs for a second, then stills. I know what's coming, but a part of me refuses to believe it'll happen.

"Now, for you… we have no use for you," Sephra says, almost crooning the words.

"I do not fear death," Mikito says stoically.

"Good."

A swing, a flash, a thump.

Mikito's head falls beside me, Hitoshi neatly decapitating her. Her eyes roll over, staring at me in peaceful calm while Harry screams in horror. I stare back at the glazed eyes while Sephra giggles and my best friend's body slumps lifelessly to the floor.

***

Time drags on indefinitely as the head of my friend, my most loyal subject stares at me. Then finally, finally it disperses, coming apart at the seams. The Mana-forged body dissolves, strands of energy fading away as the doppelganger comes apart. Her vanishing form is not unnoticed, as the shouts begin.

"What did you do?" Sephra snarls, spinning on me. Hitoshi swerves, aiming straight at my face, even the blood on the polearm fading.

"Tricked you, of course," I say, grinning with bloody lips.

Sephra snarls, stalking toward me. She glares at me, her eyes flashing with rage, as she brings the polearm above her head. I track the attack, ready to throw myself out of the way, but the hands holding me tighten. As the blade comes down, I brace for the pain.

It never arrives.

Kasva has grabbed the polearm, stepping into Sephra's place. His voice drops, thrumming with restrained anger and command. "Alive!"

Sephra growls, pushing down, incensed at the defiance. I see her eyes glaze over, the split that happens when someone taps into the System. Kasva's grip slips, and when he pushes back, she hits him. Hard. Kasva flies backward, bowling over his own people.

Then Hitoshi is swinging again.

I flinch. When the attack doesn't hit when I expect, I turn toward Sephra. I'm graced with a perplexed-looking Administrator. She's turning her hand side to side, searching for the missing polearm. I find myself grinning a little, realizing that Mikito must have recalled the Legacy weapon. So long as she lives, she can recall the weapon. And as a Legacy weapon that's bathed itself in the blood and lives of multiple Level 150+ creatures, its abilities are powerful. Powerful enough to break through the Dimensional Lock to bring itself back to her.

"Got you. Again," I can't help but taunt the Administrator. It's not the smartest thing to do, but resecuring Mikito's weapon was always a gamble. We couldn't be sure she would succeed, but since they had captured me, I assume they had relaxed their restrictions, focusing whatever locks to just us. Missing the weapon itself.

The blow from Sephra's fist doesn't hurt my face much. She hits me three more times, each time across the cheeks. I roll with the attacks as best I can, but even without that, Sephra is just not geared for hand-to-hand combat. The fact that she's not using the System Edit to boost her attacks means it's painful but not world-ending. It still helps the Administrator to vent her frustration.

That kind of makes her the perfect torturer, since the damage she does is just slightly above my debuffed healing speed. Her attacks end up replacing my injuries as she beats on me, her eyes wide and wild. I catch a glimpse of Kasva returning, but he sees I'm doing fine—for definitions of fine—and leaves it.

Long minutes later, they prop up my broken and beaten body, blood dribbling from open cuts across my face and one eye swollen shut. She's crushed my orbital lobe and the eye has popped out. I'm reeling, notifications of being Stunned and in Shock flashing across my screen, fading in and out like my consciousness.

Eventually, my regeneration pulls me back, at least sufficiently that I can pay attention to the world again. The cold floor pressing into my knees is kind of nice, especially compared to the sticky and warm blood that covers the front of my clothing. A slight stench tickles my nose, a mixture of fear and pain, sweat and the alien musk of the creatures standing around me.

"Where is she, Pirate?" Sephra is screeching at Dornalor's image, the Pirate Captain looking uncomfortable but resolute.

"I told you, I don't know." Dornalor gestures at her image. "You've got a half-dozen people listening and weighing my words. They can tell you. I haven't lied. I haven't even tried to shade the truth. I don't know."

"You planned this with the Redeemer," Sephra says.

"I did no such thing," Dornalor replies. "Not a damn thing."

"Why did you delay in signing the Contract then? Why?" she snarls.

"That was you! You refused to agree to our terms," Dornalor growls. "It would have been over earlier if you had stopped trying to sneak in your damn gotcha clauses. And I can see you're barely holding on to your side of the bargain."

"Be grateful I haven't chopped his head off!" Sephra says, her voice cooling and something dangerous growing in her eyes. "You might have made us sign a System Contract with penalties, but don't forget. We are System Administrators. We can change that."

"Can you?" Dornalor says, his voice dropping. "I think you're bluffing. If you could change the Contracts that easily, I think you wouldn't have hesitated at signing that long."

"You think I lie?"

"Not lie. But you forget, I've flown with John. You have limits." Dornalor smiles grimly. "I think you can edit Contracts, but it's going to cost you. More than you're willing to pay. More than the Council is willing to pay. Maybe it's an Edit to something much more important than a minor Pirate Captain. One whose role in all this is barely known. And the Reporter has rights, rights that they've dragged out of you before."

"Not us. The Council," Sephra says softly. "Tread carefully, Captain. You have earned yourself reprieve by delivering the Rebel, but you still aided him."

"Only till we could come to an agreement," Dornalor says, shrugging. Then his gaze turns from Sephra to me, meeting my bloodshot gaze as he shrugs one large shoulder. "It's nothing personal, Redeemer. I just had to look out for myself. It was clear you weren't going to."

I open my mouth to reply, only to find that my mouth is uncountably dry. I have to clear it a few times, working what little saliva I can into it, before speaking. "Seems pretty personal from where I'm… kneeling." I shrug, shoulders sending a sharp, shooting pain along my neck and down my arms as the manacles yank backward at my movement. "But I assumed it might happen."

"So you tricked him," Sephra says, turning to me, a finger coming to tap her lips. "Yet I don't understand. What if you did manage to get to the planet? Were you going to leave your friend stranded? Why split the party?"

"Because I was hoping I was wrong." My voice drops and I see Dornalor flush orange. "And there were plans, if I failed."

Sephra saunters over to me and pulls my face upward. She grips my chin with her fingers, staring into my brown eyes with her green ones. "And you don't intend to talk, do you?"

"Talk? I can talk... about how bad your breath smells. Or the best places to buy chocolate on Earth and how Galactics still haven't gotten it right, even after stealing our best plants," I say. "I can talk about the System and how you can... urk!"

I gag as she crushes my throat, forcing me to shut up. After a second, the equivalent of a ball gag slips over my mouth. I can't help but flash to fun times with old friends. Somehow, I don't think my future will involve much fun at all.

"Very well then, I guess we'll just have to do this the hard way." Sephra straightens, eyes falling upon Harry, who looks confused and horrified. She purses her lips before gesturing at the guards holding him. "Bring him."

"Administrator—" Dornalor says.

"He will sign a Contract with us. With penalties that include the loss of his protections if he breaks them. Then we will release him," Sephra says, cutting off the Pirate. "Is that acceptable?"

Dornalor nods.

"Good. Dock your ship. You will be our guests until this matter is fully resolved," Sephra says. "My men will check it for the Samurai. And if she is there..."

"She isn't. I've told you. But check for yourself."

"We will."

A gesture and Dornalor's image disappears before Sephra gives a few orders to her waiting minions and over the communicator. Kasva still stands, glaring at me. There's no love lost between him and the Administrator. Fault lines between the Administrators and the remainder of the Shadow Council. Something to remember to use, if I can. If I wasn't hurting so damn bad.

"As for you…" Sephra turns to me, her eyes glinting. "You'll be our guest for a while. We'll make sure to find out where your friend is. When we find her, you'll get to watch her die. For real this time. But don't worry, we'll keep you entertained while we hunt her down. However much you think you are ready for what is to come…

"You're wrong."

I gurgle around the ball gag before she gestures. The blow on the back of my head throws me forward, shooting pain and a flashing notification that I resisted a Skill pulsing. Another strike comes after the first, and the same thing happens. Twice more, they hit me, the blows sending shards of agony echoing through my skull. At last, a new Status window pops up.

I slip into darkness, the ringing pain in my head gone.

To wake with a new notification.

You Have Entered a Safe Zone (Prison of the Lost, Xylargh)

…

I dismiss reading the rest of the notification because I hear something approaching my cell. I flex, realizing I'm still shackled, still trapped, still a prisoner.

Still, I finally made it to the planet.

The End of Forbidden Zone

John will be back in the final book of the System Apocalypse—System Finale

Epilogue

The emptiness of space surrounds her as she floats. Alone, silent, and lightless, hovering a bare few thousand kilometers from her destination. In the vastness of space, she is less than a speck of sand on a beach, not even significant enough to be a rounding error. The dark surface of her space suit soaks up the ambient light, offering no indication of her presence so close to the space station.

In the distance, she can see the metal bastion of civilization in the void, a larger dot in space. Closer by, the shards of the Angler Fish expand from where it was destroyed, the debris field widening with each second. A part of her knows that searchers are going through the wreckage even now, scavengers and official investigators.

In one hand, its light dimmed, its edge faded, sits a polearm. She caresses the raised edging of its shaft, the familiar feel of the Legacy weapon. It had taken a focused conjuration of will to draw it to her, across time and space, but she and the weapon are linked. Closer than anyone could ever suspect. Anyone but her liege.

He still lives. She knows it, can sense it.

It still burns her, knowing that he sacrificed himself to allow her to escape. To create this opportunity. It should have been her job, should have been her who was captured and subjected to unimaginable tortures. Her job. Her calling. Her raison d'être.

That bakayaro…

She draws a breath, forces her ire down. Giving in to the rage is useless. That is John's way, to use anger to empower his actions, to drive his passions and in so doing, excel. For her, calm is required. Peace. What is, is, as her liege says. Even if he never seems to understand that himself.

For now, she will wait.

A tear in space opens, and a creature pokes its head out. Slant-eyed, scaled, sharp teeth, and glowing flames in its mouth. She tightens her grip on her weapon, staring at the scaled creature that so easily ripped a hole through the dimensions, bypassing the renewed Dimensional Lock. It stares at her curiously.

Then a voice, a familiar one, calls to her from inside the gap in space. "You coming or not?"

A slight nudge of the controls and she jets forward into the gaping slash of disassociated space the dragon formed so that she can join the Dragon Lord. They have a lot to do if they are to save their friend from his arrogance.

Then again, what else is new?

Author's Note

I'd ask you to forgive me for leaving you at this point, but it's the appropriate ending for the book, closing out John's desperate run to Xylargh and leaving a slider for the next, final work. Forbidden Zone is a middle book, one that needs to set up a few things for a satisfying ending to the series. And the series will end in book twelve—System Finale—though the System Apocalypse universe will continue to chug on.

In fact, you might have heard about the series I'm co-writing with Craig Hamilton—**A Fist Full of Credits**—and K.T. Hanna—**System Apocalypse: Australia**—that will be releasing in the next six months or so. The world will not end, there's so many stories to tell still. However, John and co.'s story will come to a conclusion, at least for now in *System Finale*.

This book was interesting to write. I ended up showing off more of the Forbidden Zone than I expected, and yet never managed to bring us to the planet where John trained like I had initially thought might happen. That's writing though, where the journey never really takes you where you think it will and the endings, well, they sometimes surprise even me.

And these characters live in my head, clamoring for me to write their stories.

As always, I'm grateful for everyone who has followed me on this long journey. I've received more support for this tale than I could ever expect. I truly do hope that you've enjoyed the journey thus far. If you enjoyed reading the book, please do leave a review and rating. Reviews are the lifeblood of authors and help others choose to continue with the series or not.

In addition, please check out my other series:

- the Adventures on Brad (a more traditional young adult LitRPG fantasy)

  https://books2read.com/healers-gift

- Hidden Wishes (an urban fantasy GameLit series)

  https://books2read.com/gamers-wish

- A Thousand Li (a cultivation series inspired by Chinese xianxia novels)

  https://readerlinks.com/l/1340822

- Power, Masks & Capes and the Eternal Night series which are both novelette series set in a superhero and VRMMORPG for vampires respectively

I've also written a ton of short stories, all of which are available on my Patreon account:

https://www.patreon.com/taowong

For more great information about LitRPG series, check out the Facebook groups:

- LitRPG Society

  https://www.facebook.com/groups/LitRPGsociety/

- LitRPG Books

  https://www.facebook.com/groups/LitRPG.books/

About the Author

Tao Wong is an avid fantasy and sci-fi reader who spends his time working and writing in the North of Canada. He's spent way too many years doing martial arts of many forms, and having broken himself too often, he now spends his time writing about fantasy worlds.

For updates on the series and other books written by Tao Wong (and special one-shot stories), please visit the author's website:
http://www.mylifemytao.com

Subscribers to Tao's mailing list will receive **exclusive access to short stories in the Thousand Li and System Apocalypse universes**:
https://www.subscribepage.com/taowong

Or visit his Facebook Page: https://www.facebook.com/taowongauthor/

About the Publisher

Starlit Publishing is wholly owned and operated by Tao Wong. It is a science fiction and fantasy publisher focused on the LitRPG & cultivation genres. Their focus is on promoting new, upcoming authors in the genre whose writing challenges the existing stereotypes while giving a rip-roaring good read.

For more information Starlit Publishing, visit our website: https://www.starlitpublishing.com/

You can also join Starlit Publishing's mailing list to learn of new, exciting authors and book releases.

Glossary

Erethran Honor Guard Skill Tree

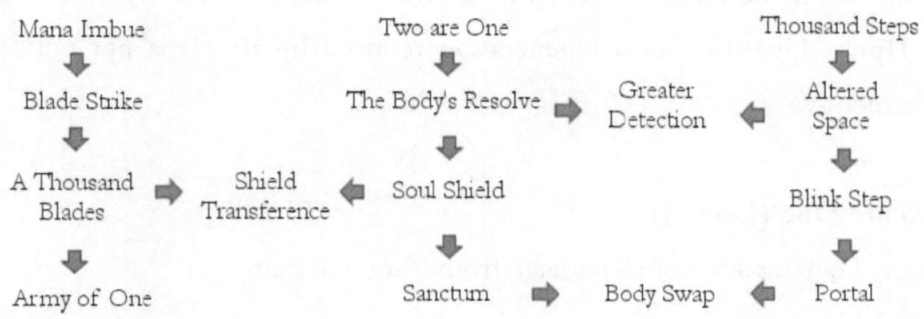

John's Erethran Honor Guard Skills

Mana Imbue (Level 5)

Soulbound weapon now permanently imbued with Mana to deal more damage on each hit. +30 Base Damage (Mana). Will ignore armor and resistances. Mana regeneration reduced by 25 Mana per minute permanently.

Blade Strike (Level 5)

By projecting additional Mana and stamina into a strike, the Erethran Honor Guard's Soulbound weapon may project a strike up to 50 feet away.

Cost: 50 Stamina + 50 Mana

Thousand Steps (Level 1)

Movement speed for the Honor Guard and allies are increased by 5% while skill is active. This ability is stackable with other movement-related skills.

Cost: 20 Stamina + 20 Mana per minute

Altered Space (Level 2)

The Honor Guard now has access to an extra-dimensional storage location of 30 cubic meters. Items stored must be touched to be willed in and may not include living creatures or items currently affected by auras that are not the Honor Guard's. Mana regeneration reduced by 10 Mana per minute permanently.

Two are One (Level 1)

Effect: Transfer 10% of all damage from Target to Self

Cost: 5 Mana per second

The Body's Resolve (Level 3)

Effect: Increase natural health regeneration by 35%. Ongoing health status effects reduced by 33%. Honor Guard may now regenerate lost limbs. Mana regeneration reduced by 15 Mana per minute permanently.

Greater Detection (Level 1)

Effect: User may now detect System creatures up to 1 kilometer away. General information about strength level is provided on detection. Stealth skills, Class skills, and ambient Mana density will influence the effectiveness of this skill. Mana regeneration reduced by 5 Mana per minute permanently.

A Thousand Blades (Level 4)

Creates five duplicate copies of the user's designated weapon. Duplicate copies deal base damage of copied items. May be combined with Mana Imbue and Shield Transference. Mana Cost: 3 Mana per second

Soul Shield (Level 8)

Effect: Creates a manipulable shield to cover the caster's or target's body. Shield has 2,750 Hit Points.

Cost: 250 Mana

Blink Step (Level 2)

Effect: Instantaneous teleportation via line-of-sight. May include Spirit's line of sight. Maximum range—500 meters.

Cost: 100 Mana

Portal (Level 5)

Effect: Creates a 5-meter by 5-meter portal which can connect to a previously traveled location by user. May be used by others. Maximum distance range of portals is 10,000 kilometers.

Cost: 250 Mana + 100 Mana per minute (minimum cost 350 Mana)

Army of One (Level 4)

The Honor Guard's feared penultimate combat ability, Army of One builds upon previous Skills, allowing the user to unleash an awe-inspiring attack to deal with their enemies. Attack may now be guided around minor obstacles.

Effect: Army of One allows the projection of (Number of Thousand Blades conjured weapons * 3) Blade Strike attacks up to 500 meters away from user. Each attack deals 5 * Blade Strike Level damage (inclusive of Mana Imbue and Soulbound weapon bonus)

Cost: 750 Mana

Sanctum (Level 2)

An Erethran Honor Guard's ultimate trump card in safeguarding their target, Sanctum creates a flexible shield that blocks all incoming attacks, hostile teleportations and Skills. At this Level of Skill, the user must specify dimensions of the Sanctum upon use of the Skill. The Sanctum cannot be moved while the Skill is activated.

Dimensions: Maximum 15 cubic meters.

Cost: 1,000 Mana

Duration: 2 minute and 7 seconds

Paladin of Erethra Skill Tree

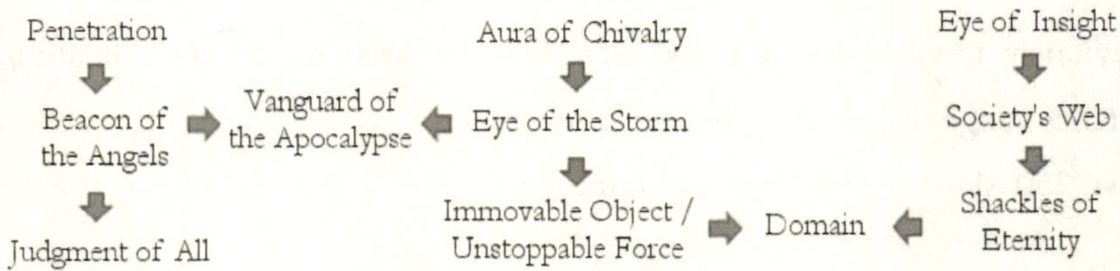

John's Paladin of Erethra Skills

Penetration (Level 9—Evolved)

Few can face the judgment of a Paladin in direct combat, their ability to bypass even the toughest of defenses a frightening prospect. Reduces Mana Regeneration by 45 permanently.

Effect: Ignore all armor and defensive Skills and spells by 90%. Increases damage done to shields and structural supports by 175%.

Secondary Effect: Damage that is resisted by spells, armor, Skills and Resistances is transferred to an Evolved Skill shield at a ratio of 1 to 1.

Duration: 85 minutes

Aura of Chivalry (Level 1)

A Paladin's very presence can quail weak-hearted enemies and bolster the confidence of allies, whether on the battlefield or in court. The Aura of Chivalry is a double-edged sword however, focusing attention on the Paladin—potentially to their detriment. Increases success rate of Perception checks against Paladin by 10% and reduces stealth and related skills by 10% while active. Reduces Mana Regeneration by 5 Permanently.

Effect: All enemies must make a Willpower check against intimidation against user's Charisma. Failure to pass the check will cow enemies. All allies gain a 50% boost in morale for all Willpower checks and a 10% boost in confidence and probability of succeeding in relevant actions.

Note: Aura may be activated or left-off at will.

Beacon of the Angels (Level 2)

User calls down an atmospheric strike from the heavens, dealing damage over a wide area to all enemies within the beacon. The attack takes time to form, but once activated need not be concentrated upon for completion.

Effect: 1000 Mana Damage done to all enemies, structures and vehicles within the maximum 25-meter column of attack

Mana Cost: 500 Mana

Eyes of Insight (Level 1)

Under the eyes of a Paladin, all untruth and deceptions fall away. Only when the Paladin can see with clarity may he be able to judge effectively. Reduces Mana Regeneration by 5.

Effect: All Skills, Spells and abilities of a lower grade that obfuscate, hinder or deceive the Paladin are reduced in effectiveness. Level of reduction proportionate to degree of difference in grade and Skill Level.

Eye of the Storm (Level 1)

In the middle of the battlefield, the Paladin stands, seeking justice and offering judgment on all enemies. The winds of war will seek to draw both enemies and allies to you, their cruel flurries robbing enemies of their lives and bolstering the health and Mana of allies.

Effect: Eye of the Storm is an area effect buff and taunt. Psychic winds taunt enemies, forcing a Mental Resistance check to avoid attacking user. Enemies also receive 5 points of damage per second while within the influence of the Skill, with damage decreasing from the epicenter of the Skill. Allies receive a 5% increase in Mana and Health regeneration, decrease in effectiveness from Skill center. Eye of the Storm affects an area of 50 meters around the user.

Cost: 500 Mana + 20 Mana per second

Vanguard of the Apocalypse (Level 2)

Where others flee, the Paladin strides forward. Where the brave dare not advance, the Paladin charges. While the world burns, the Paladin still fights. The Paladin with this Skill is the vanguard of any fight, leading the charge against all of Erethra's enemies.

Effect: +45 to all Physical attributes, increases speed by 55% and recovery rates by 35%. This Skill is stackable on top of other attribute and speed boosting Skills or spells.

Cost: 500 Mana + 10 Stamina per second

Society's Web (Level 1)

Where the Eye of Insight provides the Paladin an understanding of the lies and mistruths told, Society's Web shows the Paladin the intricate webs that tie individuals to one another. No alliance, no betrayal, no tangled web of lies will be hidden as each interaction weaves one another closer. While the Skill provides no detailed information, a skilled Paladin can infer much from the Web.

Effect: Upon activation, the Paladin will see all threads that tie each individual to one another and automatically understand the details of each thread when focused upon.

Cost: 400 Mana + 200 Mana per minute

Immovable Object / Unstoppable Force (Level 1)

A Paladin cannot be stopped. A Paladin cannot be moved. A Paladin is a force of the Erethran Empire on the battlefield. This Skill exemplifies this simple concept. Let all who doubt the strength of the Paladin tremble!

Use: User must select to be an Immovable Object or Unstoppable Force. Effect varies depending on choice. Skill combines with Aura of Chivalry to provide a smaller (10% of base effect) bonus to all friendlies within range.

Effect 1 (Immovable Object): Constitution, Health and Damage Resistance (All) increased by 200% of User's current total. All knockback effects are mitigated (including environmental knockback effects).

Effect 2 (Unstoppable Force): Agility, Movement Speed, Momentum and Damage Calculations based off Momentum increased by 200% of User's current total. Damage from other attacks increased by 100%. Only active while user is moving.

Cost: 5 Mana per second

Domain (Level 1)

With chains that bind, and threads that extend from one to another, a Paladin is the center of events. In his Domain, enemies will break and allies will bend knee. Let the enemies of the Empire tremble before a Paladin with his Domain.

Effect 1: All enemy combatants receive -10% attribute decreases, a +10% increase in Mana cost and lose 25 HP per second while within range of the Domain.

Effect 2: All allies receive a +10% increase in health regeneration, a 10% increase in attributes, and a reduction of -10% in Mana cost (semi-stackable).

Range: 10 Meters

Cost: 500 Mana + 5 Mana per Second

Judgment of All (Level 6)

An Emperor might sit in judgment of those that defy them, but a Paladin sits in Judgment of All who fall before his gaze. Desire bends and debases itself. Duty shatters under the weight of ever greater burdens. Morality shifts under the winds of circumstance. In the eyes of those he serves, a Paladin's judgment must be impeccable. Under his gaze, those underserving will fall. So long as his honor holds true, judgment will follow.

Effect: Skill inflicts (Erethran Reputation*$HonSysCal*1.5 = 671) points of on-going Mana damage to all judged unworthy within perception range of user.

Duration: 65 seconds

Cost: 1000 MP

Grand Paladin Skills

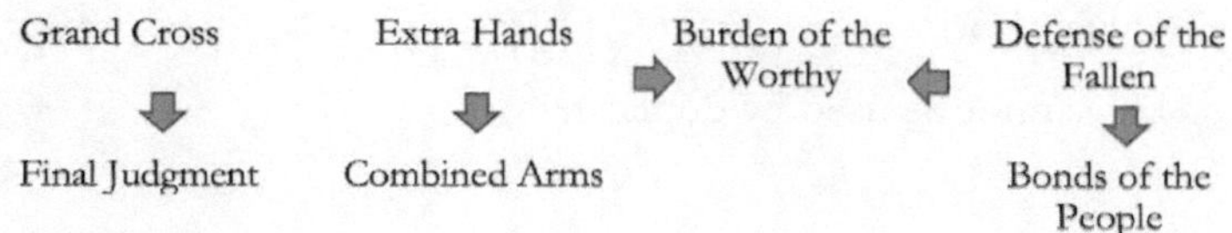

Grand Cross (Level 2)

The burden of existence weighs heavily on the Paladin. This Skill allows the Paladin to allow another to share in the burden. Under the light of and benediction of the Grand Paladin, under the weight of true understanding wayward children may be brought back to the fold.

Effect: Damage done equals to (Willpower * 2.2) per square meter over radius of (1/10th of Perception^2) meters. Damage may be increased by reducing radius of the Grand Cross. Does additional (Willpower) points of damage per second for 11 seconds.

Cost: 2000 MP

Extra Hands (Level 3)

A Paladin can never be everywhere he needs to be. But with this Skill, the Grand Paladin can certainly be in more places. Mana Regeneration reduced by 5 permanently.

Cost: 5000 Mana per duplicate.

Upkeep cost: 5000 Mana per day per duplicate. Must be paid by original Skill user.

Effect: Creates maximum four duplicates of the user. Duplicates have 90.2% of all (unboosted) Attributes, gain no effects from Titles and may not equip Soulbound weapons but has access to all (non-purchased) Skills of user. Each duplicate has their own Mana pool but regenerate at 50.2% of normal regeneration levels. Mana levels take the place of health points for duplicates.

Original Skill user has a telepathic connection to duplicates at all times and will receive a download of duplicate memories upon their destruction or cessation of upkeep costs.

Note: This Skill cannot be used by duplicates

Defense of the Fallen (Level 3)

Guardian and protector, judge and executioner, the Grand Paladin has succeeded as much as he has failed in his duty. Not everyone they seek to save can be saved, all too often the Paladin arrives after the tragedy. Defense of the Fallen armors the Paladin to deal with mental and physical demands of the job.

Effect: Increases Mental Resistance by 60%, Increases Physical Resistance by 35%. Effects are stacked on existing resistances. Effects are imbued in an aura surrounding the user, including all worn and active shields and armor.

Administrator Skills

System Edit

A core Skill for System Administrators.

Effect: Make trivial to minor amendments to System processes

Cost: Variable (HP & MP)

Class Skill: Ticket Board (Level 1)

Middle System Administrators are tasked with not just solving issues at Administrative Centers like Junior System Administrators but with finding solutions in the farthest reaches of the System.

Effect: Form a System Ticketing Board and resolve tickets wherever you might be

Other Class Skills

Frenzy (Level 1)

Effect: When activated, pain is reduced by 80%, damage increased by 30%, stamina regeneration rate increased by 20%. Mana regeneration rate decreased by 10%

Frenzy will not deactivate until all enemies have been slain. User may not retreat while Frenzy is active.

Cleave (Level 2)

Effect: Physical attacks deal 60% more base damage. Effect may be combined with other Class Skills.

Cost: 25 Mana

Elemental Strike (Level 1—Ice)

Effect: Used to imbue a weapon with freezing damage. Adds +5 Base Damage to attacks and a 10% chance of reducing speed by 5% upon contact. Lasts for 30 seconds.

Cost: 50 Mana

Instantaneous Inventory (Maxed)

Allows user to place or remove any System-recognized item from Inventory if space allows. Includes the automatic arrangement of space in the inventory. User must be touching item.

Cost: 5 Mana per item

Shrunken Footsteps (Level 1)

Reduces System presence of user, increasing the chance of the user evading detection of System-assisted sensing Skills and equipment. Also increases cost of information purchased about user. Reduces Mana Regeneration by 5 permanently.

Tech Link (Level 2)

Effect: Tech Link allows user to increase their skill level in using a technological item, increasing input and versatility in usage of said items. Effects vary depending on item. General increase in efficiency of 10%. Mana regeneration rate decreased by 10%

Designated Technological Items: Neural Link, Hodo's Triple Forged Armor

Analyze (Level 2)

Allows user to scan individuals, monsters, and System-registered objects to gather information registered with the System. Detail and level of accuracy of information is dependent on Level and any Skills or Spells in conflict with the ability. Reduces Mana regeneration by 10 permanently.

Harden (Level 2)

This Skill reinforces targeted defenses and actively weakens incoming attacks to reduce their penetrating power. A staple Skill of the Turtle Knights of Kiumma, the Harden Skill has frustrated opponents for millennia.

Effect: Reduces penetrative effects of attacks by 30% on targeted defense.

Cost: 3 Mana per second

Quantum Lock (Level 3)

A staple Skill of the M453-X Mecani-assistants, Quantum Lock blocks stealth attacks and decreases the tactical options of their enemies. While active, the Quantum Lock of the Mecani-assistants excites quantum strings in the affected area for all individuals and Skills.

Effect: All teleportation, portal, and dimensional Skills and Spells are disrupted while Quantum Lock is in effect. Forceable use of Skills and Spells while Skill is in effect will result in (Used Skill Mana Cost * 4) health in damage. Users may pay a variable amount of additional Mana when activating the Skill to decrease effect of Quantum Lock and decrease damage taken.

Requirements: 200 Willpower, 200 Intelligence

Area of Effect: 100-meter radius around user

Cost: 250 + 50 Mana per Minute

Elastic Skin (Level 3)

Elastic Skin is a permanent alteration, allowing the user to receive and absorb a small portion of damage. Damage taken reduced by 7% with 7% of damage absorbed converted to Mana. Mana Regeneration reduced by 15 permanently.

Disengage Safeties (Level 2)

All technological weapons have safeties built in. Users of this Skill recklessly disregard the mandatory safeties, deciding that they know better than the crafters, engineers, and government personnel who built and regulate the production of these technological pieces.

Effects: Increase power output from 2.5-25% depending on the weapon and its level of sophistication. Increase durability losses from use by 25-250%.

Cost: 200 Mana + 25 Mana per minute

Temporary Forced Link (Level 1)

Most Class Skills can't be linked with another's. The instability formed between the mixing of the aura from multiple Mana sources often results in spectacular—and explosive—scenarios. For the 02m8 Symbiotes though, the need to survive within their host bodies and use their Skills has resulted in this unique Skill, allowing the Symbiote to lend their Mana and Skills. (For more persistent effects, see Mana Graft)

Effect: Skill and Skill effects are forcibly combined. Final effect results will vary depending on level of compatibility of Skills.

Cost: 250 Mana + 10 Mana per minute (plus original Skill cost)

Hyperspace Nitro Boost (Level 1)

When you've got to win the race, there's nothing like a hyperspace boost. This Skill links the user with his craft's hyperspace engine, providing a direct boost to its efficiency. Unlike normal speed increases for hyperspace engines, the Nitro Boost is a variable boost and runs a risk of damaging the engine.

Effect: 15% increase in hyperspace engine efficiency + variable % increase in efficiency at 1% per surplus Mana. Each additional 1% over base raises chance of catastrophic engine failure by 0.01%

Cost: 250 Mana + (surplus variable amount; minimum 200 Mana increments) per minute

On the Edge (Level 1)

Shuttle racers live their lives on the edge, cutting corners by feet and dodging monsters by inches. There's only one way to drive a ship with that level of precision, and no matter what those military Pilots tell you, it's with On the Edge.

Effect: +10% boost in ship handling and maneuverability. +10% passive increase in all piloting skills. +1% increase per increment of surplus Mana

Cost: 100 Mana per level + (surplus variable amount; minimum 100 Mana increments) per minute

Fate's Thread (Level 2)

The Akashi'so believe that we are all but weavings in the great thread of life. Connected to one another by the great Weaver, there is not one but multiple threads between us all, woven from our interactions and histories. Fate's Thread is but a Skill expression of this belief. This Skill cannot be dodged but may be blocked. After all, all things are bound together.

Effect: Fate Thread allows the user to bind individuals together by making what is already there apparent. Thread is made physical and may be used to pull, tie and bind.

Duration: 2 minutes

Cost: 60 Mana

Peasant's Fury (Level 1)

No one knows loss more than the powerless. The Downtrodden Peasant has taken the fury of the powerless and made it his own, gifting them the strength to go on so long as they Manage to make others feel the same loss that they did. -5 Mana Regeneration per Second

Effect: User receives a 0.1% regeneration effect of damage dealt for each 1% of health loss.

Spells

Improved Minor Healing (IV)

Effect: Heals 40 Health per casting. Target must be in contact during healing. Cooldown 60 seconds.

Cost: 20 Mana

Improved Mana Missile (IV)

Effect: Creates four missiles out of pure Mana, which can be directed to damage a target. Each dart does 30 damage. Cooldown 10 seconds

Cost: 35 Mana

Enhanced Lightning Strike

Effect: Call forth the power of the gods, casting lightning. Lightning strike may affect additional targets depending on proximity, charge and other conductive materials on-hand. Does 100 points of electrical damage.

Lightning Strike may be continuously channeled to increase damage for 10 additional damage per second.

Cost: 75 Mana.

Continuous cast cost: 5 Mana / second

Lightning Strike may be enhanced by using the Elemental Affinity of Electromagnetic Force. Damage increased by 20% per level of affinity

Greater Regeneration (II)

Effect: Increases natural health regeneration of target by 6%. Only single use of spell effective on a target at a time.

Duration: 10 minutes

Cost: 100 Mana

Firestorm

Effect: Create a firestorm with a radius of 5 meters. Deals 250 points of fire damage to those caught within. Cooldown 60 seconds.

Cost: 200 Mana

Polar Zone

Effect: Create a thirty-meter diameter blizzard that freezes all targets within one. Does 10 points of freezing damage per minute plus reduces effected individuals speed by 5%. Cooldown 60 seconds.

Cost: 200 Mana

Greater Healing (II)

Effect: Heals 100 Health per casting. Target does not require contact during healing. Cooldown 60 seconds per target.

Cost: 75 Mana

Mana Drip (II)

Effect: Increases natural health regeneration of target by 6%. Only single use of spell effective on a target at a time.

Duration: 10 minutes

Cost: 100 Mana

Freezing Blade

Effect: Enchants weapon with a slowing effect. A 5% slowing effect is applied on a successful strike. This effect is cumulative and lasts for 1 minute. Cooldown 3 minutes

Spell Duration: 1 minute.

Cost: 150 Mana

Improved Inferno Strike (II)

A beam of heat raised to the levels of an inferno, able to melt steel and earth on contact! The perfect spell for those looking to do a lot of damage in a short period of time.

Effect: Does 200 Points of Heat Damage

Cost: 150 Mana

Mud Walls

Unlike its more common counterpart Earthen Walls, Mud Walls focus is more on dealing slow, suffocating damage and restricting movement on the battlefield.

Effect: Does 20 Points of Suffocating Damage. -30% Movement Speed

Duration: 2 Minutes

Cost: 75 Mana

Create Water

Pulls water from the elemental plane of water. Water is pure and the highest form of water available. Conjures 1 liter of water. Cooldown: 1 minute

Cost: 50 Mana

Scry

Allows caster to view a location up to 1.7 kilometers away. Range may be extended through use of additional Mana. Caster will be stationary during this period. It is recommended caster focuses on the scry unless caster has a high level of Intelligence and Perception so as to avoid accidents. Scry may be blocked by equivalent or higher tier spells and Skills. Individuals with high perception in region of Scry may be alerted that the Skill is in use. Cooldown: 1 hour.

Cost: 25 Mana per minute.

Scrying Ward

Blocks scrying spells and their equivalent within 5 meters of caster. Higher level spells may not be blocked, but caster may be alerted about scrying attempts. Cooldown: 10 minutes

Cost: 50 Mana per minute

Improved Invisibility

Hides target's System information, aura, scent, and visual appearance. Effectiveness of spell is dependent upon Intelligence of caster and any Skills or Spells in conflict with the target.

Cost: 100 + 50 Mana per minute

Improved Mana Cage

While physically weaker than other elemental-based capture spells, Mana Cage has the advantage of being able to restrict all creatures, including semi-solid Spirits, conjured elementals, shadow beasts, and Skill users. Cooldown: 1 minute

Cost: 200 Mana + 75 Mana per minute

Improved Flight

(Fly birdie, fly!—Ali) This spell allows the user to defy gravity, using controlled bursts of Mana to combat gravity and allow the user to fly in even the most challenging of situations. The improved version of this spell allows flight even in zero gravity situations and a higher level of maneuverability.

Cooldown: 1 minute

Cost: 250 Mana + 100 Mana per minute

Equipment

Spitzrocket Powered Armor Version 18.9 (Tier I) (Grandmaster)

The product of Grandmaster Artisan Madopnem Spitzrocket, the Spitzrocket is a hand-made, unique build Power Armor created in the Forbidden Zone. Continuing with his belief that less is more, the Spitzrocket is both built to adapt to old battles as well as having minimal additional Skills. Rather, the focus of Artisan Spitzrocket has always been in aiding the user in his battles.

Core: Class I Forbidden Zone (Spitzrocket Adaptation) Mana Engine

CPU: Class A++ Wote Core CPU

Armor Rating: Tier I (Enhanced)

Hard Points: 8 (8 Used—Interstellar Ares Flight System, Integrated Mana Warped Beam Cannon (Primary)* 2, Ares Type Primal Shield Generator, Spitzrocket Mana to Armor Adaptive Nanoreplicators * 3, Spitzrocket Neural Muscular Enhancers)

Soft Points 6 (4 Used—Neural Link, Wote HUD Imaging, Airmed Primary Body Monitor, AI integrator)

Battery Capacity: 718/718*

Active Skills: Overcharge, Spatial Twist, Adaptive Conditioning

Attribute Bonuses: +187 Strength, +244 Agility, +31 Constitution, +82 Perception, +183 Stamina and Health Regeneration per minute

Skill: Overcharge (Artisan Equipment Addition—M)

Increase power output of the Spitzrocket for a short period, increasing all damage and attribute bonuses.

Effects: Increase all attribute and damage bonuses by 200%

Duration: 5 minutes

Cooldown: 2 hours

Skill: Spatial Twist (Spatial Equipment Addition—M)

Rather than breaching dimensions or cutting through space, the Spatial Twist Skill instead bends space, bypassing the majority of Dimensional Locks. It allows the user to cross distance in but a flash of a step or a burst of energy.

Effects: Bends space to allow user to bypass intervening distance (max 219.3km). Must have clear line of sight and movement. Cannot go through occupied space.

Capacity: 3

Recharge Rate: 5 minutes per charge

Skill: Adaptive Conditioning (Artisan Equipment Addition—H)

Don't you hate it when your expensive piece of equipment breaks down? While we don't promise the Spitzrocket will never break, we do promise that the more it does, the better it'll be at not breaking the next time around. Embedded in a secondary dimension, the mainframe of the Spitzrocket is safe from normal everyday destruction. This allows it to replicate the Spitzrocket while adapting to the previous battle and conditions that destroyed it.

Effect: Recreates a full copy of the Spitzrocket with additional, adaptive changes to the equipment. Maximum change is 2.8% of armor, resistances and attributes per iteration.

Duration: 274.8 hours to recreate a full copy

Spitzrocket Sunwarmer (Artisan Equipment Addition—H)

Got a moon you need removed from orbit or a sun that is a little on the chilly side? The Sunwarmer is the Spitzrocket answer to this problem, by condensing the energy of unaspected Mana into a weapon.

Effects: Fires a concentrated beam of concentrated unaspected Mana that disrupts physical, spiritual and System links

Damage: 18,318 Base

Capacity: 1

Recharge Rate: 14.3 minutes

Hod's Triple Fused Armor

The product of multiple workings by the Master Blacksmith and Crafter Hodiliphious 'Hod' Yalding, the Triple Fused Armor was hand-forged from rare, System-generated material, hand refined and reworked trice over with multiple patented and rare alloys and materials. The final product is considered barely passable by Hod—though it would make a lesser craftsman cry.

Core: Class I Hallow Physics Mana Engine

CPU: Class B Wote Core CPU

Armor Rating: Tier I (Enhanced)

Hard Points: 9 (6 Used—Jungian Flight System, Talpidae Abyssal Horns, Luione Hard Light Projectors, Diarus Poison Stingers, Ares Type I Shield Generator, Greater Troll Cell Injectors)

Soft Points 4 (3 Used—Neural Link, Ynir HUD Imaging, Airmed Body Monitor)

Battery Capacity: 380/380

Active Skills: Abyssal Chains, Mirror Shade, Poison Grip

Attribute Bonuses: +93 Strength, +78 Agility, +51 Constitution, +44 Perception, +287 Stamina and Health Regeneration per minute

Note: Hod's Triple Fused Armor is currently under limited warranty. Armor may be teleported to Hod's workshop for repairs once a week. All cost of repairs will be deducted from user's account.

Skills in Hod's Armor:

Abyssal Chains

Calling upon the material connection to the shadow plane, chains from the abyss erupt, binding a target in place.

Effect: Target is bound by shadow chains. Chains deal 10 points of damage per second. To break free, target must win a contested Strength test. Abyssal Chains have a Strength of 120.

Uses: 3/3

Recharge rate: 1 per hour

Mirror Shade

Mirror Shade creates a semi-solid doppelganger using hard light technology and Mana.

Effect: Mirror Shade create a semi-solid doppelganger of the user for a period of ten minutes. Maximum range of doppelganger from user is fifty meters. Doppelganger has 18% physical fidelity.

Use: 1/1

Recharge Rate: 1 per 4 hours

Silversmith Jeupa VII Anti-Personnel Cannon (Modified & Upgraded)

This quad-barrelled anti-personnel weapon has been handcrafted by Advanced Weaponsmiths to provide the highest integration possible for an energy weapon. This particular weapon has been modified to include additional range-finding and sighting options and upgraded to increase short-term damage output at the cost of long-term durability. Barrels may be fired individually or linked.

Base Damage: 787 per barrel

Battery Capacity: 4 per barrel (16 total)

Recharge Rate: 0.25 per hour per GMU

Ares Platinum Class Tier II Armored Jumpsuit

Ares's signature Platinum Class line of armored daily wear combines the company's latest technological advancement in nanotech fiber design and the pinnacle work of an Advanced Craftsman's Skill to provide unrivalled protection for the discerning Adventurer.

Effect: +218 Defense, +14% Resistance to Kinetic and Energy Attacks. +19% Resistance against Temperature changes. Self-Cleanse, Self-Mend, Autofit Enchantments also included.

Silversmith Mark VIII Beam Pistol (Upgradeable)

Base Damage: 88

Battery Capacity: 13/13

Recharge Rate: 3 per hour per GMU

Tier IV Neural Link

Neural link may support up to 5 connections.

Current connections: Hod's Triple Fused Armor

Software Installed: Rich'lki Firewall Class IV, Omnitron III Class IV Controller

Ferlix Type I Twinned-Beam Rifle (Modified)

Base Damage: 39

Battery Capacity: 41/41

Recharge rate: 1 per hour per GMU

Tier II Sword (Soulbound Personal Weapon of an Erethran Honor Guard)

Base Damage: 397

Durability: N/A (Personal Weapon)

Special Abilities: +20 Mana Damage, Blade Strike

Kryl Ring of Regeneration

Often used as betrothal bands, Kryl rings are highly sought after and must be ordered months in advance.

Health Regeneration: +30

Stamina Regeneration: +15

Mana Regeneration: +5

Tier III Bracer of Mana Storage

A custom work by an unknown maker, this bracer acts a storage battery for personal Mana. Useful for Mages and other Classes that rely on Mana. Mana storage ratio is 50 to 1.

Mana Capacity: 350/350

Fey-steel Dagger

Fey-steel is not actual steel but an unknown alloy. Normally reserved only for the Sidhe nobility, a small—by Galactic standards—amount of Fey-steel is released for sale each year. Fey-steel takes enchantments extremely well.

Base Damage: 28

Durability: 110/100

Special Abilities: None

Enchanted, Reinforced Toothy Throwing Knives (5)

First handcrafted from the rare drop of a Level 140 Awakened Beast by the Redeemer of the Dead, John Lee, these knives have been further processed by the Master Craftsmen I-24-988L and reinforced with orichalcum and fey-steel. The final blades have been further enchanted with Mana and piercing damage as well as a return enchantment.

Base Damage: 238

Enchantments: Return, Mana Blade (+28 Damage), Pierce (-7% defense)

Brumwell Necklace of Shadow Intent

The Brumwell necklace of shadow intent is the hallmark item of the Brumwell Clan. Enchanted by a Master Crafter, this necklace layers shadowy intents over your actions, ensuring that information about your actions is more difficult to ascertain. Ownership of such an item is both a necessity and a mark of prestige among settlement owners and other individuals of power.

Effect: Persistent effect of Shadow Intent (Level 4) results in significantly increased cost of purchasing information from the System about wearer. Effect is persistent for all actions taken while necklace is worn.

Ring of Greater Shielding

Creates a greater shield that will absorb approximately 1000 points of damage. This shield will ignore all damage that does not exceed its threshold amount of 50 points of damage while still functioning.

Max Duration: 7 Minutes

Charges: 1

Simalax Hover Boots (Tier II)

A combination of hand-crafted materials and mass-produced components, the Simalax Hover Boots are the journeyman work of Magi-Technician Lok of Irvina. Enchantments and technology mesh together in the Simalax Hover Boots, offering its wearer the ability to tread on air briefly and defy gravity and sense.

Effects: User reduces gravitational effects by 0.218 SIG. User may, on activation, hover and skate during normal and mildly turbulent atmospheric conditions. User may also use the Simalax Hover Boots to triple jump in the air, engaging the anti-gravity and hover aspects at the same time.

Duration: 1.98 SI Hours.

F'Merc Nanoswarm Mana Grenades (Tier II)

The F'Merc Nanoswarm Grenades are guaranteed to disrupt the collection of Mana in a battlefield, reducing Mana Regeneration rates for those caught in the swarm. Recommended by the I'um military, the Torra Special Forces and the No.1 Most Popular Mana Grenade as voted by the public on Boom, Boom, Boom! Magazine.

Effect: Reduces Mana Regeneration rates and spell formation in affected area by 37% ((higher effects in enclosed areas)

Radius: 10m x 10m

Daghtree's Legendary Ring of Deception (Tier I)

A musician, poet and artist, Daghtree's fame rose not from his sub-standard works of 'art' but his array of seduction Skills from his Heartthrob Artist Class. Due to his increasing infamy, Daghtree commissioned this Legendary ring to change his appearance and continue Leveling. In the end, it is rumored that his indiscretions caught up with the infamous artist and he disappeared from Galactic sources in GCD 9,275

Effect: Creates a powerful disguise that covers the wearer. The ring comes with six pre-loaded disguises and additional disguises may be added through expansion of charges

Duration: 1 day per charge

Charges: 3

Recharge via ambient Mana: 1 charge per Galactic Standard Unit per week

F'Merc Ghostlight Mana Dispersal Grenades (Tier I)

The F'Merc Ghostlight Mana Dispersal Grenades not only disperse Mana in the battlefield, the Ghostlight Dispersal Grenades degrade all Mana Skills and spells within its field of effectiveness. Used by Krolash the Destroyer, the Erethran Champion Isma (prior version) and Anblanca Special Forces. Five times Winner of the Most Annoying Utility Item on the Battlefield.

Effect: Reduces Mana Regeneration rates, Skill and spell formation use in affected area by 67% ((higher effects in enclosed areas)

Radius: $15m^3$

Evernight Darkness Orbs

When the world goes light, the Evernight Darkness Orbs will bring back blessed darkness. If you need darkness, you need Evernight!

Effect: Removes al visible light and mute infrared and ultraviolet wavelengths by 30%

Radius: 50m³

Seven Heavenly Spire Wards

Quick to set-up, the Seven Heavenly Spire Wards were crafted by the Thrice Loved Bachelor's Temple of the Sinking Domain as their main export. Using the total prayer and faith of the temple, they produce a set of wards every month.

Effect: Set's up a 30' by 30' defensive ward; protects against both magical and technological attacks and entry

Fumikara Mobile Teleport Circles

These one-off use mobile teleport circles allow connection to existing and open teleport networks.

Effect: Connect to open teleport networks within a 5,000 kim radius of the teleport circles. Allows teleportation of individuals to the networked teleport centers

PoenJoe Goleminised-Mana Generator Mark 18

The latest Mana Generator by the infamous PoenJoe, the Mark 18 is guaranteed* to not blow up on you in optimal conditions. This partially sentient Mana Generator can extract up to 98% of a Mana Crystal's saved energy in 0.003 seconds. Currently loaded in an Adult Kirin Mana Core.

Effect: It's a Power Generator. Guaranteed to provide up to 98 x 10*99 Standard Galactic Mana Units

*Not actually guaranteed. In fact, we're 100% certain that containment failure will occur.

Payload (Level 2) (Embedded in Anklet of Dispersed Damage)

Sometimes, you need to get your Skills inside a location. Payload allows you to imbue an individual or item with a Skill at a reduced strength.

Effect: 71% effectiveness of Skill imbued.

Secondary Effect: Skill may be now triggered on a timed basis (max 2:07 minutes)

Uses: 22

Recharge: 10.7 charges per day in SGE